Ties That Bind

Ties That Bind

CATHERINE DEVENEY

Acknowledgements

With gratitude to my sisters Jean and Mary, my brothers Peter, Andrew and David, and all Colin's family for their love and support. Special thanks also to the good friends who advised, encouraged and believed, especially Eileen Kling, Brian Devlin, Anton FitzSimons, Maureen Reid, Clare Trodden, and Tom Little. Finally, to everyone at Old Street who made it happen and to Kate Quarry for being such a pleasure to work with.

* * *

First published in 2010 by Old Street Publishing Ltd
40 Bowling Green Lane, London EC1R 0BJ
www.oldstreetpublishing.co.uk

ISBN 978-1-906964-13-9

A CI[illegible] ibrary.

Typeset by Martin Worthington

Printed and bound in Great Britain.

With love for my dear mum Mollie, and my dad, Peter Black Rafferty, whose passing changed everything.

Also for Colin, for everything we have shared, and for my beautiful children Conall, Niall and Caitlin.

CHAPTER ONE

Carol Ann

Most people do their running away when they are fourteen, but I waited till I was forty-two. Maybe my mother was right after all. Lily always said I was a late developer.

I left Scotland in the late spring, when the rape fields and the cherry blossom were in full bloom. I love those few weeks each year when the two overlap: marshmallow pink at the side of the house and, out front, the bright, puff-candy yellow of the rape. I watched it through the picture window at the front of the house for days before I left, the yellow turning up gradually like a light on a dimmer switch, until it glowed as strong and vibrant as the midday sun. Then, when it was at its peak, I got a terrible pang knowing it was dying already, that the colour would fade slowly now into sunset. After that, the spring breezes came, and the cherry blossom rained down pink and white on the path, the colour of coconut ice, soft and gentle as a baby's kiss.

I guess everything starts dying when it's at its height. You think it's the beginning, but it's really only the beginning of the end. Like the day I married Alex.

In the weeks before I disappeared, the swallows were constantly fluttering round the eaves of the house. I watched them, their wings quivering as they hovered under the roof with mouthfuls of straw and mud, building houses while mine was being dismantled. Mother said they weren't swallows at all. They were too small to be swallows. They were house martins. I didn't argue. Lily always knows best.

We sat in the garden together the day before my disappearance. Neither of us knew I was going. That was the best bit. The unexpectedness. The way a long-harboured dream that had drifted into fantasy suddenly became reality. People say you hug a secret to you, and I did, but at the same time, I can't say my secret felt entirely like that. It wasn't small and insular. It was vast and expansive. It was like riding surf waves in your head. Like hearing the air whistle past you when you skydive. Not that I've ever skydived, obviously. Carol Ann Matthews would never do anything that daring.

It felt like the first day of summer. Lily had her tights off and there was a watery sunshine hitting her white, old-lady legs, the bulge of varicose veins running like blue mountain ranges in white snow. She was wearing a striped blouse, strips of coral pink and lemon, so that it was hard to know where she ended and the deckchair began. Her lipstick had gone ever so slightly over the edges of her lips, I suppose because her hand shook when she applied it. There were deep little lines, needle-thin trenches, running from her mouth, and the lipstick colour had seeped in, spreading like tiny rivers from a burst bank.

'What's your nail-polish colour?' she asked, looking at my fingers as they dangled over the wooden arm of my sun lounger.

'Parisian Rose, I think it's called.'

'That's silly, that,' she said. 'What's a Parisian rose?'

I didn't answer.

'Eh?' she prodded. 'What's the difference between a French rose and any other kind of rose?' She was a bit querulous that day. She'd had a few already when I picked her up at her house for lunch, though it was only quarter-past eleven. I could smell it from her. It hung around her like the smell of damp in an old house.

'I don't know,' I said, eyes closed.

'No … well … you wouldn't, would you?' she said crossly. 'That's because there isn't any difference.'

'Maybe not.'

'*Definitely* not, Carol Ann. Some silly marketing man's come up with that.'

'Or woman.'

'A woman would know there's no such thing as a Parisian rose.'

'Maybe.'

The sun intensified suddenly, briefly, on my closed eyelids, a blast of warmth like the rays from a grill.

'Carol Ann, will you please stop saying maybe,' Lily snapped.

'Sorry.'

I think it was annoying her that I wouldn't open my eyes, but they felt stuck together with warm glue from the sun. I could hear her fidgeting in her chair.

'It's chipped,' Lily said.

'What?'

'And I don't like the colour anyway. Too strong. Neutral, I like.'

I opened one eye and raised my fingers to examine the nails. There were small chips out of the tips of the rose-pink shells.

'Yes,' I said. 'It's chipped.'

'Very common-looking,' she muttered.

I let my thoughts roam free then, where she couldn't reach me, fantasising about the going, the walking away. I had imagined it so many times that it was like a favourite novel, reread so often I almost knew it by heart. Except it was only the first chapter I kept reading and rereading. The going. I never thought about what came after because I simply couldn't imagine it. I just imagined the walking, up past the bridge at the end of the house, past the pond where I like to walk, heels clumping rhythmically on the road, the smell of mown grass on the wind. And each time I imagined it, the hundreds and hundreds of times I imagined it, there was always something new and undiscovered, a tiny detail I hadn't imagined before that would give me pleasure.

'Carol Ann,' said Lily. 'Be a darling and get my handkerchiefs from the house. I think I left them in the kitchen.' She sniffed theatrically, and I looked at her with the cynical, insider knowledge of a lifetime's game-playing.

'They're in there,' I said, 'in the side pocket of your bag,' and I nodded down to the sprawl at her feet: a light canvas bag that she had brought some chocolates for me in, and a square black vinyl handbag. Lily doesn't invest in expensive leather goods. She has contributions to Gordon's gin to maintain.

'Oh yes.' She had slumped down into the deckchair and now she wriggled her bottom up to sit straighter. But she reached for her glass rather than the tissues.

'Any ice?' she said.

'In the house.'

'Any chance?' A light ripple of aggression marbled her voice.

I held my hand up over my eyes and squinted at her against the light.

'Mother,' I said, with uncharacteristic firmness, 'you want me to go into the house so that you can take the quarter bottle of gin out of your handbag without me seeing and pour it into your lemonade. So I tell you what. Why don't I just close my eyes. Like this, see? And that will save me getting up. Then you can fill your glass and pretend it's lemonade, and I can sit here and pretend I haven't seen. Hmm? Why don't we just do that, the two of us?'

There was silence for a second. Lily's lipstick-stained trenches were quivering with indignation. She smoothed her skirt down over her knees. 'Sometimes, Carol Ann,' she said, refusing to look me in the eye, 'you can be terribly vulgar.'

* * *

Sometimes, if I close my eyes, I can feel him. The way he was. I can feel him so clearly that his breath is warm on my neck. 'Carol Ann,' he whispers, and my name sounds sung, like a hymn. His voice is an echo in my head. *'Carol Ann.'*

Our shoes are kicked off at the side of the bed, but we are fully dressed. My hair is spread out on the cool white cotton of the pillow and he coils it lightly round his finger before letting it drop. Later, I will find strands of my blonde hair side by side with his dark.

His lips taste of red wine. He brushes them softly over my mouth, fluttering down over my throat. In my memory, I remember the desire, not the sex. He pours it over me, his longing, till I am drunk with it, my eyes closed lightly, like a cat in the sun.

I am lying on my back. Alex is on his side, leaning on his elbow. He rests his hand on my waist, slips it under my shirt so that I feel his fingers run lightly over the taut skin. Skin on skin. His fingers slide to my back, and he exerts pressure on my spine to pull me towards him. His lips find my mouth. When he pulls away, he leaves his face just inches from mine. I can see the pupils of his eyes dilating as he looks at me. You can't hide attraction.

'You're gorgeous,' he says provocatively, and I smile lazily at him, run my index finger over the outline of his lips.

'Do you know where I want to be right now, right this very minute?' he says. His voice is low, playful.

I like fantasy games.

'Paris?'

'Nope.'

'Venice?'

He shakes his head.

'Where could be more romantic than Venice?' I ask, brow furrowed, because I am only eighteen and my ideas of romance are still textbook.

I even think it lasts for ever.

He smiles.

'Where?' I repeat.

His hand pushes slowly upwards from the soft curve of my stomach to my breast, and he leans forward, burrowing into my hair to reach my ear.

'In. Side. You,' he whispers.

I take Lily back early. She's had her lunch. Scrambled eggs and smoked salmon. Thin slices of wholemeal toast. Fresh raspberries and drizzled honey. I always buy little delicacies when Lily comes. Maybe it's guilt. I pretend everything is normal when I shop for her in the supermarket. I walk round the aisles telling myself that my mother is coming for a nice lunch and what does a good daughter buy for a beloved mother who is coming to lunch? She buys small, pearly, queenie scallops, and ripe vine tomatoes blushed with the sun. She buys fresh-ground Italian coffee and dark chocolate florentines, fat with cherries and plump sultanas and green angelica.

Lily always eats like a bird. She never has anything lining her stomach to soak up the alcohol. Her appetite is shot to pieces and so is her co-ordination. Her hand trembles as she lifts her fork to her mouth, nuggets of scrambled egg spilling onto her skirt. Tiny particles cling to her lipstick.

'Very nice, Carol Ann,' she says, laying down her fork after only a couple of mouthfuls. 'I taught you well.'

Everything in the world is seen through her own reflection. She is very egocentric. It is part of her illness.

I feel guilty when I take her back. When I picked her up this morning I promised myself I would keep her all afternoon. Till four at least. Then I'd run her home to her small flat before Alex returned from work. Best to keep them apart. But at two o'clock, I lie and tell her I am filling in for a couple of hours at the charity shop this afternoon. She doesn't complain. It would have been a long afternoon for her without free access to the bottle. She picks up her canvas bag and it clunks against the chair leg. Her shirt is stained dark down the front with scrambled egg and raspberry juice.

I insist on taking her upstairs to the flat. Must be attentive. Less guilt. I guess if I could actually carry it through, if I could only be as attentive as I mean to be, there *would* be less guilt. The windows are all shut in the flat and when the door swings open the air smells stale, of trapped heat and dead flies and booze. Toby, her cat, streaks by us as the door opens. Who can blame him? A whiff of oxygen would go to anyone's head after being locked in here. Lily goes over on the side of her shoe as he shoots past, reaches out a hand to steady herself against the wall of the hall.

'I'll be fine now, Carol Ann,' she says. 'You'd better get to the shop.'

'I've got time to make you a cup of tea, Mum,' I say brightly.

When I feel at my most guilty, I call her Mum. Inside – and sometimes, when I forget, to her face – I call her Lily.

'Off you go,' she says. 'I don't want any tea.'

'Are you sure?'

She flaps her hands at me with a shooing motion but says nothing. I am frightened she knows how much I want to leave, so I go into the sitting room and open a window.

'This place needs airing,' I say.

Lily stands by the window.

'I'll wave,' she says. 'Off you go.'

'I'll phone tomorrow.'

Downstairs I open the car door and look up, wave exaggeratedly. In the frame of the window Lily looks tiny. Her hair is wild, manic, always backcombed into dishevelment like a crazy lady's. Lily *is* a crazy lady. She is stuck in old beauty habits that she can no longer carry out or carry off. Even from the street I can see her bright-red lipstick, applied so liberally it looks like a little girl's first attempt. She lifts her arm to wave as I turn the key in the ignition, her hand moving solemnly, concentratedly, like waving is the most important thing in the world. The indicator clicks rhythmically, beating in time with the pendulum of guilt inside me, and I open the window to wave up to Lily as I drive off. I feel a sharp pain in my gut, like I have left my child behind instead of my mother.

The sunshine is streaming through the picture window onto the television, a shaft of dancing dust forming a vortex between windowpane and screen. I draw the curtain slightly to block the light, listening to the monotonous voice of the commentator.

'And it's Paris Rose on the inside coming through fast now ... Paris Rose looking like she'll cause a major upset this afternoon. Terry's Girl is way, way behind, the odds-on favourite fading spectacularly here at Haydock this afternoon. Paris Rose thunders by ...'

'Come on,' I whisper through clenched teeth. 'Come on, Paris Rose.'

The commentator's voice rises to a squeal.

'Paris Rose is finishing strongly now, followed by Red Demon in second place and Flapjack making up ground in third. But what a SURGE from Flapjack … Flapjack neck and neck now with Red Demon …

'COME ON!'

'… Flapjack in second place and pushing Paris Rose all the way. But jockey Jimmy Cochrane is keeping Paris Rose steady, holding on bravely in the dying seconds of this race ... and Paris Rose has DONE it. The thirty-three-to-one outsider crosses the finishing line from Flapjack in second place, followed by Red Demon, Olive Branch and Terry's Girl ...'

The voice becomes a drone. I look stupidly at the betting slip in my hand. Of course, I couldn't resist Paris Rose when I saw the name. After

Lily and everything. And roses always make me think of pink, which is a very special colour for me. I always bet by name, which is why I don't usually win.

I'll tell you how it is. Nobody knows I have a flutter. It's my small rebellion. It started two years ago, when the dream first started, the dream of walking away. I chose a hiding place. An old biscuit tin with a picture of Monet's 'Poppy Field' inside a plastic bag, inside a big old handbag, hidden at the back of my wardrobe. I wanted to walk away with only cash. See, that way there would be no trace. I couldn't just go and make withdrawals from an ordinary bank account. There's no point walking away if you leave a trail. The secret is to disappear into nothing.

And maybe I knew five-thousand pounds was an impossible dream. I'd always be reaching the target, always dreaming but never quite going. Safe dreams. I don't earn much. Two mornings in the village tearoom, just to get me out. Six pounds an hour. Alex earns plenty, of course, which is why he goes through life like he's worth something, and I tag along like behind him like the buy one, get one free offer.

For a new life, there must be new rules. The most important one is that I pay. My dream, my funding. It would be easy to take money from the joint account – in other words, Alex's account – but I can't. He's not mean with money, but it wouldn't be right. So for two years I have put fifteen quid away almost every week, barring the month before Christmas and birthday weeks. It has grown slowly. Each week I gave myself small targets of how much I needed to raise. It pleased me somehow, when I got away with little economies without anyone noticing. A tin of tomatoes in the bolognese instead of fresh. Alex hates tinned tomatoes, detests the smell of them. But I purée them and he never notices. Saving: £1. Rustic casserole instead of sirloin. Saving: £3. Walking from the tearoom instead of taking the bus. Saving: 60p. Five days a week I have a target, with Saturdays and Sundays off.

The trick is that you make the saving and put the money in the tin *instantly*. You don't wait a week, round it up, round it down. That's not how it works. It's an abstract saving until you put the money in the tin, so you have to do it right away to make it real. There is just over a thousand pounds in there now. Not enough to leave for at least another couple of years.

Once a month or so, I have a small bet. I set up a telephone account with Bob Smith Bookmakers in town, so I don't have to go in. I don't use the house phone, obviously. I can't have the number appearing on bills. Not that Alex deals with that stuff, but still. You can't take chances. I have never won more than a tenner before and I have lost more than I have won – the punter always does. But today a surge of madness made me put on twenty quid. I don't know why. In fact, I felt sick at my own stupidity when I put the phone down. I'd never get away at this rate. But now, I stare at the betting slip in disbelief. One treble: Dream Time 11-1; Forbidden Fruit 5-2; Paris Rose 33-1. Oh, beautiful Paris Rose! I get out my son Stevie's calculator. £28,560.

There is only a pulse beat between victory and the ring of the telephone, between triumph and disaster. The shrill insistence barely registers in the enormity of the moment. Maybe it's a sixth sense that makes me pick it up automatically, something being transmitted to me from Lily. I believe in that: a way of communicating that is not about words. Though when it comes to me and Alex, a few words would do just fine. I'm just not sure we know the same ones any more. As far as he's concerned, I might as well speak Punjabi.

'Hello? Yes. Yes, I'm Lily Matheson's daughter.'

The words that follow are a jumble, senseless but shocking, the chaos clearing to leave specific words that cut like shards of ice, sharpened to a dagger point of precision. Lily. Hospital. And then, in the middle of the confusion, a single word slices the dagger straight through my heart and nails my life to the floor: stroke.

CHAPTER TWO

Carol Ann

Lily looks shrivelled in the white shroud of the hospital sheets and pillows. Her eyes are closed when I arrive. I sit beside the bed, gently lift the hand that lies on top of the coverlet and hold it in both of mine. Her skin feels dry, wrinkled like ageing parchment. The muscles on the left side of her face have slackened, the left-hand corner of her mouth drooping downwards like the sad clown of a child's drawing. Saliva dribbles into the fold that has formed from mouth to chin.

The silence is broken only by the whispered exhalation of her breathing, rising and falling steadily, and by the muffled noise of voices and trundling trolleys and sudden bursts of laughter that filter through the cocoon of closed doors, a world away. The tune of her breathing is fragile, as if the music is fading slowly at the end of a track.

Lily wears a pale blue hospital nightdress, open at the neck; the bones of her chest spread in an artery of ridges. You'd look at her now and you wouldn't know. You'd have no idea. How beautiful she was. As a child, I'd open her wardrobe and sniff her clothes, sit amongst her shoes, just holding them. She found me once, when I was about four, on the floor of the open wardrobe, the outline of her lipstick on my mouth, my baby feet slipped into the gargantuan magnificence of her best patent shoes. It is my earliest and happiest memory. On my head, her black, wide-brimmed straw hat, and on the floor a discarded striped hatbox and crinkled puffs of pink tissue paper. She scooped me up and laughed, raising me high above her face till I gasped; the rock-solid safety of a mother's hands under my oxters, the insouciant tenderness of a mother's kiss planted on the snub of my nose beneath the brim of the hat.

She was dark haired in those days, her locks swept back from her face to reveal marvellous, delicate cheekbones. And while schoolfriends' mothers were dumpy and frumpy and smelled of bleach, I rejoiced in my glamorous mother with her circular skirts and nipped-in waists, her tight-fitting trousers that skimmed boyish hips, her black, Jacqueline Kennedy shift dresses. She was gamine then, not wasted, and I thought she was the most beautiful woman in the world. My mother.

Sometimes, my tenderness for her threatens to overwhelm me, consume me, but then almost immediately it becomes tempered by the resentment of responsibility. I cared for her when she should have cared for me. Now she is old it should be her turn, but it still feels like mine. It's been her turn all my life.

Sitting here by her bed, my nostrils fill suddenly with a wave of hospital smell, the sickly aroma of antiseptic and decay. I hate hospitals. Earlier, scurrying wildly through the corridors trying to find Lily's ward, I had passed maternity and the newborn wails shot a faultline of memories through me. A couple came through the swing doors towards me, all smiles and tenderness, leaving the hospital with a baby lost inside an enormity of padding, a tiny little nut inside a great big shell. I tried to smile as I held the door for them, but they passed through, barely seeing me, and anyway, my eyes were fixed on the trailing pink blanket they had wrapped round the infant. Soft pink, baby pink, the colour of wild roses in the rain, as delicately protective as a bird's egg shell.

Through the glass windows of the room, two figures appear. Alex and Stevie. Stevie will be sixteen next week. He walks self-consciously, shoulders hunched forward against the world, eyes cast upwards from under the dark lick of his lashes. He walks several paces behind Alex, as though they are not together really. Alex, in his business suit and a crisp white shirt and tie, walks briskly, as though late for a meeting. He looks ten years younger than his age, whereas I look five years older than mine. He gets younger, I get older, and sometimes, I think that before long I will look like his mother. I watch him, head bobbing as he walks past the window towards the door. A young nurse turns her head back surreptitiously to look at him once she has walked by him. He's still got it.

Sometimes, I can reduce my feelings about Alex to a kind of emptiness. But mostly, there's repressed anger, anger that it's too late to talk about. We've passed the moment. I cannot look at Alex but I see *her* face. Her haunting face with its bone-china beauty and clear-eyed intensity. She stands between us always, a constant presence, a silent ghost. A hand on my shoulder. A hand on his.

'How is she?' asks Alex, opening the door. He glances at the bed and his expression doesn't change.

'Drifting in and out of consciousness. The doctors say they think it has been a fairly minor stroke, but it has left her groggy and temporarily paralysed down her left side. It's too early to say how much damage has been done.' I bite my lip, the skin dry and tough beneath my teeth, desiccated by hours in the dry, hospital heat. 'There's always the danger of a bigger stroke, particularly in the next forty-eight hours.'

Stevie hangs back from the bed, not looking directly at Lily, as if he's just an onlooker, not really there because of any connection to anyone else. But there is fear in his face. I try to smile encouragingly at him, but he doesn't respond.

'Steve, get rid of that chewing gum, will you?' says Alex. His voice is sharp with irritation. He never sees Stevie's fear.

Stevie's neck juts forward aggressively from his shoulders. He looks at his father with hostility.

'Why?'

'It's not very respectful, is it? Standing chewing gum round your grandmother's bed when she's in that state.'

'It's okay ...' I begin quickly, soothingly, but neither of them hear.

'What?' says Stevie incredulously. 'What difference does it make? She's hardly gonna know, is she?'

His dark brown eyes are hooded with resentment. Sometimes, he looks as if he hates Alex.

'And anyway, what's *disrespectful* ...' He says the word so that you can hear inverted commas round it. '... about chewing?'

'Steve, you've got too much to say,' says Alex with a quietness that I know from experience is deceptive.

'Alex, there are chairs over there if you ...' I begin.

'Try engaging your brain before you open that big mouth,' continues Alex, and Stevie tuts, shooting him a glancing look of utter disdain. Neither of them are aware I have even spoken.

'Oh, bloody hell,' I mutter, putting my head down momentarily on Lily's bed.

Alex hears that bit, of course. He looks at me belligerently, like it's me he's arguing with instead of Stevie, like it's *my* fault. He raises his hands helplessly in the air in a gesture of angry despair. 'Carol Ann,' he says. 'It's no wonder that kid marches about like he owns the place.'

'I'm not a kid,' mutters Stevie.

'Alex,' I say, and my voice flutters uncertainly as I look into his eyes and remember hers – long, black lashes sweeping upwards in spidery curls. Then I feel that familiar kick-back of anger I experience when I think of them together, which hardens my voice again. 'Alex, my mother has had a stroke.'

'Yes, I know that, Carol Ann,' he says. I hate the way he only ever uses my name now as a kind of angry emphasis. 'We all know that. We're here, aren't we?'

Yes. They're here. 'Carol Ann,' whispers an echo from the past in my head. '*Carol Ann.*' I don't take my eyes off him. Does he know what I'm thinking?

'I can't stay long,' says Alex. He looks at his watch. 'I need to meet Dave Bannerman in half an hour.' Alex doesn't like Lily. She may be an alcoholic, but she sees through him. She ought to; she's an expert in deception.

'I'll stay,' says Stevie, so he doesn't have to share a car back with Alex. He scrapes a chair back against the wall opposite Lily's bed and sits down, his long, gangling legs sprawling in front of him.

'I'm sorry,' says Alex. 'I'd stay a bit if I could. I just popped in ... you know ... but I'll be back ...'

I shake my head. 'It's all right. You go.' I sound like Lily.

Alex hesitates. 'Right,' he says. 'Try not to worry too much. I hope things are a bit better when I come back.' He pats my shoulder as he goes, a small gesture of comfort. He cannot bring himself to hold me any more. Somewhere inside, I am glad. If he held me close it would only emphasise our distance. When he holds me, I cannot help thinking of the way he held her. I want him gone. I feel less lonely when I'm alone.

Alex stops at Stevie's outstretched legs, though he could easily walk round them. I hate the way he does that, forces confrontation when he could avoid it. Slowly, slowly, Stevie shifts slightly in his seat, moving his legs back a little. Still chewing, he refuses to look at Alex.

'Is she gonna be okay?' asks Stevie when Alex is gone, nodding towards the bed.

'I don't know, son.'

Stevie jerks his head in acknowledgement that I have spoken but says nothing.

'What are you missing in school this afternoon?'

Stevie looks at his watch. 'French just now. Chemistry last.'

'Maybe you should go back now you've seen her. The doctors say she's stable. There's nothing you can really do here.'

He tilts his head back and leans against the wall.

'I don't want you in any more trouble.'

'I won't be in trouble.'

'Did you and Garry finish painting the bike shed?'

'Yeah.'

He scowls, irritated with me for bringing it up again. Stevie doesn't like being reminded of anything where he's in the wrong. He's a bit like Alex that way. He got caught spray-painting the school bike shed with his pal, Garry. Stevie said it was urban art. Mr Martin, the headmaster, obviously doesn't 'get' urban art, because he said it was vandalism. I said, well what's the difference between urban art and vandalism, and Stevie said grey matter. Brain cells. Mr Martin made them the offer of painting the whole thing in their own time or being reported to the police. I thought it was pretty reasonable, but Stevie just said it was typical of the fascist wee shite.

'Is Mr Martin happy with the job you've done?'

'I don't know, do I?'

'Hasn't he said?'

Stevie stands up. 'I'm going back,' he says, without looking at me. I know he's going for a wander round town.

'Stevie ...'

'I'll see you later.'

The door swings shut behind him with a bang.

Lily stirs slightly, as if at the noise. I reach out a hand, run a finger down her cheek. Her eyes flicker open, then close again. Her left eye droops sinisterly. They don't know the full extent of the damage yet, but she'll probably need help to talk again. Help to walk. Help to eat. Help to dress. When she opens her eyes and looks at me, I see suddenly how it's going to be. There is something short of recognition in her expression, a puzzlement, a weariness. She doesn't even know me. But then, who does? Who in the name of God does? There is a sudden ping inside, like an elastic band being stretched beyond tolerance and snapping. I stand up. Gently, I push the hair back from Lily's face.

'Bye, Mum,' I whisper, and bend to kiss her cheek. She says nothing, but I feel her suddenly alert as I walk to the door. If I didn't know better, I'd say her eyes were following me. I turn quickly and look at her again, as if trying to catch her out, and see her eyes are open, burning like black, shining stars. Burning so bright, it's as if they are floodlights, casting light on me from the inside out. I swear to God, in that moment you would almost think she knew.

CHAPTER THREE

Karen

Fucking wanker, Mackie!

The words are in my head and then all of a sudden they're spitting into the atmosphere, echoing round the bathroom. The water in the bath is cooling rapidly and I reach out with my foot and turn the hot tap on with my toes. The water tank rumbles angrily.

'FUCKING WANKER!'

I shout it this time, above the sound of the gush from the tap, and it's like a release.

Jesus, I hate that guy. Fat, sweat-drenched, disgusting Mackie. He started in the police force at the same time as me and I haven't been able to shake him off since. Even in the first few weeks he thought he could put those octopus arms of his round me until I twisted round one day and kneed him in the groin.

'Fuckssake!' he spluttered, doubling up.

I don't like anyone touching me without permission.

'Aw, Macks, did I get your balls?' I said softly. 'Sorry. Didn't realise you had any.'

The steam is rising from the bath and I switch the tap off again. I always run a bath after a shift, take some wine in with me. One of those plastic wine glasses people use for picnics. It has scratches on it from the dishwasher, looks permanently cloudy. I'm not fussy like that. The bath and the wine help me relax before bed. I don't sleep well, never have. I got into bad habits as a kid, sleeping light, listening out. It was always important to listen out.

Mackie is only a PC, like me, but it always feels like he's testing me, watching me constantly with that smug smirk to see if I'll crack. In the early days, I'd feel his piggy little eyes on me at road accidents, waiting for me to show weakness, to turn away, especially if there was a kid splattered across the carriageway. Now he has to resort to wind-ups in the station because he knows that out in the streets, where it matters, the others would rather be paired with me than him. I've got more bottle.

The bathroom window is half mottled glass, but the top half is clear. The evening is darkening rapidly, light summer clouds skidding by in a red-stained sunset. It felt like a long day today. I heard about the CID vacancy and felt the first flicker of hope in a long time. Uniform work does your head in. It's all teenage kids nicking cars, old guys getting drunk and disorderly, and the dreaded fucking missing persons inquiries. I really hate working on that stuff. Bored housewives running off with their new boyfriends. Deranged nutters trying to drown themselves in puddles ...

I take a sip from the glass, feel the warmth of the wine and the heat from the bath engulf me. The water is too hot; my cheeks flushed red, the mirror above the sink frosted with condensation. I stick my legs on the side of the bath to cool them, the water dripping below onto cool white tiles. I quite liked uniform at first. People knowing who you were, having to take note of you. Bit of a turn-on in the early days, but I'm so over it. I really, really want that CID vacancy. I need it. Stop me going crazy. Trouble is, Mackie wants it too.

He took great delight in telling me today that he thought Chief Inspector McFarlane would favour him over me. I just looked at him for a moment, then shook my head with as much of a sneer as fear would allow me. No fucking chance, I said, before hearing someone moving behind me. McFarlane, creeping around as usual. Need to watch my language, apparently. Said it was inappropriate for the workplace. He also muttered something about femininity, which was out of order but typical of McFarlane. He's a fucking wanker, too.

He's one of those book types – can't have a thought unless he's had it confirmed in print somewhere first. He'd be totally useless on the streets, which is no doubt why he's got where he has. Those who can do the job get on with it; those who can't read about it before spitting it all out again in front of promotion panels. It's obvious he doesn't like me. Seems to want me to behave like a vicar's wife instead of a cop. That's the thing about men, though. Half of them are turned on by someone with long hair and tits who can handle herself like I can. The other half are threatened. You're not as smart as you think you are, Karen, McFarlane always screeches like some demented parrot. I've tried a bit of extra lipgloss on him, but there's never a flicker. Bet he's a poof.

The bathroom is airless now, stale with condensation and heat. My cheeks are pink and I can scarcely breathe. I don't know why I always run baths too hot. Somehow I never feel clean otherwise. If the water is near scalding it makes me feel stripped, like there's new pink skin where the old dirty scales used to be. Hard to feel clean. A sudden thought runs through my head then out again before I can grasp it properly. Mackie vaguely reminds me of someone, but I can never quite place the recognition because it's not entirely physical. A couple of times it has almost come to me and it nearly did again there. But the comparison always disappears just as I have almost grasped it.

I walked back to my desk after McFarlane told me off about my language and was surprised when he followed me. There was something he wanted to talk to me about, he said. In his office. He had a case for me. I could feel everyone's eyes on me and I shot a furtive glance at Mackie, trying to see how he was taking it. McFarlane led the way and as I walked past Mackie's desk, I raised an eyebrow at him. McFarlane favour him? I feel hot all over again at the memory. The way it turned out …

I pull the plug with my toe, feel the water level dropping. My skin feels flushed and wrinkled with the water. I lie in the heat, waiting for my body to cool, eyes closing, suddenly too tired to move.

Mackie … McFarlane … bastards, the pair of them.

CHAPTER FOUR

Carol Ann

I go for breakfast in a patisserie that is warm with the smell of dough, the air lightly dusted with the scent of roasted coffee beans. It's smart, chic, unfamiliar. A tiny kernel of excitement flickers inside. A beginning.

Already it feels like a lifetime ago that I was someone else, yet it is only a few days. After leaving Lily in the hospital, I walked to the car, hearing nothing but the crashing waves inside my own head. Was this a crisis? Dr Hammond said if I ever found myself in a crisis, I should phone him. Any time. But if this was crisis, it beat normality. I felt calmer than I had in years. Not on the outside where it's easy to look calm. Deep, deep inside me. In there, I found somewhere hidden, an uninhabited island.

In our appointments together, Dr Hammond would say quietly, 'Tell me, Carol Ann, what is the worst thing that can happen?' I loved his calmness. It made me feel safe. I was capable of anything in there. Depression, he said, could be a transient phase, not a permanent state, and a little bit of hope, soft as a sigh, would surface inside me. And then I would leave his office and head back into the storm and almost immediately I was powerless again.

He would work patiently, soothingly, to show me I could *survive* the worst. And maybe he was right. Right now there should be nothing left to salvage. I had become the worst possible person, the one who runs, who abandons everyone in her life. I was weak, trivial, flimsy as a dandelion clock in a breeze. Worthless. As I had always known I was. And yet look. Look at me. My heart still pumped. My fingers tapped a rhythm on the steering wheel to a radio tune I did not realise I even listened to. I looked down and saw them moving and was full of wonder. I was still here.

I drove slowly, deliberately, from the hospital. When I reached the village, I saw Linda Strachan coming out of the post office. She waved but I didn't wave back. I didn't care enough to wave, didn't care what she thought. Imagine that! Carol Ann Matthews not caring what other people thought. I knew, then, a little part of me had left already.

I drove the car up past the pond, the place where I often walked when I needed to be on my own, and then to the house, parking neatly in the drive. I didn't need to go back to the house before going, I suppose.

The funny thing is I didn't go back to collect anything. I went back to leave them.

The car. My keys. My pay-as-you-go-mobile, £2.23 in credit. I took the cheque books, the credit cards, the bank statements from my handbag and put them in an old one in the bottom of the wardrobe. I didn't pack a bag, not even one with clean underwear in it. I didn't want Carol Ann Matthews' underwear. I didn't want her life. I didn't want anything that she owned. I wanted to take her life off like an old dress and hang it in the wardrobe. Then I wanted to put on a new one that she had never seen before.

You'd think it would be hard to walk away, to leave a whole life. But it's really very simple. You walk and you keep on walking. I closed the door, heard the click of the lock. The heels of my ankle boots rang on the paving outside the house. I passed by the picture window but didn't look in. There was no nostalgia forming, no need to see things for a last time. One time more was one time too many. Deliberately I looked outward to the open road. A swallow swooped above my head on its way to the eaves.

The noise of my jeans rubbing as I walked was comforting, the rhythm of a new tune. Swish, swish, swish, a metronome marking time. A lorry thundered by, too fast on the narrow country road, brakes squealing, its load tilting dangerously. When it disappeared past, there was silence again. A glint of pink foil glittered in the grass of the ditch, a discarded chocolate wrapper. A white butterfly landed on it, wings trembling, mistaking it for a flower.

I tried to imagine what they'd think when they discovered I had gone. It is not as if there would be weeping and wailing and gnashing of teeth. Alex would be shocked at first, of course. And Stevie ...well, Stevie ... he was young still, of course, but already he was severed from me. His head, his life, were elsewhere. He no longer needed me. Sometimes, it's as if he looks right through me.

It had been my job to keep Alex and Stevie apart as much as possible, to keep the peace. What happened now? Strangely, I didn't feel the usual nagging sense of responsibility. They would simply have to sort it out themselves.

Lily ... My footsteps slowed. Lily produced the biggest stab of guilt. So helpless. I stopped, hesitated. The fact that I could walk from her shook my sense of self. What kind of person could abandon their sick mother? Then I thought of that look as she lay in the hospital bed, the look that went right through me and out the other side. She didn't know me. Anyway, the truth was that Lily had been dead for years. She didn't really exist any more. And neither did I.

Looking after her would be impossible. She and Alex could never co-exist in the same house. If I even tried, there would only be turmoil ahead and I'd had enough of that to last a lifetime. No, the only thing to do was to put these people in a box and tape it up, then put it in the loft of my mind where it could slowly gather a comforting film of dust.

I can do nothing for them. That is why it is right to walk away. I can't help them. I never have been able to help any of them. They will be better now I am gone. Alex will wait the decent amount of time and then have me declared dead – so that he can remarry – and I feel relieved about that. Carol Ann Matthews *is* dead.

There are businessmen in the patisserie, with papers spread across the table. Like Alex. Who are their wives, I wonder. Stay-at-home wives? Or women-with-their-own-lives wives? Liberation boils down to economics. I knew that as I stood outside the bookie's on the last day, my senses heightened to the nth degree. The warm smell of tar from roadworks prickled inside my nostrils. The heat had been sucked out of the day and my cheeks were stinging with the chill of spring breezes. I heard the rattle of a stank as a car trundled over it, the scoosh of a water hose on a shop window, the distant echo of a siren.

You want to know what £28,560 feels like? The notes were new and sharp and crisp and difficult to separate, the paper not yet worn limp. It did not curl or fold when held between my fingers. The colours seemed artificial. I imagined I could smell ink. But none of that matters because, actually, the feel of £28,560 pounds is much, much simpler than any of that. I'll tell you what it feels like. It feels like freedom.

I took the last train to Glasgow. It was after eleven when I arrived in the city, so I bought a toothbrush in the late-night chemist at the station and booked into a hotel. I had to give myself a new name. I only realised as I started to write that I could not use my real one. I had already written the 'Ca' of Carol when it occurred to me. I would have liked more time to think up a name, to choose something significant. But I had to decide instantly. I wrote Cara May for a Christian name and am ashamed to say I panicked and wrote Smith for a surname because it was the first thing that came into my head. How little imagination for a new beginning. I suppose I could change it any time I like, but somehow signing the hotel register felt like signing some kind of baptismal certificate. It felt like my new identity was fixed: Cara May Smith.

I washed my underwear out in the sink in the hotel room and hung it over the radiator to dry. The room was pretty basic, but there was a television, so I switched it on and lay back on the bed. Highlights of the European football. I switched over. Alex and Stevie would be watching it, though not in the same room, obviously. If I'd been home, both televisions would still have been used up, so I'd have read.

The late night Scottish news flashed up and I froze. It made me nervous. In case, you know, in case there was something about me being missing. How silly. People go missing all the time. Thousands every day. Nobody's going to care about Carol Ann Matthews going missing, or think it even remotely newsworthy, are they? And, anyway, it's too soon. But I still switch it off. I've thrown the stone in the water and now I simply want it to sink without trace. I don't want to watch ripples.

I tell myself I have to stop thinking about that woman, Carol Ann. I don't even like her very much. I'm certainly not taking her with me, carrying her like a big solid lump on my back. I'm not thinking about her and I'm not thinking about her family. They're nothing to do with me any more.

I slept naked that first night. Like a newborn. Next morning, it felt like the beginning. You might think it would be frightening, being in a strange town, being completely without possessions, having no idea of where you are going. But I wasn't frightened. £28,560 took care of fear.

This morning, I went to Marks & Spencer before breakfast to buy underwear. But I didn't buy it there. That's Carol Ann's shop. I decided that Cara May Smith is not the kind of woman who buys her underwear in Marks & Spencer. It's very creative, building a new life. You have to take it seriously. Details count.

I bought in a specialist lingerie shop. Soft, creamy satin trimmed with deep lace and threaded with ribbon. Delicate, shell-pink French knickers and balcony bra, the straps a handful of spaghetti-thin strands of twined pink lace. Blue-black voile, the colour of winter midnight, shot through with silver thread, like a thin trail of falling meteors. The assistant wrapped them carefully, in deep-purple tissue paper, and scattered scented beads into a purple paper carrier bag with black string handles. I love the feel of that bag in my hands, the way it swings, the paper rustle of it against my leg. I love the decadence of what lies buried in tissue paper in the heart of it. I am a woman who likes nice underwear.

The waitress in the patisserie is young, slender and stylish with tight curly hair and an open smile. She is dressed in black trousers and top with the ties of her long white bistro-type apron wrapped round and round her waist and tied casually. What would I like? The question makes me smile. A whole menu. I can finally have anything I want.

Cara May has blueberry muffin for breakfast and a large espresso. Possibly two. The muffin is warm still, and soft, crammed with berries that bleed blue into the light cake. I do not have to practise being Cara May. I understand her life immediately. I do not live in her; I *am* her. She is the me I have never allowed myself to be.

CHAPTER FIVE

Karen

Just as we reached the door, McFarlane stopped and turned back.

'Mackie,' he said, like it was an afterthought, 'you'd better be in on this, too.' I was rooted to the spot, but McFarlane marched on out, letting the door swing behind him. Mackie grinned and swivelled his seat round towards me, sitting in one of those gross, legs-akimbo, cock-o'-the-north male poses he specialises in. As he turned, I was hit with a wave of sweat followed by an after-ripple of cheap aftershave. The buttons of his shirt strained over the swell of his middle, mounds of belly fat creasing into concertina folds. His chair creaked with the strain as he stood up. He winked.

'C'mon Karen. Best not keep the boss waiting.'

So we're sitting there, the pair of us, in front of McFarlane's desk while he drones on. He knows we're both interested in CID work and he'll be giving us both a few tests over the coming months and watching how we respond. As he talks, there's a picture on his desk that keeps catching my eye, a snap of his wife and his four sandy-haired, turnip-headed kids. Four kids is trying too hard. It's denial. I still think he's a poof.

My eyes flick back to his face when he says he wants Mackie to be involved in a fraud case, because he thinks if Mackie has a weakness, it's organisation, and he wants to see how he copes with detailed analysis.

'And you, Karen,' he says. 'What's your weakness?'

'I think I'm pretty much an all-rounder.'

'Maybe you're not as smart as you think you are, Karen,' he says, pulling a tub of paperclips towards him. I fold my arms. Heard it all before. A voice like a parrot screeches in my head. *Who's a pretty boy, then?*

When he says he has a missing person's case for me, it takes all my control not to kick his desk over. Mackie doesn't have to say anything. I can feel suppressed laughter rippling through the quivering jelly of his fat. It isn't the usual missing-person case, McFarlane continues, trying to sell it to me. Not someone vulnerable who is mentally ill. Not an alcoholic or a dementia patient or someone with a history of walking. A nice, middle-class woman, apparently – McFarlane's sort in other words – who simply disappeared two days ago. I am supposed to do the initial investigation and see if there are any suspicious circumstances, if CID need to be pulled in.

'I am assigning you to this case because I think you need to empathise more, Karen,' McFarlane is saying. 'I know you can do the tough stuff, but I need to see that you're able to relate to people.' I don't think he sees the irony in the fact that he's refusing to look me in the eye. All the while he's talking about empathy, he's sorting paperclips into separate plastic tubs for red, yellow, green and white. Red for urgent stuff. Yellow for stuff that will be urgent next week. Green for stuff that won't ever be urgent. And blue for *who the fuck put this on my desk anyway?*

'Of course, she may turn out to be a bored housewife who's run off with her new boyfriend,' says McFarlane, as he tries to untangle a red paperclip from a blue. 'That's what I want you to find out, Karen. If CID need to be involved, we'll keep you in there as family liaison officer.'

Mackie turns to me with feigned interest, eyes full of malicious laughter. I stare back.

McFarlane swivels slightly to reach for some papers, and the light catches his thin, brown and gold streaked hair. From the side he has an angular, hooked nose and slightly flared nostrils. He is tall and thin and looks like a hawk. A buzzard, maybe.

I watch his clip-sorting for a minute, feeling utter contempt.

'You shouldn't be taking on a job that size on your own, Chief,' I say. He's so engrossed, he doesn't react at first, just keeps droning on, but a minute later he lifts his head.

'What did you say?' he says.

'What?'

'What did you say a minute ago?'

'Dunno,' I say vacantly. 'How gorgeous you are, boss? What were we talking about?'

He flashes a cold smile.

'Get us a cup of tea, Karen, would you?' he says. 'There's a love.' And then he goes back to sorting.

I headed for the toilets to compose myself when we came out, but as soon as I walked back in the door, Mackie started.

'Karen's got a missing person's case all to herself,' he told his mates. 'McFarlane thought she was the only one who could handle it. I said you're right, boss. It needs a woman's touch. And Karen's the closest we've got to a woman in here.'

Someone sniggered.

I smiled coldly and walked over to him. 'Ooh Mackie,' I said, slapping both my hands sharply either side of his cheeks in faux good humour. 'I'm amazed any woman has been close enough to you for you to recognise one.' I hit him so hard my fingers left red marks down the side of his cheeks.

'Tell you what, Karen, why don't you teach me about women? Show me the ropes,' he said, his slitty little eyes almost disappearing into his head. There were a few guffaws.

'I'm a good teacher, but I don't do remedial, Mackie,' I said, kicking his sprawling legs out of the way and heading over to fill the kettle for McFarlane.

Mackie's voice followed me, low and dirty.

'Ooh, Karen, I love it when you get rough with me.'

He rubbed his hands and shivered. I ignored him and filled the kettle. I could feel Mackie watching me still.

'Karen?'

I turned back instinctively.

'You wouldn't get me a cup, too, would you?'

I smiled at him and flicked the kettle on, then walked over to his desk. I leaned forward on my knuckles, and his eyes flicked down to my tits. He ran his tongue over his lips. There was something serpent-like about the movement.

'Mackie ...' I said.

'Yes, darlin'.'

'Piss off.'

CHAPTER SIX

Carol Ann

His fingers work deftly, the hair falling in soft, wispy clouds to the floor. Hacking through the forest of an old life, stumbling into the clearing of a new.

I walked up and down until I found a salon that looked right. One that looked younger than the kind of place Carol Ann would go. I'm offered a choice of hairdresser. Clive or Sarah? I chose Clive deliberately. Carol Ann would have chosen a woman.

Maybe because I have hopes that Carol Ann wouldn't dare to have: that a man might know how to make a woman look good. That makes sense doesn't it? Or does it? I don't seem to know what I think about anything. But if you're attracted to women, wouldn't you know what to enhance? If you love a woman's eyes you cut her hair like Audrey Hepburn. And if you love a woman's lips you make her hair tumble like a young Brigitte Bardot. Right now, it's obvious no one loves anything about me because I have hair like a Dulux dog.

The hairdresser is young, skinny hips clad in tight jeans. He wears a soft blue shirt and has rolled the sleeves back over his forearms, the way …

'What are we going to do today, then?' Clive says, running his fingers through my hair and eyeing it critically, as if it is a separate entity from me. His fingers on my scalp feel light, crisp, dextrous. 'Bit top heavy, isn't it? Needs a bit of shape.'

I nod. 'Are we going short or keeping the overall length?' he asks.

I like the way he says 'we', like we're in this together. Like there's someone on my side.

'I want ...' I say, and stop, looking at my reflection in the mirror. I don't know what I want. He stops fiddling with my hair and looks at me. Not critically or judgmentally, just like he's waiting. I smile at him. 'I want a bit more ...'

'Oomph?' he says.

'Sex appeal,' I say, at the same time.

We laugh.

'If that's possible,' I add. I am surprised the words in my head have been spoken aloud. Carol Ann would feel really silly saying that. I am glad she's not here.

He smiles back then. He understands. See, men who get paid to understand women can do it. Doctors. Psychiatrists. Hairdressers. It's only when love comes into it that things go wrong.

'I want,' I say more definitely, 'to look completely different. Unrecognisable.'

He doesn't think I mean that literally.

'Anniversary coming up? Special date?'

'Something like that.'

'You leave it to me,' he says, and he couldn't have said anything better. We're in it together, but now that he knows what I want, he'll do it. Leave it to him.

He sings softly as he works, knows all the words to the songs on the radio. He doesn't dance exactly, but I can tell he has rhythm the way he moves. When I look at him in the mirror he's catching the eye of one of the young blonde girls who's washing hair. She has one of those long fringes that sweeps her eyes, and the way she has to glance up from under it makes her seem almost coquettish. Her hair is past her shoulders and falls in sharp edges round her face, like forks of lightning. In the mirror, I see him wink at her and she smiles, glancing upwards from under long, mascara-thick eyelashes. A new, growing intimacy I think, rather than a long-established one. The most exciting part.

I like feeling his fingers in my hair. Don't get me wrong. It's nothing to do with fancying him. Not my type. He's got smaller hips than me and that's not a good start, is it? But it's intimate somehow, having a man run his fingers through your hair, lavishing that much physical attention on you outside of the bedroom. Sensuous. I miss intimacy. Intimacy stops long before sex does. I mean, I slept with him still … when I was … Well, let's just say sex and intimacy are not the same.

He stops cutting and pulls strands of hair forward onto my face. I feel the soft brush of his fingers against my cheeks. His hands are warm. He's looking in the mirror, watching the effect of the hair falling.

'See, that's softer,' he says. 'Suits your face. If we go just a little bit shorter, and lift it a bit more on top, it'll make your eyes look bigger.' He looks critically in the mirror. 'You've got great eyes,' he says. This will emphasise them.'

That's the other thing about men who are paid to listen to you. They compliment you. Once a man marries you, you can barely get good morning out of him. *Hair like spun gold.* That's what I had. I hear his voice. *Carol Ann.* I laugh suddenly, inexplicably, at the black humour of it and Clive glances at me in the mirror, surprised, questioning. I shake my head, lift a hand in apology and blush.

I watch as the hair falls, snip, snip, snip, feeling relief as it hits the floor. Dead weight falling away. Carol Ann used to get so anxious in hairdressers that she stopped going. Instead, she would stand in front of the mirror with a pair of nail scissors and snip small sections from her fringe, then grow bolder and hack chunks from the top. It'll do, she'd think. But it won't do now. I love this feeling of sitting here watching a whole life cut away. I have never felt more free in my whole life.

Clive moves constantly as he works, a continuous energy flowing from him. He flourishes the scissors like a paintbrush, cutting not just with his hands, but with a movement that takes over his whole body. And after each few minutes of cutting, he stops and ruffles the hair, watching how it lies, adjusting his movements.

The young blonde is leaving. 'Alison,' he says, picking up a can of mousse and shaking it. She is putting on her jacket, glances up self-consciously at him. I see him hold up his hand, spread his fingers. 'Five minutes?' he mouths. She nods and her eyes flick quickly from him to me, a rose blush staining her cheeks. She half smiles at me, and wanders back into a side room to wait. And whoosh, it's there, unbidden, unwelcome, my consciousness yielding to the unexpected ambush of a half-forgotten memory.

He is there, across a restaurant floor. Glasgow in the rain. I'm working as a waitress, laughing with my friend who has just messed up an order. I catch him looking at me again, cornflower-blue eyes steady and watchful. A look, a moment, a sudden knowledge of what was to come. A feeling of being on the brink of something momentous before I was ready. This has not happened yet, his look said, but we know it will ... both of us.

'Are you all right?' For a second, the voice is his. Clive puts down the scissors, watching me in the mirror rather than looking straight at me. Talking to my reflection, which is the way conversation often feels these days.

'Yes,' I say, 'oh yes, fine.'

I feel my eyes blinking rapidly, involuntarily, and shake my head in an attempt to break the tic. He sprays the mousse into his hands in an uneasy silence and then works it in deep, throwing my hair roughly, like tossing waves. Watching him dry it, it's like watching a magician. He runs his hands up through it, blowing the hot hair over his hands and I'm transfixed, watching someone else appear in the mirror. Really someone else. The wet hair is turned over the brush, until the damp limpness is transformed into a sleek, golden sheen.

'Got plans for the weekend?' he asks conversationally, above the roar of the dryer. The conversation of taxi drivers and hairdressers. I shake my head.

'Family will keep you busy, no doubt,' he says. 'You got kids?'

I barely even hesitate.

'No,' I say. 'No kids.'

CHAPTER SEVEN

Karen

I went over to the missing woman's house after taking McFarlane his coffee. I thought about spitting in it, but I couldn't risk being seen. Had to be content with putting four spoons of sugar in it. Petty? Don't give a fuck.

She's been missing two days now. Her husband didn't report it right away because he says he kept thinking she would walk back through the door. Carol Ann Matthews, forty-two, bored, middle class, earning pin money working in a local café for a few hours a week. Oh, and volunteering in a charity shop now and then just to up the excitement quotient. Christ. Mid-life crisis, I'd guess, though looking at her life, I'm surprised it took her this long to combust. Maybe it's early menopause. Except … what age *is* menopause? I don't know. Doesn't seem relevant. I can't imagine being middle-aged. There's something not real about it. It's like knowing everyone dies but, well, not you. Certainly not yet.

Anyway, she lives – lived – on the outskirts of a small village about a ten-minute drive from town. Wife, mother of a surly teenager, waitress – and that's it as far as I can see. Oh, and daughter ... to an alcoholic mother who's just had a stroke. No bloody wonder she walked.

Her husband Alex was hot, though. When it comes to supporting the family I'll volunteer for duty there. Don't know what he was doing with Carol Ann. He gave me pictures of her and she looked pretty good when she was younger, but she'd really let herself go in recent years. Why do women do that? Shapeless hair, Marks & Spencer's T-shirts, elasticated waistbands. They get a man by flashing a leg and a tight backside and as soon as they've got him they let it all go to hell. They have kids and suddenly their brains and their bellies turn to dough. Well, no way.

My mum was on at me the other night about getting married. 'You're nearly thirty, Karen,' she said. I'm twenty-seven, actually. 'Well, that's nearly thirty. And you don't want to leave having children for ever.' Want a bet?

I reckon Gav would walk down the aisle if I would. But I'm quite happy where I am, thanks very much, especially when I look at Carol Ann Matthews and see what domesticity does to a woman. He was talking the other night about *how to move our relationship on*. Bit oblique, but I knew what he was on about; he was going to suggest moving in together. I shut him up in the usual way. Fantastic the way you can short-circuit a man's brain with a little anatomical know-how. Gav's thick as pig shit sometimes, but he has a bloody good body, which is why I keep him.

Trouble is, he's thirty-six now and reckons it's time he settled a bit. Which means he thinks it's time he got himself a wife and housekeeper. Me too. I fancy having a wife as well. Now, Frenchmen ... they're smartest of all. Mistresses as well as wives. I'd rather be a mistress than a wife, any day. You get the secrets, the presents, the midnight chats, the frenzied sex over the breakfast bar. No childbearing, no sock-darning ... no contest. Come to think of it, that's what I need: a no-strings, married man. Bet Alex has a mistress. Someone that good looking isn't going to be faithful. It's just against the laws of nature.

I did the usual formal missing person stuff with Alex, entering the details into my pocket computer, then phoning the central control room to carry out hospital and custody checks. Nothing. I asked the press team to release a very brief statement about the fact that she's missing so, no doubt, by tomorrow we'll have all sorts of dubious sightings. But so far, I suppose the one interesting thing is that she's managed to disappear so neatly. Usually, there's *some* kind of clue.

The village is too small to have any CCTV, but I asked around and there was one old biddy who saw her driving by when she came out of the post office. Said Carol Ann didn't wave, that she looked preoccupied. But no one saw her after that. Of course, it could be that her old man bumped her off, but I don't suppose it's going to be as interesting as that. Far more likely to be some dreary mid-life crisis. Jesus, I hope someone just shoots me if I ever start that stuff.

The one I actually felt sorry for today was the Matthews kid, Steve. Surly wee bugger, but it's a hard age, fifteen. I, of all people, know that. I can smell fifteen, taste it still. Sometimes I think something stopped inside me at that age, that I'll have it inside me forever. Steve Matthews is at that awkward stage, like his body has grown too tall for the rest of him. As if the casing has grown and grown on the outside, but there's still something small inside, and the noise of it rattling around in there in all that space, like a marble on a wooden floor, freaks him out. But he can't say. He can't say, 'I'm frightened,' because he doesn't know being frightened is normal when you're fifteen.

I'd been there an hour when he came in, looking like he'd had a cider or two. As soon as he saw a stranger, he turned to walk out the door again.

'Hold on a minute, Steve,' his dad said.

The kid shuffled back in. He looked a bit of a handful, actually. He's so tall he looks older than almost sixteen. He's only an inch or two smaller than his dad.

'Wha's goin' on?' he said, his voice just slurring slightly at the edges.

'Have you been drinking?' Alex Matthews asked, really aggressively, like he wanted to belt him into the middle of next week.

'Nuh,' he said, staring at him, hostility forming in dark clouds on his face. Then it seemed to dawn on him. 'Wha's she doin' here?' he asked, nodding at me. His speech suddenly sobered, sharpened. 'What's happened? Have you found Mum?'

'No …'

'She's not …' The blood drained out of his face and he shrank back into being a kid somehow, leaving this empty shell of bravado behind. I saw his eyes dart towards his dad and there was panic in them.

I took over then. Tried to get him to sit down, but he wouldn't.

'If anything's happened to her …' he said to Alex with a flash of anger. I recognised that anger, the feral fear in it. 'This is your fault. What did you say to her now?'

'Steve, I didn't say anything to her. I didn't even see after I left the hospital. You saw her after I did. Now sit down and don't be stupid.' For all his sharpness, Alex looked unnerved.

'I'm not sitting down,' Steve said, but he sounded fretful, like he wanted to be defiant and couldn't find anything big enough to be defiant about. I stood up and put my hand on his shoulder, but he shrugged me off. Up close, I could smell the booze.

'Go to bed, then,' said his dad irritably.

'This better not be your fuckin' fault,' I heard him mutter, and then he went out and slammed the door behind him.

'Sorry about that.'

I shook my head dismissively.

'Why did he say that? About it being your fault?'

'Oh, for God's sake don't start reading too much into the ramblings of a half-pissed fifteen-year-old.' He rubbed his face wearily in the palms of his hands.

'Look, Mr Matthews,' I said, dead gently, like they teach you on the training courses, 'I know this is a really hard time for you, but you must understand we want to find your wife for you and I have to follow up any possible leads ...'

He mustn't take it personally when we ask questions and search the house … just a formality ... blah, blah ... best to eliminate from our enquiries ...

He stares at me throughout the spiel. He has eyes the colour of cornflowers.

'Search the house? What's the point of searching the house?'

I let the silence talk, watch the light switch on in his head. To tell the truth, I always like that little moment when you see a flicker of fear in someone's eyes, when they suddenly realise just how much power you have to turn their lives upside down.

'What? You mean ...'

'As I say, just a formality, Mr Matthews. But if there's any reason why your wife was upset, perhaps ...'

'Carol Ann's always upset, as far as I can see.'

He leaned his head back on the sofa. He has a good body. Lean and athletic but broad shouldered. I'd say he must be six foot two, anyway. He looks like he's in his late thirties, early forties at most, but he's six years older than Carol Ann, according to the notes. He had this white shirt on from work still, tie loosened and top buttons undone, cuffs turned back to the forearms. The white of it made his skin look bronzed.

'What now?' he said.

'Like I said, we have to search the house. And the garage and the farm outbuildings up the track there. I'll also need some details from you about friends and family. And we'll go through all of Carol Ann's belongings, just making sure there's no clue about what's happened to her. Obviously, with her mother being so ill ...'

'Christ – Lily!' he said, and sat bolt upright. 'With all this, I forgot to phone the hospital ...' He slumped down again. 'Don't suppose it matters.'

'Are you close to Carol Ann's mother?'

'No,' he said, almost rudely. He clearly didn't care what I thought. He didn't even bother looking at me.

'Well, it may be that Carol Ann's just really upset about her mum and will come back in a couple of days when she's come to terms with things ...'

He nodded. 'Yeah, I suppose so.'

'But we can't bank on that so, in the meantime, we'll start going through anything we can that's left here. We'll run a check on her bank account to see if there's any movement there.'

'Oh yeah, of course. Will the bank tell us where she's withdrawn from?'

'They can tell us if there's movement in the account, but they won't tell us where she has withdrawn from, Mr Matthews. If a person deliberately goes missing, it is their right to retain privacy. The most we can do is ensure they are safe and let their family know, but if they don't want to be found, we can't do anything about it.'

'So if there's no movement in the account, how do we know she's not lying murdered in a ditch somewhere?' he demanded.

It seems a pretty brutal question for a husband to ask.

'We don't,' I say, equally brusquely. Maybe too brusquely. An expression passes through his eyes, a mixture of pain and fear and uncertainty. He looks rattled. I find it hard to work out what he feels about her.

'You said Carol Ann's mobile is here?'

'Over there.' He nods at the kitchen work-top.

'We'll go through phone records, try and piece together who she was talking to before she left, what she was doing.'

He nods, but he's not really listening. He leans forward, his forearms resting on his knees, hands clasped.

'Do you think you'll find her?' he says, and the way he asks the question is suddenly so naive, so completely transparent, that I feel almost thrown.

'I don't know, Mr Matthews,' I say. 'I hope so.'

Leave hope, but make no promises – that's what we're told. I don't know, there's something about Alex Matthews. Something detached, cut off. I can't quite figure it. It's not that I think he killed his wife, not exactly … well, I don't know. But he has a kind of guilt, somehow, as if he thinks on some deeper level he might be culpable for her disappearance. It intrigues me. There's a story behind this pair, that's for sure.

Gavin comes over unexpectedly. I hate surprises. The bell goes and when I answer it, he's standing there on the doorstep, grinning, like he's brought me a surprise present of … him. Drum flourish. Taraaa! Like I'm going to be pleased to see him.

I'm not.

'What do you want?' I say rudely.

His hair is damp from the shower and he's carrying a gym bag. He points to it like a gypsy pedlar who is carrying untold riches of sparkling beads and bangles and jewelled hairclasps.

'Would the pretty lady like to see my wares?' he says suggestively.

'Nope,' and I push the door as if to close it.

He sticks his foot out and the door bounces off his shoe.

'Playing hard to get,' he says. 'Hmm. I like a challenge.' He leans against the door-frame, still thinking I am kidding. He is wearing black jeans and a black short-sleeved T-shirt that shows off the firm bulge of his muscles. He is in good shape, Gavin.

The thing is, I have my space. I like to remain in control of it. I don't like people coming in uninvited. Gav thinks because we've been seeing each other for six months that gives him some kind of territorial right to call round when he wants. I walk away from the door, leaving him on the step, knowing he'll follow me in. I want to tell him to piss off.

I hear the thump of his bag as he dumps it in the hall.

'Thought we could eat together tonight since we were both off,' he shouts. 'Just a chill-out night with a film or something.' He starts to whistle, except it's not a proper whistle. It's this silly, grating sound that he makes with his tongue on the roof of his mouth. It drives me nuts.

I stick my head out of the kitchen door.

'Yeah? So what were you thinking of making?'

'Oh,' he says, surprised. Clearly he thought I would do the making, which shows how much he's learned in six months. 'Ehm ... I could do some spaghetti ... or something.'

'Like hell you will.'

I am not having him cooking in my kitchen. Four dirty pots, tomato splashed everywhere, garlic clinging to the press because he hasn't rinsed it right, cold, slimy worms of congealed pasta blocking the sink. And the smug expectation of thanks. Darling, you are so clever. You must be so tired now, so you lie back and I'll do the dishes. A whole night's work to shift his mess while he lies out on the sofa watching sport on television. Fuck off to that.

Gav looks startled, wide Bambi eyes.

'You okay?' he says. 'Something happened?'

'I'm fine,' I say. I flash him a smile, a ray of winter sunshine reflecting on deep, cold snow. He's too stupid to know the difference.

'Nip down the Chinese, though, eh?'

'Oh, right. Yeah, okay,' he says. 'What do you fancy?'

Gavin chop suey and rice. That's what I fancy.

He's going to have to go.

CHAPTER EIGHT

Carol Ann

I simply went with the wind, submitting almost sacrificially to the direction it blew. A thought, a whim, a chance direction. A train, a bus, a missed destination. A change of plan. A tossed coin. A random thought.

The closest thing to strategy was a memory that surfaced and resurfaced, each time clicking in my head with increased clarity. When I was a child, Lily and I went on holiday only once. We caught the Irish bus in the Gorbals and headed to Donegal. I was so excited about that holiday, thinking that for one magical week, everything would change. Lily and I would be normal. For the first day maybe we were, but Lily couldn't keep it up. As the week wore on, the disappointment cut deeper. There was no magic. There was no normality. By the day we left, we might as well have been back home already.

And yet Donegal, with its healing palette of soft colour, had its own magic. That week, it wrapped its landscape round me in a comfort blanket that I never forgot. A smirr of rain that pitter-pattered gently on burgeoning greenery; sun that broke through skidding cloud; a breeze that whispered comfort in my lonely walks while Lily slept off the booze. Despite everything, I always wanted to go back. Alex never thought it much of a holiday destination. Only I wanted to go there. Now there is only me to consider.

I take the bus to Donegal, just as I did all those years ago with Lily. I ignore the ghosts who try to whisper in my ear. In Donegal, I take a random selection of buses and end up in a village called Killymeanan. I was really heading for the town of Balgannan, ten miles on, but there is something about Killymeanan that calls to me instantly. The small whitewashed church with blue stained glass. Hanging baskets outside a post office. I shout to the driver, asking him to pull in and am surprised at the sound of my own voice. I wonder about the decision as soon as the bus drives off, kicking back a cloud of dust and gravel and leaving me in the stillness. I have won some money but not security for life. I have to work and I suspect I would be better off in Balgannan.

I test the capricious instinct. One of life's chance conversations, in the Killymeanan post office. *A house to rent? Well, there's Peter Murnaghan's place. Jenny, is Peter Murnaghan's house to rent yet? I heard the builders were gone. Sure, why don't you ask him, he can only say no. Left at the phone box. Second on the right. House with a green door.* Strange the way life is. The way you end up going where you go, seemingly on a whim. The way the random, the insignificant, is at the root of everything that matters.

My new house is a simply furnished holiday home, a terraced cottage at the end of the village. It is basic, but recently renovated and therefore bright and fresh. The owner has only just modernised it, was about to advertise it in the brochures. I have it on a four-month let before he markets it properly in the autumn. He is pleased, I think, to have found a long term-tenant without even having to advertise.

The house is pretty, with square-paned windows and an arched front door. It has clumps of unruly honeysuckle and hedges of wild roses. Two bedrooms, a small kitchen, a sitting room with 'character', beams which means they aren't real and come from B & Q. The only drawback to the place is the neighbours: the side window overlooks the cemetery. It is more than I ever dared dream of, but then the dream never involved Paris Rose romping to victory.

The sitting room has a light blue carpet and two light blue canvas two-seater sofas with cream scatter cushions. On a small table in the corner is a blue vase with artificial creamy poppies, heads scattered with black seeds, and a handful of cornflowers. So much blue. I think I will have to get rid of the cornflowers. They unnerve me. It feels like he's in the room when I look at them. I picked some wild flowers today, a paler blue, to put on the windowsill. Forget-me-nots that I saw crammed in the ditch outside, beautiful, dainty little heads emerging victorious from the slurry of rainwater and mud that gathered in a dank pool at the bottom.

The house smells of wood, new wood, freshly varnished. I love the bedroom. It is the colour of sunshine, the colour of rape seed, not when it is in full bloom but when it first begins to burst open and is still mixed with lots of green stalks. In this room I am bathed in sunlight. It will be summer even in winter.

I have never been to Killymeanan in my life before. But this is where the wind blew me. Had there been no accommodation I would almost certainly have headed on to Balgannan. But Killymeanan somehow opened its arms to me in welcome and perhaps, eventually, I can buy a little second-hand car. For now there is the country bus, a red single-decker that trundles round by the coast and on through rich green farmland.

Killymeanan is slightly inland, half a mile from the coastal tip where breakers crash against rocks on stormy days, where the wind whips seaweed up like candyfloss and leaves it strewn across the stony section at the top of the sandy beach. There is enough wind in Killymeanan to whip up a life and rearrange it.

CHAPTER NINE

Karen

All in a week's work: one drunken old bastard who threw up in the back of the car on the way to the night shelter; one office 'break-in' conducted by two twelve-year-olds who threw a brick through the window and got away with less than a tenner from a charity bottle and a packet of KitKat Chunky from the tea cupboard; and one complaint from this posh bird who says her neighbour insists on walking about starkers in front of the window in the flat opposite hers. Mackie was almost drooling as we took her statement. He kept raising his eyebrows and pouting his lips suggestively at me when she turned her back on him. She was gaggin' for it, he declared on the way back to the car. Probably has her binoculars trained on his window.

It's been a relief to have an excuse to get off on my own and nose about the Matthews case. I like working alone. That way, you don't have to stick by the rules. The more I'm round at the house, the more I think there's something strange about that family. They're all so ordinary on the surface, but you get the feeling it's a house where no one really talked to anyone else, where everyone had their secrets. Especially Alex.

It's not that Carol Ann Matthews is unique. People go missing all the time. Over 200,000 of them every year. Unless there are obviously suspicious circumstances, we can't do much. Most are teenage runaways, but even when it comes to adults, the majority are found within days.

Usually, you know immediately why they've gone. Mental health problems. Drug problems. Debt problems. Trouble with their partners. They wander out of their lives and, most of the time, they wander back in. Of course, we target the vulnerable, the at-risk, but we can't go chasing everyone who fancies a long walk.

Carol Ann is a little more mysterious. Posh house. Good-looking bloke. Boring as fuck, but not the kind of life you run from. I've done all the usual checks and the complete absence of explanation, clues or motive makes her disappearance a bit more suspicious than the usual. In those circumstances, McFarlane would expect me to alert CID. But I'd rather stall, nose around some more. As soon as they get involved, I'll be on family liaison duty, which means hand-holding. Here, cry on my shoulder, boo-hoo. I want to at least go through her mobile phone records first. It would do me no harm if I could pass this on as a partially constructed case.

I switch Carol Ann's mobile on for the first time; there is a voicemail message. Sally from a Dr Hammond's office. Something about Carol Ann not turning up for an appointment and would she like to reschedule. I scribble down the number and quickly sift through old text messages for anything that jumps out, making a note of call details as I go. They will all need to be properly checked.

If the phone settings are correct, it looks like the call from the doctor's office came the morning after she disappeared. My first thought is that maybe she recently got told something awful, like she had terminal cancer, and she topped herself by jumping off some cliff or other rather than face chemo. But as it turns out, Dr David Hammond is not a proper doctor. He's a head doctor, a shrink.

His office is up two flights of stairs in a run-down part of town. He's an old guy, I'd say in his early sixties but he could be more. He has a head of thick grey hair and a trimmed grey beard and he smells of mint.

Small hands; neatly filed white nails. He wears a navy jacket and a deep blue shirt and a blue handkerchief in his top pocket. I hate men with matching handkerchiefs.

Hammond has that really irritating, old-codger way of talking, formal and prissy, and he looks at you in a way that suggests he thinks the world is falling about his ears because nobody has manners any more. Usually people are a bit wary of being too snooty to police, but Hammond clearly isn't impressed. He irritates the hell out of me almost immediately.

He doesn't exactly call me 'young lady', but he has that kind of tone. I can hear the click of a mint against his teeth as we talk. He leafs through a large desk diary. Mrs Matthews, he says, had an appointment with him at 5 p.m. on Thursday, 24th May. She didn't turn up, which was unusual. He had Sally, his receptionist, phone her to see if she had merely forgotten, and if she would care to make another appointment.

'Why did Sally not phone her house – why the mobile?'

Hammond picks up the phone on his desk and pushes a button.

'Sally, can you come in a moment please?' he says quietly, then replaces the receiver. His every movement is somehow small, restrained and contained.

When Sally comes into the room, I can't help thinking that people should stop being called Sally when they hit forty. There is something girlish about it. How do you draw a pension when you're called Sally? Can't they call themselves Sarah or something once they start wearing crimplene trousers?

This one's a smug Sally. She gazes at me from behind slim-rimmed glasses and as soon as I speak I see a switch being flicked. I often see that switch flicked in middle-class women like her. There is something about me that makes them retreat behind their fine new wool cardigans and a thin-lipped smile. I don't know what it is. I don't care enough to find out.

'My understanding is that Mrs Matthews preferred to be contacted on her personal line,' Sally says when I repeat the question. 'We were instructed not to phone her home number. In fact, we didn't have a home number for her, though I dare say we could have got it easily enough if it were required.'

'Is she an NHS patient?' I ask Hammond.

'Yes.'

'How long had she been coming to see you?'

'About nine months.'

'What about?'

'A variety of things.'

'What things?'

Hammond hesitates. 'I have to respect my patient's confidentiality.'

'Your patient is missing, Dr Hammond.'

'People sometimes *choose* to go missing,' he says. 'That is their right. And sometimes they choose to return in their own time.'

'Yeah? Well, let's see if we can just speed the process up a bit, eh?'

He says nothing, but the muscles of his cheeks tense momentarily, quivering like butterfly wings above his jaw line. He really doesn't like my style, though I think he recognises my efficiency. Then suddenly, unexpectedly, he smiles.

'How, exactly, do you think I can help you?'

His voice is very calm, soft. He practises hypnotherapy as well as psychotherapy apparently, though you wouldn't catch me letting myself be put under by some old bloke in a room behind closed doors. Half of them are pervs.

'I need to know about Carol Ann's state of mind.'

He looks at me unblinkingly, his face a barren, lunar landscape. 'There is no CID investigation into this?' he asks. 'This is not an official demand – just a request?'

Hmm. Not stupid then.

'Dr Hammond,' I continue, 'I understand that privacy is important, but it may be that Carol Ann Matthews is in danger. That's *more* important. And if she is, I need to move fast. What I need you to think about is whether there was anything Carol Ann told you that would make you believe she was about to leave her home and her family. If she did, then hopefully I'm looking for a live person. If she didn't, then …' I look at him expectantly. 'You take my point?'

'It's really not that easy.'

Sally hovers uneasily still, clutching a folder to her chest. 'I'll just ...' she says.

Hammond glances briefly at her and nods. Their eyes lock momentarily, a wave of silent communication running between them.

'Well, did she or didn't she?'

'Did she or didn't she what?' says Hammond

'Did she say anything to make you think she was about to leave?'

'Not directly, no. But just because she didn't express the intention doesn't mean she didn't have the desire.'

'Dr Hammond, would you say Carol Ann was the kind of person who would simply walk away from her life?'

'Carol Ann struggled with a ... a sense of duty, perhaps, that kept her ... close to home. But of course, that creates its own burdens.'

'A sense of duty?'

His mouth turns up into a flicker of a smile. 'An old-fashioned concept.' He sounds sarcastic.

Okay, things are not going to fit this way. I am going to have to turn them round slightly.

'Let's leave Carol Ann out of this for a moment. Somebody who walks away from their life ... what makes them do it?'

'Well, fairly obviously, people who simply walk away are usually not thinking normally. Many will be clinically depressed.'

'Was Carol Ann depressed?'

He continues without pause, as if he hasn't heard me speak.

'Some will have alcohol problems.'

'Did Ca–'

'While for others it will be connected to the onset of dementia.'

'Carol Ann was too young for that.'

'She would be outwith the highest risk cohort for dementia,' agrees Dr Hammond. His calmness irritates me somehow. It's like when you see a too-perfect head of hair and you want to stick your hand in it and ruffle it up. That's what Hammond is like: a too-perfect head of hair. His elbows are resting on his chair, the tips of his fingers steepled together. His desk is not just uncluttered but almost bare. A telephone. A large A4 pad in front of him. A black pot with pens. That's not natural, is it? Looks like he's sitting waiting for the phone to ring.

'Sometimes,' Hammond says, 'people's lives simply become intolerable. It's like that children's game ...'

He frowns.

'Cluedo?' I say dryly. 'Hunt the thimble? Postman's knock?' I don't think he detects the sarcasm.

'Buckaroo!' he says suddenly. 'Buckaroo – where you pile all sorts of things on the horse's saddle but eventually there comes one final thing that triggers the horse bucking. One tiny little thing. The straw that breaks the camel's back. A person may be living under a great deal of stress, but they are keeping up a pretence of normality. And then one day something happens ... *something*... that simply flicks a switch and they can't pretend any more. At that point they can no longer cope and they remove themselves from the stressful situation. They run away.'

'Or top themselves?'

Hammond looks at me disapprovingly.

'Sometimes a person will commit suicide, yes.'

'How much stress was Carol Ann under?'

'She wouldn't have been coming here if she didn't have her stresses,' he says carefully.

'But not suicidal?'

'I wouldn't have thought so.'

I take my pen and start doodling on the side of my pad. Other possibilities, I think, drawing a square in the margin. What are they? *Other possibilities*. I keep adding squares on the page, box after box. I look up suddenly to find Hammond staring.

'Is it possible, Dr Hammond, that the person who suddenly disappears literally forgets who they are?'

'It's possible but unlikely. A person can suffer a kind of temporary amnesia, during which the brain simply shuts down. That situation can go on until there is a trigger that reminds them of their old life and who they really are. But it's rare. More often a person simply dissociates themselves from their life and their stresses in order to walk away from them. It's like not being able to cope with the person that you are, so you walk away and create another one that you *can* cope with being. At least for a little while. But you don't actually believe you *are* another person.'

'But won't things get out of hand again in the person's new life?'

'Possibly. It's hard to say.'

Hammond makes me frustrated. All that control. 'Is there *anything* you can tell me about Carol Ann that might help our inquiry?'

He tilts his head back slightly to lean on his chair.

'I think at this stage, probably not.'

'At this stage?'

'I think we need to see if Carol Ann returns in a few days or even a few weeks.'

'I'm not sure you understand, Dr Hammond. She hasn't gone on holiday. She's missing.'

'"Missing" is a word for those left behind. I very much doubt Mrs Matthews is missing to herself. I imagine she knows precisely where she is.'

At first, I think he's playing word games. Then I realise it is his way of telling me that if Carol Ann has disappeared, she's in control of both the leaving and the returning. She's not a victim. Clearly, he's not convinced she's come to any harm.

'I'll say good afternoon, Dr Hammond. I'll be in touch.'

He inclines his head but says nothing, rising from his seat to open the door.

You know, sometimes you have an instinct when you're leaving a room that as soon as you close the door, whoever you leave behind it is going to talk about you. I have that sense very strongly when I leave his office. Maybe it's the way Sally looks up from under her lashes as I walk by. When I catch her eye, she gives me one of those polite, official smiles.

'Bye,' she says.

Or maybe it's the way Hammond stands in the doorway of his office waiting for me to leave instead of closing his own door. Waiting to talk to Sally. He's probably having it off with her. They both look dull enough. By appointment only. In fact, it's probably in that desk diary of his. Wednesday, 5.30 p.m.: sex with Sally.

I stand for a second behind the closed door, listening. I can imagine her eyes shooting up to him, the glance running between them.

Sally's light, trilling laugh drifts outward.

'Can you imagine ...?' she says and the rest is lost in a low murmur.

Hammond's voice is soft, level. 'I rather think ...' he says, but I don't wait to hear what he thinks. I don't care what either of them thinks.

Fuckwits.

CHAPTER TEN

Carol Ann

My sleep is dreamless here in Donegal. White sleep, a blank sheet unmarked with images. I have no past life, no memories to call on. As peaceful as the sleep of the dead in the cemetery that sits opposite the house. It does not disturb me as I thought it might, sleeping beside the dead. In the daylight, I watch the visitors and then, in twilight, when the summer blue of the sky darkens and the green trees turn black with the night, I see the votive lights, encased in red glass, flickering on the graves. And then when night falls completely, the lights glitter like animal eyes in the darkness, living things amongst the dead.

In the daytime, I walk. Miles and miles along the undulating country roads, past hedges of creamy honeysuckle and blood red fuchsia side by side. Past moorlands peppered with stones and bracken and yellow ragwort, and ditches choked with meadowsweet. Today I walked over the hill that leads from Killymeanan to the coast, only this time I headed west, over the path that winds round the hill and down over the sand dunes. The sand is ivory white, dry and soft underfoot. Clumps of reeds and grasses shoot tall through the sweep of it, tufts of hair on a balding pate. Over the last bump of the dunes the landscape opens out, a vast expanse of secret beach, damp and firm as concrete under foot. Down by the water, the sand is marked with the tide, the imprint of the waves rolling silver across the shore.

And then I saw it. On the east side of the beach, on the hill above a rocky outcrop, was a concrete beach hut, the outer walls blue-washed like the sea. I scrambled across the rocks and climbed the short burst of hill to the hut. It lay open to the elements, the door missing and the floor carpeted with sheep dung and jagged broken glass from the windows. A small discarded cooker lay on its side, and above, a strip of kitchen paper still clung to the walls, squares of red spoons and kitchen jugs printed on a white background.

The proportions of the hut were tiny, a small square for a bedroom, with only the rusting metal frame of bunk beds fitting into the space. A cupboard-sized area at the back of the house with an old WC, the wooden seat twisted and hanging off the green tarnished porcelain. But while the rooms were small, the windows were huge. Only remnants of glass remained in the frames. Even in the state it was in, you could imagine what it was like to wake here, to come to with the sound of the sea washing onto the rocks below, or to hear the windows rattle in their frames with the wind and look out over the deserted beach, the water clear and blue, and white with choppy froth.

I stood there in the quiet, the June sunshine streaming through the empty window frames, and I looked at it with the same kind of look Alex had all those years ago in the restaurant. A look that knew certain events would unfold. It was just an old, desolate ruin, with no water or light and a floor that crunched under foot. But I have never had any trouble imagining how perfect the imperfect could be. And somehow, it felt like coming home.

Sometimes at night, I stand at the window and stare into the darkness, just thinking, my fingers tracing the pattern on the blue brocade curtains. Watching the clouds cross the moon, thinking of a soldier's description I once read of the stars above the Egyptian desert. No clouds, no smog, just a jewelled sky that spoke of an infinity greater than the grains of sand beneath. You have big thoughts in the Egyptian desert, the soldier said. Thoughts of eternity, of the endless possibilities of existence. But you do not need the Egyptian desert to think big thoughts. I think them here beneath the star-studded sky of Killymeanan.

A car headlight rises and dips slowly in the road outside the house, driving past the front window, then turning left so that the beam falls round the side of the house, next to the cemetery. I switch the light off in the sitting room so that whoever is there will not see me watching from behind the curtain.

The car swings round, stopping at an angle to the gate, deliberately casting light over a section of the graveyard to the right of the entrance. The driver's door is almost side-on to my house. The engine dies but the beams of light remain focused. There is only one person in the car. I move the curtain a fraction more, straining to see who is at the wheel. The car door opens and then the driver, an elderly man, bends, before swivelling round. He is lifting one leg with both hands, from the pedal to the ground, as if it is a dead weight, incapable of independent movement. He swings the other leg round and places his hands on the open frame of the door to manoeuvre himself to standing.

I let the curtain drop a moment as he turns to face my window and shuts the car door. It's just instinct; he's not aware of my presence. When I look again he has the back door open and is lifting out a walking stick. He is dressed formally, as though for a visit, with a tie and what looks in the half-light to be a tweed jacket, and on his head, a cap. He is his late sixties, perhaps early seventies, and walks with a slight roll, like a listing ship, the walking stick bearing the weight of his right leg.

The cemetery gates are never locked here. Neither is the church. The man walks slowly, heading up the slight incline of the graveyard and into the light cast by the headlights of his car. The grave he visits looks to be roughly in the third row up. Irish graveyards have surprised me;

each lair here is surrounded by a little kerb that gives the outline almost of a bed that the dead slumber in. There are pictures on some, and flowers, and little religious artefacts: medals and statues of the Sacred Heart and stone prayer books carved with a few lines of remembrance. I cannot see from the window what lies on the grave that he visits, but the stone is a simple Celtic cross.

He takes off his cap. Then he reaches out a hand to the cross, and at first I think he is holding on to it for balance. But I see then that he strokes it, caressing the cold stone with the gentleness that you would stroke an infant's soft face. I feel guilty watching this intimacy, and yet I cannot let the curtain drop. He stays for some minutes, then bends forward and lightly kisses the stone before slowly walking back to the path. He turns then, gives a last look, replaces his cap and limps to the gate. A minute later I hear the car door bang, the engine start, and the light moves slowly back along the main road.

There is a shop here that sells bottled milk, something I thought was a thing of the past. It gives me a strange feeling when I lift the bottle from the chiller cabinet in the village store and hear it clink against its neighbour. There is no sound I associate more with childhood than the chink of Lily's bottles. Not milk bottles, obviously.

The milk bottle is cold against my hand, chilling my fingers. Just looking at it roots me to the spot, unable to move. I shake my head, desperately trying to clear the memories, trying to push Lily from my mind.

She was sly. All alcoholics are sly. They can't help it. In the years after my father left she was often drunk, but I rarely saw her actually drinking. She drank when I was at school. When I was in bed. Whenever I was out. I think she drank in the bathroom because she kept a bottle down beside the toilet, hidden in the caddy that held the bleaches and toilet cleaners and cloths. In the end I became aware the bottles were everywhere, in nooks and crannies all over the house.

I used to hear her cry sometimes. Her bed was on the other side of the wall from mine. Sometimes I'd lie with my face to it, aware that she was doing the same on the other side. It was like we lay on a double bed with a barrier down the middle. Her crying was low and terrible. Sometimes I would wrap my head up in a pillow and turn the other way, trying to block it out, trying to pretend the room at my back on the other side of the wall didn't exist. Sometimes I hummed softly, hearing the muffled sound ring tunelessly inside my own head, blotting out the sound of pain.

I never went in to comfort her. I didn't know how. She cried for things I knew nothing about, though I can guess at them now. But sometimes I tried to help in little ways. When I was twelve, I came home from school once and found her asleep on the couch. The room was cold. The house was untouched from when I had left that morning, two days' dishes strewn around the kitchen, the light flashing on the washing machine. I covered her with a blanket and quietly tidied up before hanging up the clothes and going upstairs to the drying cupboard to get the basket of ironing. I had never done the ironing before. But I thought that maybe it would make her happy. Maybe when she woke she would see that I loved her and she would smile. I would make us both something to eat, and we would sit together and watch television. Maybe tonight she wouldn't cry.

The basket felt heavy, inordinately heavy. I lugged it through to the bedroom, dumped it on the bed, and lifted the top layer curiously. There was something hard wrapped in a T-shirt. A bottle. Further down the basket was another, wrapped in a woollen jumper. And another in a towel. And another. And another. I looked blankly at the pile of dark green glass assembled on the white counterpane.

Lily was still asleep downstairs. I went into her bedroom, pulled her dressing table stool across to her wardrobe and stood on it. I reached up and tentatively put my hand into the dip on top of the wardrobe. My fingers ran a trail through a layer of dust, then they hit an obstruction. Cold. Hard. I lifted it up, threw the bottle onto Lily's bed, watched it sink into the duvet with a small firework of dust. There were three up there. And two in the back of the wardrobe amongst her shoes. And one at the bottom of the wicker basket where the dirty washing was kept. And another two in the drawer in the base of the bed where she kept her sheets.

The bottles frightened me. I wanted them out of the house. I went down to the kitchen and rummaged in the cupboard for some black bin liners. Then I collected up the bottles and shoved them roughly into the bag. Clink, clink, clink. I threw it over my shoulder like Santa's sack and carried it downstairs, listening to the sound of banging glass, the bottles chinking and tumbling inside the bin liner as if they had taken on a life of their own. Lily woke as I came downstairs, rushed distractedly into the hall like she didn't know where she was. For one second our eyes met and the worst bit was the streak of shame that I saw flit through her eyes and away again, fast as a man on a galloping horse.

'Don't put them all out at once,' she said, voice low.

I said nothing but continued with the bag to the bin at the back door. In my fear and my distress I was pitiless, ignoring her stricken face. They were going out. Out.

I always escaped to bed as early as I could as a teenager, but I could rarely sleep. I would lie, tense and alert, listening for the sound of crashes from downstairs: the glasses tumbling from the cupboard into a pool of shattered glass; the thump of the carved wooden statue that sat on a small table in the hall, and which Lily regularly knocked over; the stumbling, fumbling, creaks and bangs of her finally negotiating the stairs for bed.

I worried if I heard the bath taps running, that she would fall asleep and drown. Or that she would use electrical equipment with wet hands.

I worried about her, but I worried about me, too. There was always the possibility that she had left something on downstairs, that we would be fried as we slept. Or that I would waken to find someone standing by my bed because Lily had left the front door wide open.

I could not rest until I knew she was asleep. Then I would sneak downstairs and check systematically, over and over, like someone who cannot resist washing their hands repeatedly. Back in bed, the thoughts would revolve in a constant circle. Did I check the cooker? The door? The tap? I did. Didn't I? And though I knew I had, sometimes I would be forced downstairs again by the nagging fear. Cooker. Check. Door. Check. Taps. Check.

It was noticed in school, my white face and heavy-lidded torpor. The teachers knew my background, of course. Broken family, they called it then. Iffy mother. My form teacher kept me behind once and asked diffidently, with awkward embarrassment, if everything was all right, you know, at home ...

'Yes, Miss,' I said and she nodded with thinly disguised relief.

'Sure?' she said, but didn't wait for a reply. 'Off you go then, Matheson.'

Off you go. Run along. Close the door behind you. Childhood was about dismissal. For a moment I am back there and I close my eyes, fighting back tears, pushing out memories, re-establishing the boundaries. A hand on my shoulder. A woman's hand. Lily? And then I realise I am still in the village shop, at the chiller cabinet, my hand gripping the milk bottle still. My fingers feel colder than the bottle.

'Are you all right there? Can I help you with that?' The voice is gentle. The middle-aged woman who runs the shop is looking at me, her pale-grey eyes pools of concern in a face devoid of make-up. It has its own beauty, that face.

'Oh ... yes, thank you ... I'm fine. I just ... I ... I felt a little faint ... I ...'

'Would you like a seat?'

'No..no … thank you. I'll just take this and get home.'

'Are you sure now?'

I pay the money with stiff, chilled fingers and try to smile.

CHAPTER ELEVEN

Karen

After the promising – but misleading – start of a psychiatrist's number on Carol Ann's phone, there has been little of interest since. The school … the dry cleaner … the dreary woman who runs the local village café she worked in. A friend she met when Steve was at playgroup and who she hasn't seen for the last nine months. That counts as bosom buddies in Carol Ann's constipated life. She has no immediate family other than her mother. When I finally found myself connected to Tesco 'shop and drop' in town, I just shook my head. Did this woman not have a *life*?

Then things changed. I don't know why exactly. I think it was the first day the phone beeped with a text message. After that, her phone becomes like a viewfinder into another life. It fascinates me. I carry it in my bag, though I know I should keep it locked away in case it becomes evidence. But I feel almost like another person when I am carrying it. Like I can slip into her life for a little while and walk around in it. It may be a dull life but it's safe. Privileged. A woman with a shrink, for God's sake. You don't get them where I come from.

It was only Steve's school calling that first day the phone went. An automated text message. 'Steven is absent today. Only contact the school if you are concerned. Please ensure a note on his return. Thank you.' God knows where he was off to. I tried to imagine what it would be like if he were my son, if this really were a message for me, but I couldn't. I decided not to tell Alex, just to save the information up and give Steve the fright of his life when I needed to. Make him think he was being watched. Make him owe me something for not telling his dad. Always useful to have people owe you.

Beep. Beep. Beep. Carol Ann's mobile sounds from deep inside my bag while I am on my way home from work. The unfamiliar tone makes me jump. A surge of adrenaline. Having Carol Ann's mobile ring out is slightly spooky, like having a message from the dead. I'm carrying a little bit of her life around, and the edges between her existence and mine begin to blur slightly when it happens. Is it for her? For me?

A small envelope appears in the phone window. Text message. My fingers press the buttons quickly. Select. Read. Back in town end of next week. Can u meet Friday? Please? Doug. I've been through all the numbers on this phone and there was definitely no one called Doug. Makes me wonder if Carol Ann deleted numbers deliberately before she left. Now why would she do that? Whoever he is, Doug obviously doesn't even know she's missing.

I hesitate only for a few seconds before hitting reply. He might know something. Where? I write, and press send. Within two minutes, the beep, beep, beep sounds again. Usual? 1pm.

Shit. My fingers fly over the buttons. Would Carol Ann use abbreviations? Don't know why, but I doubt it. I write in full. No. Somewhere different. Rossi's. Across the bridge. 1.30. I'll book. The message back is less brief. You'll book? Very practical! You sound different. Bossy! Thanks for meeting. Longing to see you again. I read the message several times and close the phone over with a snap. Nearly two weeks to wait before finding out who Doug is. I don't risk another message. Even in a few words, it seems, you reveal yourself. The phrase goes over and over in my mind. 'Longing to see you.' *Longing* to see you. Not 'looking forward to seeing you'. Not 'can't wait to see you'. Longing. Longing to see you. Like a lover.

Steve let me in when I went round to the house again today. Alex had taken the day off work and was sitting in a chair, lost in thought. He didn't bother even getting up when I came in. I needed to speak to him again about Carol Ann's bank account.. There's been no movement in the main account he told me about, but I need to double check with him that there are no other savings accounts with other banks or building societies that she might have tapped into. You can ask people the same question over and over before they suddenly remember something they haven't told you before.

'No movement?' he repeated, ignoring my question. 'Nothing?'

But there's another reason I'm here.

'Does the name Doug mean anything to you?'

I can't tell if he really hasn't heard or is pretending not to.

'Alex?'

'What?'

'Does Carol Ann know anyone called Doug?'

'Doug? Not as far as I know. Why?'

The phone went. He jumped immediately, but it was the hospital about Lily.

'I see,' I heard him say. 'Yes, that's good.'

Steve was listening, scowling as usual.

'Yes, I'll try and come in later today for a bit,' Alex said. I could see his teeth gritting.

Steve threw himself onto the sofa and watched his father through half-shut eyes.

'Well, she can't come here!' Alex exploded. 'No, no, I understand. But ... yes ... yes, I know.' He walked to the window, shoulders hunched with tension. 'She's my wife's mother and as you know, my wife's gone missing and ... yes. Yes, she … it's difficult.' He listened for a minute, saying nothing, but his eyes glanced up at me watching him. 'I'll discuss it with you when I come in,' he said tersely. He stood still for a minute when the call ended, then walked out to replace the phone on the base station. I think he just wanted out of the room for a minute.

He said nothing when he returned.

'How is she?' I asked carefully.

'Early days,' he said 'But she's okay. Her speech is a bit confused and her walking is impaired, but the stroke was actually pretty minor. The biggest danger is that this is just a prelude to a bigger one, so they've put her on blood-thinning medication, which is about all they can do. They want to talk already about plans for her when she is discharged. They've said she can continue to get physio and speech therapy from home.'

He folded his arms and his head dropped slightly. I could see his lips setting in a grim line, his chest heaving with a deep, controlled inward breath. I glanced sideways at Steve. He was watching his father with intense, pitiless eyes.

'Bloody National Health Service,' said Alex. 'No sooner through the door than they're trying to get her out of the bed. Wheel them in and wheel them out. '

'She ought to come here,' said Steve.

Alex rounded on him. 'Don't talk daft, Steve. Your mother isn't here. Who is going to look after her? You're going to wash her clothes and make her meals, are you? Help her to the toilet? I don't think so.'

'She's Mum's responsibility.'

'Yeah, well, Mum's not here, is she?' he retorted.

'Doesn't that mean she's ours?'

'Steve, if I had said she was coming here, you'd have made a fuss. You're only saying this so that you can take the opposite line from me. You're just bloody contrary.'

'No I'm not.'

'You're going to spend time with her, are you?'

Steve shrugged.

'Well? How are we going to look after her?'

'You could pay someone.'

'I could pay someone to look after her somewhere else,' Alex said bluntly. Then he looked as me as if he had suddenly remembered I was there.

'I'm out all day,' he said. 'There's no point in her being here instead of in her own surroundings. It would be better for her to be in her own home.'

What's he explaining to me for? Do I look like the kind that would look after some old granny in my own house? I shook my head non-committally.

'I see your point.'

'Well, I don't,' said Steve.

'You never do.'

'She's our responsibility.'

'Yeah, you've said that, Steve. I've heard that bit now,' snapped Alex. His anger was the anger of a man who knew inside that his opponent was right, but who didn't want to admit it, even to himself. He paced to the window.

'They shouldn't be pushing us like this,' he said. 'It's far too quick. She's not ready to come out.'

'You mean you're not ready for her to come out,' muttered Steve. 'And you're talking as if Mum's never coming back. Why are you doing that?'

He's brave, I'll say that for him. He just doesn't know when to shut up.

'Oh, for God's sake,' said Alex, and he walked from the room, banging the door behind him.

'Well,' I said witheringly to Steve, who was slouching on the sofa with his feet resting on the coffee table, 'that went well. Don't you think?'

CHAPTER TWELVE

Carol Ann

I keep thinking that she's dead. I keep wondering if I'd know. There were times in my life when I thought it wouldn't make any difference; that she might as well be dead. But now there is a real possibility, I have a cold, cold feeling inside me. It starts with a small chip of ice that just keeps lengthening and lengthening, until it feels like there's a giant stalactite running through the core of me, drip, drip, dripping down through my legs to the very tips of my toes.

'I can only give out information to relatives. Are you a relative?' the voice on the phone says. It sounds crisp, starchy.

'Yes, I'm ... she's my sister.' Oh damn, no. That was stupid. My voice is too young.

'I mean, my mother's sister. She's my mother's sister. My Aunt Lily.'

There is a pause.

'Sorry, I'm upset, all mixed up.'

'What's your name?' says the voice suspiciously.

'Please ...' I say. 'Is she ... is she all right?'

'She's ... she's as well as can be expected and making reasonable progress. Now, who shall I say has called?'

'No message,' I say, and put the phone down in a rush.

She's alive. The relief is overwhelming.

* * *

When Stevie was small, he had a boxed game with a little hammer in it. Plastic crocodile heads popped up out of a grid and you had to use the hammer to hit them on the head. Each time you beat one down, another would pop up somewhere else, then two, then three, so that you had to respond faster and faster. It was about reflexes, training little hands and fingers to co-ordinate with the brain and become nimble. I used to watch him and laugh at the solid intensity of his responses, the chubby hands curled with frowning concentration round the hammer. But right now, I feel like I'm playing that game and my attempts to hammer down memories are as ham-fisted and unco-ordinated as a baby's.

I have tried to keep all the memories in their boxes. But each time I lash out wildly to beat one down, another springs up, and then another. Back home, life was dominated by memories of only one person. She was always there, hovering somewhere between me and Alex. But here in Ireland, I am bombarded by all of them.

It is a Sunday afternoon in winter, the light soft and low in the late afternoon. Lily in the big leather chair with my baby in her arms, crooning the Eriskay Love Lilt, a beautiful old Hebridean song that is a mixture of Gaelic and English. Sometimes, I am so certain I hear that tune that I turn to find the source of it, then realise it comes from inside my own head.

'*Bheir me o, horo van o*,' Lily sang softly that afternoon, the chorus of it washing gently over the sleeping figure in her arms. *'Bheir me o, horo van ee, Bheir me o, horo ho*, Sad am I, without thee.'

I was standing doing some ironing, the rush of the steam like a percussion instrument to Lily's singing. It was a song she'd sung to me as a child too, and I'd joined in momentarily without thinking. Lily had looked up at me in gentle surprise and smiled.

'You remember?' she said.

'Thou'rt the music of my heart, Harp of joy, *o cruit mo chruidh,*' I sang and then stopped, fishing mentally for the words.

'Moon of guidance by night, Strength and light thou'rt to me,' she finished.

And then we sang the chorus together, Lily never taking her eyes off the baby.

'You're a beauty aren't you?' she whispered then, into her arms. 'Aren't you my darling?' The steam whooshed over the babygro I was ironing. 'Yes, yes, you are. You're a beauty. Yes, you are.'

Through the cloud, Lily looked peaceful, almost happy. I had the feeling she thought that baby was me, that somehow life was offering her a second chance.

CHAPTER THIRTEEN

Karen

There's a major murder inquiry going on in town, a drug-related shooting, and McFarlane has pulled Mackie off the fraud case and made him available to CID to help with the investigation. Mackie's so puffed up with smugness these days he looks like he might burst. I look at him sometimes and fantasise about him simply blowing up and up until he pops like a balloon, little fragments of oily Mackie raining down until there's only a puddle left.

'Found your missing woman yet, Kar?' he says. He knows I fucking hate it when he calls me that.

'Between you and me,' I say, 'I wouldn't be surprised if this turns into a murder inquiry. I think that's why McFarlane wanted me involved.' I have the two-second satisfaction of seeing a moment's uncertainty cross his smarmy chops before the default smirk setting is back.

Mackie was right about McFarlane. He's taking him more seriously for this CID vacancy than me. McFarlane passed me several times today and then, suddenly, it was as if seeing my face prompted some half-forgotten memory.

'Has she come back yet?'

'Sorry?'

'The missing woman. Andrews.'

'Matthews.'

'Yeah, Matthews.'

'No, but I've got things in hand.' He suddenly looked a bit more attentive.

'What do you mean you've got things in hand? If there are any suspicious circumstances in this case, CID should have been pulled in immediately. That's what I asked you to check, Karen.'

'Of course I've checked!'

'Hospital admissions? National Insurance numbers? Bank accounts? Friends?'

'Think there might be a boyfriend involved.'

'Oh.' The alertness leaves him and he nods. Just another marital breakdown, then. 'Keep me posted,' he says before wandering off, presumably to shuffle some more paperclips.

Marital breakdown. It not necessarily a lie. There's something about Alex … I have a hunch he knows more than he's saying. He's very controlled, has that masculine steel that Gav is so completely lacking. There's also an ambiguity that makes me wonder what he's capable of. He seems distressed about Carol Ann's disappearance but also vaguely guilty. Maybe he found out about Doug. Maybe he got jealous. Maybe things got out of hand…

There's a surprise when I call round to see Alex on my way home. Lily's out of hospital, staying with him and Steve. I can't believe the kid got his way. She freaks me out with her twisted mouth and glittering eyes, hovering over proceedings like an old crow.

Alex wasn't in when I arrived. Steve sullenly showed me into the sitting room and said his dad wouldn't be long. Then he went upstairs and I heard the thump of music. He's not one for conversation.

I heard Lily coming down the hallway, her walking stick thudding on the polished wooden floor. A sharp thump, followed by a dragging sound, as she hauls her left foot along. Thump! Dra-a-a-g. Thump!

Dra-a-a- g. The door springs open with a jerk; she can't control her movements properly any more.

'Hello, Lily,' I say brightly, trying to smile. Christ. Hurry up, Alex. Lily pulls herself into the room and stands over my chair, watching me. I hate having to try and stumble through some kind of conversation with her. She looks at me intently, her eyes unnaturally bright. It is very unnerving. The left side of her mouth droops badly still, giving her a look of malevolent absurdity. I watch as her mouth begins to move, but it is some time before she produces sound.

'Aahalan,' she says, concentrating hard. She is receiving speech therapy, but progress is slow.

'Sorry, Lily?'

'Aahalan,' she repeats, 'Aahalan.' Her mouth twists slowly, as she fights to form words. Her lips are a barrier rather than the instrument of sound they once were.

I get up and take her arm.

'Come and sit down, Lily. Shall I get you a cup of tea?'

'Ohhh,' she says, shaking her head.

Her eyes are shimmering with impatience and frustration, two hooded jewels beneath dark, heavy lids.

'*Cah…ahlan*,' she says, with a huge effort.

'Carol Ann?' I say. 'Is that it? Carol Ann?'

Her head nods forward, once. 'Ahah,' she says eagerly.

'We're trying to find Carol Ann for you, Lily.' I put an arm on her shoulder, trying to lead her to the chair, but I can feel the resistance in her frail body. She's like a bundle of old bones with a bird's nest on top of her head, but there's steel in there somewhere.

'Aachs,' she says.

I watch her mouth closely. 'Aachs,' she repeats, then her eyes dart across the room to a photograph on the sideboard. Her stick thumps hard on the floor, then softens as she hits a rug, Thump, draa...ag.

Thump, draa...ag. Slowly she reaches the photograph and points to Alex.

'Alex,' I say. She nods.

'He'll be in soon, Lily. Steve says he won't be long.'

'Ooh,' she says, shaking her head. Her lips purse deliberately. 'N...n...nooo'

'Aax,' she says.

'Alex,' I say, watching her lips closely, interpreting.

'Hhh...ht'

'Hat? Alex has a hat?'

Lily's face contorts with irritation.

'HH...HRT!' she explodes. For a minute I think she's going to have another stroke in front of me.

'Heart? No ... hurt?'

She nods eagerly. 'Hh..,hrt Cahahlan.'

'Alex hurt Carol Ann?'

'Yy...yiss!' She says with relief, and then she sinks into a seat and closes her eyes with exhaustion.

I've been round so often recently that Alex isn't surprised when I open the front door to him. What he doesn't realise is that most of the time I'm on unofficial business, conducting my own little investigation. I want him to accept my presence, to start talking openly. Lily's words are running round and round my head. Alex hurt Carol Ann. Of course, the old crow is batty. I know that. But still. Alex hurt Carol Ann. Is it possible? 'Steve let me in,' I say, and he just nods.

'Where's Lily?' he mouths.

'Sitting room,' I mouth back, enjoying our complicity.

He veers away from the door and heads to the kitchen, dumping his keys and case with a clatter on the breakfast bar.

'Want anything?' he asks, flicking the switch on the kettle.

'Coffee if you're making it, thanks.'

I watch him. He looks like a stranger in his own kitchen. He opens the wrong cupboard for the coffee, has to think where the sugar is. Theresa, the woman who has come to look after Lily, has been doing most of the practical stuff since Carol Ann left. Alex made it a condition of the job that she would work weekends even though he's off then. He makes sure his contact with Lily is minimal.

He loosens his tie while he waits for the kettle, undoes the top button of his shirt.

'There's nothing new, I take it?' he says.

I've come round to ask him about his marriage, but I can't just jump straight in.

'Not really. I ran another check and Carol Ann still hasn't registered with a doctor or employer using her own National Insurance number.'

He frowns, shakes his head. 'What the hell is she playing at?' he mutters. 'How is she living without money?'

'The thing is, Alex,' I say, watching him carefully, ' when there is no movement in bank accounts, no visible signs of life ... well, it doesn't mean anything definite, but obviously we do have to consider other possibilities. It has been a month now.'

I see the ripple of muscle as he clenches his jaw.

'Carol Ann isn't dead,' he says flatly.

'Why so sure?'

'I'd know. I'd feel it, wouldn't I? After twenty-five years. I'd feel it.'

I am surprised by this. It's the kind of thing mothers come out with when their kids are missing. 'I'm their mother, I'd know,' they say, usually when their kid is lifeless at the bottom of a ditch somewhere, or sprawled under the wheels of a lorry. Men don't often say that stuff.

'You and Carol Ann were close then?'

'We were married.' He hands me a mug.

'Not the same thing.'

'No.'

I wait, but Alex is in no hurry to fill the silence. He takes his mug and moves into the small conservatory off the kitchen. It's like a geranium garden; creamy cushions with big, sprawling pink flowers scattered along the cane furniture. I follow him. He does not sit, but stands at the window, looking out over the rape fields to the front of the house. I hate that stuff. It stinks.

I sit in one of the armchairs, the cane creaking in the silence.

'Alex, we've talked before about the state of mind Carol Ann was in before she left, but I have to ask you a bit more about your relationship.'

Alex doesn't miss a beat.

'In case I bumped her off, you mean?' he says, and looks at me with a malicious smile, like he's playing with me. It irritates me because I wonder if he'd do it with a male police officer, but there's no denying it: I find Alex's arrogance a turn-on.

He sits in a soft chair now too, and puts one foot up comfortably against the coffee table.

'So what would you like to know, Karen?'

It strikes me that it is the first time I have been aware of him using my Christian name. And it also strikes me his tone is so polite it's dangerous.

'Just how things were between you.'

Alex puts his head back against the back of the chair and closes his eyes. After a minute I seriously begin to wonder if he's fallen asleep.

'Were we close?' he says finally, like he's examining the words from every angle.

'I think that's the question you are asking. And the answer is no, not any more. Not in an obvious way, anyway. But we were once. And sometimes ... sometimes people are bound together for reasons other than love. There's a cord there they can't break even if they grow to hate each other.'

'Did you and Carol Ann hate each other?'

'That's not what I meant.' He puts his mug on the table. 'How old are you?'

'Is that relevant?'

'Yeah, I think it probably is.' He doesn't push it.

'What *did* you mean then, if you didn't mean you hated one another?'

He folds his arms and breathes out deeply, his cheeks ballooning with the exhalation. 'I just mean,' he says slowly, 'that even when things are not good in a relationship, there can be stuff underpinning it that makes it difficult to end it. Sometimes it's just about the length of time you've been together ... years and years of ... stuff. Shared experiences, if you like. A deep understanding of what the other person is about.' He glances at me. 'Do you know what I mean?'

I can't say I do. I've always walked away, never bothered waiting around to create any kind of history with anyone. The realisation makes me feel a bit inadequate, so I nod.

'Sure,' I say.

'We were very different. Carol Ann is such a ... she's not … she doesn't cope very well with things. She's a dreamer. I try to toughen her up sometimes, make her see things properly ... and that just leads to tension.'

'What about?'

He shrugs.

'Everything. We see things differently.'

'Did you ever hit her?'

'No,' he says, the word flicking sharply like a whip.

'Lily says you hurt her.'

He does not respond angrily, but his eyes darken and he shakes his head. He doesn't look at me, but I see his lips twist as he bites the inside of his cheek.

'I'm quite sure that's true,' he says quietly.

'So she means emotionally?'

Alex doesn't reply.

'Were you faithful to her?' The question comes out so bluntly, it seems to ricochet round the room like a bullet. It is only partly professional interest. Frankly, I am just curious.

'None of your business,' says Alex sharply.

'Do you want to find Carol Ann or not?'

'What's me being faithful got to do with it?'

'I'm trying to find her motivation.'

'Well, it wasn't infidelity.'

'That's what men always say.'

'Oh, do me a favour ...' He gets up and walks across the kitchen and I watch him silently. He looks irritated. He washes his cup out, throwing the water into the sink as though trying to douse a fire.

'What's the matter. Does the question make you feel guilty?'

'*What*?' he says incredulously, turning from the sink and looking at me like I'm an idiot.

'You look like you feel guilty.'

'Oh, really? Do they teach you psychology at plod school these days, then?' He turns off the tap. 'Who takes the class – Noddy?'

Outside the door I can hear the approaching thump, thump, thump of Lily's stick progressing up the hall.

'Shit,' says Alex. He looks at me with a warning in his eyes. 'Leave this just now,' he says.

There's a bang as Lily uses her stick to push open the kitchen door. The door bangs off the kitchen cabinet behind the door and she stands in the frame, looking accusingly from one of us to the other, like a hawk ready to pounce.

CHAPTER FOURTEEN

Carol Ann

Scrambling across rocks. Stone hard beneath my fingers, glistening like granite with seawater. Slippy beneath my feet with moss and wet, straggling seaweed. The sun like a blowtorch on my back as I negotiate the warm water pools where tiny fish dart so suddenly I see only their movement. Concentration. There is nothing to exist for except this moment right now: heat and exertion and the crab-like movement from the beach across rock to the silver-sanded cove in the distance. The light is shining on it in a headlight beam, beckoning me from afar.

By the time I finally jump onto the powdery sand, I am breathing heavily. Behind me, rocky hillside; in the distance, the blue of the beach hut. I stretch out in the sand using my cardigan as a pillow and listen to the whoosh of the waves breaking on the shore. The sea is never completely calm here, even when the weather is hot and there is no wind. A light sweat prickles my skin. Wriggling up onto my elbows, I look out at the expanse of water, white froth bubbling at the edges. Instinctively, I glance behind me, checking the hillside. No one. Completely alone.

Can I? It feels good to slip my jeans off, feel the sun on my legs, but something inside me disapproves. I fold my shirt carefully. Another glance round. Silence. Stillness. What's the difference? My underwear will be like a bikini. Except I would never normally dream of wearing a bikini any more. A towel? My cardigan. A tentative embarrassment when I stand up, a fear that someone watches silently from the bracken-strewn hill. Silly. At the water's edge, even the wet sand is cold and I hop from foot to foot, laughing, though I am alone. Laughing *because* I'm alone. Water round my ankles. God, it's freezing! Sun burning my back and icy water up to my knees.

Then a rush of emotion, a kind of exultation. Suddenly I run out of the water and up the sand, unhooking my bra as I run and throwing it up the beach to the neatly folded pile, where it lands stretched out like an exclamation mark. The knickers stick on my wet legs as I half hop back down to the water, finally rolling them into a ball and chucking them up the beach. Straight back into the sea, no pausing, no hesitating this time. Embrace the cold, open myself up to it so that it doesn't hurt. Throw myself into the waves, feel them hurl against me with such force that a mouthful of salt water surprises me.

I lash out, spluttering, swimming against the tide. Moving … moving … so that I feel nothing but the movement itself, not the burn of icy water beneath. And finally there really is no cold. My body is comfortable in the water, timing the waves, jumping against them at their fullest point, the water slapping against every inch of my nakedness. The hillside is bare. The beach is empty. I am suspended in a world where only I exist. There is freedom and there is loneliness. Only the water caresses me.

We were two outsiders against the rest of the world, Lily and me. But the night of the third-year school parents' evening stayed with me for years, a jewel of a memory that made me understand, despite everything, the way the universe was constructed. When things were tough, we were on the same side against everyone else. We were an imperfect pair, but at least we were a pair.

Lily said she wasn't sure she could make parents' night when I asked. I said nothing, fixing my eyes on my bowl of soup, tinned soup that I had heated for us both. Lily toyed with a spoonful, but her hand kept shaking and she spilled most of it before it reached her mouth. She complained it made her squeamish. I guess mulligatawny squishing round on gin cocktails would make anyone squeamish.

'Miss Bailey said she wanted to see you,' I said. I looked at her speculatively. I guessed I would be in trouble if she didn't come. But how much worse would it be if she came drunk?

'What does *she* want?' Lily stared at me, her eyes streaked pink as a morning dawn. She looked like a rabbit that had been experimented on. She propped her head on one arm and looked at me, and her eyelids began to close. I pushed her bowl away from in front of her, lowered her arm and placed her head on top, then carried on eating. It was too regular a procedure for there to be any tenderness left in the action. I finished my soup and bread and washed the bowl, then covered Lily's and stuck it in the fridge for later.

Miss Bailey was my physics teacher and I hated her even more than I hated physics. She was a stick-thin old crone who wore the long silver river of her hair scraped into a tight bun at the back of her neck. It fascinated me the way there were streaks of yellow in it, like aged parchment. Her skin was so dry that, up close, it looked in places as if it had a thin film of white flaking powder on it, a half-shed skin.

I had fallen asleep in her class the week before, having been up half the night trying to get Lily to bed. Miss Bailey picked up a heavy book and dropped it with such force onto my desk that it cracked like a gunshot.

'Christ!' I shot from my seat, catching the desk lid, which banged down with a clatter. There were some suppressed giggles round the room, but nobody dared laugh out loud when the thin, mean, coldness of Miss Bailey's anger was on display.

'Foul mouthed as well as lazy, Matheson,' she said. She spoke quietly but venomously, each word given unnatural emphasis, her tongue flicking in her mouth like a snake's. I was uncertain what to do. Having leapt from my seat I was now standing, but I bobbed my backside uncertainly, half sitting, half standing, trying to make myself smaller.

'DON'T DARE SIT!' she yelled suddenly, her arm darting out for my chair with the lightning speed of a snake's forked tongue. I jumped again. The room was deathly quiet.

'If you cannot keep awake sitting, Matheson, you will have to stand,' she continued. 'Stand until the end of the period. And make sure that mother of yours attends parents' evening on Thursday. Do you hear me, Matheson?'

On Thursday night when I came home, Lily said we'd have an early tea so we'd be in plenty of time. I looked at her closely. I guessed the slight tremor in her hand wasn't from drinking, but from the effort of *not* drinking. I said nothing.

She scrubbed up pretty well. Sometimes when Lily 'made an effort' she managed to look even more like some crazy old lush, with Cruella de Vil hair, ladders in her tights and too much rouge. Tonight she had overdone the eye liner, and her skirt could have done with a press, but she looked pretty normal for Lily. Until you got up close and smelled the stale booze mixed with fresh. I think she must have got nervous and poured herself a stiff one in her bedroom when she got ready, but for Lily she was stone-cold sober.

The teachers' desks were laid out in the assembly hall. Miss Bailey watched us with cold, marble eyes as we approached.

'Mrs Matheson,' she said. 'Or Miss Matheson ....?'

'*Mrssss* Matheson, *Miss* Bailey,' said Lily. Miss Bailey's bleach-clean, short-nailed finger, which was running down a marks list, stilled momentarily. She looked up.

'I am not happy with your daughter's performance in class,' she said, her mouth pursing sourly.

'Really?' Lily didn't physically move, but I sensed the stiffening in her, the quiet danger in that one word. When your life is a crash scene, you don't take kindly to people trying to bulldoze the one part of it that is still standing.

'She's lazy and inattentive and will achieve nothing if this carries on,' continued Miss Bailey.

I sat beside Lily with my eyes down, listening. Old bag. I wasn't that bad. Not anywhere near it.

Miss Bailey's hard little eyes focused on Lily expectantly but Lily remained silent.

'I hope you will encourage her to work harder and explain the importance of good exam grades to her future,' she said, a little impatiently.

'What – exactly – do you see as Carol Ann's problem?' Lily wrapped her cardigan tightly round her chest and folded her arms, still holding the edges of the cardigan.

'Lack of application,' said Miss Bailey crisply. 'She also needs discipline. She fell asleep in class the other day. Are you ensuring she gets sufficient sleep?'

Miss Bailey talked with strange formality. It was her barrier to the world. But questioning Lily about what she did and didn't make sure of was like running a fingernail down a fresh scar. Lily wanted to be a good mother, but an alcoholic can't be that. Only she didn't want to acknowledge that. I could see the bubble of resentment blowing up inside her, ready to burst.

'Of course there's another possibility for falling asleep in class,' Lily said finally. 'She could be bored.'

'I am here to teach, Mrs Matheson, not to entertain. I am not a hired circus performer.'

Lily leaned forward over the desk.

'I think you are picking on my daughter.'

Miss Bailey moved back from the desk with exaggerated distaste.

'Have you been drinking, Mrs Matheson?' she said. 'Because I really see no point in continuing this conversation if you have been drinking.'

Lily half stood from her chair and leaned her hands on Miss Bailey's desk.

'Listen you ... you ... you shrivelled-up old *moose* ...' she said, and I gasped. Cheryl Sweeney, who was sitting with her parents speaking to Mrs Walters from the maths department, swivelled her head and looked at me with wide eyes. 'Just keep your nose out of my business and stick to trying to do your job,' continued Lily. She turned from the desk and that's when it happened.

Of course, later everyone said Lily Matheson had been blind drunk and shouting abuse on the famous occasion when she went sprawling across the assembly-hall floor, revealing red silk knickers to the world. (Red silk! Was she a whore as well as a lush?) But the truth was she wasn't really drunk at all; she just caught her foot in the handle of the bag that lay at the foot of her chair.

It was a bit of an exit.

On the bus on the way home, Lily and I sat in companionable silence.

'What on earth made you call her a shrivelled old moose?' I asked eventually.

'Dunno,' said Lily, 'Think it was the hairs on her chin.'

We both giggled then, one of the rare occasions when we laughed together.

'Does a moose have hairs on its chin?'

'No idea. But it sounds like it does.'

Our shoulders shook all the way home. When we got off the bus, I took Lily's arm – for once out of companionship rather than a desire to keep her upright – and we walked together under the streetlamps, the pavements glistening with jewels of rain and reflected light.

CHAPTER FIFTEEN

Karen

Dr Hammond is leaning his elbows on his chair in his familiar pose, the fingers of both hands steepling together to make a triangle. He pulls his thumbs up to form a base and looks down through the empty space of the triangle thoughtfully, as if looking through a telescope. He does not look at me directly.

I try to curb my impatience as I watch him. It's like watching the innards of a clock, whirring, ticking, the pendulum pulse steady, slow, inexorable.

'I think we have already had this conversation,' he says finally.

'It is six weeks since we spoke, Dr Hammond. We do not have a single lead to help us find Carol Ann. If she has gone of her own free will, and we manage to find her, then she will stay where she is. No one will force her to return. But we need to know that it *is* her own free will that has taken her from her home and her family. We need your help.'

He says nothing, but continues to stare through the triangular space onto his desk.

'We need your help,' I repeat slowly. 'We need to know Carol Ann is safe. That no one has harmed her. I understand your professional etiquette. But it's six weeks now, Dr Hammond. Six weeks. We need to find her. I'd appreciate your help.'

Dr Hammond's soft black leather chair squeaks as he stands up and moves to the filing cabinet in the corner of the room. He says nothing, does not look at me, but I can tell that in his own way he is unnerved by the fact that Carol Ann has not reappeared. He pulls a file from it and places it on his desk unopened, in front of him.

'Perhaps if you tell what you need to know, I can consider whether I can help you or not.'

'Did Carol Ann talk much about her relationship with her husband? Was it a normal ... I don't know ... healthy ... relationship.?'

'What's normal and healthy?' he asks.

'Was there friction between them?'

'You think friction is abnormal? Can you think of any couple you know where there is not friction?'

Oh, for God's sake. He knows what I mean.

'Anger then,' I say tightly. 'Destructive anger.'

Dr Hammond looks through the window on the side wall of his office, as if he hasn't heard the question. 'Interesting you should focus on that,' he murmurs and continues to look out of the window. 'When I was a boy,' he continues eventually, 'I lived next door to a very angry, vicious Alsatian dog.'.

'Uhuh?'

'Any time anyone in the street went near it, it snarled. If you had tried to stroke it, it would have bitten your hand off.'

What is this? *Jackanory*? I am trying to push down the irritation that is rising inside me, running like a poisoned vein from my gut up through my chest. There is something about Hammond that makes me feel patronised. He thinks I'm stupid because I never went to some posh university? He thinks he's got to talk in parables? Fucking intellectuals.

'The dog was very, very angry. You understand about anger, Officer McAlpine?' he asks softly.

The question makes my heart beat rapidly, then steady to an over-syncopated thump.

'The owners had their own reason for keeping this animal,' he continues, as if he never asked the question. He leans back in his chair, his head resting on the back cushion, and momentarily closes his eyes. 'It was, as you might imagine, a superb guard dog. If anyone came in the gate, it barked the place down. So they kept it on a short lead in the garden so that it couldn't actually reach anyone who came in, and sometimes they put it on an extended lead to exercise it. The dog never actually bit the owners because they brought its food, but it became so aggressive that even *they* became frightened to go too close.' He opens his eyes and looks at me. 'I became fascinated by this dog. I spent a long time watching it.'

'Doggie psychology?'

Dr Hammond smiles vaguely, without looking at me. He picks up a pencil on his desk and doodles on the corner of a sheet of paper as he talks.

'The thing is that the more angry the dog got, the less freedom and exercise it got. And the less freedom it got, the more angry it got. You see?'

He's drawing straight lines across the page with arrow heads leading to another straight line.

'More anger, less freedom,' he repeats, and his eyes focus directly on me.

'Yes. And ... ?'

'And eventually, I realised that one of the dog's habits was to rub at its neck. It would lift one of its paws and worry away at the neck, not roughly but very gingerly. I used to do my homework at a desk in my bedroom which looked down over the front garden of the house next door. So I'd watch it, you see? Over long spells. Sometimes I wouldn't look at it for quite a while as I was working, but eventually, when I was thinking, I would lift my head and look down on the dog. Well, after a long time of watching this process I realised that there was something wrong with the dog's neck. I spoke to the neighbours about it. And the thing was really very simple: the dog's collar was chafing at his neck and, underneath the collar, sores had developed. But nobody really went near enough to the dog, and when they did get close up they were more concerned about guarding themselves from the dog's anger than they were with actually looking after it. They threw it food. They hosed it down with water. The dog's anger meant people maintained it, but they didn't actually engage with it. And, you see, if you don't engage, it's amazing what very, very obvious things you can miss.'

He sits back in his chair and smiles at me again.

'Right.'

'You are wondering what the point is, Officer.'

My smile back is vicious. 'You are a mind-reader, Dr Hammond.'

'The point is that the anger was not simply anger. The anger was caused by a pain that nobody knew about.' He is drawing circles on the paper now and I watch the grey lead whirls build up like cloud formations in a white sky. 'A vicious circle. You asked about destructive anger. The thing to remember is that pain can be the most destructive thing of all in any relationship. Pain causes anger and anger causes pain. That's normal.'

Oh God. We're into riddles now. If pain equals anger, and anger equals normal, what does fucking irritating equal?

'Are we talking about Carol Ann's pain? Or her husband's?'

'Maybe both,' he says.

I wait for him to elaborate, but he doesn't. He opens a small tin on his desk. It looks like it's full of aspirins, but they are extra-strong mints. He offers the tin, but I shake my head. Hammond pops one into his mouth.

'I also find myself wondering, Officer – Karen, isn't it? – about *your* anger.'

'What are you talking about?'

'*That*. Exactly that … the note of belligerence that stains your every conversation. I wonder about it … about the possible cause of it …'

'Yeah? Well, you keep right on wondering Dr Hammond,' I say with controlled sarcasm, but my heart is leaping in my chest, banging against my insides like it's shouting to be heard.

'Let's concentrate on Carol Ann Matthews,' I say brusquely. 'What are you saying was the cause of *her* pain?'

'You've spoken to Alex?'

'Yes, of course.'

'Has he told you about Josie?' He looks at me keenly.

'Josie? Who's Josie?'

'I see,' he says, and picks up the file from his desk, still unopened, and replaces it in the filing cabinet. I don't know what the point of getting it out was. Some kind of symbolic gesture, I guess. The drawer of the filing cabinet rolls shut softly.

'Speak to Alex,' he says.

'Who's Josie?'

'I can't help you any more than I have. Speak to Alex.'

'You've counselled Alex too?'

He shakes his head.

'Never met him.'

'So how do you know ...'

'I don't know anything other than what Carol Ann told me.'

'And what conclusion did you come to?'

'I don't come to conclusions.'

He's really getting on my nerves now. I think he knows it. He raises his eyebrows lightly at me.

'My patients come to conclusions after talking to me.'

'I see.'

'I think if you really try, you will understand the connection I am making between pain and anger,' he says. His voice drops, becomes soft and almost intimate. The words slip out, smooth and dangerous. 'And forgive me if I spoke out of turn. It's just that in my line of work, one gets to recognise suppressed anger very quickly.' The mint in his mouth click, clicks against his teeth.

'Sometimes, people in your line of work, Dr Hammond, get a bit too bogged down in theories.'

'Perhaps,' he says with a hint of a shrug. 'Then I can be of no further assistance to you, I'm sure.'

We sit in silence but he's not going to budge.

'One more thing,' I say finally. 'Carol Ann's mother is worried that Alex might have harmed her. From what Carol Ann said, do you think she was in a violent relationship? Did her husband ever attack her?'

'She gave me no reason to believe that. Of course, I could not say definitively, but I would be surprised. As I said, I think this relationship was fuelled by pain rather than violence.'

Time to go. His eyes are no longer engaged, even in his own thoughts about Carol Ann. The drawer on that particular file is now closed and locked.

'You can't tell me anything else?'

'I think I've told you rather a lot.'

'Yeah,' I say. 'Thanks a lot.'

You know about anger, Officer McAlpine? His voice soft and slippery as a wet sliver of soap. You know about anger? Almost like he knows, but he doesn't. He knows nothing. He knows stuff from books. He knows what his nice middle-class lady patients tell him about their troubled middle-class lives. Their negative equity. Their empty-nest syndrome. Their husbands' affairs. Is that who Josie is? Some affair? Bad boy, Alex.

Dammit! The tin opener I am using slips clumsily from my hands, my knuckle grazing painfully against the side of the tin. A bubble of skin is torn back, leaving a raw pink graze beneath. That's what Hammond thinks he can do, see under your skin. He sees nothing under mine except what I let him see.

Only the rich have time for psychosis. The rest of us are too busy surviving to get traumatised. I don't trust those people who jump a class, you know, who start out in a housing scheme with snot on their nose and holes in their shoes and end up with a poodle on a lead and a shrink. Doesn't add up. You don't change what you are inside. What you are is what you are.

I empty beans into a pot. Slice of toast. Bit of grated cheese. Dammit. Grated skin. Fills a hole. Functional. What does Hammond know about function? My mother never needed a Hammond to get her through. She had me, of course. I got her through. Do you know about anger, Officer McAlpine? Yes, Dr Hammond, I do. You, on the other hand, know fuck all.

CHAPTER SIXTEEN

Carol Ann

I wake shortly after dawn, early rays streaming into my bedroom and gradually warming the walls from pale sherbet to a richer, deeper lemon. I cannot sleep. I lie for a while watching the light move, then sit on the edge of the bed, running my bare toes through the carpet tufts and yawning.

Half an hour later, when I cross the road outside, it is still quiet. Not a car to be seen. Across in the graveyard, jewelled morning light sparkles in the granite of the headstones. I have seen the old man for four consecutive nights now. I count back from the gate, three rows, try to fix the grave he visits in my head. It is easier from a distance than up close. Inside the gates, I hesitate between two, then remember the Celtic cross headstone.

The stone is new, the inscription near the top with space for a later addition to the grave.

Patricia Kirkpatrick. Born 18th June 1944. Died 4th January 2009.

Beloved wife of Harold, adored mother of Patrick and Conor.

Your life ended, our pain endures.

Only five months gone. He will come again this evening, for sure. Tomorrow would have been her birthday.

In the day, I visit the local pubs, looking for work. Killymeanan is a small, straggling village with only one cluttered local store and post office, but three pubs in a one-mile stretch. The most central, McGettigan's Bar, is looking for someone for three evening shifts, all day Saturday and alternate Sundays. It has a bare wooden floor and smells of stale ale and, vaguely, of manure because it backs onto a dairy farm. And because it's stuffed with farmers who trail work boots across the floorboards, and wear overalls they used to muck out the byres.

It would be fair to say McGettigan's doesn't do chintz and flounces. It has rough wooden tables and the plastic chairs you get in school canteens. The heavy green curtains are tied back with rough hairy rope, the kind used to tie up boats, and the scoop of the folds are lined with dust. Above the old wooden bar is a surprisingly clean mirror.

Sean McGettigan is eating lunch at one of the rickety old tables when I come in: a plate of chips and a pint of Guinness. It might explain the size of his gut, which sits in an extraordinarily regular dome underneath his red checked shirt. I have to fight not to let my eyes fix on it. It is almost like a separate entity that has been strapped on. He's a man who looks to be in his early fifties, but whose face still retains the boy he was. Round, ruddy, a generously proportioned mouth and eyes that invite confidences.

'Sit down,' he says cheerfully, waving a fork, when he's told why I am here. He spears a long chip and crams it in sideways, doubling it over with his mouth.

'You're the woman staying in Peter's cottage aren't you?'

Looks like you might not know anyone round these parts, but they certainly all know you.

'That's right.'

'Have you worked in bars before?' he says.

'No, I'm afraid I haven't. But I can learn fast. I've worked in a tea-room so I'm used to dealing with customers.'

'Tearoom?' he says. 'Jesus, Mary and Joseph!'

'Not when I was on duty. As far as I know.'

He grins and jabs his fork at me.

'Funny lady!'

Funnier than Carol Ann, anyway, I think.

'Where you from?' he asks.

'Scotland.'

'Is that right now? Glasgow?'

'Originally. But not now.'

He notes my reticence and an awkward silence blossoms.

'And what brings you here?' he says eventually.

'I needed a change.'

I know by the way Sean McGettigan looks at me that he doesn't understand. In truth, it's not much of an answer. A woman on her own moves from Scotland to Ireland because she 'needs a change'? I need an answer he can understand.

'My husband ...' I say. 'My husband ... well, he died.'

The look of unease disappears from Sean's face like chalk being wiped from a blackboard. It is replaced with pity and, despite a little obvious discomfort, I know there's a kind of relief in that pity. A widow, well he can understand that.

'Ah, God, I'm sorry now to hear that,' he says, gently. 'God rest him. Was it sudden?'

I don't look at him. 'It was a long time coming,' I say, 'but in the end ...' I look up at the mirror above the bar. 'In the end ... yes, the end was sudden, I suppose.' There's a tear beginning at the corner of my eye. I can feel it forming into a bubble, like it's held in protective plastic, but suddenly the casing bursts and it spills over, running down the side of my face, round into the curve of my chin. The tear is real; no pretence needed. My husband is dead. He really is dead. And I loved him once.

My hand is flat on the table in front of me. Sean McGettigan reaches out and squeezes it; his big, muckle hand closing round mine briefly, his fingers like soft, fat sausages around my bony ones. My hands are the thinnest part of me. My body is soft, curved, but there is something about my hands that reflects my life: they are thin, hard, the network of blue veins standing out like tunnelled ridges against the paleness of my skin. I do not move; my hand does not return the pressure but simply rests momentarily in his.

He clears his throat. 'I'm sorry,' he says, and lets my hand drop. I wipe the track of the tear with the flat of my hand.

'It's okay.' I smile at him, a watery smile.

'Here,' says McGettigan gruffly, and pushes his plate across the table, 'have a chip.' It's a dangerous moment and it hangs in the balance for a second. Then I look at him and we both laugh, spontaneously, unexpectedly, and it's like a burst of sun breaking through cloud after rain.

'There,' he says. 'That's better.'

'Do you think you could make a barmaid of me?' I say.

'Ah, God now, I dunno,' he says, 'but I'm desperate enough to try.'

He shows me round there and then. Gives a first lesson in how to pull a pint.

'Hello there, Davie!' he shouts when an old boy in a overalls comes through the door.

'How're ya,' says Davie. He eyes me suspiciously.

'New barmaid, Davie,'

'I'm seein' that. Pint of Guinness, please,' he says and slams the exact money down on the counter.

'Nice and easy now,' says Sean to me. 'Nah, nah, nah ... if you go too fast you get too much head. Nice and slow. Start again. Clean glass. Slow now, slow. Tha-a-a-t's it! Right, stop there. Let that bit settle now before you pour any more.'

'Sometime this week would be fine,' mutters Davie.

'Sure, don't rush her, man,' says Sean. 'She's used to teashops, not pubs.'

'My God, she's no good to us, then,' says Davie, 'There's no tay will quench this thirst!' But his mouth twists up at the side in a half-laugh when I look at him. 'Here,' he says, 'I'll take them slops while you pour another, save yous throwing them away, now.'

'Aw, go on, you auld chancer,' says Sean, pushing the glass along the counter.

I only stay an hour or two. My first shift will be Thursday evening, but I agree with Sean to come early. I walk the half-mile home, feeling like I have laid a foundation brick in my new life. The money at McGettigan's is minimal. But it doesn't matter here. I don't need it. That's the strange thing. At home, all that you're aware of are the things you need and don't get. The holes. The emptiness. The unfulfilled expectations. But when you're on your own, it's different. You expect nothing. Right now, I feel happy. In this moment. Not looking backwards. Not looking forwards. Just existing, right here and right now.

CHAPTER SEVENTEEN

Karen

Anger? Do I know about anger? I watched the shadow on the wall for years, lying in bed, heart hammering in my chest. Waiting, just waiting for him to make a move. The light in the hall would be on, and he'd stand outside the door, an elongated shape drawn clearly on the full length of the wall, the shadow quivering sometimes as he swayed. Once I saw the shadow reach out, the door creep forward an inch, two inches, and stop. I held my breath then, eyes peering into the semi-dark, until my lungs felt like they would burst and I had to breathe in. I'd open my mouth in a silent lion's roar, trying to breathe noiselessly. And then the shadow would disappear, the light would snap off and I'd lie in the blackness, waiting to see if he would come back.

I still sleep like a coiled spring. Sometimes I wake suddenly, even now, all these years later, heart thumping, looking for the shadow, waiting for its dark presence to creep gradually onto my wall.

I have the advantage over the mysterious Doug that while I am looking for him, he will be looking for someone else entirely. Carol Ann. When he comes in, he'll be scanning the restaurant for her and, of course, he won't see her. It'll give me time. I sit in the corner of the restaurant and watch for men on their own. I read the menu cover to cover twice. Tagliatelli carbonara. Grilled monkfish and whole prawn kebabs. Tiramisu.

Just before the appointed time, a guy comes in. His glance around is casual, but then he's early. Maybe he doesn't expect her to be here yet. Maybe Carol Ann is the kind who comes late. He wears a dark suit, a business suit. But his hair is slightly longer than a businessman's, slicked back at the front and curling up over his collar. Some people transcend their uniforms, stamp their style on it. This guy certainly transcends his. Put it this way: I'd take him home after the tiramisu. Well, well, Carol Ann, you old dark horse. I rise and walk towards him.

'Excuse me,' I say, 'are you Doug?'

He looks startled, then smiles. 'Eh ... no,' he says. 'I'm Ed.'

'Shame,' I say, walking away.

'Hey,' he calls, 'It's only a name. I'll change it!'

I grin over my shoulder at him. He takes a table on his own, catches my eye now and then. I hold his gaze just a little longer than seemly. It passes the time.

When Doug arrives, I know it's him. Like, with a certainty. It's 1.28. God, Carol Ann, how could you? Talk about having steak at home and dining on hamburger. Doug has sandy-coloured hair, bordering on red, and a baggy suit that barely covers an ample middle. Not quite Mackie levels, but close. He wears a striped shirt and the stripes don't hang straight but are curved with the tension of covering his stomach. He looks like a second-hand-car salesman.

'Doug?' I say, and he turns, smiling a surprised but instantly affable smile. He hesitates, looking at me with confusion.

'I'm a police officer. PC Karen McAlpine,' I say, flashing my warrant card. 'I believe you are waiting for Carol Ann Matthews?'

'Oh my God.' His ruddy face blanches. He looks instantly clammy somehow, like a fish on a slab, still glistening with sea water. 'What's happened to her? Is she okay?'

I fill him in. He listens with a mixture of horror and relief that I haven't told him she's lying in some hospital morgue, sliced open by some joyriding kid's car. He takes a cloth handkerchief from his pocket, wipes his brow. I am aware that people have begun to turn their heads curiously towards us. Doug hasn't noticed. We are still standing in the middle of the floor and he looks lost, as if he's not sure which direction he's meant to go in. I press his shoulder lightly, guiding him towards the table.

'Shall we sit down?'

A waitress come over immediately, but I hold my hand up and she moves away.

'Do you want lunch, Doug?'

He shakes his head. Dammit. I am starving.

'Maybe a coffee,' he says distractedly. He rubs the palms of his hands down his face, stopping on his cheeks.

'I can't believe it,' he says. 'I can't believe it. Carol Ann ...'

I beckon the waitress over.

'Two coffees, please. And, eh ... sure you don't want anything, Doug?'

He shakes his head.

'Maybe a panini with goat's cheese and roasted red pepper,' I finish. I smile apologetically at Doug when the waitress leaves. 'Thought I'd better order something since we're taking a table at lunchtime.'

'Yes,' he says blankly. 'No one has any idea where she is?'

I shake my head. 'Unless you do?'

'I've been away for six months.'

'Where?'

'I was only here as a relief manager in the first place. I went back home after ...'

'What's your relationship with Carol Ann?'

'We're friends,' he says, too heartily, too self-consciously to be convincing. He squirms under my gaze.

'Not lovers?'

He clears his throat.

'No.'

'Your choice or hers?'

'Hers.'

'How did you meet?'

'I sold her a car.'

Bloody knew it.

'She came in a few times,' he continues. 'I said I'd call her if anything came up that might be what she was looking for. When something came in, she called round again. But she didn't buy that first one.' He shrugs. 'We just became friends.'

'How do you go from trying to flog her a car to becoming friends?'

He shrugs. 'The second car she came to see, she called just before lunchtime. I was on my way across the road for lunch and said I'd show her it on the way out. She liked it, but said she'd need to bring her husband to see it. We talked for a while and then she said she felt guilty she'd kept me back from lunch. I said I was only going to get a sandwich and why didn't she come across the road with me and I'd go over the possible finance deals for the car. She hesitated but she came.' He smiles. 'Beautiful South were playing on the radio when we went in.

'What's that got to do with it?'

'She was a fan and so was I. Funny, really.'

Another insight into Carol Ann Matthews. Pish taste in music.

'Her favourite was the one about being a perfect size ten. You know, but a fourteen really. Carol Ann always thought she was fat.' His voice dips so I can hardly hear him and he murmurs something about figures.

'Sorry?'

'A lovely figure. I thought she had a lovely figure. Rounded. Womanly.'

'Are you married, Doug?'

He clears his throat.

'Yes.' He does not look me in the eye. 'Does my wife need ... ?' His voice trails away. How pathetic men are. But I know instinctively Doug isn't crucial to this investigation. I can tell him more than he can tell me. I won't be passing him on to CID.

'Just so long as you tell me everything you know, Doug – and I mean everything – I think we can keep your wife out of this. Of course, if I think you aren't telling me everything, I might have to start investigating a bit and talking to your wife and, you know, that's when things start getting messy. But I am sure you won't let it come to that.'

'No, no,' he says. 'No, I'm sure there won't be any need.'

He has begun to sweat, a bead running down his forehead and plopping onto his eyelid. He takes out a handkerchief and wipes his face. I hope it's me that's causing it. I enjoy making men sweat. It gives me a kick, I mean a *real* kick. See, I know how often the bastards get it all their own way. The way they make women dance to their crazy psychotic tunes. And then the dance gets faster and faster until there's ...

'Excuse me?'

I look up. The waitress is standing staring at me, holding a plate. Doug is looking expectantly at me. I move my arms back from the table quickly, leaving space for her to put the plate down.

'Oh, right, yeah ...' I say.

'Panini with goat's cheese and roasted red pepper?'

'Yeah.'

'I'll bring the coffees.'

'So, how come you and Carol Ann didn't get it together?'

'I ... I'm sorry?' he says.

Sorry? I'll bet he was.

'You and Carol Ann. How come things didn't ... progress?'

He looks acutely embarrassed. I cut into the crisp, golden, toasted skin of the panini and melted goat's cheese oozes onto the plate like molten lava. A sliver of pepper is carried like flotsam in the flowing river, its curled red skin charred black at the edges.

'I ... I feel a bit ...' he says.

'Oh, don't mind me, Doug,' I say cheerfully, spearing a square of panini on my fork. 'I'm unembarrassable.'

'Right,' he says miserably. He wipes his handkerchief back and forward against his forehead.

'You got close ...' I prompt. I guess I don't need to remind him that I need to know everything or he gets shopped to the wife. Might sound a bit like blackmail if I repeat it. I can be subtle sometimes.

'Yes, we got close.' He empties a sachet of sugar into his coffee and stirs slowly. 'I wasn't happy and I recognised it in her, that same... thing, the same kind of unhappiness. I think in her it was even more pronounced, you know? She sort of carried it round with her. I said to her one day, you know ... I said, "Carol Ann, are you lonely?"'

'What did she say?'

'She looked startled, I remember that. Her eyes were really ... really ... kind of soft, sort of ... she used to make me think of a butterfly. She would look at you only for a few seconds and then her gaze would flutter elsewhere. Even when she was looking at you, it was as if she was already taking flight.'

Bit of a poet, old Doug.

'God, this is good,' I say.

'Sorry?'

'Panini,' I say, tapping it with my fork

'Oh. Oh right. Yes.'

'So ...' My mouth is full and I try to chew quickly, but the cheese is so hot I can feel it burning the roof of my mouth into splinters of skin. 'Oh ... oh ... oh,' I say, waving my hand in front of my mouth like a fan. 'Ouch.'

Doug blinks.

'So what did she say?' I manage eventually.

'About what?'

'About being lonely.'

'She said, "Not always." And I knew what that meant.'

'What? What did it mean?'

'It meant yes.' He takes a sip of coffee.

'Did she mention her husband, Alex, much?

'Not directly and I didn't ask. I think to mention him directly, or to say yes, she was lonely and unhappy all the time, not just sometimes, would have seemed like a betrayal to her. She was that kind of person.'

'Did you get the impression she was frightened of him?'

He frowns, looking puzzled. 'Frightened? No, why?' His eyes widen suddenly. 'Has he done something? Has he ...'

'No, no. We have no idea what has happened to her. I'm just trying to find out the possibilities, that's all. Carol Ann never gave you any reason to think she was in any danger?'

'No,' he says, and his voice is thin, bewildered. 'No, no, I never felt ...'

'How often did you see her?'

'At first, we never actually arranged to meet, you know. It would have been ... deceitful somehow. We just kind of ... drifted. As I said, she didn't buy the first car I phoned about and after that I'd phone regularly with things for her to come in and see. And you know, if Carol Ann was in town, she'd pass by on the off chance I was there just to see what had come in. Then I'd suggest going across the road for coffee or a drink or something ...'

'She didn't buy so she could keep coming in?'

'Maybe. And maybe I offered her things I knew weren't quite right because once she bought that would have been it.'

I know this story is going somewhere. I can feel it building. He's tense, periodically taking his handkerchief out and wiping his brow then stuffing it back into his pocket.

'How did it finish?'

'I ... I asked her what she had planned one weekend. Her son was going on a school trip and her husband was away on a business trip. She said she would be glad to have the house to herself.'

'And you offered to come round to keep her company?' The melted cheese on my plate has solidified into a firm puddle. I scrape it with a knife, butter it onto some purple salad leaves. He watches me carefully and when I look up, something passes through his eyes. Not disdain exactly, but wariness.

'It wasn't like that. She wasn't like that. She didn't want me to come to her house. But I said … you know… I wanted the relationship to go further. Carol Ann said it couldn't. She really wasn't looking for anything, but I told her how much I cared for her, how much I wanted ...' His voice trails away.

'Wanted what?'

'Her. How much I wanted her.'

'Did it make a difference?'

'I thought so. We met three times that week and talked and talked and eventually she agreed to meet me on the Friday night.'

'Where d'you go?'

'Just a hotel a good bit outside of town. About ten miles away. We had dinner. I ...'

He pauses and I look up from my salad, raise my eyebrows. 'Yeah?'

'I booked a room.'

The metal of my knife is scraping against the china plate as I try to lift the last stringy remnants of cheese from it.

'Are you hungry?' he says, curiously.

'Yep.'

I catch the waitress's eye.

'Tiramisu and another coffee please,' I call. 'Doug?'

'Coffee please.'

'Two coffees,' I shout and the waitress half turns back, jerks her head in response.

'So you've got the room, you've got Carol Ann at the hotel – what next?'

'We talked all night. I asked her to come up to the room even just for a nightcap. I just wanted to ... to be alone with her. We were always in public places, never on our own. But later I realised that was sort of the attraction for her. She liked the company and the attention and being with other people made it safe.'

'Did she go up to the room?'

'Eventually. She'd had a bit to drink by then. We both had.'

The waitress arrives with two more coffees. Doug half smiles at her.

'Thank you,' he says quietly. Neither of us continue talking until she goes.

'What next?' I say. Doug watches as I fork up a creamy mouthful of tiramisu.

'I kissed her.'

'What did she do?'

'I thought she sort of kissed me back but …'

He shifts in his seat. I notice his neck is flushed, a red rash-like flush creeping up between collar and chin.

'Can we just shorten this bit?' he says. 'Things didn't go any further because while I was kissing her I suddenly realised there were tears streaming down her face. And then I asked her why she was crying and she ... she just broke. She was sobbing in a way that ...' His voice trails away.

'That what?'

'Well, it frightened me. It was like she was completely ... you know, that she would never, ever stop. I kept saying I was sorry, I hadn't meant ...'

He stops, unable to continue. The memory is distressing him. He takes out his handkerchief again and wipes not just his forehead but his whole face.

'What did you do?'

'Held her. Just held her. And then she said it wasn't me should be sorry, she was sorry. She was sorry she'd ever started this because she knew it couldn't go anywhere, that she couldn't go through with it. She couldn't because she still loved him.'

'Who? Alex?'

'Her husband, yeah.' He can't bring himself to say his name.

'So what was wrong between them?'

'I could never work that out. I think he was just one of those detached men who didn't deserve her.'

'Ever meet him?'

'Once. He came in the garage with her once. That was the strange thing. When you saw them together ... it was like ... it wasn't love that you would have thought ... they just didn't seem ...' He shakes his head. 'I thought he was a bit of an arrogant bastard myself.'

'Did you see her after that?'

'Only once. Before I left to go home. I called her up, told her I was leaving. She agreed to meet for a coffee.'

'Did you talk about what happened?'

He shakes his head. 'I thought we would, but when it came to it, we didn't. We had coffee, said goodbye, walked away. That was it.'

'And now you're back.'

'Only for two weeks.'

'Why did you want to see her?'

'Because I've never stopped thinking about her.'

His voice has a catch in it. He looks at his watch. 'Look, I ... I really need to get back to the garage.' He takes out a card and scribbles a mobile number on it. 'You can get me on that if you need me. Is it okay if I go?'

'There's nothing else you can tell me? You haven't seen her since that day?'

He shakes his head.

'Okay. On you go. I'll settle up here. If I need you, I'll be in touch.'

He nods, leaves. I watch him as he closes the restaurant door carefully behind him. He pauses just for a second, leans one hand on the wall and breathes deeply. His jacket shifts as his hand raises, drawing attention to the baggy seat of his trousers, hanging shapelessly over a broad backside.

My God, Carol Ann, I think, taking a toothpick out of a holder in the centre of the table. You must have been desperate to even consider it, girl.

CHAPTER EIGHTEEN

Carol Ann

I get used to watching for the car lights in the twilight, but tonight it is pitch black when the rise and fall reflects through the curtains. He turns the car in the usual way, leaving the full beam on to light the path in the cemetery. I watch him lift the dead weight of his leg out. He moves slowly towards the grave and I drop the curtain and go to switch the kettle on. I check again when I return with a mug and for a moment I cannot see him. Then I realise that in the darkness he has become one with the headstone. He is clinging to it like a lifebuoy, his body curled round the base of it. His head rests against it.

I do not know what to do. I drop the curtain again, sit on a chair opposite the window. The day's paper rests on the arm of the chair and I pick it up half-heartedly, stare uncomprehendingly at the front page. In front of me, the wisp of steam from the mug dies. Outside, the light has not moved. Tentatively, I move towards the side of the window, lift the curtain just a fraction. I do not know what I hope to see, but he is still there, curled tightly in a ball.

I slip on a pair of shoes, wrap a cardigan round my shoulders, open the door to a draught of cool air. Uncertainly, I look across at the graveyard, change my mind and step back in the door, then change it again. Quietly, I walk across, then, inside the graveyard, my feet crunch on the gravel. He hears the sound and tries to clamber up, but he cannot move quickly. 'It's okay,' I say in a low voice. 'It's okay.' I crouch down beside the stone as he unwinds himself. He does not look at me.

I place a hand on his arm. 'I live across the road,' I say. 'Are you okay?'

'I'm fine, thanks,' he says stiffly. His cap is scrunched into a ball in his hand.

'Would you like me to get anyone to help you?'

'No.'

'Perhaps you would like to come in for a minute? Some tea, maybe.'

'No. Thank you,' he adds. He wants to move quickly but his body won't let him. His stick lies on the ground beside him and he uses it to manoeuvre awkwardly to his feet. I take his elbow, raising him gently.

'Sorry to have troubled you,' he says. Still he has not looked at me once.

'No trouble,' I say. 'Please, don't drive when you are so ... so upset. Come and sit for a little.'

But he shakes his head.

'Thank you,' he says. 'I'll be fine.' He limps away from me on the path and I follow. I stand uselessly at the side of his car while he lowers himself into the driving seat. The door bangs. Slowly, he does a three-point turn to face back down the road and I watch as the car moves off into the night.

When slivers of my old life intrude into my new one, they cut like glass. I try and keep them out, but sometimes they slice through my will like a knife slitting through tender skin. For a while after he goes, the old man's loss is my loss. I sit in the armchair willing it away. I imagine a box round me. A box full of doors that I can slam shut. No one can reach me inside my box. Slowly I imagine closing those doors to everyone I once loved ... to everyone Carol Ann knew. But there is one face I cannot shut out. I never could. She fades in and out at her own will, like the Cheshire Cat in *Alice in Wonderland.* One minute there, the next gone.

And I hear the music when she comes and goes, a background of Lily singing and the whoosh of the steam iron. 'In the morning when I go … in the morning when I go …' but the next line will not come to me. When I go where?

I wake early and walk each morning, out into the air that is becoming fresh with approaching autumn. I walk to the sea, drawn to watching the rising sun over the beach hut, the light brushed with a dew-washed delicacy, and every morning I wish I could be that clean, be reborn like the light. The sea froth dances white in front of me and the forgotten line from the song comes back then, 'In the morning when I go, To the white and shining sea, In the calling of the seals, Thy soft calling to me.'

Some mornings I go and buy soft white rolls from the village shop. I walk round the hill and across the dunes, but when I cannot see the sea still, I hear the whisper of it, calling, calling in the background. And I hear her in the whisper, plaintive and unmistakably Josie.

CHAPTER NINETEEN

Karen

I hear Lily playing Frank as I walk up the path. She was playing him a few days ago when I left. I think perhaps it has been non-stop Sinatra since. The croon with the little kick at the end. '*I've got you ... under my skin, I've got you, deep in the heart of me ...*'

'Under my skin,' I echo. It gives me a small shiver. I ring the bell.

'*So deep in my heart that you're really a part of me, I've got you under my skin.*'

Alex answers. It's around eight, maybe eight-thirty. When he sees me, he rests his head on the door.

'If I hear that bloody song one more time ...' he says.

He stands back to let me in.

'Whositt?' I hear Lily call. Her voice is slurred still but she is making huge progress.

'It's okay, Lily. It's Karen,' shouts Alex.

I hear the volume going up.

'*I've tried not to give in, I've said to myself this affair never will go so well.*'

Then suddenly it goes off completely.

'Come through,' Alex says.

His eyes scan my clothes, a straight black skirt and fitted leather jacket, black stilettos with a silver buckle. I often wear plain clothes rather than uniform when I come to the house, but this ain't plain. I changed twice before I left.

'Going out?'

'On my way to the pub,' I say. 'Just called in to see how you were.'

'Social call,' he says, raising his eyes. I can feel him looking at my legs when I walk in front of him into the sitting room. 'Are you allowed to do that?'

'Probably not. I have a habit of doing things I am not allowed to.'

'Naughty girl.'

'The best fun ones always are.'

'And the ones who get you in the most trouble. Drink?'

'Better not.'

'Not that naughty then,' he says.

'Oh, go on then. Gin. Small one.'

'So what are you doing here?' he says, unscrewing the bottle top.

'I told you, to see how you are.'

'Thanks.'

I can't tell if he's being sarcastic or not. He astute enough to know I always have an agenda. Now that I've met Doug, I'm pretty sure he's not at the heart of Carol Ann's disappearance. I can't see Alex bumping Carol Ann off in a jealous rage over a dumpy second-hand-car salesman. But I still have to find out who Josie is. Did Alex need Carol Ann out of the way for Josie's sake?

'Work has been really busy this week but I just wanted you to know I'm still working away on Carol Ann.'

He hands me a drink.

'What is there to work on?' he says. I take it as a rhetorical question.

'How's it going with Steve?'

He shrugs. 'Okay.'

The way he says it, I suspect it's not okay at all.

'He doesn't say much, but I know he misses Carol Ann. Not that he spent much time with her when she was here, but he had a choice, didn't he? He doesn't have a choice now and he doesn't like it.'

'And what about you?'

'What about me?'

'Are you missing her?'

He pours himself a drink.

'I don't have a choice any more, either.'

There's a bang at the door. Lily pushes it open, holding a portable CD player in her good hand. Her other hand looks a bit withered still, but the droop in her face has lessened. She tries to push the socket into the wall but hasn't the strength. I take it from her and push the plug in.

'What are you doing, Lily?' asks Alex.

Lily holds up a CD, *Hits From the Movies*.

'Oh God, not in here, Lily!'

'Karenikeit,' protests Lily.

'Karen *won't* like it, Lily.'

That surprises me. Alex can understand Lily quicker than I do. He must be spending *some* time talking to her.

Lily looks resentfully at Alex. She is dressed all in black with a grey scarf at her neck and she looks like an old hoodie craw.

'Drink,' she says, like a child demanding juice.

'No. No drink.'

Lily waves the CD at me.

'What have you got on there, Lily?'

'Listen,' says Lily, and the word is clear as a bell. She puts the disc into the player and Fred Astaire's voice spirals out, wrapping itself round us all like a thin light mist.

'Heaven, I'm in heaven,
And my heart beats so that I can hardly speak,

And I seem to find the happiness I seek,
When we're out together dancing cheek to cheek.'

Alex folds his arms and looks at his feet. Lily sways slightly where she stands, then stumbles, grabbing hold of the wall to steady herself.

'Dansse,' says Lily.

'I think your dancing days are over, Lily,' says Alex, taking a swig of gin like he needs it.

Lily's eyes glitter shrewdly.

'You dansse, Ax. Wi Karn.'

'I'm not dancing,' says Alex flatly.

'Yiss!' exclaims Lily. 'Karn.'

I think I know what the old bird is up to.

'Come on, Alex,' I say. 'Let's keep Lily happy. What harm can it do?'

Alex looks like he's panicking.

'Here,' he says, trying to make an effort, smiling grimly at Lily. 'I'll dance with you, Lily, if you're that bothered.' He walks over to her, but she waves her good hand dismissively at him.

'Oohh. nome, Ax,' she says. 'Karn.'

Alex looks trapped.

'Come on, Alex,' I say, holding out my hand to him, 'show us what you're made of.'

I put my hand round his waist and hold his other hand.

'Like this?' I say to Lily. I don't know the man's bit from the woman's bit, but I don't care. I'm just going to enjoy being that close to him.

'What the hell is all this about?' says Alex grumpily.

I lean forward and whisper in his ear.

'Just go with it.'

'Dance with me! I want my arms around you
The charms about you will carry me through to
Heaven ...'

We do little more than shuffle, but I make sure I move real close to Alex. I can feel the warmth of him where my hand sits on his back. I let my hips rest against his. Lily's eyes are boring into our backs.

'Toilet,' she says, and she moves out from the wall and thumps her stick into the floor as she goes.

I know what she's doing. Testing. Probing. She thinks Alex is a womaniser and in her deluded old head this will be proof. If he's not heartbroken enough to resist me, then he didn't think much of Carol Ann and maybe he bumped her off. She thinks she'll leave the two chemical elements together and see if there have been any explosions when she gets back.

Her mind is unpredictable after the stroke. She's childish, moody, emotional at times. She invents plots all around her. According to Lily, the doctors are using untested, experimental medicine on her. She's barking. Still, I'm with her on the dance experiment. I'd quite like to examine the chemistry myself. Though maybe for different reasons.

When Lily leaves the room, Alex drops his hand and stops moving.

'Bloody hell,' he says. 'She ...'

'Hey,' I tease lightly, 'I was enjoying that ...' I grab his hand again, pull him closer.

Alex looks at me calculatingly.

'Are you coming on to me, Karen?'

'What would you do if I was?'

He looks down at me and I see his eyes shift to the scoop of my neckline and then back to my face. And then down to my neckline again and back to my face. Bet he doesn't even know he's doing it.

'I think ...'

'You think I'm very attractive.'

'Oh, do I now?'

'Well,' I say moving in closer, 'since we're on a movies theme night, let me paraphrase Mae West here. Is that a gun in your pocket or are you just enjoying this dance?'

'It's a gun in my pocket.'

I hear the flush of the cistern from the toilet.

'I'd better be careful then,' I say.

'Yes,' says Alex. 'You better had.'

Lily appears round the door, her eyes darting eagerly, looking for sparks. I doubt she's disappointed.

CHAPTER TWENTY

Carol Ann

I love McGettigan's. I love the rawness of it, the lack of polish. The scratches on the table; the grey yellow of the light that filters through dusty bulbs above our heads. The sound of shoes on wooden floors. I love the banter and the craic and Sean's good-hearted teasing. Because it's the summer months just now, and the holidaymakers from the caravan site up the road are around, he opens all night if the customers want it. Nobody bothers. He closes the curtains at the front of the pub so that the Garda don't see the lights from the road. They came anyway one night, in the early hours of the morning. Sean saw the car swing in and looked through the curtains.

'Garda,' he said, and the pub went quiet.

They rapped at the door, but they were only looking for some petty criminal who had last been seen five miles away.

'Might be time to lock up now,' said one of them, and Sean nodded.

'Sure,' he said, 'we were just thinking that.'

They drove off and Sean grinned at us all.

'What're yous having?' he roared, and everyone cheered.

The Garda don't bother, really. Not if there's no trouble. They know people like Sean make two thirds of their year's profits in those summer months. Sean says I'm boosting his. The old men like me and I like them. I don't feel like a slightly overweight fortysomething when I'm around them. They make me feel like Marilyn Monroe.

There were whispers when I first started, of course, half-conversations that ended when I approached. And when the drink flowed people were less discreet.

'Your new barmaid,' I heard old Davie say to Sean one night, 'What in God's name is she doin' round here?'

Sean shushed him them, spoke low and urgent and when he finished Davie cried out, 'My Gawd, she'll not be long in findin' another one, a fine lookin' crater like her.'

Sean looked down the bar at me, apologetically. I half smiled.

The old guys like it when I'm sassy. *I* like it when I'm sassy. When you are stuck in a life, hemmed in by other people's expectations of who you are, hemmed in by your own expectations of who you are, you think you can't change your personality. But what I've discovered is that you can. You can add things in and take bits away at will. Once you become free, you can do whatever you like.

Every day I create who I am. I say to myself, Cara May Smith is a confident woman, a woman who can talk to anyone. And I am, because I am free to be. I am free of expectations. Yet if someone I knew in my old life came up and said, 'Carol Ann!' I know I would shrivel back into her. Just the call of her name. If I think too much about her, I will become her again. I cannot afford to think. I shut doors on unwanted thoughts every day.

It was the best thing I could have done, to tell Sean my husband was dead. To all intents and purposes he is. There is a sense of closure about it. And it stops people asking too many questions. They don't talk about him in case it upsets me, but they treat me kindly. And the bonus is that I can feel positively about my husband. Widows who loved their husbands have something divorcees don't. On paper, they are in the same position: they don't have a husband. But widows get to keep the memories. Divorcees get to keep the bitterness. The widow's future is stolen but the divorcee's past goes, too. It was never what she thought it was in the first place. That's what I think, anyway. I just know I'd rather be a widow than a divorcee in my new life.

'Don't look up now,' I say to Sean as I dry some beer glasses at the bar. I have my back to the counter, facing the mirror above the gantry, and Sean is facing the other way, hands submerged in soapy water. 'There's an old man in the corner ...' I break off abruptly. 'I said, don't look up!' I hiss, and Sean casts his eyes quickly back down in the water. 'He'll know we're talking about him,' I scold.

'What about him, anyways?' asks Sean.

'Who is he?'

'That's Harry. Harry Kirkpatrick. Why?'

'I've just seen him about and wondered who he was ...'

'Up at your bit? Up the graveyard?' says Sean.

'Aye.'

'Ah, poor fella,' he murmurs. 'Is he still goin' up there?'

'Is it ...'

'His wife,' nods Sean. 'Patsy. Nice woman, she was.'

He glances at me and smiles sympathetically, as if Harry and I are in the same boat. For the first time, I feel a stab of guilt at my deceit. And then I feel angry, like my old life is getting in the way again. I could be me, could be free, if the past would just leave me alone. If the circles of the old and the new would simply stay separate and stop trying to overlap, stop trying to find common ground.

'Hey,' says Sean, and runs his hand gently on my arm.

'I'll go and get the rest of the glasses.'

Harry Kirkpatrick keeps his eyes cast down when I pick up the glasses from the table next to him. His fingers nurse a small whisky glass, the peaty remnants of a double measure. When I pick up his empty half-pint glass he glances up at me, and though he says nothing, he acknowledges me briefly with his eyes and a soft incline of his head.

'Thanks,' he says, as I turn away. The single word is enough to make me turn back.

'I didn't mean to intrude ... you know, the other night. I'm sorry if I ...'

'No … I–I didn't ... it was kind of you. I never even said ... I didn't think to ...'

I shake my head. 'It's fine.' I smile at him. 'Come in some time ... when you want ...'

'Aye,' he says. 'Aye, thanks.'

'Cara May!'

Sean is calling from the bar. The name takes me unawares; it takes a moment to register Cara May as me.

'Cara May!'

Sean beckons me over, leans across the bar towards me.

'Mind now you were asking about that auld beach hut? That's the fella there that owns it, Kevin Howard.'

'In the black jacket?'

'No, the one next to him with the stripy-lookin' shirt.'

'Do you think it would be all right to talk to him in here?'

'Where better? This, Cara, is the centre of all Killymeanan business.'

We agree a price. €25,000. Sean thinks I'm mad because sure, it's only an auld ruin and there's no proper ground with it. It's perfect, I say. It's a postage stamp, he says. But I can't keep the excitement in me contained, the wings of it are battering against my chest like an imprisoned bird.

CHAPTER TWENTY-ONE

Karen

'I'll need to get a taxi home, pick up my car tomorrow.'

Alex pours another gin into my tumbler and hands it to me.

'Don't suppose it would look too good if you got breathalysed.'

The gin is beginning to bite, just a little, but I am still in control. Alex looks like he hasn't had a drop, though I'd guess he's had almost half a bottle in the last few hours. Lily has given up and gone to bed and Steve isn't in yet. We're playing some music – not Frank Sinatra. I never made it to the pub. Obviously. I sent Gav a text. Cnt mk it. C u 2mrw. I didn't add, 'Got a better offer.'

'I need to ask you something.' I say. I kick off my shoes, flex my toes. Alex's eyes flick down to my ankles.

'What?'

'Who's Josie?'

He's so startled, his eyes whip instantly from my legs to my face.

'Who told you about Josie?' he asks sharply.

'Alex,' I sigh, 'I am a police officer. It's my job, remember?' He says nothing.

'Who is she?' I repeat.

'Not that good a police officer, then,' he says.

'Come on, Alex.'

'I'm not talking about Josie. She is nothing to do with you. Nothing to do with any of this.'

'I asked you right at the start if you were faithful to Carol Ann.'

Alex shakes his head. 'You're way off track, Karen,' he says and his voice holds a muted warning. He drains his glass. 'Way off.'

'She was your mistress, right? Is that why Carol Ann was seeing a shrink?'

Alex looks stunned.

'A what?'

'A shrink. She was seeing a psychiatrist.'

'No, she wasn't.'

'Oh, she was, you know.'

He gets up and walks over to switch off the music.

'What psychiatrist? What are you talking about?'

'I'm right, aren't I? Josie was your mistress?'

'No, she wasn't my mistress,' he says tightly.

He turns and stares at me and it's like a challenge. He's daring me and I can never resist a challenge. I put my glass down and slip my feet back into my shoes, then walk towards him. I'm tall, but even with my high heels he's taller. I can feel my breath quicken sharply, a mixture of anxiety and adrenaline, the way it used to be ... in the dark ... when I waited in the dark, when I watched the shadow. Right now Alex seems as tall as the shadow, as imposing, as dangerous, but alluring rather than threatening. I can smell him close up, a smell quite unlike Gav's lightweight mixture of soap and aftershave.

'Who was she, Alex?' I say, and I can hear the almost taunting tone in my own voice. 'Your bit of stuff? On the side from Carol Ann?'

I sense the movement in his body immediately, the ripple, and instinctively I put my hand up, thinking he's going to lash out at me. I've learned to be quick. But his hands don't leave his side and a flash of surprise registers in his eyes. I can hear his breathing, the anger in it, and we stand together, waiting. I won't look away first. A door bangs. Steve opens the door abruptly and stops dead.

'What's going on? What's she doing here?' he says.

Alex's eyes don't leave mine.

'She's just going.' Steve looks from one to the other of us as if he hates us both. He crosses the room and drops into a chair, sticking his feet up on the coffee table in front of him.

Alex's eyes finally focus on him.

'Have you eaten?'

'Nuh.'

'Do you want something?'

'I'll get a sandwich or somethin',' he mumbles. He refuses to look Alex in the eye.

'There's some bacon in the bottom of the fridge and ...'

'I know,' Steve says, and he gets up again, as if impatient at Alex speaking to him. He walks from the room.

I can hear Lily in the hall. The noise has wakened her. I hear the slow, painful drawl of her voice and then Steve's voice, low and soft, a different tone from any I've heard before.

'I'm not finished, Alex,' I warn. 'And I know I'm right.' He looks at me contemptuously.

'I'll call a taxi now,' I say. Out in the hall I almost run smack into Lily and Steve. Steve has his arms round her comfortingly, hugging her, not like a child, but protectively, like a man. He wraps her small, old-lady body up in those long, gangling arms. Her head is sideways, on his shoulder, and there are rheumy tears running from her eyes.

'I know, Gran,' Steve is saying softly, 'I know. I do, too.'

They become aware of me behind them, but their moment is too important to be hurried. Steve straightens slowly. I walk round them.

'Come on, Gran,' Steve says. 'Go back to bed. I'll bring you a cup of tea.' The voice has lost its teenage truculence. It is trapped somewhere in a limbo between childhood and adulthood. Lily seizes his proffered hand gratefully.

They say that making love produces some kind of chemical that binds you emotionally to your partner. You're meant to be all loved-up in the afterglow. I can't say I've ever felt that. Maybe that's because if I am honest, I don't think I have ever actually made love. I've always just preferred sex.

Gav rolls over on his stomach and kisses my neck.

'Was that good for you?' he murmurs, and I resist the urge to kick him right out of bed for talking like someone in a crap movie. Alex wouldn't say something so stupid.

'No,' I say, closing my eyes. 'It was rubbish.'

He laughs then, burrowing his face in my shoulder.

'I love you, Karen,' he says quietly.

I don't suppose this is the minute to tell him it's over.

'Karen?'

'What?'

'I said, I love you.'

'I know, and I don't blame you. I love me, too.'

He rolls onto his back and guffaws. He's so thick, Gav. He always thinks I'm joking.

CHAPTER TWENTY-TWO

Carol Ann

Work has started on the beach hut. The son of a friend of a friend of Sean's, which is how everything works here. He's doing it as a homer, so it will take all winter. He's young, late twenties I'd say, or early thirties, so I'll be lucky to get weekend work out of him. On the other hand, he doesn't have a family. Nothing to keep him in at nights.

His name is Michael. He barely talks to me. I ask a question and his answer is a surly kind of grunt. His eyes are permanently cast downwards and he refuses to directly catch my eye, though sometimes he sneaks glances at me from under thick black eyelashes.

The first job is simply clearing up, getting rid of the sheep shit and the broken glass and the old iron shell of the bunk beds and the chipped enamel cooker that lies on its side. Then getting the roof put back, making it watertight. But though I listen intently to Michael stumbling out an explanation of the necessary work, I am looking ahead already. Yellow in the kitchen, the colour of the pale spring daffodils that will be dancing on the hill by the time I move in here. All the while Michael talks about the specifications, and the plumbing and the generator, I am imagining the springtime, sitting on a window seat in the tiny, postage-stamp living area, listening to the whoosh of the waves from behind the glass, watching the white foamy wash bubble and froth along the silver sand.

* * *

Harry and I are gentle with each other when we next meet. The gentleness of empathy, of understanding. He comes from the graveyard and knocks softly on the front door, though it is past ten. I open the door and he is standing on the step, as if we have a prior arrangement. I suppose we have. I ask for no explanation; he offers none. I kick the draught excluder from behind the door so that he can get by and he limps past me into the sitting room.

The next night the pot of tea is on the table already when he comes, two mugs beside it. I get into the habit of putting the kettle on the minute I see the flash of his lights pass by the window. The water trickles noisily into the mugs and I hand one to Harry.

'Working tomorrow?' he says, speaking for the first time.

I nod. 'Afternoon.'

Harry puts down his mug and stretches forward for a digestive biscuit, snapping it in two with a crisp movement, a small flurry of crumbs snowing into his lap.

'Snooker's on,' I say. 'Do you watch?'

'I like the snooker,' he says, and I press the button on the remote control.

The silence in the room is companionable, not awkward, broken only by the hushed voice of the commentator. We sip our tea while the balls click rhythmically. Occasionally Harry oohs audibly when someone misses a pot.

'Best be off,' he says, at the end of a couple of frames.

I lean forward to take his cup and he grabs the arm of the chair to haul himself up. There's a blast of cold air in the hall as the door opens and then he's gone.

It becomes a pattern. I look forward to him coming. I don't analyse it much, just accept that maybe we fill a need in one another. It's a novelty to have an older man in my life; there was only ever Lily. Harry and

I talk more as the weeks pass, but he never mentions his graveyard visits or his loss. I don't ask. And then one night, on his way out, he stops.

'I was wondering ...' he says.

'Yes?'

'I was wondering if you'd like to pay a visit ... maybe Sunday afternoon. There's things … things I'd like to show you.'

Maybe the surprise shows in my eyes.

'Patsy,' he says, 'My wife, Patsy ...' He looks at me tentatively, like he's worried I'll rebuff him.

'I'd like that,' I say

'Sure,' he says, and there's relief in his voice. He looks at me with a nod, a half-smile, and suddenly one of those moments runs between us that happen sometimes in life, a cord forming invisibly, a tie of understanding and empathy and sheer naked humanity that flares like a sudden, warm flame inside.

'See you tomorrow, though,' I say. It is not a question.

'I'll be here.'

'Night, Harry.'

'Night, Cara.'

The door of his car bangs shut. I stand on the doorstep watching, wrapping my arms over my chest, rubbing my hands down my sleeves to keep warm. Harry waves briefly. I close the door and turn the bolt.

The woman in the mirror emerges slowly, gradually wriggling free of the old, tired skin that confines her. I watch her with fascination, as if she is not part of me. As if she is an experiment in a laboratory, and the mirror is the glass side of the scientist's test tube. The face grows thinner, more defined, the white, doughy pillows of her cheeks falling away to reveal cheekbones. The tentative eyes grow bolder, more direct. The chemistry of her body is changing, bubbling, brewing. Sometimes, I feel I hold my breath when I look, and then I simply wait to see what the next explosion will bring. There is an excitement, an anticipation. I know what this woman was; I do not yet know what she is to become.

I stand naked in the yellow bedroom before the glass. It is a curious feeling, like I am standing outside of myself. I look objectively, as if examining a scientific specimen. I see the swell of my breasts and the creamy curve of my hips as though they belong to someone else. My stomach has sagged since giving birth, the skin like an overstretched elastic band that has simply never regained shape. A bit like my mind. There is a little mound over my abdomen that never goes away. I used to look at it with frustration, even distaste, but now I feel detached. I run my hand over it, the skin loose, saggy. It was the calling card nature left behind; it will never go away.

I have lost weight. I have no scales, but perhaps half a stone. Objectively, I am, say, still ten pounds overweight. Maybe more. A stone perhaps. I stand sideways to see. There is a little cellulite on my thighs and on my buttocks. When I make the muscles taut, the dimpling is worse. My body changed and I resented Alex for that. As if he made the rules. My body changed and his didn't and that seemed merely a reflection of the bigger picture; his life went on much as before and mine didn't. That is the thing about Alex. The world stands still for him. He is always unassailable.

The wind smells of salt today, brine and seaweed and damp sand carried from the coast. There is a cold sunlight, like a too-brittle smile, and the wind is fresh and keen, ruffling the grasses on the hill behind Harry's house, blowing up a thin trail of fine, white sand amongst the reeds and grasses. The house is small, trim and whitewashed, the window frames and wooden doors a deep blood red. Across the hill, back towards the village, the brown scrub of rocky moorland, and the peat-blackened walls of outhouses, and the bare outline of drunken trees left leaning by winter storms. And in the other direction, the track that leads round the cliff before dropping towards the sands and the blue beach hut on the hill.

There is only the sound of the wind to complement the click of the metal latch on the gate when I lift it. The door of the house is open before the gate is closed, and Harry stands on the step waiting, in the way that instinctively I know he has been waiting for the last hour. He wears a shirt and a tie and a cardigan and there is something of the small boy, scrubbed for Sunday visiting, about him. I realise I have rarely seen him without the tweed cap that sits on his head, even in McGettigan's. His hair is black and grey like a badger's, prone to dryness at the front where he has smoothed the unruliness into a neat, fat slick.

There is awkwardness as I hand him the small box of assorted biscuits from the village store, a clumsiness in my gesture, a certain stiffness in his thanks. The moment that sparked this invitation, the gentleness of understanding that it was born of, has temporarily vanished, and we stand, the two of us, on his doorstep, a little uncertain how either of us got to be here, uncertain now if that closeness will be recaptured.

'Come in, now,' says Harry, and he turns stiffly, leaning on his stick.

In the sitting room, I see the table at the window, which overlooks the back garden, is laid with a tray. Floral china cups and saucers; a milk bowl and sugar bowl covered with a white lace cloth that is weighted with beads. A plate of biscuits on a little dainty china platter. Patsy is in that tray. I never met her but somehow I know she is there, in the delicacy of the lace, in the prim attention to preparation. Harry has laid the tray just like Patsy would.

'Take a seat.'

I sit in the middle seat of the sofa, Harry on an armchair by the hearth.

'Not a bad day.'

'Yes, it's bright enough. The wind's sharp, though.'

Harry nods.

'Things still going okay at McGettigan's?'

'Yes ... yes. Sean's been good to me.'

'Good family.'

'Yes.'

He nods.

'Good family,' he repeats.

'Have you a ... do you have any children, Harry?'

'Two boys. Both in England now. They come when they can.'

'Grandchildren?'

'Three. Two girls and a boy.' He lifts his stick and points to a photograph on top of the television cabinet. 'That's them.'

'Who is ... is that Patsy with them?'

'That's her.' He shuffles his bottom forward on his seat, rocking to lever himself out of the chair.

'No, you stay where you are,' I say, walking over to the photograph and lifting it. The frame is ornate silver and surprisingly heavy. Patsy is photographed on the sofa, in the very seat where I have been sitting. She is flanked by two small girls, perhaps two years apart, and dressed in identical pink outfits. A little boy leans on the back of the sofa behind Patsy, as if growing out of her head. He is taking his weight on his hands; his cheeks are flushed with the devil, his eyes like two bright pin heads. He sticks his tongue out above his grandma and one of the girls is looking up at him and giggling. Patsy, I am sure from her expression, is unaware.

I say nothing, but smile at Harry and he gives a little cough of a laugh, jerking his head.

I put the photograph back and look at the one next to it, Harry and Patsy together.

'You look smart,' I say, 'like you are off to a wedding.'

'Oldest boy's wedding. Patrick's.'

Patsy is dressed in soft green, a dress with a little thin coat over it. She has a way of smiling at the camera that is not quite direct. In each photograph, it is as if she is not entirely there, as if the camera lens cannot quite capture where her mind is. She is not defined by her expression, because it is already flitting away when the camera flashes to steal it. She is somewhere else already. Patsy cannot be stolen.

'She's pretty,' I say, smiling at Harry, more because I feel I should say it than because she is. In truth, Patsy is not pretty exactly, but slightly quaint, ethereal, other-worldy. Her hair is dark but thin, a little wispy, her eyes a grey-blue. She is tall for a woman, almost as tall as Harry – though, granted, he is not a big man – and she is a little too thin, too bony, for clothes to hang well. Well, these clothes. It is as if she has pushed herself into a conventional mother-of-the-bride outfit to mask her strangeness, and all she has done is emphasise it. She wears the clothes like they are someone else's uniform, like they don't quite fit. I know all about that.

'Lovely eyes,' I say, which *is* true.

'Sure, doesn't she?' says Harry, with a gratitude I don't quite understand until later.

My thumb has accidentally touched the glass of the frame and I carefully wipe the mark away with my sleeve before setting it down again.

'Shall I show you now?' says Harry. 'Show you Patsy's things?' I feel his tension, his need to embark on what we have arranged.

'Only if you'd like to, Harry. Only if you feel up to it.'

A little part of me hopes he won't.

He climbs the stairs ahead of me, hauling himself on the banister with one hand and using his stick with the other. Slowly we go up, me two stairs behind, pausing on each step, never narrowing the gap. Despite the age gap, it feels awkward to be climbing the stairs to the bedroom with him, too intimate for a friendship that is still in its early stages. I think he feels it too, the silence heavy with broken taboos.

And yet, I know that this is important to him. He needs to introduce me to Patsy.

The room is light and feminine, a confection of peaches and cream and candy stripes of palest lemon. There are little signs of Harry's existence: a biography of George Best and a pair of reading glasses on the bedside cabinet ; a can of spray deodorant on the dressing table and an unopened bottle of aftershave, probably an unwanted Christmas present; then the tiny edge of men's pyjamas, like a little tongue sticking out, from under the pillow. But though they shared this room, though Harry exists in it, it was clearly Patsy's space. She is gone but Harry still lives only on the edges of it.

Her make-up bottles, an assortment of nail varnishes and lipsticks and perfume bottles, stand in two neat circles either side of the dressing table. There is a painted pot, a jumble of lipsticks and eye pencils. Harry picks up a bottle of varnish, a deep rose pink. A vague memory stirs, a sense of déjà vu. Pink varnish ...

'Patsy always did her nails,' he says, 'beautiful long nails she had, like a lady. She was proud of them. When she did the housework, she wore rubber gloves.'

I nod.

'She didn't go in for red,' he says. 'Too tarty for Patsy, red varnish.'

I think of telling him I wear red varnish, but I stay silent. 'She liked the softer colours, pinks and peaches. See?' he continues, holding up the bottle to the light. He hands it to me. 'Open it,' he says. 'Go on.'

I unscrew the bottle; it is sticky, the varnish starting to solidify around the top. Inside the bottle, the varnish is marbled, the colour beginning to separate at the bottom.

'It's nice,' I say, looking at the label. Moroccan Rose.

'I bet there'll be a lipstick to match in that pot,' he says. 'She likes things to match.' Present tense. I put the bottle down, back where it was.

'Over here,' he says, moving stiffly to the window, 'this is where she kept her jewellery.' There is a small cabinet under the window, cream-coloured wood with painted peachy flowers on the front panels. He opens the shallow drawers, and inside, neatly labelled, are gift boxes and jewellery rolls and a square box for holding rings. The ring box is pretty, silver and heavily ornate and lined with red velvet.

'See, that,' says Harry, lifting it out, 'is from Spain. It was our first holiday abroad and she took a fancy to it in a market.' He lifts the lid. 'She wouldn't spend the money on it, but I went back on my own and bought it for her birthday. Never told her. Kept it a month and she couldn't believe it when she opened the parcel.'

Inside the box, a collection of rings nestles amongst the red velvet. A small emerald, surrounded by what looks like diamonds.

'Cubic zirconia,' says Harry. 'We never had the money for proper diamonds.' An opal and garnet Victorian ring that had belonged to Patsy's mother. And a rather sad-looking chipped, cheap pearl in a gold setting.

'Try one on if you like ...' says Harry.

'Oh no, I ...'

'Go on, now,' he says, and he lifts out the emerald. 'Sure, Patsy wouldn't mind. That was her favourite.'

The emerald flashes in the light streaming through the window. I feel uncomfortable seeing it glint on my finger, a dead woman's ring.

'It's lovely, Harry,' I say, slipping it off as soon as I decently can and putting it back in the box. 'Did you buy it for her?'

'Near the end,' he says, and his voice, dry and brittle, cracks slightly, a tiny fissure in his composure. 'Near the end. An eternity ring ... kind of.' He swallows hard.

'And here,' says Harry eagerly, moving quickly now, dragging his dead leg as fast as he can across the dark apricot carpet, 'here is where she kept her clothes,' and he throws open one of two wardrobes. 'See?' he says. 'See?' He runs a hand over a deep midnight-blue velvet evening dress. 'This was her favourite. Feel it,' he says. 'Feel how soft it is.'

I am behind him now, standing awkwardly, my own desperation growing towards his, two magnetic forces drawing together. I lift my hand half-heartedly to the velvet, but he does not wait for me to comment.

'And this,' he says lifting out a silk shirt in a deep fuchsia pink, 'she got this for our granddaughter Sarah's christening. She wore pearls with this. Now, where did those pearls go? The box was too big for the cabinet and she always kept them in the original box. Patsy liked things in the right place.'

He rummages in the top of the wardrobe, and pulls out a red box of Majorcan pearls. The box has gold writing on the lid and he lifts it to reveal a single strand of beads nestling inside. He turns to the bed and lays out the shirt and puts the pearl at the neck.

'Like that,' he says, and turns back to the wardrobe. 'She liked velvet, and silk, and lace.'

The wooden hangers scrape along the metal bar of the wardrobe as he pulls them towards him.

'That green, that's the outfit she wore to the wedding,' he says, and he lifts it out and throws it on the bed. 'The one in the picture. 'And this was just her everyday skirt. Like a work-day skirt. And this blouse was a bit big on her, but she liked the colour.'

Another scrape along the bar, the hangers flying fast now. A chunky-knit cardigan for the winter, a pair of charcoal-grey trousers. 'And *this* ... this,' he says, stopping at a bright sleeveless dress in a floral print and lifting it out, 'this sundress she bought for our Spanish holiday. Patsy said the Spaniards were more exotic than us and she had to try a lot harder.'

Again, he throws it onto the bed behind him, and immediately pulls at the other hangers in the cupboard, like a man demented. Pulling, throwing; pulling, throwing. There's a growing sense of desperation in the room, so strong it feels like a heat. I watch him silently, wanting to remove myself, but unable to take my eyes off him. He's lost inside himself. It's almost like I'm no longer in the room. I don't know what to say.

'Did she like clothes, Harry?' I say softly , more to remind him that I'm here than anything.

Harry doesn't look at me, but his hand stops rifling, and hovers over the next hanger.

'No,' he says, and he suddenly looks deflated, turning towards the bed and flopping onto it. 'No.' His hand reaches out to the fuchsia-pink silk, stroking it lightly, and then he lifts the pearls into his hands. 'Patsy hated clothes shopping. She never felt right in anything she wore.'

The clothes lie piled on the bed, a themeless assortment, each item random in colour and style, a one-off, a desperate search for identity. The walls of the room seem to be moving inwards, making it smaller. What am I doing here with a stranger? I don't know him. Not really. He's not my responsibility..I look towards the door, turn to Harry to mumble my excuses. But he looks so lost now, miserable, the floral sundress crushed underneath him where he sits, one sleeve of the fuchsia-pink silk trailing across his knee. I hesitate, then sit down on the bed, a few feet apart from him, my hands on my knees, and the silence engulfs us both. I glance sideways and see the muscle in his cheek quivering. I hold out my hand to him. Harry does not look at me, but his hand reaches out, still clutching the pearls, and we sit holding hands, the beads entangled between our two palms.

'Harry,' I say, 'Harry ...' But he won't look at me. 'Patsy was so lucky ...'

The words seem to distress him; the muscle quivers more strongly, the whole of his cheek shaking, but he looks straight ahead still.

'She must have known you loved her, Harry ... loved her like this.'

I look round the peach shrine, the room that is alive with a dead woman. 'It's important not just to be loved, but to *know* you're loved,' I say softly. 'And Patsy must have known.'

The wall of his cheek is crumbling now, granite imploding inwards into powdered rubble. His grip tightens on my hand, the pearls between us digging into my palms.

'In the end,' I plough on, 'it matters that you have spent your life with the right person. What could be worse than reaching the end and knowing none of it was right, that it was all a waste. Could there be any realisation more cruel than that when you are dying?' The tear that has filled Harry's lower lid for the last few seconds, like a small pool, finally bursts its banks and spills over, running down his cheek, splashing onto his shirt, a single damp spot on the collar.

In my stupidity, I think that despite his sadness, my words are somehow helping, that the tear signals catharsis, not hopelessness. Later, those words will come back to haunt me.

'But Patsy, she didn't have that awful realisation ...' I continue softly, shaking his hand gently to rally him. 'She had you.'

He turns to me then, his hand dropping mine.

'But she didn't,' he says, his voice low and still and awful. 'She didn't. Because I didn't. I ... I ...' He stops. 'I didn't love Patsy all those years,' he says. 'All those years. I never loved her like I ought. See? Not till it was too late.'

He gets up from the bed then, leaning on his stick, propelling himself forward onto it. Quietly, he picks up the pearls and places them neatly in the box, then back on the shelf. I sit on the bed in silence and watch him as he works, lifting each garment and placing it on a hanger, hanging them methodically back into the wardrobe. There is a stillness about him now. Almost eerie. It reminds me of that unnatural calm that follows a storm when you can't quite believe the tumult has died down. But when it's gone, it's gone. Harry closes the cupboard door and walks from the room without speaking, thumping down the stairs with his stick, leaving me sitting alone on Patsy's side of the bed.

CHAPTER TWENTY-THREE

Karen

McFarlane called me in for the biggest bollocking of my career. Apparently Mackie had dropped in some 'casual' comment about how I thought the Matthews case would turn into a murder inquiry. Fat bastard. McFarlane went ballistic.

'What are you playing at, Karen?' he yelled, after calling me into his office.

I focused my eyes on the turnip heads in the photograph on his desk. Cut off, that's the thing. Ignore him. Ugly little bastards, his kids.

'CID should have been in there if you had any suspicions,' McFarlane continued. You told me this bloody woman had run off with her new boyfriend!'

'I said she might have. Turned out she didn't.'

'So why didn't you ask me to pull CID in for a full investigation if you were suspicious?'

'Mackie's exaggerating. I only said …'

'Imagine,' McFarlane interrupts, 'what this would look like if any harm has come to her and we've been sitting on our backsides doing nothing.' His narrow, glittering eyes pin me. 'Have you checked CCTV?'

'What CCTV? She lives in a toytown village the size of Camberwick bloody Green!'

'Don't get lippy with me, Karen, I'm talking about the train station, the bus station, the shopping centre in town – have you checked?'

Shit. Brazen it out.

'You never asked me to check town-centre CCTV.'

McFarlane's hands slap down on his desk. He looks like he might have a heart attack. Of course, he's only mad because he forgot about the case and he's taking it out on me.

'Karen, when you eat your cereal in the morning, do you hold your own bloody spoon? For God's sake, show some initiative.'

'I …'

'Oh, get out of here! CID will be round there in the morning. You're on family liaison duty now. I expect you to fill Sergeant Kennedy in on anything that's been done so far – if you have actually done anything, of course.'

'Of course I have!'

'Out, Karen!'

There was a sudden flurry of activity when I emerged from his room, and nobody looked directly at me. I could tell they'd all been rooted to the spot, listening. After a few minutes, Mackie came over to my desk.

'Sorry if I got you in trouble, Karen,' he said innocently. 'I had no idea it wasn't official …'

Like fuck he didn't.

All it means is that I'll need to do things even more unofficially than usual. Might even work out in my favour if I can find out what's going on when CID are involved. I reckon I've got a better chance of cracking Alex than they do.

I think I know men pretty well. I know their buttons and their switches. How to make them jump through hoops; how to make them sit up and beg. (McFarlane aside, of course, but I can hardly be expected to iron out the kinks in the pink-shirt brigade.) But I can't completely 'get' Alex. I quite like the challenge. I've known from the start there's something bothering him. I think he knows more than he's saying. What I don't – yet – know, is if it's to do with this Josie woman.

I started following him in the car about a week ago, not on official business, but just out of curiosity. Now I can't stop. And I haven't seen any sign of him meeting up with another woman. Whoever Josie is, she's keeping a low profile. But what was her role in Carol Ann's disappearance?

I have one afternoon left to myself before CID move in. No time now for rules. I call round at the house when I know Alex will be at work, telling Theresa, Lily's carer, that I just want to check a few things of Carol Ann's in her room. She shrugs – as I knew she would. Lily is being stroppy about taking medication again and that's enough for Theresa to concentrate on. As far as she's concerned, I'm police and, after all, it's not her house, is it?

Carol Ann and Alex's room is enormous. I can't help feeling a tinge of resentment walking into it. You could have fitted half my house when I was growing up into this place. I glance round at the white-washed walls and the tastefully highlighted raspberry-coloured detail: a throw, a picture frame, a magnificently ornate mirror with a mosaic of pink and red around the rim, like stained glass. A vase of deep-coloured flowers on the chest beneath. A white wicker chair with cushion to match the throw. It's a haven of peace. I take my jacket off and throw it on the bed just to see how it looks lying on the cover, to see what ownership of this place would feel like. It looks good there.

I take my shoes off and let my feet sink into the deep-pile carpet, turn around in it, imagining. I like the left side of the bed – Alex would have to have the right. The top drawer of the chest is slightly open and idly, I pull it further. A make-up drawer, scattered with pink powdery bloom from a blusher with a broken lid. An assortment of lipsticks. I open one, looking up to the mirror and streaking it on my lips. Don't think much of the colour. I chuck it back. There's one in Christian Dior packaging and the colour's not bad, so I slip it in my pocket. No one will ever know. Certainly not Alex.

I close the drawer and open the ones below. Most of them have clothes, but one has an assortment of junk, the kind of drawer that exists in every house, even posh ones like this, I guess. Sellotape, odd paperclips, old kirby grips, a broken necklace, a packet with a few photos. I open the packet, concentrating on the ones with Alex in. God, he looked good when he was younger, too. I guess that's Steve with him, the childlike smile lighting up his face before his teenage years ate up his enthusiasm and openness. A few of Carol Ann that I flick quickly over. Carol Ann with Steve. Carol Ann sticking out her tongue at the camera. And one of her kneeling down beside a little girl in a party frock and cuddling her like she was her own. Some local kid, I suppose, at one of Steve's early birthday parties. I look at the next one and then flick back instinctively to the one with the little girl. Carol Ann has a different quality in it to other photos I've seen. She looks happy, enthralled in the moment. I stuff the photos back into the wallet.

In the wardrobes, I look at Alex's fancy dark suits, the array of different coloured shirts and ties. Nothing in the suit pockets apart from a pen in the breast pocket of one and a dry cleaner stub in another. No evidence of Josie.

Carol Ann's side is full of frumpy stuff, but there is something about it that strikes me. It's high-quality frump. I pick up a soft blue sweater and rub my cheek against it, smell the remnants of Carol Ann's Lou Lou perfume from it. I check the label. Cashmere. Another flash of irritation. She had everything. Alex isn't short of a bob or two. She has a beautiful home – though I'd make it look better – a cupboard full of clothes, a jewellery box over there that I bet has proper stuff in it ...

and Alex. What was wrong with her? Unless, of course, she didn't walk. Who would walk from this?

This room really gets me thinking. Who would walk? I repeat to myself, over and over. Who would walk? Alex, Alex … what's he capable of? There's a faint kind of … what would the word be? Excitement, maybe, when I wonder what Alex is capable of. What if … what if he … Then I realise something. I really don't care. Because, unlike Carol Ann, I could handle him.

One of Carol Ann's scarves is trailing from the closet and idly I pick it up, wrap it round my neck. That scent again. As if she were still in the room.

'What the hell are you doing?'

I spin round to see Steve standing at the door. He has really startled me, but I suppress the fear and gaze as calmly as I can at him.

'A much more pertinent question, Steve, would be what are *you* doing here? Why are you not at school?'

'That's my mum's,' he says nodding at the scarf. 'Get it off.'

His eyes are darting round the room to see if there's any evidence of what I've been up to. They flick back to me. 'What are you doing in her wardrobe, anyway?'

'I'm a police officer. I'm trying to do things that will help me find your mum.'

'Well, I doubt you'll find her in there,' he says and his eyes bore into me with the penetrative honesty of a teenager who doesn't give a shit. 'Go on,' he says belligerently. 'What are you going to find in there?'

I calmly find a place for the scarf in the wardrobe and ignore him.

I'd hoped for longer. I've found nothing in Alex's pockets but I don't dare stay now. I'll turn the tables on Steve and insist on dropping him back at school. Focus on his wrongdoing. Say I'll need to tell Alex if he keeps skipping off. He'll know what I mean: open your mouth and I'll open mine. I take a last look round the room. Did she walk? But one thing's for sure. Whatever the reason for Carol Ann's disappearance, it creates a vacancy that I wouldn't mind filling.

From the top of the stairs I hear the front door bang. Alex is back early from work. Feeling the strain. Fuck. I hold onto the balustrade, trying to think rapidly. As it happens, I don't need to think up excuses for what I'm doing because things just take off within minutes. I sit on the top stair and listen while Alex tells Theresa she can go. She doesn't hang around. It's been a difficult day for her.

Steve emerges from the sitting room and confronts Alex just as I begin to walk down the top half of the stairs. 'Why is she *always* here?' Steve demands, without even saying hello.

I stop dead on the stairs, listening intently. There are two parts to the staircase and from this upper part I can only hear, not see what's happening.

'What are you on about now?' says Alex.

'Her. PC Weirdo. Always here, sneaking about, rifling through Mum's things. Why are you letting her? Do you fancy her or something?'

It's such an obvious teenage wind-up, an expression of general anger, that I am surprised Alex responds, but he seems to be losing the place a bit these days. Guilty conscience or the grieving husband?

It all gets a bit confusing after that. A couple of shouted comments, the general roar of male voices shouting in anger, and on top of that, Lily squawking in fear. I run down the remaining stairs to the halfway landing and look down.

Alex has Steve by the shoulders up against the wall, two fistfuls of Steve's T-shirt squeezed into his hands, lifting him almost out of his shoes. The two of them have been ready to explode with tension for weeks. Lily is wild-eyed, breathing heavily.

'Krnn,' she shouts when she sees me, but the rest is gibberish.

'YOU'LL DO WHAT I TELL YOU,' Alex roars, oblivious to anyone else.

'I WON'T!' Steve shouts, 'I'll do nothing you tell me, you bastard. It's your fault she's gone.'

'Me? I didn't drive her away. Dealing with a teenage delinquent drove her away.' Alex yells, pinning him to the wall still.

I grab hold of Alex from the back, pulling him away.

'Right. Enough,' I say, tugging at him. 'ENOUGH!'

Alex refuses to loosen his grip at first but then I feel him go limp. He drops his hands from Steve's shoulders, runs one hand through his hair.

'Bloody hell,' he mutters.

Steve is crying tearlessly, gulping air and whimpering. He crouches down suddenly, onto his hunkers in the hall, like a cornered animal.

Alex looks at him and puts out a hand awkwardly.

'Come on, Stevie, up you get,' he says, but the boy doesn't move. Alex bends down and tries to pull him up, but Steve shrugs his shoulder violently to try and push him off.

'Come on, Stevie,' Alex says, 'come on. This has gone far enough.'

Tears are pouring down Steve's cheeks but he says nothing. Gently, Alex raises him, ignoring Steve's resistance until he has his son standing. Even upright, Steve seems to have collapsed somehow, his shoulders curling inwards at the edges like stale sandwiches. And then suddenly he's bawling, bawling like a baby, and Lily's eyes are frightened and distressed, darting from me to Alex, waiting for one of us to take charge. Alex's hands are still on Steve's shoulders and he pulls his son then, pulls him in to his chest and wraps his arms tightly round him, holding him like he'll never let go. Lily hobbles over, tentatively stroking Steve's back, like he's some strange little animal, then she turns to the stairs and sits down suddenly, inelegantly, on the step.

Bolt upright. Sweat. Shadows. Not for years as bad as this. Not for years. The smell of stale alcohol. Jesus, he's in the room. Where is he? Throw back the sheets, grab something, anything. Thump. The thump of his fall. Is it? Is it? Jump from the bed. No ... no ... the lamp has fallen. I've knocked the lamp over. Listen. Listen. Heart beating, boom, boom, in the stillness, like a tribal drumbeat. Breathe. Deeply. Breathe. Nothing. No one. Place the lamp upright. Fall back onto the soft, down pillows. Breathe.

He had me once, by the neck, grabbing my school shirt until I almost choked. Like Alex had Steve – yet not like it, too. Sadistic, he was. Alex isn't sadistic. The old man came at me and my mother one day when I was about fifteen, and something snapped. I grabbed a bat from a cricket set under the stairs that my brother Jerry and I had played with when we were kids.

'Come any nearer and I'll take your bloody head off,' I roared, blood rushing in my head. My mother shrivelled against the wall when she heard me and he lunged forward, but I swung the bat up and he thought twice about it, jumping back instinctively. He stood silently then, his black eyes glimmering like coals from hell fire. But he didn't move. 'Touch her again and I'll have you,' I said, nodding at my mother. The old bastard just looked at me and lifted a finger and wagged it at me, like he was warning me.

'Come on, then,' I said, the adrenaline pumping through me, the bat twitching above my head, sweat sticky on my back. My feet were spread apart, bent slightly at the knee, waiting. He inched forward and then stopped, smiled. He never said a word, and a minute later I heard the door bang. I slept with the bat under my pillow after that.

In the darkness, I feel under my pillow for the cricket bat. It is not there. Of course it's not. He is not here. There is no smell of stale, rank booze. No shadows. There is nothing at all but my need.

CHAPTER TWENTY-FOUR

Carol Ann

The kitchen door is open downstairs and I hear the surge of the kettle beginning to boil. I rise slowly from the bed, and stand in the centre of the floor, uncertain what to do. Part of me wants to sneak out the back door and run across the hill to the safety of my own house. I thought I'd left emotional turmoil behind.

I look round at Patsy's things, neat, ordered, as if she's temporarily away and coming back. A bottle of perfume sits on the bedside cabinet and I lift the lid and sniff. The first smell is fresh, light, the tang of citrus mixed with the sweetness of vanilla. But there's an after-kick of staleness, as if it's beginning to ferment. Nothing lasts for ever.

Harry is pouring the water in the pot when I come down. He looks calm still, as if the agitation has left him and been replaced with a tired resignation. He doesn't glance up, so I go straight into the sitting room, sitting awkwardly on the edge of a seat at the table where the tea tray is laid. A few minutes later, Harry carries the pot in from the kitchen and puts it down on the tray. He lifts the lid and stirs in silence, then pours.

'Now you know,' he says, handing me a cup.

'Know what?'

'About Patsy.'

'Harry, we *all* think we could have done better when people die.

That guilt is ... it's just *part* of it, of the grieving.'

'No.'

I know from the calmness of his voice, the lack of passion, the absolute *clearheadedness* of it, that my words are not true.

'Guilt?' he says. 'It's more than that. There's no word for guilt this big.'

'Tell me.'

Harry sips from his cup.

'I don't know how.'

'How did you meet Patsy?'

'My best friend was going out with Patsy's sister. Patsy and I got together at a village dance, went out for a couple of years.' His cup chinks on the saucer. 'Then I decided I was going off to London to work. This place wasn't big enough for me in them days. Patsy was ... she was upset.'

'She was in love with you?'

He nods, but says nothing.

'But you weren't with her?'

'I wasn't in love with anyone. Unless it was with meself.'

I smile instinctively.

'I was a few years older than Patsy, but I was just a boy, really. I liked her, though. She was different to the other girls. She didn't have a great figure or know how to dress or have a really outgoing personality, but she was sort of her own person, if you know what I mean. And she had lovely eyes… really beautiful eyes. Soft grey-blue…'

'So what happened? Did you go to London?'

'I got a job in a bank. I met this girl, there, Caroline ...' He shakes his head. 'I'd never seen anything like her. This mane of dark, wavy hair to her waist and a figure like you wouldn't believe…'

I suppose he would have been handsome when he was younger, Harry, in a craggy kind of way. Remove the pouches from under the eyes that give him that slight lugubriousness … tauten the slackness under his chin … darken the thick, coarse hair … the young man he was is still in there, drowning slowly in the tide of age.

'Fiery, though,' he says, taking a sip of tea. 'She was so sure of herself, Caroline. She didn't need me but she wanted me, and that felt pretty good, having a woman like her want me. She had a lot of friends in London and we were always at parties or pubs or the house of some posh pal of hers. Drinking too much, living too hard. For a boy like me, coming from here … I loved it.'

Loved *it*, I think to myself. Not loved *her*.

'Did she love you?'

'Who, Caroline?' He smiles. 'I was her bit of rough.'

'What happened to Patsy?'

'Nothing. She stayed at home, got a job locally. The next summer I came over with Caroline. I was showing off, I suppose. Caroline looked like a model. I wanted people to see us.'

'And Patsy did?'

'Patsy did,' he nods. 'What a bloody carry-on, that night.' He raises his eyes and smiles wanly. 'D'you remember,' he says, 'when you were young and turned everything into a big drama? By the time you are old enough to have real drama in your life you try and smooth it out, pretend it's not there, but with young folk, everything's a crisis.'

I laugh.

Harry pushes the plate of biscuits across to me and I shake my head.

'I took Caroline to a village dance, though by this time she was being a bit snotty about what a dump this was and how she wanted back to London. Patsy kept looking at us that night. I could see she was upset. She was never very good at hiding things. Anyway, my mate Brendan told Caroline that Patsy was an old girlfriend of mine and Caroline wasn't very nice to her. Caroline and I had words, later. We'd both had a lot to drink.

I surprised myself, but I was angry at her for the way she spoke to Patsy. Maybe I cared more than I knew. I don't know. But it was the worst row we'd ever had and that's saying somethin'. Caroline had a habit of lashing out when she got in a strop. Split my lip open once. Blood everywhere.'

'My God!'

'It was just one of those relationships,' says Harry matter-of-factly. 'Too hot and too angry and just … too everything, really. Addictive. You'd get days where you didn't want to be with anyone else and other days where you couldn't stand the sight of one another. You know those relationships?'

Not really, but I don't say so. I look at the salt-and-pepper stubble on his face and his old cable cardigan and wonder where all that passion has gone.

Harry smiles thinly. 'You make me feel very old when you look at me like that, Cara.'

'Like what?' I say, flustered. 'I wasn't ...'

But I was.

I lift the teapot to cover the moment and refill Harry's cup. He puts a spoon of sugar into the tea and stirs the teaspoon round and round the cup, long after the sugar has dissolved.

'Anyway, I stormed away from Caroline and went back towards the hall,' he continues. 'Patsy was coming towards me, crying, with these big black streaks of mascara running down her face. She wasn't very steady on her feet. Her friend Val was running after her and once she saw me, she started shouting that it was all my fault. Making a fuss. The way girls do.'

'Girls look after each other.'

'Hmm. Sometimes.'

I laugh.

'Though I suppose it was. My fault, I mean. Anyway, I felt awful seeing Patsy that upset … she looked so young, somehow, with all that black stuff running down her face … I put my arms round her and at first she tried to pull away, but then she put her head down on my shoulder and cried and cried …'

Harry breaks off. 'Are you fed up listening to this?'

I shake my head and smile.

'You remember it in such detail, Harry.'

'That's because everything stemmed from that night. Everything. One night and your whole life is set.'

'Why? What happened?'

He sits back and for the first time I sense real hesitation. Maybe he hasn't known me long enough. Yet on some level, that's the very reason why he is drawn to me. A clean slate. No preconceived judgements. Besides, there has been something instinctive between Harry and me from the start. Almost as if we recognise and reflect back each other's need.

'Why?' I repeat gently.

'You know those times in life when you talk to someone and it's like, something just clicks. You don't know why exactly it happens at that particular moment but it just does. A bit like now … with me and you … here.' His eyes almost plead with me to confirm it.

'Yeah, I know what you mean.'

'Well, that's what happened with Patsy and me that night. We walked for two miles, right down to the coast. It was a warm night and we sat on the sand and talked, talked in a way I'd never talked to anyone, certainly not to Caroline. About things we felt, things we wanted from life. We were young. It was all ahead of us then. '

Harry stares at the table.

'What are you thinking?'

'Just daft stuff.' He wrinkles his face dismissively. 'It was kind of special. Big moon. All that.' He clears his throat. 'I can be a sentimental auld eejit when I want.'

'What did Patsy say?'

He laughs lightly.

'She just listened to everything I wanted from life and then she said, "You want the moon, Harry." And I said, "Yeah, and don't forget the stars."'

Our eyes connect and we smile at one another across the table.

'And then I said, "Well, what do you want Patsy?" And she said, "I just want tonight. This. Right now." She said she wouldn't ever feel for anyone what she felt right then for me. And she meant it. I knew she meant it. She lay back in the sand and I kissed her.'

We sit in awkward silence. I become aware of the clock ticking on the wall.

'So what happened?' I say eventually.

'One thing led to another ...' he says, looking out the window and studiously avoiding my eye. 'One thing led to another,' he repeats quietly.

'I didn't take advantage of her,' he adds with a hint of defiance. 'I really cared for Patsy, but we both had too much to drink. I knew ... I knew that in the morning, I might feel ... well, I'd still care for her and everything, but I might feel ... different. But I couldn't stop myself because everything was right about it at the time and I didn't want to listen to any little warnings inside myself about tomorrow. And Patsy just didn't care about tomorrow. She really, honestly didn't care.'

'And *did* you feel different?'

'I had a thumping head for a start.'

'But about Patsy ...'

'Caroline came round in the morning. Made it up. We always did that. Lots of fights. Lots of making up. Lots of ...' His voice trails off.

Sex, I finish mentally. Poor Patsy. How could she compete?

'Caroline said she wanted me to take her back to London, so I did.'

'Jesus, Harry! What about Patsy?' I say instinctively, like it was last week he did it. Like I knew Patsy.

'I know … I know … I drove away that day without even speaking to her and all the time I was thinking, You bastard. How can you do this? But I did. I just tried to shut it out, shut *her* out. Then I got back to London and gradually it all faded. I did miss Patsy. I did think of her sometimes. But I was back with Caroline and life just ... well it went on. Then two months later I got this awful letter from Patsy's mother. Patsy was pregnant.'

'Oh God. What did you do?'

'I didn't have any choice ... my family, her family ... You know, it was different times. And in Ireland and all ...' He looks up at me. 'There wasn't any way Patsy would have had an abortion,' he says, answering a question I haven't even asked.

'So ...'

'So I came home and I married her. Got a labouring job on a farm for a while.' He nods his head towards his leg. 'Agricultural accident.' He shifts in the seat. 'Caroline didn't want to know me anyway when she found out Patsy was pregnant. She went wild. She cut the sleeves off every garment in my wardrobe. Threw paint at my front door.'

I give a little snort of laughter in spite of myself and Harry looks surprised, then half smiles.

'She was a wild one, Caroline. But funny, too, and sexy and smart ...'

'You missed her?'

'I thought my life was over. And I spent the next twenty years telling Patsy at every opportunity that my life was over. I never let her forget that I only married her because she was pregnant with our Patrick. '

'Was that true?'

'What?'

'That you only married her because she was pregnant.'

Harry looks at me shrewdly.

'Good question. I told myself that, but I don't think now it *was* true. I think part of me knew that Patsy was always going to be ... kind of inside me somehow. But I didn't see it properly until it was too late. I was so angry with her ... with life. I wanted more, always wanted more, and I blamed Patsy. I didn't … didn't always treat her right.'

He has sounded quite composed until now, but his voice breaks very suddenly, coming in little uncontrolled gasps. 'But through all those years, she … she never ... stopped ...'

I reach out and touch his arm across the table.

'*Loving me*,' he whispers.

Harry stands up from the table and limps to the window, his body stiff and tense. He talks now with his back to me, so that he doesn't have to look at me. All these weeks, I thought it was grief that was destroying him, but I see now it was guilt.

'You know the worst thing?' he says. His voice is low, tinged with bitterness. 'The only time we ever recaptured what we had on that beach that night was when she was dying. The tenderness then … the depth … it was unbearable, really. I realised what I was losing when it was too late.'

He reaches out and leans an arm on the window frame, lifting his leg from the floor to relieve the pressure on it.

'You told her, though?'

I hardly dare ask.

Harry nods.

'She was diagnosed and it was such a shock. And gradually – no, not gradually really, suddenly – we began talking, like we did all those years ago. I've thought since that Patsy thought there was only going to be that night on the beach and that's why she said everything she did. Because you only say the things that are really important when you know there's not going to be a tomorrow to say them. When our tomorrows started running out, we began living the todays.'

'How long did you have?'

'A year. Only a year.' He pauses. 'There were a lot of laughs. You'd be surprised. Patsy didn't waste that year. She didn't mourn. She just grabbed hold of it. She ... she blossomed in a strange way.'

More than anything, that makes tears well in my eyes. He makes her sound like a daisy trying to soak up as much sun as possible before its petals close in the dusk.

'I said Patsy was lucky earlier, Harry. I still think she was. Even after everything you've said.'

Harry shakes his head, unwilling to let go of his self-hatred, to let himself off the hook.

'She didn't get what she deserved.'

'Who does?' I say. 'Maybe she got enough. More than some.'

Harry folds his arms at the window, still doesn't turn round.

'Your visits to the graveyard, Harry ...'

'Patsy didn't like the dark,' he says quietly. 'She said being in the dark was like being dead. She always slept with a light on in the hall. That last year, she slept with the bedside light on. I come to see her at night. Leave the light on for her.'

I feel impotent, useless.

'Always come in afterwards, Harry, even if it's late. I like it when you come in.'

I try to see the time on my watch without making it obvious that I am looking. Earlier, I wanted out. Now I feel bad that I'm going to have to leave him. Harry is right that some conversations simply change everything. I don't know how I feel about that. It confuses me. I came here to cut ties, to find freedom, and already there are new ties forming that make me feel responsible for someone else.

'Harry, I'm so sorry. I need to go. I'm going to be late for my shift at McGettigan's. Will you be okay?'

He nods but doesn't turn round. I know there are tears falling on his cheeks that he doesn't want me to see. I cross the room and briefly place my head on his back and my hand on his arm. He doesn't move, but his arms are still folded and he slips one hand round to mine, where it lies on his arm, and he clasps it.

'Take care, Harry,' I say, and I leave him by the window and walk out the back door, out where the sun still shines cold and the scent of brine blows sharp and bitter from the sea.

CHAPTER TWENTY-FIVE

Karen

'Lily!' Alex shouts. 'Lily! Do you want something to eat?'

I arrived only a few minutes ago, am standing watching him make cheese on toast.

'Where is she?' He shoves the pan back under the grill impatiently.

I look out of the kitchen door. Lily's room is at the other end of the hall. The door opens. She peers round, jerking her head clumsily to summon me towards her.

I walk down the corridor towards her, frowning.

'Ddd e make it?' She is mouthing the words at me, pointing down the hallway to the kitchen. I walk towards her and she opens the door further.

'Aax,' she says. Her mouth struggles to make the shape she needs and falls short. 'Oryoo.'

'Alex made it.'

She beckons me further with her head, willing me to move further towards her.

'What is it Lily?'

'Poison me,' she says, speaking more distinctly than I have ever heard her. In the effort to enunciate clearly, she speaks loudly.

Alex appears at the other end of the hall and leans on the kitchen door.

'Oh, for God's sake,' he says, 'is she wittering on about poison again?

Lily's mouth sets mutinously, like a child's.

'Lily, don't be so bloody stupid. I am *not* trying to poison you. Why would I be trying to poison you?'

He starts walking down the hall towards us and Lily hobbles back into her room quickly and slams the door shut. I can see the sudden flare of temper, like the strike of a match, in Alex's face. He rushes forward so fast he brushes against me with the speed and I step back instinctively against the wall. He throws the door open.

'Lily!' he yells.

Lily looks startled as the door bangs back against the wall. She sits down suddenly on the bed and looks up at Alex, her eyes a whirlpool of fear and confusion. She looks frail and tiny and confused.

Alex stops suddenly when he sees her, like the fire goes out of him, and his head drops. He puts his hand to his head and rubs, as if wondering where he is, what he is doing, how the world got to be this way.

'Lily,' he says, glancing up from the carpet. 'You've got your slippers on the wrong feet.'

Lily looks down and recognition and distress flash across her face. She shakes her head. She is vexed that she made the mistake, vexed that she can't put it quickly right.

'Wrong,' she says, looking at her feet, and then she shakes her head again. She makes a strange little clicking sound with her tongue. 'Wrong.' She doesn't know what to do. She looks from one to the other of us and then tries to use her stick to manoeuvre the back of one slipper off. I can see a tear beginning to form like a gel over one eye.

'Here,' says Alex gently. 'I'll help you.'

I watch as he sits down on the bed next to her and removes the slippers, swapping them from one foot to the other. Lily doesn't resist.

She sits passively now, until unshed tears finally cascade down, leaving tracks on cheeks that are thick with streaked orange powder.

'Come on, Lily,' says Alex gruffly. But Lily's shoulders are shaking now. She has lost control.

'CarlAnn,' she says, her voice a thin, bleak wail.

Alex puts his hand on her back and pats her awkwardly, like someone who has been asked to pat his head and rub his stomach at the same time.

'I know,' he says. He reaches out and takes her fingers in his for a moment, and Lily looks at their hands entwined and then up at his face.

'Come on,' he says, shaking her fingers gently. 'Cheese on toast.'

She nods.

Alex gets up off the bed and walks out of the room past me. I follow him, leaving Lily to compose herself.

In the kitchen he fills the kettle, the water rushing in so fast it splatters up on him but he barely seems to notice. There is a stillness about him now.

'Hard going,' I say.

'The hospital said her emotions might be all over the place,' he says quietly. 'You know ... tears and frustration ... and ... it affects people's personalities. They said she might get depressed. And Lily has spent a lifetime getting through everything with the help of booze. Obviously, she dried out a bit in hospital because she couldn't drink, but I think she's finding it hard now she's home. Now there's a choice.'

'Has she said?'

He shakes his head. 'Lily never admitted she drank. She wouldn't even talk about it to Carol Ann. But I know the consultant has warned her that if she mixes alcohol with the medication she's on she's going to be in serious trouble.' He glances up at me.

'I went to see him,' he explains.

Well, well.

'Does she really believe you are trying to poison her or is that just the only way she can rebel against you?'

Before he can answer, the door opens. Lily hobbles in, not looking at either of us, and sits down at the table with a very deliberate dignity. She leans her stick against the table. Alex is solicitous. He gives Lily hers first, cutting it into small bite-sized pieces for her, slicing up some cherry tomatoes into tiny segments to decorate the top. She doesn't smile, but she looks up at him kind of deeply somehow, and nods. Alex and I sit either side of her. Alex has put Lea & Perrins on the cheese on toast, and it has bubbled under the grill into small, brown crusts, like brown sugar volcanoes.

'Whassat?' Lily asks Alex, pointing to the bubbles.

He looks at her dryly.

'Cyanide,' he says.

Lily's lips twitch but she doesn't smile exactly, and then she lifts a square and takes a bite.

CID are working through interviews and taking statements. I haven't told them about Carol Ann's phone yet. A small control. Another day or two and I'll have finished going through the numbers anyway.

Two things have happened, I tell Alex. Firstly, I have been in touch with Missing People to establish a contact for him. He can phone any time. Just a bit of additional support. The charity has suggested putting Carol Ann's picture on the side of milk cartons. It's been done before, I assure him. Would he like to give it a go?

The second thing is that some weirdo claiming to be a psychic has offered to help us find Carol Ann. Alex looks bewildered, but every high-profile missing persons case attracts psychics – without exception. And it's so long now since Carol Ann went missing without any clue of where she is that it has attracted a good few column inches.

The psychic says she saw the story in the paper. Says it 'drew' her. She just knew she could help. Officially, the police keep 'an open mind' on these things. McFarlane once worked on a case where a psychic was brought in and says it was bloody spooky, but mostly it's just a waste of time. Kennedy from CID doesn't want to know, says I can handle all that kind of shite and let him know what happens.

'Christ,' says Alex, 'the ouija board or the milk marketing board. Some choice.' He runs his hands through his hair, digging his fingers in deep. It's a new habit.

'You think Carol Ann's dead?' I say sharply.

'What are you on about now?'

He's like a bear with a sore head today. Says he didn't sleep well.

'You said ouija board. That's for contacting the dead.'

'Oh, stop trying to be Miss Fucking Marple,' says Alex irritably. 'You're not old enough or smart enough.'

He goes out of the room without saying another word and I hear the toilet door bang. A couple of minutes later, he's back. Lily comes in the room at his back, nods at me.

'Why milk cartons?' he says abruptly.

'They go all over the country.'

'Milk?' says Lily frowning, lowering herself into the seat next to him on the couch.

'They want to put Carol Ann's picture on cartons,' Alex explains, and I am surprised how patient his voice is. He actually sounds like he's asking for her opinion.

'Worth try,' says Lily. Her speech is improving all the time. At times it is almost normal, until she gets tired and the words seem to slip away from her again.

Alex nods.

'I suppose so,' he says wearily. He runs his hand across his cheek. 'Nothing's private any more. It's like having your whole life pegged out on a public washing line.'

CHAPTER TWENTY-SIX

Carol Ann

Being with Harry, it's like holding up a mirror to my life. The mirror reflects back dispassionately, even coldly, all the things I do not want to see. All the things I am running away from. I don't hide from that, or call it something else. I *am* running away.

On the walk back from Harry's I see my loss and his intertwine. Standing on the outside of his life, I can forgive his infidelity, almost understand it, in a way I can neither forgive nor forget Alex's. The standards are more exacting for a partner than a friend.

I can tell you the exact night Alex's affair started. Five years ago. He said he was going for a business dinner and not to wait up. I couldn't sleep. Stevie was in bed and I was curled on the sofa in the sitting room. The television was on, but only for appearances. I couldn't tell you a single programme that was on that night.

It was well after one in the morning when he came back and even now I can remember the way he looked. He had his dark suit on, the one I always like best on him, and a white shirt. He was carrying his jacket over his shoulder and his shirtsleeves were rolled slightly up his forearm. I guess it's a Pavlovian reaction, but when I see him in a white shirt I always think of the first day I met him, in a café in Glasgow, where he sat drenched from the rain. Whatever it was, I remember glancing up and feeling a stab, a stab of the old desire for him mixed with regret and a little confusion. Sometimes, it just creeps up on me.

We had hardly spoken for those few weeks. Just polite enquiries. Practical information. There was no need for Alex to talk that night, but he seemed compelled to, which was very unlike him.

'Still up?' he said. 'I said not to wait up.'

'I didn't.'

He nodded, ill at ease.

'Steve okay?'

'Fine.'

'I'll look in on him and check he's asleep.' His eyes kept flickering away from me, unable to hold my gaze. He hadn't even come properly into the room, but was standing at the door still, lurking. He seemed so tall and all of a sudden I felt I couldn't last another minute in this atmosphere. I wanted to lie in his arms. I was ready for an outbreak of peace.

'I'm going to make coffee,' I said. 'Want one?'

Alex looked startled. 'No th–' he began, then stopped. 'Well, yeah, if you're making one. I'll just go and have a quick shower first.'

'Now? It's so late. You always have a shower in the morning.'

Usually when you question Alex he gets a bit aggressive. But I noticed he was more hesitant than usual. More appeasing.

'I know,' he said, 'but the restaurant was really hot and I feel a bit sweaty and my hair and clothes stink of cigarette smoke from the bar.' He backed out of the door. 'You put the kettle on and I won't be a minute.'

Maybe it sounds odd, like I made too much out of a tiny snatch of conversation. But I knew instantly why he was having that shower. He was washing another woman off him.

He expected me to wait downstairs, but I made the coffee quickly and crept upstairs with his. The door of the en suite to our bedroom was open and I saw him standing in the shower with his head leaning forward on the door in a gesture of supplication, the warm water cascading onto the back of his neck.

I put his coffee down on the dressing table and he heard me then, standing upright immediately, washing himself briskly with soap and lifting his face to the shower head. I lifted the dirty clothes from the basket for the wash, putting his white shirt on top.

'Are you putting that washing on now?'

'Might as well,' I said, 'it can do while we sleep and I'll hang it up in the morning.' I was amazed to hear how steady my voice was.

On the way downstairs, I lifted the bundle of clothes in my arm closer to my face and sniffed the shirt. There was no lingering smell of nicotine. Neither was there anything so convenient for my diagnosis as the lingering remnants of perfume. Afterwards, I tried to tell myself that perhaps I'd got it wrong, but the words had only formed in my head when an inner voice was saying scornfully that I was a fool. It wasn't just the shower. It was everything that Alex transmitted that night. Instinct isn't as unscientific as people think. Just because you can't identify exactly what the signals were doesn't mean you didn't receive them, that they weren't transmitted. I knew almost immediately and I think, eventually, Alex knew that I knew.

I watched over the next few weeks. He got more sure of himself, more confident of his ability to hide things. More brazen. We hardly spoke to one another but when we did, Alex was more polite than usual, less offhand. He felt guilty, but I know he felt alive, too. He had something new, something different and it was taking his mind away from the situation at home and maybe, more importantly, from himself. He had a secret life and he loved it, the way it made him have to plan and think ahead, the way it made him devious, even the way it made him sweat a bit at the prospect of being caught.

Lily came round one night for dinner when he was going out.

'Lot of business dinners these days, Alex,' she said and her voice, as it always did when she spoke to Alex, held a slight challenge.

'That's right, Lily. Some of us have to work.'

'Poor old Alex,' said Lily, and took another serious swig of a gin and tonic I had just given her. She looked at him critically as he put on his jacket. 'I always say, Alex, that you scrub up very well.' She waved her glass at him and the ice cubes chinked against the side because the gin was almost drained already. 'I do hope your dining companions appreciate how much effort you have gone to.'

Alex smiled at her coldly. 'Lily,' he said with that deadly, venomous politeness that always sent a shiver through me, 'we're neglecting you. Let me fill your glass before I go.' He turned to me. 'Carol Ann, that was far too niggardly a gin and tonic for Lily. There's a pint glass in the cupboard.'

'Alex ...'

'Bye, bye Alex,' said Lily airily. 'Don't do anything I wouldn't do.'

'Oh, I think it best if I'm better behaved than that, Lily, don't you? I'm a married man.'

'Yes,' said Lily. 'I'd forgotten. I thought you had too.'

'You'd best go, Alex,' I said, 'you're going to be late,' and I handed him his keys.

'Mum,' I said, when Alex had gone. 'You're not helping.'

Lily merely shrugged and glugged back the gin. 'I know his type,' she said, putting her glass down on the table with a bang. 'I was married to one for long enough.'

I thought it might fizzle out in a month or two, but it went on right up to Christmas that year. I figured it was someone he worked with. I said nothing until early on in December when I asked Alex what night his works Christmas party was.

'Twentieth,' he said.

'I'll get a baby-sitter for Stevie,' I said.

Alex looked up from his paper, startled.

'You're coming?'

'Don't you want me to?'

Alex widened his eyes and shrugged his shoulders, as if it was nothing to him, one way or the other. 'You don't usually, that's all. You never come.'

'That's why I thought this year I would.'

'Whatever you like,' he said, but I could see he was panicking. 'It'll be the usual dull affair. I doubt you'll enjoy it much.'

I only had two weeks, but I starved over the next fortnight. It made little difference. I lost a few pounds, but I was still at the fat end of my wardrobe. Size fourteen nudging towards sixteen. I picked out a black dress that I thought wasn't too frumpy because it said size twelve on the label. Even though it was bigger than some fourteens I had, psychologically it made me feel better. It was fitted over the bust but flared out slightly from the hips, hiding the lumps and bumps of my thighs.

I hadn't worn make-up for a while, but I sat at the dressing table for half an hour, lining my eyes, my lips, wiping it off and starting again when my hand shook and missed the lines. I streaked my eyelids with gold highlights to match my hair and buffed my cheeks with soft plum blusher. There was, despite everything, a kind of awakening inside at these preparations, a feeling that life wasn't over yet.

Alex barely glanced at me at first when he came in, but then I saw his eyes dart back in surprise. He said nothing. But I recognised that look. It lasted only a second but it gave me a short-lived surge of confidence. What is it they say about men and the number of times they think about sex every hour? I think that was one of Alex's.

'I'll not be long,' he said, and went to get changed.

Every time I think of that night I feel again that sense of sick anticipation mixed with excitement. I cannot sit down. Underneath the plum blusher, my cheeks are beginning to fire anyway with adrenaline. I put my fingers to my cheeks to cool them but my fingers, too, are warm. The sensation is not altogether unpleasant. It's like being suddenly aware of being alive after months of being dead; of blood pumping to my extremities, to my scalp, to the tips of my toes; of gas bubbling and fermenting in my stomach, making me hiccup with nerves; of feeling that my emotions are loaded in a Russian roulette gun with empty cartridges. Spin the cartridge and you just don't know what you'll get. Laughter. Tears. A deadly explosion of anger.

All this, I keep to myself. I sit beside Alex in the car and we say nothing to one another the whole way. At the traffic lights around the corner from the restaurant, Alex pulls the handbrake and looks down. 'You've got a ladder in your tights,' he says, nodding at my right leg.

I glance down, see it running from the knee. I was aware when I got in the car of catching my leg against the door, but hadn't seen the damage. Shit. *SHIT.*

'Is there a chemist round here?' I say.

'Won't be one open at this time.' The lights change and he moves off. 'Pull it up under the hemline and make do.'

'No.'

'Nobody will notice if you pull it up.'

'They will. I will.'

'Don't make a fuss. I wish I'd never said now.'

Don't make a fuss. Don't make a fuss! I'm going to see his bloody mistress and he says don't make a fuss.

'There's a supermarket,' I say. 'Stop!'

'For God's sake!' Alex is startled and instinctively slams on the brakes. 'I can't stop here!'

I jump out and grab my bag.

'Go round the block. I'll get you back here.' And I'm out before he can do anything about it.

I cross the road. It has begun to rain, a fine, steady drizzle. The shop is brightly lit, a glowing, warm orange against winter darkness. Inside, the displays are festive, the aisles piled with tins of biscuits and chocolates and boxed nuts and raisins with silver elastic ribbon.

Down the meat aisle. I feel silly in my party dress and shoes, walking amongst the chicken legs and the packs of steak. A few curious glances come my way. Up by the washing powder. I find the tights near the end but the selection is limited. No nude colours, like I'm wearing. American tan. The colour is strong, brown and orange like a sunbed tan. I buy black instead. My dress is black so they will do, but I wish they'd had more choice. Younger women all seem to wear nude with black just now. His mistress would wear nude with black.

A gust of wind catches me as I run from the shop. The rain has become heavier. I can feel it flattening my carefully blow-dried hair. The thin material of my dress becomes damp quickly. Alex is not there, but I need to catch him on the other side of the road. I stand shivering, moving close to a garden hedge with an overhanging tree to shelter slightly. He is only a couple of minutes but I feel cold, damp. The blast of the car heater is warm when I open the door and slide in.

'I had to go twice round the block,' Alex complains. 'What kept you?'

I say nothing but open the new packet, lift out the tights. I wait until there is no other car level with us, and slide my skirt up to remove the laddered tights, wriggling against the leather of the seat. Alex keeps looking in the mirror.

'There's a car coming,' he says, and I lower the skirt over my knees and sit still as the car draws level with us. By the time several cars have gone by I am hot and flustered. Oh, to hell with this, I don't care who sees. I bend to pull the tights over my feet and the seat belt locks against me. The space is too cramped to manoeuvre properly and though I try to pull the tights up properly, they stop just short of the crotch. The back of my dress is rolled up against the back of my seat and the material is limp and crushed.

I pull down the passenger mirror. My hair is damp and dulled by the drizzle and my cheeks are pink with exertion. I pull out a powder compact to dull the shine, retouch the lipstick, but it's too late. That feeling of being alive has gone. I read an account once of a boxer before a world title fight. He was up for it, alive with the desire to win. And then just before he was led on, his team watched the fight leave him like air from a slowly deflating balloon. By the time he got in the ring he was defeated before the first punch even landed. That's the way I feel right now. Defeated.

The Russian roulette cartridge is spinning dangerously close to tears. I snap the mirror up and look out into the darkness.

'The others looked better,' says Alex.

'What?'

He nods down at my legs and then switches his eyes back to the road.

'The other colour of tights looked better.'

There is a drinks reception first. I hate that bit. The mingling, the polite chatting. But tonight my eyes are everywhere. Is it her, with the flame-red hair and the statuesque figure? Or her, the petite little brunette with the sexy wiggle? Or ... no, *her*, with the red dress. God, she's so Alex's type. Long blonde hair. Tall. But then I see the real mistress. Surprisingly, she's not blonde. She has a head of short, chestnut curls and lips painted a glossy tangerine to go with her dress. I know it's her because she looks across at Alex, and gives a tiny flicker of a wave, no more than a waggle of the fingers, with a tight little smile that is the wrong side of smug. And she's the only woman in the room who shows the slightest interest in me. She keeps glancing over at me, then him. I catch the way their eyes lock and then look away. And then back. And then away. What, she thinks I'm stupid? She thinks I don't notice?

I hate her confidence. Her self-belief. If it were me, I'd keep on the other side of the room. But she's coming over. She's actually going to speak to me. She's assessing as she walks towards us. I know she's taking in my thick waist, my dress with the crumpled skirt. My size fourteen body – whatever the label of my dress says. She's relieved. She thinks I'm no competition. She slips her arm into Alex's in a faux friendly way.

'Hi, Alex,' she says, then she looks at me with a wide, bright smile. She likes the danger of this, the fact that she and Alex are hanging close to the edge here. I can tell she thinks it's sexy. Her and Alex one side, me the other.

'Hello, I'm Vicky,' she says, and holds out her hand. Alex takes the opportunity to shift position, disentangle himself from her arm.

'Vicky, this is Carol Ann, my wife.'

'Pleased to meet you, Carol Ann. I do a lot of work with Alex.'

'Yes, I believe you do,' I say pleasantly, but I let a little edge harden in my voice. 'I believe you know him very well indeed.'

Her smile locks slightly, unsure how to take that. Good. Her smug security knocked even for a second. She is in her twenties, an age where she is still too certain. Certain of the world, of herself, of her power. Time has not challenged her yet. Up close, I can see the beautiful creamy paleness of her skin, the tiny smattering of faint brown freckles over the bridge of her nose. Alex is sipping from his glass with such forced casualness that I know he's embarrassed. Just so long as she knows I know.

And then suddenly it doesn't matter any more. It doesn't matter what she thinks. Because time will challenge her. I don't need to burst her bubble because time will burst it for me. She thinks that she and Alex sit at the secure base of this triangle, with me at the high pinnacle, ready to be toppled. She's wrong. Sometimes, you have no choice who you are with: you're bound. That's just the way it is. She will lose Alex. I know it. Alex knows it. The only one who doesn't know it yet is her.

CHAPTER TWENTY-SEVEN

Karen

Brenda the psychic arrives off the train from Glasgow just after lunch. McFarlane has paired me with a young trainee for a few days, Pam Ferguson. She's nice enough and I don't mind her being with me on other cases but I don't really want her around Alex. She's quite good looking. I tell her she can do the driving today.

I scan the crowd coming off the train looking for suitable psychics. The bohemian-looking creature with the big bust is a possible, I think. Or the one with wild hair and big jewellery.

Then I see Brenda.

Instinctively, I know it's Brenda. Without any doubt.

'Oh shit,' I mutter.

'What?' says Pam.

I nod my head down the platform. There's an elderly woman with a tartan shopping bag over her arms and it has the white cup of a thermos flask sticking out of the top. She has on a brown tweed skirt and flat lace-up shoes and a pale blue zip-up jacket. She rolls slightly from side to side as she walks. But the reason I know she's Brenda for sure is that her lips are moving, like she's having a conversation with herself. In other words, she's a nutter.

'Is that her?' asks Pam incredulously. 'How do you know?'

'I consulted my crystal ball.'

'But she doesn't look like a psychic, she looks like my Auntie Nora.'

'She might as well be your Auntie Nora.'

Once ensconced in the back of the panda car, Brenda doesn't say much, but after a few minutes, I hear a whispering from the back seat. I glance sideways at Pam. She looks at me, then glances in her mirror.

'Sorry, Brenda, did you say something?' I ask.

'Naw, it's awright, hen,' she says. 'I'm just havin' a wee chat. People think it's only at seances that psychics chat, but sometimes our friends on the other side don't wait to be asked a question.' She laughs. 'Always butting in, you know what I mean?'

'Is that right?' I say, looking out the window.

'Oh aye, they're always around. That's how I first knew I had the gift,' says Brenda, reaching down to the bag at her feet and rummaging around. 'The voices, you know. When I was wee, ma mammie used to say I talked more to the other side than I did tae the livin'. She wasnae wrong there,' she adds. 'Though there were so many auld biddies round oor bit it was kinda hard to tell the difference between the deid and the livin' sometimes.' She stops searching in her bag. 'Though I suppose I'm an auld biddie masel' now. When did that happen, eh?'

Brenda fishes out a packet from her bag, wrapped in crumpled silver foil. She opens it up, then sticks the packet through the gap between Pam and me to reveal a couple of limp ham sandwiches. They look a bit damp. I think her flask might have leaked on them.

'Would either of yous like one, girls?' she says.

'You're all right, thanks Brenda,' I say. 'We're not long after our lunch, are we Pam?'

Pam nods and mumbles, unable to look at me, unable to risk an answer. Her shoulders shake slightly under my gaze and I look out of my side window and grin.

Brenda takes a sandwich out and wraps up the packet. She takes a bite and sits back again, watching the countryside speeding by.

'It's awful nice here,' she says. 'Awful nice. All these green fields. Yous are dead lucky. I've not got a garden but I have a few wee window boxes for colour, you know?'

'Where is it you live, Brenda?' asks Pam.

'Pollok,' she says. 'Do you know it?'

'No,' says Pam.

'Well, you just go to Pollok shopping centre, then go a couple of hundred yards past and take a left. You walk down and come tae wan of they wee mini roundabouts, straight through, a right and then a left and you're in ma street. Flats,' she says.

'Right,' says Pam.

A few minutes later the whispered hiss begins again.

When we reach Alex's house, he opens the door before we even ring the bell. Brenda is already on the doorstep. I tell Pam she can go and have a coffee in the village teashop that Carol Ann used to work in. Re-interview the owner, I tell her. I'll call her when I need her. She leaves happily enough.

'Hello, son,' Brenda says, holding out her hand to Alex. 'I'm awful sorry for your trouble.'

'Thanks,' Alex mumbles, and Brenda wraps him up in a hug. Alex looks questioningly at me over her shoulder, but I hold up my hands and shrug.

'Tea?' says Alex politely, and Brenda finally lets him go and follows him into the kitchen. Lily is there, waiting, and she and Brenda chat non-stop. Well, Brenda chats. Any time Lily slowly tries to say anything, Brenda pats her hand. 'That's right, Lily,' she says. 'You said it.'

Afterwards, Brenda says she wants to get the 'feel' of Carol Ann.

'Now, I don't want to intrude in your hoose, son,' she tells Alex earnestly, 'but maybe you could take me somewhere to get a wee idea of Carol Ann's spirit.'

'Ehm ...' says Alex, vaguely, hopelessly.

'Bedroom?' I say helpfully.

'Aye,' says Brenda. 'Bedroom.' She reaches out for Alex. 'I don't want to upset you,' she says kindly, 'but I need to get a wee idea of ... you know ... if she's still with us.' She pats his arm encouragingly.

We all troop upstairs, even Lily. Alex leads the way and I bring up the rear.

'That's the way, Lily,' says Brenda, taking her arm and hauling her up the steps.

Alex opens the door and goes to stand over by the window, as if he thinks the less he says, the sooner it will be over.

'Aw, my,' says Brenda, walking in. 'Aw, my. That's lovely, that.' She heads over to the bed and fingers the white broderie anglaise duvet cover and deep raspberry-coloured throw. 'Very tasteful.' She looks at Alex. 'Did Carol Ann pick that?'

'Ehm, yes. Yes, she did,' says Alex.

'Beautiful intit, Karen?' says Brenda, turning to me. Her fingers linger over the throw. 'Aye, very nice,' she says, and then she sits down suddenly on the edge of the bed and closes her eyes, breathing in deeply.

Alex flashes a 'get-her-out-of-here' look at me, but what am I supposed to do? We can only let this run its course now. Brenda sounds like she's in the throes of a heart attack. Lily stands in front of her and stares curiously. Alex turns to the window and bangs his head gently against the glass in despair.

'Ssshe aw ... aw ... aw right?' stammers Lily.

'God knows,' I say.

Brenda is whispering to herself, but suddenly she stops and opens her eyes. She stands up and walks to the window, then throws her arms round Alex, who stands like a Tussaud's dummy with Brenda attached to his waist. Brenda's eyes are shining.

'I'm so pleased for you, son,' she says. 'So pleased.'

She beams round at us all.

'She's alive. Carol Ann's alive. Absolutely no doubt aboot it.' She turns back to speak specifically to Alex. 'I'd know, son,' she says. 'I wouldnae tell you any lies aboot that.'

Lily looks confused.

'Ehm, any idea where she is, Brenda?' I ask.

Brenda looks almost insulted, like she's already given me half her scone and now I have the cheek to ask for the other bit.

'Oh, I couldn't say *that*,' she says. She holds out her arm for Lily to take.

'Come on, Lily,' she says, 'I'll take you back downstairs.'

Lily hirples along at her side.

'Though I think,' says Brenda, turning back when she reaches the door, 'that if I'm not mistaken, she's gone over water.'

The door clicks.

'Well,' says Alex, looking at me challengingly, like it's my fault. 'That's good, isn't it?' His voice drips sarcasm. ' That *really* narrows it down.'

CHAPTER TWENTY-EIGHT

Carol Ann

In the corner of the graveyard is a tree that spreads its branches over half-a-dozen graves like a comforting arm. By late September it had turned from green into a rich russet red and now, in mid-October it is giving way to orange, the leaves fluttering down over the graves, dry and brittle, scratching over the stones when the wind whips up. I look at that tree through the glass of my living room and think my life is like that: slowly changing hue, gradually becoming a completely different colour from what it was just months ago.

Most of the time, I understand the importance of not looking back. I have become more accomplished at batting down the crocodile heads when they emerge, my fingers more skilled, my reflexes faster. But sometimes still, the old life catches me unawares, a cold sliver of shock like an indrawn icy breath in frosty winter air. In fact, usually, it is not the old life, but a reflection of it. When Harry talks of Patsy. When Sean's boy comes into the bar and tries to tap his old man for a fiver. When I see a young child with his arms around his mother, and I think of the soft fatness of limbs around my neck, the fierceness of my child's hug. No adult can hug you with the naked ferocity of a child.

If I am honest, there are times when I feel a longing for old familiar things, for people and places that resonate deeply, that have long-established roots. Nothing in my new life has deep roots. Harry invites me over for Sunday dinner sometimes. He makes pot roast, cooking it in red wine with root vegetables and chunks of floury potatoes. But it is the smell of cabbage that makes my stomach flip over when I open the door, the smell of it so unexpected, so evocative, that it takes my breath away. Boiled cabbage, like Lily made, the smell of it drifting from her flat out into the close, lingering in the stairwell. She burned it once, let the pot boil dry when she had been swigging gin straight from the bottle one afternoon and fell asleep. I came round that day, could smell the burning as soon as I opened the close door. The smell hung around like an uninvited guest for two days.

'Okay?' says Harry.

'Fantastic Harry,' I say. 'This is *so* good,' and I fork a mouthful in, feeling the squeaky, wet limpness of boiled cabbage against my teeth, the taste of abandonment rising like bile in my gut. Lily. I can only try harder to shut Carol Ann out. I am Cara May. I am motherless. I am childless.

Forgive me.

Time has stood still. The past has halted the present and I will be late for my shift. I should have walked straight back from Harry's, but I detoured round by the beach hut and stand here on the hill listening to the call of the sea. I hear Josie louder than ever in the sea, a plaintive echo of the waves. I see her face. She destroyed us.

Listening to Harry, to his story of love gone wrong, made me miss Alex. I grieve for him, for myself, for what we were, what we could have been. But I can live with missing Alex because I have missed him for such a long time. I always missed Alex, even when I lived with him. I missed the Alex he was. Now I even miss the Alex he became.

Harry's life is not my life, and yet it is. The pictures of our lives are woven from the same tapestry threads. Blue for blame. Red for anger. Green for sadness. Perhaps we are drawn together because we recognise ourselves in each other. But he stayed in his life and I walked from mine. I chose to walk out of the tapestry and build another picture. Except the one I'm building is not without its complications, either, because Harry's sadness draws me. I feel responsible for trying to ease it. Not because we are connected, just because I am alive and standing next to him. And the more I do that, the more connected we will become. You think by walking away from a life you will be free. But maybe, unless you choose to live on a desert island, freedom is just an illusion. I guess that's what happens in life. You leave behind one set of problems and you go and build another set just like them.

But it's done now. I do not have enough courage, maybe enough desire, to go back. Back home, their pictures will be different now, too. It has been just a few months, but already there will be new pictures, new horizons. I am not part of that. No, there is no going back – even if I wanted to. I walk back from Harry's past the beach hut, sitting half finished on the curve of the hill above the sea. Soothing, timeless, a haven that beckons me and offers sanctuary. This is my life now, the only future I can have.

CHAPTER TWENTY-NINE

Karen

After Brenda, I have nothing really to go round to the house for, but I don't want to wait a week before going back. So a couple of days later I bump into Alex when he's leaving work. Well, when I say I bump into him, I arrange to bump into him. Unknown to him, I'm still following him, so I park a street away from his office in town, take a window seat in a café and wait.

Trailing him has meant no time for seeing Gav and since I can't be bothered with excuses or justifications, I've chucked him. He got a bit high-handed. Said his mates had never known what he saw in me anyway. Tossers. I knew they didn't like me.

'That first night I met you,' Gav said, 'I knew you were trouble. But I thought, and I have always thought, that there's something else inside you. Something worth fighting for. But you won't let it out. And one of these days it's going to disappear completely and nobody will be able to get to it any more, not even you. There will be plenty of guys willing to screw you, Karen, but not many prepared to look for more. If you realise any time soon what you're giving up here, you know where I am.'

He thinks he's so bloody smart with his amateur psychology. An untrained Hammond when, God knows, the trained one is bad enough. People like Gavin, nice middle-class boys with paper qualifications, think they're cleverer than the likes of me, but paper stuff means nothing. People like him are still thick when it comes to the ways of the world. They know nothing. He's a forensic scientist, Gavin. But if I can be forgiven for quoting someone who produces such crap music as Shania Twain, that don't impress me much.

From the café, I keep scanning the streets, waiting for Alex to appear. I think he'll turn down the street opposite, where he normally parks his car, so I have to be quick if I'm going to time it right. But in fact, he doesn't turn down. Instead I see him walking straight on at the crossroads and coming right by the café. I bang on the window at him and he looks up startled. I wave him in.

'What are you doing here?' he asks.

'Never mind that. Do you want a coffee?'

'Yeah, that would be good. I'll get it. Want another one?' He throws his jacket over the back of the chair. He looks weary.

'I'll take another cappuccino, thanks.'

I watch Alex as he moves to the counter and asks for the coffees. He smiles vaguely at the woman, not flirtatiously exactly, but like he's aware she's a woman. Like he's aware she'll take extra good care with his coffee.

'You're sure of yourself, aren't you?' I say when he puts the cups down.

'What?'

I just smile.

'What are you on about now?' he says, but without any real interest in knowing. Not like a woman, who would be suddenly alert if you expressed an oblique opinion about her, who would chip and chip until she got an answer.

The cappuccino is overflowing with brown-and-white-marbled froth, so I spoon the froth out of the top of the cup. I don't want to sit opposite him with a white moustache.

Alex shakes his head

'Sometimes I don't understand you,' he says, and then lets his eyes wander round the interior of the café, as if suddenly realising he's somewhere alien.

'That's the way I like it.'

His eyes flick back to focus on me. He raises his eyes but doesn't enquire further. I kind of understand it, that lack of curiosity. Self-containment. I'm more man than woman in that sense. He didn't even bother pursuing how I come to be round the corner from his work, how I just happen to be sitting at the window when he walks by. He asks a question, I don't answer it, he shrugs. That's men for you.

'You're late going home,' I say.

'Work ...' he replies vaguely, his voice trailing away.

'Not avoiding going home?'

He gives a twisted, lopsided smile, then turns sideways in the seat, moving his long legs from under the table and stretching them out into the passageway.

'How is it at home, then?' I ask.

'Bloody awful.'

I wait for him to elaborate, but he doesn't. He takes a sip of coffee and the cup chinks quietly on the saucer as he puts it down.

'Is that it?'

'What?'

'Is that all you're going to say – "bloody awful".'

He shrugs. 'What else is there to say?'

'Why are things so bad?'

His eyes wander again, watching the woman behind the counter lift a slice of chocolate cake from the glass display. Soft tendrils of honey-blonde hair fall onto her cheeks, escaping from the confines of a bun at the back of her neck.

'I just ... I can't seem to ...' he says slowly, and stops. 'I hate the feeling that everyone is waiting for me to walk in the door, you know? That things rely on me, somehow. I've hired Theresa and she's a big help but ... oh, I don't know how to explain it exactly. It's like ... like your brain being invaded by other people. Uninvited guests or something, who strip all the food from your cupboard until there's nothing left for you, and then disappear. But you know next time you turn around, they're going to be back, sitting there silently with their faces turned expectantly towards you.'

'Waiting for you to do what?'

'Oh, I don't know.' He shoves his coffee cup away from him impatiently. 'Stuff. Just stuff. Things Carol Ann used to take care of, I suppose. Little things. Things that take up too much head space.'

I look at my watch. Seven o'clock.

'You should probably be home right now.'

'Yeah, I suppose so. Though Theresa is there until eight tonight. At least she'll feed them.'

'But you still don't want to go?'

'No. Steve will be there, floating round the house like some ghostly apparition, suddenly appearing at my elbow, then disappearing again. And Lily!' He shakes his head. 'Lily will be muttering about some mad plot by the pharmaceutical companies to use the elderly as human guinea pigs, and how her medication isn't really to help her at all but is research for them. Probably not for stroke either, but for cancer, and if it has terrible side effects she won't be able to say what's happened and people will just think she and all the other victims have had another stroke. She's dictated the whole story to Steve and made him write it down in case anything happens. Mad. And then she'll talk about going to see Flora. Flora is her sister and has been dead for ten years ...'

'You think she's losing her marbles, then?'

'God knows. No,' he adds, thinking better of it. 'No. She's just ... ach she's just confused. She gets names mixed up sometimes, you know? Sometimes when she's talking about Flora I think she maybe means Carol Ann. It's just a labelling thing. Common after stroke.'

Hasn't he become the expert, I think. He shifts in his seat, then rotates his head and rubs his neck as if easing tension in his shoulders.

'She's worried sick about Carol Ann.'

The waitress walks by our table with cakes for a family at a table behind us. She's late thirties, maybe, and looks like she's on the cusp. Pretty face that could easily settle into plumpness, clothes that border on not caring any more. A faint waft of perfume. Alex watches the movement of her as she goes by. It makes me angry that he's sitting here with me, watching her. I turn very deliberately, as if following his eye-line to see what he's looking at, though I know fine. I make it clear he's staring.

Alex looks away.

'She reminds me of Carol Ann,' he says, and his voice shakes suddenly, catching me unawares. 'Her hair ...'

He can't say any more. There's a visible battle going on in his face. It's quivering, like it's going to collapse. It's like looking at a building knowing that if one small, crucial brick goes, it's going to be catastrophic; the whole edifice is going to crumble in a cloud of stour and dust.

I panic, looking at him. Not tears. And not here.

'Let's get out of here,' I say in a low voice. 'You go outside, I'll settle the bill. Meet me on the corner.'

Alex doesn't argue. He lifts his jacket and throws it over his arm. His folders. He walks quickly from the café.

Outside, he says with terse embarrassment that he'd better go now, better get home. No, I say, not yet. He's not ready. Come to my flat. But he doesn't know where I live. And anyway, he protests, he needs to go. They'll be expecting him. But, I say, Steve will look after Lily. They have his mobile number if anything is wrong, if they need him. Come and have a drink. Where's he parked? All he has to do is follow me. I'll lead the way.

He hesitates.

The conversation is a little whirlwind of pressure. I am pressing Alex's buttons because he doesn't want to go home. And because he hasn't recovered from his upset yet, he can't think clearly enough to know how to say no. He is vulnerable; everyone seeks out comfort when they're upset. But there is something else making him say yes. He doesn't actually want to say no. Inside himself, he really wants to come with me. I am not like Carol Ann. I intrigue him. I challenge him. I know it.

Wants to and doesn't want to. Attracted and repelled. It's the same instinct when someone says, don't touch that, it's hot. You've got to test, haven't you? You've just got to put your finger out tentatively and see *how* hot. And see that instinct? It burns you every time.

Back in my flat he sits down silently, looking as if he already regrets the decision. I pour him a drink. 'Listen,' I say, as I hand him the glass. 'We've got unfinished business, you and me. It's time to tell me about Josie.'

CHAPTER THIRTY

Carol Ann

The beach hut has a roof on. Michael is running the job, bringing in other workmen as required. He says that once the roof is on, once the place is watertight, he can take his time with the rest. He does not seem to sense my impatience for it to be finished. He has taken to coming into McGettigan's, staying for a pint, watching me from the corner, chatting when I have a free moment.

'Be kind to him,' says Sean.

'Who?'

'Your admirer,' says Sean, nodding at Michael. 'He's a nice guy but sensitive, you know?'

'What? Don't be silly Sean.'

'I'm telling you,' says Sean, throwing a tea towel over his shoulder.

'I'm nearly old enough to be his mother.'

Sean grunts.

'I think that's an exaggeration. And I don't think being mothered is quite what our Michael has in mind, Cara ...' He turns to the bar.

'Yes, Davie, what can I get you?'

The notion is as thrilling as it is ridiculous. To be seen in that way again ... to feel alive.

I busy myself with washing the glasses, looking up surreptitiously from the sink, glancing curiously at the dark crinkle of Michael's collar-length hair, the film of chalky dust on his work shirt, the dark hair on his forearm where he has rolled up his sleeves. He catches me looking and my eyes dart away immediately, a stain the colour of port wine rising upward from my neck.

I always saw building a new life as an escape from the old one. But it suddenly occurs to me one day that my new life is a trap, too. I can never again be totally honest with anyone. Never again be totally free to say who I am because I don't really know any more. That thought, the feeling of being trapped, persists. A feeling of confusion builds up inside my head, becomes a vague pulsing headache that lasts for days. The bars of my new life clank shut around me.

Harry notices. I think he thinks it is caused by bereavement, that he must encourage me to talk. 'Cara, I told you about Patsy. But you've never said about, you know … about your husband.'

The sharp intake of breath in my chest. The interrupted heartbeat.

'What about him?' I say.

'I'm a good listener.'

I look at Harry now and I see the understanding in his face. I can't bear the guilt that understanding makes me feel. The closer you get to someone, the worse a lie feels.

'I know Harry, thanks.'

Harry looks at me still, and I know thanks is not enough. He is waiting. Waiting for me to talk. My shift at McGettigan's is finished and since Harry is in, I stay for a quick drink with him. The two of us are in a dusty corner, away from the main body of the pub.

'His name was ... was Alex,' I say.

Harry merely nods.

'We met twenty-odd years ago,' I say vaguely. 'In a café in Byres Road. I was a student.'

I was also a waitress, though I don't explain that to Harry. I am too busy leaping ahead frantically, trying to think what I can tell him about my old life that won't trip me up.

'It was raining,' I say, irrelevantly, and Harry smiles.

Steady slashes of rain driving against the pane, the inside smeared with steam. Small puddles on the floor under the dark wood panelling, fed from drips plopping from the umbrellas lined against the wall. Coffee machines hissing a background tune against the steady hum of voices. And Alex in the corner, white shirt stuck damply to his chest, a faint shadow of dark hair visible underneath. Suit jacket hanging on the chair next to him, papers spread in front of him. Long legs sprawled sideways into the passage because they don't fit neatly under the table. I take his order, and the way he looks at me makes a strange kind of panic rise in my chest.

He becomes a regular. Philip, the waiter who works the same shift as me, winks at me when he comes in the door.

'He's here,' he hisses and my heart stops the way Philip grabs my arm so suddenly.

'Will you bloody stop that!' I say crossly, slapping him, but Philip just grins.

'Go on, go serve him. You know you want to.'

'He's at your table.'

'He's your man.'

'Not your type?' I ask sarcastically.

'Oh, he is,' says Philip. 'But somehow I don't think I'm his.'

I gasp then as Philip walks off with a backwards grin at me. I guess that's what you call coming out.

'Cara?'

Harry is looking at me.

'Sorry, Harry. What did you say?'

'I said, did you always love him?'

I am silent.

Always love Alex? My eyes feel strained now with the headache pulsing inside me. Always love Alex?

'Yes,' I say, and I am surprised to hear myself speak and even more surprised by what I say. Is it true? Have I always loved Alex? Do I still?

Harry lays a hand on my arm.

'I am sorry, Cara,' he says. 'Loss is ...'

'I lost him a long time ago,' I say, trying to tell a kind of truth without telling it properly. Harry eyes register confusion. He hesitates.

'I thought he … I thought it was quite recently that he died.'

'Alex just kept on dying,' I mumble. 'He died over and over.' I am leaning on the table, my cheek resting against my hand and I roll it sideways to look at him because I can't summon the energy to lift it.

'I'm sorry, Harry. I'm not making any sense.' Harry's brow creases but he says nothing, waiting. But it is true. Alex died more than once, little bits of him over time. Like me, really.

'Harry, did you ever have an affair when you were married?' I ask suddenly.

He looks startled.

' I…' he says. 'Well …'

'I'm sorry. I shouldn't have asked that. Forget it.' There is silence. Then Harry says,

'Once. Not an affair exactly, because it was only the once.'

'A one-night stand?'

'Caroline,' he says. 'It was Caroline. She got in touch with me about five years after we parted. I was in London for a family funeral and I went to see her. She'd broken up with her husband and ... ach sweet Jesus, it was just a mess. The boys were too young to leave and ... it should never have happened. Patsy ...' He shakes his head.

'Did she find out?'

'No. But I always had the feeling she knew.'

'She probably did. Just like I did.'

'Alex had …?'

I nod.

'I'm sorry, Cara.'

I shrug.

'How did you know?'

'He was nicer.' We both smile, as though at a joke that we shouldn't laugh at.

'It doesn't mean …' says Harry slowly, 'it doesn't mean he didn't love you …'

Harry talks almost apologetically. He can't hold my eye. He's making excuses for Alex, but I think he's actually trying to excuse himself. Much later, I realised that when Harry tried to sort my life out, he was really trying to correct the mistakes in his own. A bit like Lily when she sang with the baby in her arms. That chorus is Harry's as much as Lily's. '*Bheir me o, horo van ho*, Sad am I without thee.'

Memories are dangerous tonight. They are everywhere, in every incidental thing. The burnt-orange-coloured cardigan of a woman who drinks martinis in the corner reminds me of the dress Alex's mistress wore to the party. Her glossy lips. The feel of the drink I hold, the touch of my fingers on glass, is a shadow of my fingers trailing down a baby's incubator. The stumble of the drunk on the way out the door is the pull of my mother. Even the scent of Harry's whisky reminds me of evenings with Alex. The effect is that my old life is beginning to bubble up above the surface of my new one, lifting the surface and tilting it dangerously.

Tonight I am weak. Tonight I could talk …

'It doesn't mean he didn't love you,' repeats Harry. 'Cara?'

'Hmm?'

'It doesn't mean he didn't love you.'

I shake myself free of the past and look at Harry.

'It is possible, you know, to love two women at the same time. In different ways, maybe, but it is possible,' he says.

It's one of the only times I resent Harry.

'Can't help yourselves, can you?'

'Me n…' he says, 'they just … they can't …'

'It doesn't matter.'

'What doesn't?'

'Whether he loved me or not.'

'Of course it matters, Cara.' Harry looks baffled. 'Why are you saying that?'

I feel so tired. As if I could sleep forever. Never ever wake up or engage with any of this ever again. It used to be like this, when I first went to Hammond with depression, when sleep was a cocoon I crawled into to escape the world. When I woke there would be a second where I was suspended in time, and then I would remember, and the cables suspending me were cut, crashing me to the earth. I simply crawled back into my cocoon, seeking oblivion. Only now they're coming back do I recognise that those feelings had ever gone away.

'Cara?'

'I should go home.'

But where's home?

Harry drains his glass. 'You're not going home on your own like this.'

'I'm fine.' Harry looks at me stubbornly.

'You're not going on your own.'

That's how it happened. As simply as that. Because if Harry hadn't come in that night, I wouldn't have told him what I told him and maybe the rest wouldn't have happened. Maybe eventually the two lives would have separated neatly and I would have been free. But it wasn't to be.

* * *

We haven't eaten, so I tell Harry I'll make some pasta for supper. The tomatoes are deep red with a fine film of dust. I take them from the net bag and place them in a colander under a running stream of cold water. Harry sits on a kitchen stool and watches as I chop them into pieces, the skins spurting as the knife punctures them, juice running over the tips of my fingers and onto the chopping board. Red pepper. Onion. Garlic. On the stove, the thin film of olive oil in the pan is beginning to smoke. It sizzles furiously when I throw in the onion and garlic, almost ignites when the juices of the tomatoes hits the oil, a rush of smoke clouding up over the pan.

'Smells good already,' says Harry. He is on edge. I can tell.

I fill a pan with boiling water from the kettle for the pasta.

'You know, Cara,' says Harry, 'You can trust me. I won't go talking round the village.'

'Oh, I know that, Harry.' I look at him gratefully. 'I know that.'

Harry looks at the floor.

'I'm not very good at saying this kind of stuff, Cara, but you know, I'm very, very fond of you already. I can't believe the difference you have made in my life in such a short time and I know it's because, for whatever reason, I have spoken to you about things I have not shared with anyone else. I don't know why that happened. I don't question it too much. But I'm glad it did and I want you to know that.'

I say nothing because I can't speak, but I cross the floor and put my arms round him.

'You're like the daughter I never had,' he whispers, and I squeeze his shoulder. Stepping back from Harry, I see the gentleness in his eyes and I feel a shit. A lying shit. My life has become fraudulent. How can I retain any sense of authenticity within this lie?

The tomatoes are beginning to stick and I walk quickly to lift the pan off the heat. For a minute, I stare into the pan, leaning my hands either side of the hob. 'It ended, Harry.' I turn towards him in the silence. He says nothing, but his eyes question me. 'Everything ended. Everything. Me … Alex … Josie ended everything.'

'Josie,' he says. 'Was she … was she Alex's mistress?'

I shake my head slowly, my eyes never leaving his, willing him to understand. There is concern in the quizzical eyes and I look at him, the grey shadow of evening stubble on his face, and he looks old and solid and vulnerable and strong all at once. 'We had a daughter,' I say. 'Alex and I had a daughter.'

He knows. I can see he knows, the way I used the past tense. Had a daughter.

'Is she …?' he says. I nod, and turn back to the hob, pulling the pan back, turning the heat up again.

'Cara, darlin' …' I hear him move from his seat but, halfway towards me, he hesitates, then stops. I cannot go to him. I pick up the spoon and busy myself over the pan, stirring and stirring and stirring. I cannot look him in the eye.

We eat in silence, pushing food around the plates. *Newsnight* is on the television playing in the background, Jeremy Paxman lightly grilling a cabinet minister for supper. I cannot stop the fork shaking in my hand. Harry reaches out suddenly, grasping my hand, stemming the tremble. 'Tell me,' he says.

'She was beautiful.'

'Like her mother.' I shake my head.

'No, not like me. More like Alex, I guess. Dark hair … huge dark eyes …'

Josie's looks, I always thought, were almost part of her illness. She was so weak and fragile that it gave her an exotic kind of delicacy, visible cheekbones and white skin. But it wasn't just the way she looked. She was sweet-natured, special. Just a beautiful, beautiful child.

'How old was …'

'Seven,' I say, taking a sip of water. 'She was seven.'

'What was wrong with her, Cara?'

'Everything. She died of living.'

Harry says nothing.

'She was ill from birth. She struggled for everything. But in the end, she got leukaemia. The kind they can normally treat, but for some reason Josie's body just didn't respond to anything. She just ... everything broke down ...'

'Awful,' mutters Harry, staring at the table.

'Sometimes nature just says no. I think her body, her immune system, was shot to pieces.' Suddenly I can't bear it, the unfairness of it rising up through the years again to grasp me. I push my plate away, sink my head into my arms.

'No,' says Harry, trying gently to raise me. 'No, don't think of her that way. Tell me what she was like when she was alive.'

What was Josie like? I want to say that she was a little sprite girl, white, ethereal, almost transparent. I want to say she had skin like white lilies and eyes that were deep and timeless – not a child's eyes at all – and a heart that knew secrets the rest of us only dreamed of.

But of course I don't. Instead I say rationally that Josie was just like any other little girl except her skin was unusually pale because she was always sick, and she was perhaps a little quieter, a little deeper, than other girls her age.

Josie tore my heart when she was born, ripped it in two like it was made of paper. She was like a scrawny little chick that had been born too early; she lay limp in the incubator, almost as if she had no backbone to support her, a soft pale down on her arms and legs. Her ankles were skinny as my ring finger. The incubator was her nest and as I looked through the glass I held my breath. I couldn't breathe with loving her.

She slept most of those early days, but every so often her body started, her arms and legs jerking suddenly into motion as if an electric current had been passed through her. And every time it happened, I gasped, exhaling my held breath with the fear of it. Alex couldn't bear to watch. I never saw Alex so broken.

I whispered when I talked to her, as if sound would break her, too. Sometimes, I would tentatively hold out a pinkie and run it softly down to her cheek but I was frightened to touch her properly. Stevie was four then, plump and dimpled and he would wrap his fat arms round my neck, his blond hair falling into his eyes, and I would marvel at the robustness of him. His head would bang carelessly against mine when he threw himself at me and he would roar, rubbing his hand against his temple until the tears stilled into a hiccupped whimper, and then finally they were gone, lost in the curiosity of some distraction, his hands reaching out to explore some new treasure in life. I knew he was indestructible. I felt it. The way a mother feels it.

I would look at him and then I would look into the incubator at Josie and my heart would stop. It didn't seem possible when I looked at her, it didn't seem possible that she would survive. And of course it *wasn't* possible. Josie was only borrowed; not ours to keep. The trouble was that when she went, she took us all, every last one of us, with her.

Josie. Josie. I dream of her now, the nights no longer peaceful. At the coast, I hear her cry again in the whine of the seagulls, the plaintive cry I could never soothe. After so many years of silence she comes to me there, by the blue beach hut, the essence of her carried like the tang of salt carried on the wind from the sea. Bitter salt, the taste of it like the taste of failure in my mouth. I failed her, Josie, my tiniest love. I could not protect her as a mother should. I let her go, and now she has returned, unleashed inside me like the fiercest storm.

CHAPTER THIRTY-ONE

Karen

'So that's who Josie was,' Alex says, not looking at me. There are tears rolling down his cheeks when he talks. To be honest, it makes me uncomfortable. I can't really handle it when men cry. I know all the PC stuff. Men are entitled to their emotions. Men shouldn't always have to be strong. I still think it's a bit poncy. I can't help it.

I saw my father cry once. Bloody pathetic. Six foot two inches of fat, blubbering lard. He'd just knocked my mother about again, but this time she was out cold, lying like a bloodless corpse with her lips slightly parted and a whacking great bruise over her left eye. He was snivelling over her then, words dripping from his mouth with all the ease of the snot running from his nose, telling her how much he loved her. It was probably the alcohol fumes from his rancid, stinking breath that brought her round.

'I'm sorry, Mary,' he cried, slobbering wet kisses all over her face. 'Jesus, Mary, I'm sorry. I'm sorry. I'm sorry, pet. I didn't mean it. Mary, Mary, can you hear me? Mary, I didn't mean it, pet. Mary, I love you, Mary. I do. I swear to God I'll never lay a finger on you again.'

I watched my mother with the black circles under her eyes, and the nervous twitch, and I swore he'd not turn me into that. I've never seen a woman with such an ability to make herself small, to turn herself into nothing.

Alex's tears are not like my father's. They are silent tears, running slowly, with jerky progress down his cheeks. Every so often, he lifts a hand and wipes both sides of his face with his fingers.

'I'm sorry.' I say.

Alex's eyes flick over me, almost dismissively.

'Yeah,' he says, like he knows it's a platitude.

What else could it be? What am I meant to do? Start blubbing into my pocket handkerchief? I never knew the kid, did I?

The sitting room of my flat feels like a contained world holding just the two of us. I had switched on only the side lights when we came in, making the room glow softly, intimately. It is decorated in red and cream and black and in the soft light, the red is warm, embracing. It wasn't difficult getting Alex to talk. He was ready. One question and he was pouring his guts out.

The half-empty bottle of whisky sitting on the table between us helped.

'How long ago did you say Josie died?'

'Five years.' He looks into the distance, thinking his own thoughts, not meeting my eye.

'Does it help talking about it?'

'Not really.'

I feel relieved at first. I'm not good at emotional conversations. As a policewoman I can deal with them, but not as myself. And Alex and I have gone beyond policewoman and client. But I don't think Alex Matthews is the kind of man who breaks emotionally very often and I know this is my best chance of getting information.

'How did Carol Ann cope when Josie died?'

Alex licks his bottom lip, trying to steady himself.

'Pretty badly.'

'Upset?'

He looks at me witheringly. 'What do you think?'

'I guess you had to be the strong one.'

He's biting the inside of his cheek, the flesh indented where he has sucked it between his teeth.

'I thought I was being strong ... I thought ...' He breaks off.

'Thought what?'

'Josie was in such pain. I couldn't bear to see her that way. The doctors were trying all sorts of experimental stuff, but none of it was working. I didn't want them to keep going because I could see what it was doing to her. She had no life, poor kid. And she deserved it, you know. She was such a sweet ... sweet ... little girl. It broke me watching her like that, seeing her upset and in pain and struggling for everything. Fighting to breathe, fighting to live. I thought the strong thing was to let her go, but later, I thought maybe ... maybe I was just being weak, like Carol Ann said.'

'Why did she say that?'

'She wanted the doctors to try everything. She wouldn't give in. She said if I couldn't face the fight to get out of the way and let her get on with it.' He stands up abruptly. 'Got anything else to drink?'

'In there,' I say, nodding at a small cupboard under the window. 'There's not much to choose from.'

He find the remains of a different whisky, pours himself a large measure.

'Do you want one?'

I shake my head.

'There was this time Carol Ann wanted me to go see the consultant and I wouldn't.'

'Why not?'

He shrugs, shakes his head.

'I ... I just didn't want any more. I couldn't take hearing what ... so I said I had to work. And anyway,' he says defensively, 'I was just hacked off with it being about Carol Ann all the time when we were at the hospital. Like I was ... like I wasn't ... and I *know* she carried Josie for nine months and it's different but ... but I was hurting too, you know? I didn't deal with it like Carol Ann dealt with it. I did it in my own way and it never seemed to be ... the right way.'

'Things must have got pretty bad between you.'

He nods, but says nothing.

There is silence for a moment as he sips from his glass, and then he says, 'She blamed me. For Josie, I mean.'

'Why would she do that?'

He shrugs. 'It's not a very ... very rational time,' he says. 'You don't think straight. You do things that ... you know ... that you regret. And say things.'

I know from the tremble in his voice that he's cracking.

'What things?'

'Just things.'

'Must be terrible to lose a child,' I say, trying to encourage him. I have no desire for a child, and no concept of what it feels like to lose one, but I think it's the right thing to say.

Alex nods. 'It's the wrong way round. It's so ... kind of unnatural. A child knows they will have to bury a parent. But a parent bury a child ...' He shakes his head. The whisky in his glass is almost gone already.

'Help yourself,' I say, nodding at it.

Alex stands up and walks to the window, trying to compose himself.

'Was it after Josie you were unfaithful?'

His shoulders slump. 'Back to that?' he says wearily.

'Was it?'

'Yes.'

'How long after?'

'I can't remember. Does it matter?' He turns back and sits on the seat furthest away from me on the sofa. 'Quite soon.'

I come across to him, and sit at the other end, tucking one leg under me to face him.

'How soon?'

'I told you I don't remember.'

'Yes you do.'

'About a fortnight.'

'Bastard!' Inside, I half laugh as I say it. His opportunism amuses me.

'Is that a professional judgement or a personal one?'

'Both.'

'Who was she?'

'Just some woman'

'Yeah, well I didn't think it was with a bearded Turkish wrestler. What woman?'

'A woman at work.'

'How did you feel about her?'

'What?'

'Were you in love with her?'

'Oh, do me a favour. Josie had just died. I didn't love anyone.'

'What was it about, then?'

'What do you mean, what was it about?'

'Why do you keep doing that?'

'Doing what?'

'Answering questions with questions. It's really irritating.'

'Stop asking questions, then.'

'Why did you do it?'

'I don't know.'

'You must know.'

Alex's body has become angular with irritation, one leg crossed in an open triangle across his knee, his elbows sprawled on the arms of the chair.

'Okay, what was it about?' he says, his voice shrivelled and bitter with sarcasm. 'I'll tell you what it was about. It was about grief and loneliness and losing myself in somebody else. It was about selfishness. It was about the feeling that not everything was black and white and grey, that there was still some colour if I just cared to grab hold of life by the throat. Oh yeah. And it was about sex. What else makes you more alive than sex? It was about proving that Josie might be dead, but I wasn't. Yet.'

'Did Carol Ann know?'

'I think so.'

'She didn't say?'

'That wasn't Carol Ann's way.'

'I'd have cuts your balls off.'

He eyes dart up at me.

'I'll bet you would.'

'How long did it last.'

He shrugs. 'About three months.'

'Why did you end it? It *was* you that ended it, I suppose?'

'Because I knew Carol Ann knew. And I was never going to leave Carol Ann for her, so that was that, really ... And once it wasn't a secret, it wasn't fun. And when it wasn't fun, I lost interest.'

'Poor cow.'

'Yeah,' he says, leaning his head against the cushion. 'Poor cow.'

'Do you miss sex?' I ask.

'Of course I miss sex,' he says, a bit brusquely. I've noticed Alex always answers with either irritation or sarcasm when he is asked about how he feels.

'With Carol Ann, I mean.'

'I've been with her over twenty years.'

'That's what I mean. You might be bored.'

'I know her. She knows me.'

'Do you think she's coming back?'

'Aren't you supposed to tell me that?' His shoulders slump forward.

'I thought she had come back a week ago,' he says quietly. 'I really thought she was here.'

'You never said ...'

He shrugs. 'What's to say? It wasn't her.'

For one horrible moment I think he's going to cry again.

'What happened?'

'It was the middle of the night. The bedroom door was closed but not shut tight. I wasn't sleeping very well, but I was dozing. I had my back to the door and then I heard the click of the door, and then the creak as it opened slowly. As I began to turn towards the door, I felt movement on the bed next to me and for a second I thought, thank God, she's back ...'

He smiles, a forced smile without any warmth or humour.

'Toby. Lily's bloody cat.' He looks desolate.

'Why did she *really* go, Alex?' I say softly.

'I don't . . .' he shrugs. 'Josie, I suppose. She blamed me.'

'But why would she do that? I don't understand, Alex.' I look at him, calculating. There is an agitation about the way he's talking, like he's pushing out a half-truth, testing his own ability to tell a whole one. Seeing how far it takes him. Seeing how far I'll push. I think he wants me to push. I can sense it. When you live with an alcoholic, when you live with fear for as long as I did, you get very intuitive about people's body language. You learn to read signs. Alex has something to unload.

'I was with Josie when she died.'

'And Carol Ann wasn't?'

'No. She never forgave me for that.'

'It wasn't your fault ...'

'I never called Carol Ann. To tell her Josie was slipping away.'

'Why not?'

'I knew she'd call the doctor. I didn't want Josie to have any more pain.' The tears are sliding down his cheeks again. He wipes one with the hand his glass is in, tilting the glass sideways and the whisky slops dangerously close to the rim. 'Or maybe I didn't want myself to have any more pain.'

A tear runs down his cheek and splashes onto his shirt and suddenly he breaks and his hands cover his face so that I can hardly make out all the stuff that's tumbling out of his mouth, stuff about pain control and Josie's morphine pump. I move over to perch on the arm of his chair and put my hand on his back. 'Okay, Alex, I think we've talked enough about Josie.'

He takes a deep breath. 'I didn't want Josie to die. But I didn't want her to live like that. You know?'

'I understand.'

He looks up at me. 'Do you?' He frowns slightly. 'Do you?' he repeats. My hand is still on his back. I can feel the heat of him. And then something strange happens. I sense the atmosphere changing. I can feel it, like heat being turned up slowly. There's a sexual charge to it and he's backing away slightly, trying to deny it. But it's there. It's not disconnected from the tears and emotion of a few minutes ago, not something separate. It's not switching off one emotion and turning on another. It's all part of the same thing. Psychiatrists like Hammond might explain it some fancy way, but I think it's pretty simple. Alex is upset. Right now, he needs to be close to someone.

'Of course I understand,' I say, though I've forgotten what it is I am supposed to be understanding. But to show him just how much I understand, I lean forward towards him, feel the rush of the alcohol in my veins, and slowly, slowly, brush my lips against his.

CHAPTER THIRTY-TWO

Carol Ann

Alex was frightened of Josie at first. I could tell, because Alex can think what he likes: I know him. Frightened to hold her, frightened to love her. Frightened she'd take his heart and leave him. Whenever he was forced to lift her, it looked like he was holding a temporary package for delivery to someone else.

When she was seven months old, I got ill. She had only been home from hospital a few weeks. I continued to nurse her through my fever, my skin fiery, burning hot against the cool creaminess of Josie's sickly pallor. I told Alex I was frightened she'd get ill like me and that night, for the first time, he got out of bed first when she cried. My temperature had soared and I heard her cries only in a distant way, bursts of sound that washed closer and then receded again like waves.

I am not sure how long I slept, but I woke with a start at 3 a.m., the furnace cooled but my limbs without strength. I raised my head and turned my pillow over, feeling the cool of cotton against my cheek. The bed was empty beside me. I lay for a moment and then slowly swung my legs round and sat up, waiting for the spinning room to still. The floorboards creaked heavily as I walked downstairs and pushed open the living room door. Alex lay on his side on the floor, fast asleep, Josie beside him in a Moses basket. He was curled round the basket, the straw resting against his stomach, his forehead against the top. He looked like a sleeping lion, in repose but alert, ready to pounce whenever danger approached.

Years later, when the chemotherapy was failing, Alex and I argued furiously. The doctors couldn't have made things clearer. They called us in to see the consultant. Alex was working and I tried to make the appointment to see him right away, on my own, but the nurse wouldn't let me.

'I think you and your husband should be there together, Carol Ann,' she said gently.

I was mad with Alex when I told him. I had waited all afternoon for him to come in, felt sick with apprehension at what was ahead. I wanted him to put his arms round me, but he just looked at me and said tersely not to make an appointment until the following week.

'Next week! We can't wait that long to see him!' I took a covered dinner plate from the oven where it was being kept warm and banged it down in front of him.

'We'll just have to. I can't get away, Carol Ann.'

'Alex, are you telling me that your bloody work is more important than Josie?'

'Don't be fucking stupid,' he said, his voice low and venomous. 'Not more stupid than you have to be.'

'I am so *sick* of you calling me stupid,' I spat furiously.

'Well, stop *being* stupid, then.'

My face flushed with temper and I had a sudden desire to bang down on the rim of his plate and tip it right over him.

'The thing is, Alex, that anything that is different from what *you* think is stupid, as far as you are concerned. I am always wrong. Well, this time I'm right. The consultant has asked to see us and we need to go right away. I'm not waiting until next week to find out what he has to say.'

'Do you seriously think anything's going to have changed in a week?' Alex said.

'Alex, I need to know. '

'Do ... you ... think,' he repeated slowly and viciously, 'assuming you *can* think, of course, that anything is going to have changed by next week?'

I could feel the hot sting of tears in my eyes, which meant I was going to lose.

'Oh God, don't start the waterworks,' said Alex, spearing a floret of singed, shrivelled broccoli savagely with his fork. 'You always do that. Bloody grow up, will you.'

I am losing. And I am losing Josie. I take a saucer from the draining board and smash it so hard on the worktop that it shatters into pieces. Alex is startled only for a second.

'Well done, Carol Ann,' he says sarcastically. 'You can always be relied on for rational, reasoned argument.'

I hate him. I hate his coldness. I hate the way he belittles me. The way he always assumes control, makes the rules, plays umpire as well as opponent. And I hate myself for never staying calm, for always throwing the match.

'You are a bastard, Alex, do you know that?' I say, trembling.

'There's the door,' he says. 'Don't let me stop you.'

I turned from him and grabbed a plastic bag from the drawer, slamming it shut with a violent bang.

'You're going to break that,' he says.

'I don't care.'

'Oh, fine,' he says, and continues eating mechanically. He reaches for the remote control for the television and switches on the news. Ignoring me. Like I am nothing. I pick up the pieces of the saucer carelessly, not caring about the sharp edges, throwing them into the plastic bag. The sharp slivers are like glass spears, cutting through the thin skin on my fingertips. The blood drips onto the china, smearing into the floral pattern, dripping down the outside of the bag. I am too angry to feel any pain.

Stevie runs into the kitchen.

'Mummy, what was that bang?'

I say nothing.

'What was the bang, Mummy?' he repeats. Then he sees the blood and gasps. 'Mummy!' he shouts. 'Look, Mummy, you're *bleeding*!'

'It's okay, Stevie, I just dropped a plate and it's cut my finger a little bit.' I lean forward and drop a kiss on his hair.

'But it's all blood, Mummy!'

'Yes, I know, Stevie, but it's okay. Mummy will be okay. You go back and play now.'

'Go and see if Josie is all right, Stevie,' Alex says. 'I'll help Mummy with a plaster.' He crosses to the kitchen drawer and takes out a box of plasters, then turns on the cold tap.

'Put your hand under,' he says in a clipped voice.

I run the blood away and dry the cut on kitchen towel. The blood immediately seeps into the white paper. Alex lifts the towel away and quickly wraps a plaster round. Then he throws the box back into the drawer and walks away. Even while I am hating him, I want him to put his arm round me, to kiss my hair. I don't understand how I can feel both those things at once. I walk from the room and close the door with a bang.

It was later, much later, that I realised Alex couldn't face what Mr Montgomery, the consultant, was going to tell us, that he needed to put it off. I could feel Alex's tension when we finally sat in front of him. The consultant spoke quietly, firmly. He spoke compassionately enough, but it wasn't his child, was it? He was controlled because it wasn't his child. It was ours. It was Josie.

It was a difficult decision, Montgomery said softly, and one that only we could make as Josie's parents. Josie was gravely ill, he said, as if we didn't know. Alex leaned forward in his chair, hands clasped, forearms resting on his knees and his head down, eyes to the ground. I bit my lip, trying not to cry. Again.

'Treatment?' I said, the only word I could force out. I didn't dare risk a complete sentence.

Montgomery nodded. That was the decision we needed to make. Josie's leukaemia wasn't responding to treatment as they had hoped. They could make one last-ditch effort, but it would be painful and unpleasant and there was no guarantee it would work. In fact, he said gently, looking at me intently, he had to say that it was very unlikely to make a difference.

'How unlikely?' said Alex, and it bugged me that he felt the need to quantify everything, even his daughter's chance of recovery. Bloody accountants.

'Ninety-eight per cent unlikely,' said Montgomery without hesitation. I got the feeling he was glad Alex had asked.

'A two per cent chance of recovery?' said Alex.

'You can't really put a precise figure on these things, but what I'm saying is, extremely unlikely.'

'We'll do it,' I said.

'No,' said Alex.

I couldn't believe my ears.

'Alex,' I said, trying to sound calm. 'We have to take that chance.' I wanted to scream at him, but I couldn't with someone watching, listening. 'We don't have any choice.'

Montgomery looked down at his desk, as if by not looking at us we were somehow alone and could hold the discussion in private.

'No,' repeated Alex. He finally lifted his head from the floor to look at me. 'Josie has had enough, Carol Ann. We can't put her through any more. Let's just take her home and make the most of the time she has.' He looked at Montgomery. 'How much time without any treatment?'

'That's hard to say,' said Montgomery gently, looking directly at Alex now. 'A month. Maybe two. Three at most.'

'No,' I said.

Alex reached out and took my hand. 'Carol Ann ...'

'It's not something you need to decide right away,' said Montgomery. 'I think it best if you go home and think this through, and talk about it, and then see me again.'

I felt like things were slipping away from me, like I was completely out of control. Life was completely out of control.

'I don't need to think about it,' I said. 'I want the treatment.'

Montgomery nodded. 'I understand how you feel, Carol Ann. I do. I understand how you *both* feel.'

'Which would you do?' I said, louder than I meant to. I could hear a querulous note in my voice. I sounded like Lily. 'Which would *you* do?'

Alex sat back in the chair. 'You can't ask ...'

'It's all right, Alex,' said Montgomery, lifting a hand. 'I don't know, Carol Ann, and that's the honest truth. Sitting in my chair right now, I think I would feel as Alex does. But if I was the other side of this desk ...' He shook his head, lifting his hands up into the air in a gesture of hopelessness. 'I don't know ... I just don't know. None of us can know until we are in that position, until we face it for ourselves. It's a terrible dilemma and that's why I say you shouldn't give me an answer right now.

'Take some time. Think it through. Think what's best for Josie. She's a brave, brave girl and she's got fighting spirit, but you know ...' He broke off. Tears were spilling down my cheeks, and I didn't bother to wipe them. I saw the compassion in his eyes, but he couldn't help me. 'Sometimes, fighting spirit is not enough,' he finished softly.

Later, I lie in bed back to back with Alex, neither of us touching. My eyes are staring into the darkness and I know, round the other side of the bed, his are too. Our bodies are only inches apart, but it's as if a great thick wall runs down the middle of the bed, dividing us, one from the other. Back then, I thought it was a question of one fighting and the other giving up. Of one being strong and the other being weak. Now I realise that we were both being strong in different ways. Or perhaps both being weak in different ways. It's just that we were both frightened of different things.

We never talked about it. Never. The consultant told us to go home and talk about it, but we went home and didn't talk about it. We didn't talk about anything. Two days later I phoned Montgomery and told him that, after some reflection, we both felt we had to take every chance for Josie, however difficult the treatment. We had to try.

'I understand, Carol Ann,' Montgomery said. 'I have to be honest and tell you that Josie faces a very, very difficult battle, but now you have made this decision, I will fight as hard as I can alongside you.'

Montgomery's voice is pouring over me gently, sweetly, like warmed milk and honey. As he talks, I wind the telephone cable tightly round my finger, deliberately causing pain to stop the tears springing to my eyes. The tip of my finger is a violent red, pulsing with the pressure of trapped blood, the cable making white lines underneath. I lean my head forward onto the wall.

'Thank you,' I whisper.

Instead of telling Alex directly, I tell him Josie will have to go into hospital again the following week for at least four days. He looks at me, his eyes boring into my skull, but says nothing. Usually, what Alex says goes. I don't have the willpower to defy him, but when it comes to my children I have the willpower to defy the devil. I don't flinch from his gaze. He turns on his heels and leaves the room.

In those weeks and months, the physical loneliness is almost unbearable. We do not touch, except accidentally, and then we almost jump apart like strangers who have accidentally invaded each other's territory. Alex talks to me only when he has to. This is his way, to freeze me out.

I feel ugly. Fat and ugly. The sicker Josie gets, the fatter I get. All of life seems to be about trying to harness comfort. I make a lot of mashed potatoes these days, whipped up to a froth with cream and cheese and laced with wholegrain mustard seeds and ground black pepper. In the morning when I go for the papers, I buy fresh bread from the village bakery, soft, doughy bread like a pillow with a light golden crust. And thin bars of dark chocolate with chunks of almond. And Danish pastries stuffed with apricots and drizzled with honey and thick white sugar icing. I buy one for me and one for the children to share. Stevie eats most of his half, but Josie only sucks a little at the sugar icing, nibbles a corner of the flaking crust. Sometimes I even finish her half-sucked pastry and then I look at the empty plate and feel sick and ashamed.

I see no reason to make the first move towards Alex because I always make the first move and I have to be strong. I cannot give him the power of being in control of my emotions because then I will have to do what he wants. And anyway, the truth is I am a little tired of being emotionally pathetic, so needy that I hand him my life on a plate. But it is also true that in all that time I long for him to touch my hand, to hold me in the night and whisper that everything will be all right. Perhaps he feels the same. Perhaps Alex is alive with raw nerve endings of need, too. But he shows no sign of it. I do not understand how we can be so much and so little to each other. I do not understand how we can offer each other so little comfort.

Until, after three weeks, I lie awake in bed, my feet cold as stone and somehow unable to get warm. Alex is asleep but he rolls over suddenly, his arm flinging out across my stomach. I sense him waking then, the sudden tension of finding himself next to me, but he does not remove his arm. I edge slightly towards him, pushing my cold feet towards the warmth of his side of the bed. For a moment neither of us move, and then he lifts his arm and puts it round me, pulling me to him. We lie like two stone statues in the dark. After a few minutes, the dark is no longer blanket blackness; I begin to pick out shapes, the bulk of the wardrobe in the corner, the slender outline of the rose vase on the dressing table.

Alex says nothing, but then I feel a tiny movement on my arm, the gentle pressure of his thumb against my skin. My whole body tingles, craving contact rather than sex. Gradually the movement becomes stronger, his hand sliding up and down my arm and then slowly over my breasts. I feel myself holding my breath, as his hand slides over my stomach and strokes the inside of my thigh. Lightly, gently, and the memory comes back to me as softly as his touch, a memory from years ago, before the children were born. It is not just the passion I remember, though certainly there was that, but the way he smiled and ran his finger down my cheek before he kissed me. When we make love these days, we do not look each other in the eye, as if there is a slight shame in the proceedings.

I hear his breath quicken when I touch him. There is sad urgency about it, the pressure of his tongue on mine, the speed of his hands pulling me towards him. I am aware, even at the height of it, of my mind separating from the rest of me; my body needs him and yet he isn't getting all of me the way he once did. And I am getting even less of him. I feel a kind of desperation when he is inside me, the desperation of solitude, of impending loss, the desperation of wanting this to be something other than it is. Afterwards, I feel a single, cold tear trickle out of the corner of my eye, running slowly into my hairline.

The loneliness is more unbearable than ever.

I move slightly onto my side and Alex takes my hand loosely, awkwardly; it lies in the palm of his hand in a half-heated gesture of reconciliation. We lie like this for several minutes.

'Alex?'

'Hmm?'

He is awake then. He usually falls asleep so quickly afterwards. I feel the urge to try and build something out of what has happened, to move closer, reach an understanding.

I rest my head against his arm, eyes open, wishing I knew what to say. For a minute, my open eyes stare into his arm in the darkness.

'Alex, this is so hard, this time right now,' I say eventually. 'The hardest thing we could face. And I know you're angry about the treatment, and have doubts, and I understand that. But this is not ... I promise you that I'm not deliberately trying to overturn what you want ... I–I just ... Alex, I am terrified of losing Josie. That's the honest truth. I just can't imagine what that would be like ... and I am so, so scared ...'

It is so hard to say what is inside. I am always frightened of saying to Alex what is really inside me because I never feel that he quite gets it, and more often than not it gets reheated and served up in a slightly different form, then thrown at me during some row or other. And anyway, right now all I feel is this overwhelming fear that is hard to put into words.

'I've thought about it so much the last few days, and I can see that maybe ... maybe your way is stronger than my way, but I can't be any stronger than I am being. This is it. This is all I am capable of. I am at my limit. I keep thinking of Josie when she was born, that tiny, fragile scrap of nothing, and the way we fought for her, and what we wanted for her, and just ... Just the way she hung on and proved them all wrong. And I think maybe she can do it again ... maybe she can fight one more time ...'

The lump in my throat is growing, obstructing my speech, but my voice is dry, tearless still. Because this is important. This is all I can say, so much and so little. 'Alex, I am sorry if what I am doing turns out to be the wrong thing, but ... but right now, it's the only way I can deal with everything ... to keep believing ...to keep trying ... I just can't deal with letting go. I am not brave enough. Do you understand what I am trying to say?'

His hand does not tighten round mine. It feels limp still, our fingers loosely entwined. My heart sinks. He does not understand.

'Alex, I–' and then something makes me stop.

'Alex?'

I hear his breathing, soft and steady, the half-whistle of sleep trilling from his parted lips like a discordant tune.

CHAPTER THIRTY-THREE

Karen

A risk. My lips on his. His fingers on my face, soft as falling snowflakes, melting into nothing. Soft heat glowing from the track of where he's been. I've never felt this way. A kiss I fall into, a caress that lifts me, calls me. A strange country this, unfamiliar territory but one where there is instant, inexplicable recognition. My eyes are closed and yet I feel he sees inside me to something I have not known existed.

Drowning, the desire just below the surface, but distanced, muffled below the lap of water above my head. Surrender; I have never known surrender. He is drawing it from me, like he holds the end of the string buried somewhere inside me. Pulling out a strange kind of tenderness that is buried deep. The glint of it as the light hits it, dazzling, blinding in its unfamiliarity. He is opening me up, slicing through me to the core. 'Karen,' he murmurs.

I do not stop to question this sudden explosion of tenderness, but take it as my own, like my due, like I've earned it, expected it, needed it all my life. And maybe I have. He's lifting me out of myself, and I am shedding anger and loneliness and disappointment like an old, wrinkled skin. I never felt this w–

'Karen,' he repeats. And then suddenly alarm bells ring. There is so much emotion inside my head that it takes a while to realise I am kissing him but he is not kissing me. The fingers, so seemingly tender on my neck, are not caressing at all; they are actually pushing me away. He is taking hold of my face, trying gently to disengage without showing repugnance.

'Karen, I'm sorry. This is not … I can't do this … Carol Ann …'

A wave of nausea rushes through me. Inside, I can feel a whoosh of emotion licking up inside me like unruly flames from a fire. The most distressing bit is the sadness. I am not used to that; I don't know how to handle it. But it is only a kernel wrapped up deep inside other feelings. Rejection is the most dangerous. Rejection fuels the anger that glows white hot inside me. I can feel it burning a trail inside, like a river of acid. I can hear Hammond inside my head. *Pain leads to anger. And anger leads to pain.* 'You're really attractive, but …'

He is trying to be polite, being so solicitous of my feelings that the humiliation is complete and overwhelming. It is not just that he is rejecting me. He is pitying me. Pity wipes me out, makes me powerless. Makes me nothing. I won't be a victim again. I want to lash out at him. I want to hurt him, destroy him. I want to make him pay. And I will.

Powerlessness puts me back with the shadows, makes me fifteen again. My sleep is disturbed and my pink, slightly bloodshot eyes sting with tiredness. I have dreamed of my father three times this week. Well, not just of him. Of his wheelchair. At first, I do not know that it is the wheelchair. It is sitting in the hall and is covered with the old curtains from the sitting room, the dark ones with the orange flowers on. The orange flowers had brown centres that always reminded me of bumblebees. A sting nestling at the heart of the petals. The curtain-covered package is like a surprise present sitting there, the mysterious shape of it, all bumps and lumps and odd angles.

My father is standing again. It is odd to see him out of the wheelchair, given power once more. Even in the dream there is a nagging feeling of strangeness about it, but I am too focused on finding out what is under the curtain. I have a sense of dread and the old man knows it. He is smiling at me, enjoying my sense of foreboding. His eyes don't leave me. He takes one corner of the curtain. His eyebrow raises slightly, as if to say, 'Shall I pull?' And I watch him tease the cloth forward inch by inch. Then suddenly he tugs. The curtain flicks viciously, then sprawls into a lifeless heap. Beneath, the chair is gun-metal grey with a grey canvas back, but the frame glints like reflected sunshine, too bright for my eyes. I turn away from the light, gasping, and waken with a jerk. The last time I had the dream, I made a V-sign at my father, viciously, as if he were standing right there in the room in front of me, and then snuggled back down under the duvet, pulling it round me like a cocoon.

In the gym, my lungs feel like they are lined with sandpaper. Each inward breath sends a rasping pain through my chest as it expands to capacity. The figures on the dial are steadily rising as my heartbeat is measured: 155,156,157. My mouth is so dry I can feel my lips shrinking inwards, my tongue rising to the roof of my mouth, swelling to become an obstruction that threatens to block my throat and force me to cough. I swallow hard. 164, 165, 166. As the heartbeat rate rises, the time clock ticks downwards. Thirty seconds to go. I try to ignore the reflection in the mirror facing me, keep my eyes on the dial. Beads of sweat trickle on my forehead.

Twenty seconds. My hair is tied back high on my head, the tail swinging from side to side as my feet pound on the treadmill. A rhythmic thump, dull and flat. The machine beeps. Check pulse. 167. I glance up briefly in the mirror now, see the normally pale skin suffused with colour. Life is about ruthlessness, even with yourself. Especially with yourself. Determination: not to lose sight of the goal, not to give in.

My legs feel weak. A tremor runs through the calf muscles, right up into my thighs. Ten seconds. Feet barely lifting now, slapping down without rhythm or co-ordination, like an old punch-drunk heavy-weight, slugging on with grit when the skill is long gone. Just a little bit longer, a little bit further. Five seconds. Four. Three. Two ... I reach out a finger quickly, press the button, watch it climb back up to thirty. Just thirty seconds more. I couldn't put it to sixty seconds. But thirty seconds is possible. And after thirty seconds I know it might just be possible to make one last thirty seconds. One step at a time.

That's the way things are. Just when you think you have come as far as you can possibly come, when you can go absolutely no further, then – *then* – you can always go just a few steps more.

After the gym session, I sit in my car, not moving, for a good twenty minutes. I have a renewed sense of urgency about this case. If Alex is responsible for her disappearance, I'm going to have the bastard, and even if he's not, I'm still going to have him. I fish out my phone from my bag and dial Jack Thornton's number. It goes straight to voicemail. 'This is Jack Thornton of the *Daily Tribune*. Please leave a message after the tone.'

For a second I consider hanging up. Then I hear myself say, 'Jack, it's Karen McAlpine. Long time no speak. I think I have something that might interest you. Give me a call.' I snap the phone closed, tossing it onto the chair beside me, and start the engine.

CHAPTER THIRTY-FOUR

Carol Ann

Josie sleeps for much of the day now. I sit beside her, like I sat beside her incubator when she was born. The beginning and the end. I watch the light change in the room, the shadows fall as the sun shifts and fades. Sometimes I raise my hands to the shafts of light and block them from my eyes as they stream through the window, just for the sheer pleasure of momentarily controlling the physical world. Light. No light.

Josie's breathing is laboured, gentle little snores each time she breathes out. Sometimes, I lay my hand on her hair, or stroke her forehead, and there is a pause in the pattern of her breathing, the sound halts, just for a few seconds, before it resumes. But she does not waken.

I see the outline of her bones so clearly, her skin a stretched, paper-thin veneer over the canal network of her skeleton underneath. It is as if she is dissolving into the essence of herself. Her cheekbones are like mountain ridges above a crevasse, her eyes the sunken hollows left by a devastating glacier.

One day as I watch her breathe, I find myself wondering how many breaths she has left. Can they be counted? No matter what I say to Alex or Montgomery, inside I am contemplating the finite. And then suddenly she goes quiet. My body tightens, rigid with fear. I hold my breath. Listen. I will her to breathe out, to make a noise, but there is only the leap of my heart in my chest, thump, thump, like it's trying to fight its way out of my body.

'Josie!'

I grab her arm roughly in my panic, but she doesn't answer. I hear Alex's key in the lock, the bang of the door, the thump of his briefcase on the wooden floor. I dart from my seat, stumbling, pulling the door open, aware of the pain as my nail bangs against the door and breaks halfway down.

'Alex,' I scream from the upstairs landing. 'Alex!'

And he knows, he knows from my voice and he runs, long legs taking the stairs two at a time and near the top he stumbles but keeps propelling himself forward, steadying himself with his outstretched hand on the curve of the stair. I run back into the room before he reaches the top and I stand, hand over my mouth. I can't believe the shock; like I'm not prepared, yet the prospect of Josie going has haunted both my waking and my dreams for years. Alex is on his knees next to the bed and he's taking her hand and then, suddenly, Josie's eyelids flutter and she opens her eyes and the relief, oh God, the relief is rolling over me, rolling and rolling, unrelenting, unstoppable, like the wash from a passing ship.

'Daddy,' says Josie, blinking, and she begins to whimper in distress.

'Okay, Josie,' says Alex, and his voice is low and intimate, the way I remember it from long ago. He strokes her hair. 'Would you like a drink?'

Josie nods and he lifts the glass from bedside her bead and supports her under her shoulders while she sips. I stand outside the door then, shaking, trying to compose myself. She's asleep again when I tiptoe in, her breathing laboured.

Alex is still kneeling beside the bed, Josie's hand in his. He lays her fingers gently on the cover and stands. He is drained, spent. He loosens the tie round his neck a little more. Then he turns to walk past me.

'No more, Carol Ann,' he says, his voice quiet. He does not even look at me. '*Enough.*' And he pulls the tie so sharply it whips from around his neck in a single movement.

Josie is taken into hospital for the next week while they try to stabilise her. Her body is rejecting every attempt to save it. I see Montgomery in a huddle with his team, but there is something about the set of them that is hopeless. There is no sense of alert tension in their bodies, as if they are engaged still in a fight of which they do not know the outcome. There is a kind of sad impotence mixed with resignation.

'I think it would be best if Josie goes home, to her own surroundings,' Montgomery tells me gently, and in that sentence there is so much unsaid, so much that I cannot address. I tell him with my eyes that I do not want him to say any more.

Josie has been fitted with a morphine pump. The morphine is pumped into her spinal-cord area through a small catheter. It means she does not have to try and swallow so many painkillers.

'There should be no breakthrough pain,' Montgomery tells me. I ask how much painkiller is contained in the pump and he says enough to last one to two months.

'It can be refilled,' he says and pats my arm.

On her first couple of days home, Josie has a good spell. She smiles. Talks. We watch television together. I feel hope pushing up inside me, like the first snowdrops pushing through the frozen earth of winter. Fragile but beautiful. But on the third day she is barely with us. She has had such a bad night that Alex stays home. He has never done that before. Later I realise how remiss it was of me not to think that strange.

The doctor calls in the morning, shows us how to increase the dose in the morphine pump to keep her as comfortable as possible. I talk to Montgomery on the phone, trying to urge him to bring the next treatment forward.

'Carol Ann, what we were trying to do is not working for Josie,' he says, gently. 'That's why she has come home.'

He wants me to face reality but I refuse. I will not be defeated, I think, cradling the phone to my ear and leaning my head against the wall. I feel the raised pattern of the wallpaper against my forehead. I will not be defeated.

'The truth is, we don't know what we can do next,' says Montgomery.

At lunchtime, Josie is awake for a little. I try to encourage her to take a few mouthfuls of thin soup, but she is fretful. In the afternoon she sinks into a sleep so deep she seems barely conscious. Alex tells me gently to lie down on the bed for a little while and he will sit with her. He will call me if she needs me. I am grateful to him, a little gesture of consideration that rekindles warmth between us.

'Thanks,' I say and touch his arm.

I sleep for two hours and wake with a start, a terrible tremor running through the core of me, like a swarm of insects flapping their wings inside me. I know. I run to the bedroom door. Josie. Josie. Josie. I push her door open.

The first thing I see is Alex's shoes. My eyes focus on those shoes rather than on Josie or on Alex. Black, fat toes, casual shoes he wears with jeans. There is a clump of dried mud clinging to the heel of the right shoe, but what strikes me most is the neatness with which they have been paired. The precision. They have not been kicked off. They have been taken off and placed neatly, deliberately together. The laces are tucked inside the shoes, not left to trail. I know instantly what that signifies. It is amazing the number of calculations the brain makes in a single second.

My eyes move slowly from the shoes to the bed. Alex sits cross-legged on Josie's pillow, cradling her head in his lap. He is not moving. His face is wet. His nose is running but he makes no attempt to wipe it. When I come into the room, he does not register my presence. It is as if I do not exist in this room.

'Josie?' My voice squeaks up at the end, trembling.

Alex turns his eyes to me at last but does not speak

'She's ...?'

He looks straight at me, and from somewhere deep, deep inside him I see a kind of compassion for me that is reflected in the watery pools of his eyes. He says nothing, but nods.

'Josie, Josie, Josie ...' I whisper, moving towards her. Alex moves away from her and holds her head gently until I take her from him and hold her close to me. I hold her so close that my chin is next to her head. I cannot stop kissing her head gently. I kissed her head like that when she was born, when her scalp was still covered in blood. I remember the doctor looked at me, not strangely, but with fascination that I kissed her bloodied head over and over so instinctively. I didn't care, though I knew the blood stained my lips, dry and cracked still from labour.

'But why? Why didn't you ...?' I question, ignoring what I know inside, pushing it down.

But I don't finish the question, because there is only one reason why Alex didn't call for me to hold my daughter in her dying moments. The beat of my heart stutters in my chest like interrupted machine-gun fire.

'The morphine pump ....' I say, looking at him wildly.

'She'd had enough, Carol Ann,' he whispers. 'We couldn't hold onto her for ever ...'

I watch the tears spill from his eyes.

I lay Josie's head gently on the pillow and stand. Inside me, I feel a level of anger that I have never felt before. I try to hold it, contain it, because I am frightened to let go of it, to set it free in case it takes on life of its own.

'You pump ... the pump ...' I say stupidly, 'You turned ... you made it ...' The words don't make sense. I walk towards him and he holds out his arms to me, to circle me.

'Carol Ann ...'

'You ... you ...'

The words are shaky, contained, and then I feel the lid lifting, the contents of the box exploding into his face.

'You fucking ...' I lash out with my fist into his chest. I rarely swear. The words sound alien in my voice. Alex looks startled, caught off guard.

'YOU FUCK–ING,' I scream, each syllable accompanied by a blow. Alex reaches out to catch my hands. 'MUR–DER–ER!' The word is screamed so loud it hurts my throat. My voice will have a rasping edge for the next few days. Alex is trying to physically restrain me, but I'm flying at him, fighting against his strength with so much passion that he cannot hold me.

'MURDERER!' I scream with every bit of strength I have in me. 'I FUCKING WISH IT WAS YOU!'

I should never have said it. Never, never, never. I didn't even mean it. But words are the one thing you can't take back. They are the most dangerous weapon in the world. Once they are said, you can't unsay them. Murderer. One small word with all the killing capacity of a nuclear bomb wrapped inside its three little syllables. Mur-der-er.

Nobody knew at the funeral that Alex and I weren't talking. They didn't see the distance between us. I suppose it doesn't matter what you do at funerals. Whatever it is, it gets put down to grief. People expect you to be odd. And anyway, despite everything, there was that moment when Josie's white coffin was lifted and I grabbed Alex's hand instinctively at the same moment he grabbed mine. Because we both knew, whatever the distance between us, there was no one else in that place who understood so precisely what we were feeling except each other. How could there be? Josie came from us. She was from our bodies, from inside us. And from our minds, from our hearts, from the instinct that brought us together. The intimacy of the moment she was conceived was repeated in her going, because in that church, for that moment, there was only me and Alex. Then our hands dropped.

CHAPTER THIRTY-FIVE

Karen

Lily is playing Frank again. 'My Way'.

'Yes, *there were times, I'm sure you knew, When I bit off more than I could chew.'*

Lily leans against the door and looks at me.

'Evening, Lily.'

I look at Alex.

'A word in private, please.' I deliberately make myself sound more official than usual.

Lily looks terrified.

'You've found her?' she says.

'No, no, nothing like that.'

Lily moves back inside slowly.

'*But through it all, when there was doubt, I ate it up and spit it out, I faced it all and ...*'

The door clicks.

Alex walks to the sitting room and I follow, closing the door behind us. Neither of us sits down. Alex folds his arms. We haven't spoken since the kiss. He's finding it hard to look me in the eye and it fuels my anger.

His eyes are so very beautiful in colour.

'I've come to talk to you about Josie.'

It is as if someone is taking a cloth and wiping all expression from his face, like chalk being wiped from a blackboard.

'What about ...' His voice goes hoarse, jams, and he clears his throat. 'Excuse me. What about Josie?'

'This is very difficult, Alex. But I am a police officer and I have to consider everything you told me. I find myself ... really ... well, perturbed ... by what you told me about the morphine pump.'

Alex's face is a mask now. A death mask, pale and fixed.

'Forget what I told you.'

'That's the thing, Alex. I can't forget. I wish I could. You know, some courts would take a lenient view of what happened with the morphine pump. Mercy killing, they would call it. But there have been a number of prosecutions in the last few years and well, I just feel that decision isn't mine to take. You know what I mean? It's not up to me as a policewoman whether to prosecute. It should be up to the procurator fiscal and, ultimately, up to the courts. I feel you told me about a potential crime that has been committed and that really, I should pass that on.'

'Karen, don't do this ...'

'It's my job, Alex.'

'I didn't realise you stuck to the letter of the law, Karen. Is that what you were doing the other night?' he calms himself, becomes almost pleading. 'Look, this is ridiculous. I told you what happened. You know that I didn't murder Josie. Not in that way. You *know* that.' His voice is beginning to rise.

He's sweating now, inside himself. He's sweating and it's me that's making him sweat. It soothes me. Of course, I have no intention of reporting this. At least I don't think so. But I need to mess with his head, make him malleable.

'I've told you, Alex. It's not up to me to "know" anything. I just feel ... it's my duty to pass this on.'

'Karen, please. Not now. You know how things are. There's Steve to think about. And Lily and ...'

'I know things are tough, Alex. I need to go away and make a decision about this, but I felt it only fair to tell you what I was thinking. I can't ... I can't just pretend we never had that conversation.'

'How can you do this? Karen, we ... I mean ... how can you even think about doing this?' He gets up from his seat agitatedly, but when he looks at my face, he stops abruptly.

'Go and do what you have to do Karen,' he says, holding my eyes coldly. 'But I'll do what I have to do, too. I'll deny it.'

'Josie's body may have to be exhumed.'

'You bitch,' he says quietly.

I pick up my bag. 'I'm sorry, Alex. I'll be in touch.'

You know, I really hope Alex learns something from this. *He* doesn't decide when this is finished. I do.

CHAPTER THIRTY-SIX

Carol Ann

Michael is in McGettigan's almost every night now. On the rare occasions he doesn't turn up, I feel a pang of disappointment that I don't want to examine too closely. He arrives an hour before closing after working at the beach hut, and sits at the end of the bar, a quiet, undemanding presence. He tells me about progress in the beach hut, a subject I never tire of hearing about. It gives me a thrill every time.

An easiness has developed between us, a friendship. Michael expresses it in very practical, masculine ways. He fixes things: a broken light-fitting; a loose carpet rail. He brings me firelighters for the open fire in the sitting room. I have never laid an open fire before and think you only need sticks and rolled-up newspaper. This will be easier, he says.

Michael has a quality that is hard to define. Like he understands things instinctively on some very deep level inside him. And yet he has never been away from Ireland. One night when we are chatting, I ask him if he never wanted to move away and he simply says no, he never had the notion. He's been away for short periods but he always comes back. Killymeanan suits him just fine. I say some people think you miss out on life if you stay in the same quiet place all your life. He smiles then.

'Killymeanan *is* life,' he says. He drains the dregs of his glass.

'There's a whole world out there ...'

'There's a whole world in here,' he says, and looks at me with an expression that makes me turn to the sink to busy myself with washing glasses. 'You don't need to look for the world,' he continues. 'It comes to you, wherever you are. You stand still and it meets you. Some people don't understand that. They keep moving on and on and on, looking for experiences, never staying still long enough to know they're actually experiencing it anyway.'

The water is running over the glass rim as I look up at him.

'Watch,' he says gently, and nods at the fine spray flying up from the glass. I look down, hastily remove the glass from the jet of water, tut at the water stain on my shirt. He smiles.

'See you tomorrow.'

He unfolds his lean, long frame from the stool, picks the keys from the counter and his leather jacket from the chair next to him. I watch him move to the door and he raises his eyes at me in almost imperceptible goodbye. The door bangs shut.

I have a strange feeling of agitation when he's gone, and I don't know why.

CHAPTER THIRTY-SEVEN

Karen

The dreams are horrific, the night sweats basting me in damp, sticky terror. I've never been a patient person, but during the day my temper is short and I feel exhausted most of the time. Things are falling apart. McFarlane is on my case, demanding to know why none of my paper-work is up to date. I was due in court yesterday morning with Mackie for a road traffic case, but I slept in. In the end, I was only twenty minutes late and the case was delayed anyway, so nobody would have known if that bastard hadn't called the station pretending to look for me.

On my day off, I walk by Hammond's office three times before finally going in. I'm not sure I'm going to be able to even pretend that this is about Carol Ann.

Hammond has a cold. He looks grey and tired, pulls a weary succession of tissues from a box on his desk. But he never looks surprised to see me. Why is that? Each time, he looks as if he's been expecting me, waiting for me. Come back in an hour, he says. He has a twenty-minute break then.

Hammond puts his pen down and indicates a seat with his hand when I return. He smiles vaguely, nods as if fully prepared for my visit. Something about the expression annoys me. It's as if he thinks he knows me better than I know myself and I don't like it. Instinctively, almost without making the decision, I change my mind about what I am going to say to him.

'Just a few things about Carol Ann.'

'Oh?' says Hammond. 'I thought the way you came in that you wanted to talk about something else.'

'No.'

He looks at me and nods, waits. My mind has gone blank. He lifts his hands, opens them in a 'go on, then' gesture.

'Dissociation,' I say.

'Yes?'

'You mentioned dissociation in my first visit. I wonder if you could just explain again what was ... what you meant by that. You know, tell me what ... like ... what would be happening for Carol Ann if ... if she was ... you know, if that was what was happening.'

Hammond watches me as I stumble through the words.

'Dissociation is simply a defence mechanism for the mind,' says Hammond quietly. 'It is a release. When a person is stressed, when they feel unable to cope, they might not be able to physically remove themselves from the situation, but they try and remove themselves mentally from it. And sometimes ... as may have happened with Carol Ann ... that leads eventually to physical removal, too.'

He is wearing a peach-coloured shirt today. I fix my eyes on the collar of it.

'But how do you remove yourself mentally?'

'All sorts of ways.' Hammond leans back in his chair, resting his elbows, joining his fingers in that familiar triangle. The movement back has cast his face in shadow. His eyes look different colours in different lights; sometimes blue, the dull blue of a stormy, rainy sea, and sometimes grey. 'Imagine,' he says, 'just as an example, living with an alcoholic.'

He reaches for a tissue from the box on his desk but his hand pauses momentarily before he lifts it out.

'I'm sorry,' he says, 'did I startle you?'

'No.'

'I thought you jumped,' he says, his voice gentle.

'No.'

'Well,' he continues, wiping the handkerchief lightly against his nose, 'as I say, imagine living with an alcoholic. You love the person, but they are impossible to live with. You lie for them. You cover up for them. And eventually, you realise that by supporting this person you are making their alcoholism worse. So you decide you must get tough. Tough love, yes? You know what this is?

'Yes.'

'So the next time, your loved one asks you to phone in sick for them to their office, you refuse. You tell them they must lie for themselves; you will no longer lie for them. And when they plead with you for the bottles you have hidden, you refuse. And when they come in drunk at midnight and find the door locked, you refuse to open it for them. Now normally, because you love the person, you cannot resist their pleas to you. But you know you *must* resist because it is the only way you can help them. By lying, by giving them the bottle, by opening the door, you are only allowing them to behave badly. But it is not easy to resist them. So you detach yourself. You go somewhere else in your head. You do not allow yourself to look at their pleading eyes or listen to their desperate voice. That, in its simplest form, is dissociation.'

I have done that all my life. Detached myself. Gone somewhere else in my head. Somewhere where I was powerful and in control, where I couldn't feel any pain. Somewhere where my father crawled at my feet begging for mercy. I become aware of Hammond waiting.

'And Carol Ann ...' I say.

'Carol Ann? Oh yes, we're talking about Carol Ann, aren't we?' he says.

Smart Alec. He wants me to know that *he* knows this is about me.

'Well, Carol Ann may have detached herself so completely in her head, that finally, she was detached enough to walk away physically, too.'

'I know about Josie.'

Hammond merely nods, as if that is insignificant. He is right. I do not want to talk about Josie. Or Carol Ann. I want to confess everything. I want to tell him about the shadows and the night sweats and the anger. I want to tell him about the fear, the fear of my father that I could only conquer by becoming invincible. The fear that even now I cannot acknowledge lest it consume me completely. I want to tell him about the secret fears that burrow down in cramped places inside me, that whisper terrible things to me about my inability to love or be loved.

'In any person's life, there are times when emotional difficulties become too much. For the sake of argument ... to show you how this works, look at your own life. Have you ever wanted to walk away?' Hammond says.

This is my opportunity. But even as I hear the words I am shrugging, turning my lips down nonchalantly in a deliberately careless, dismissive gesture.

'Can't really think of anything. I'm not a walking-away kind of person.'

'No relationship worries? No money troubles? No personal difficulties?' He smiles. 'You are a rare person, Karen.'

'Yes.'

'Of course, people detach from situations in different ways. In its most acute form, some people develop layers to their personality. Or even multiple personalities. Dissociation is very common when a person has been involved in a traumatic event. A rape, a violent attack, a freak accident, abuse of some kind ...'

'I see.'

'And if they have a history of traumatic events – continual fear, continual violence – over a period of time, then one really big event triggers dissociation more commonly than for people who *don't* have that history.'

'Did Crrr ...' My voice cracks. I'm not sure why. That way when your mouth is dry. I clear my throat.

Hammond's eyes watch me, but his hand reaches out for another tissue from the box.

'Did Carol Ann have a history of traumatic events?'

'She had her share.'

I feel low down in my seat, somehow, as if I have slipped too far into it. I push myself up with my elbows on the arms of the chair, straighten my back, cross my legs at the ankle.

'I wondered about Carol Ann's father,' I say.

'Yes?' says Hammond and his eyebrows twitch into an arch. 'What did you wonder?'

'I realised nobody had mentioned him. I wondered if she saw him still, you know, before she left?'

'Now I wonder,' says Hammond speculatively, 'why you should ask me such a question?'

'It's another person to contact. Somewhere she might have gone. I should check it out.'

'Yes, but the obvious thing to do is to ask Lily. Or Alex. They surely know the practical details of Carol Ann's family circumstances best of all? But then, perhaps it is not the practicalities you want to ask about?'

He sneezes.

'Bless me,' he says, perhaps a little sarcastically. Like I should have said it.

He pulls another tissue from the box.

'Did she get on with her father?'

'So it's *not* the practicalities?'

'Did she?'

'You want to talk about fathers today?'

'No.'

'Sure?'

'Just Carol Ann's.'

'I don't think her father is a person who has been in Carol Ann's life since she was a child. Anyone else's father you are interested in?' Suddenly it's too close. I don't want to confess anything, not even to myself. I don't want self-knowledge, self-awareness. I don't want to acknowledge anything that means I have to relinquish control.

'This is all too clever for me,' I say suddenly, smiling mockingly at Hammond and folding my arms. 'I am too stupid to follow your logic.'

Hammond smiles, as if he's not taken in by the shift in gear, the sudden acceleration away from the conversation.

'On the contrary, Karen, you're not stupid at all, are you? Though I think perhaps you are more intuitively clever than intellectually clever. Wouldn't you say? Animal cunning? Instinctive survival? I wonder what has sharpened those skills in you?'

'Oh please, Dr Hammond, don't,' I say sarcastically, standing up and moving to the door. There is sweat prickling on my back. 'You're making me all confused. If you keep this up, I'm going to need a psychiatrist.'

CHAPTER THIRTY-EIGHT

Carol Ann

Late October. I hear a cacophony of sound, like the noise of gunfire, from outside, and rush to my back door to see what the noise is. I throw open the door and see hundreds of ducks filling the sky, flying above me in pointed arrowheads. I have never heard such a noise fill the skies. I shield my eyes from the light with my hand, and watch as they head south. I wonder how many of them will not make it home.

Sean is organising a small fireworks party at McGettigan's. He is temporarily removing the outside table benches from the garden area. I have agreed to work that night; all hands to the beer pumps. I am glad to be occupied. Stevie was born on bonfire night.

Stevie was his own man from the start. I always knew there was a little part of him that belonged to no one but himself. Even the way he stood as a child was a trumpet blast of independence, a V-sign to the world. Legs slightly apart in a triangle to his body, feet planted firmly to the earth like rocks, hands on his hips. He certainly developed Alex's certainty, his absolute belief in his right to a place in the world. I loved Stevie, but I never completely understood him, which I guess is a bit the way I felt about Alex, too. They never understood each other, either, which is strange, considering how alike they were. How alike they are. Perhaps now that I am gone, they will find that out.

* * *

Out in the back garden of the house, there is a fence with a thin wire running along the top. In the summer, the swallows line up in a row along it, just as they do at home. Or house martins, if Lily is right ... whatever they are. A little chorus of birds, trapeze artists, their tails dipping, heads jerking this way and that, an occasional pirouette to face the other way, yet they hold fast, secure on their thin perch. This last week has been cold and the line of birds I see on the wire have creamy breasts puffed out against the brittle wind that whistles from the coast.

When Stevie was wee, a bird flew into our window at home. In fact, it happened from time to time as they flitted round the house; they would see through the glass and keep flying into the space, unaware that an obstruction lay between. Sometimes, they would lie huddled on the path for as much as an hour and just when you had given up hope, they would stir a little, gradually coming to, fluttering their wings before sinking back into themselves, necks bent into their chests. Then suddenly, they would be off, flying free. It seemed like a small miracle every time.

But this day, the bird was sprawled on the path, wings half outstretched as if still in flight, and his tail feathers were bent at a peculiar angle. It was the first time Stevie had seen it happen, and he came running to fetch me, distress fighting with excitement at being the one to tell me.

'Mummy, Mummy!' he yelled, his sturdy little boots thumping on the wooden floor as he ran up the hall to the kitchen. 'Mummy!' He threw the door open.

'What's wrong, Stevie?' I said, running to him in fright. 'What is it? Is it Josie?'

'No,' he said, and my heart stilled a little. Josie was asleep still, safe. I knelt beside him then, rubbed his chest. 'Bird ... mummy ... outside,' he gasped, and I felt his chest heaving. He could hardly get the words out; they tumbled haphazardly in the wrong order. 'Hurt, mummy ... the bird.'

'Take your time, Stevie,' I said. 'What's happened?'

He took me by the hand then and ran down the hall, pulling me behind him, to see. The two of us peered down at the small form on the path. I saw the way the feathers bent, as though something was broken. The bird's eyes hovered between open and closed; a small beat still visible in its chest. But I knew.

'See?' said Stevie.

'Poor little bird,' I said.

'Make it a bed, Mummy.'

There was no point, but I got a shoe box and lined it with newspaper and a layer of cotton wool on top and gave it to Stevie. Sometimes you have to go through the process, learn for yourself without being told. And I knew what it was to believe when others only preached despair. I made up the bed in the shoe box like I was making it up for my own child. For Josie.

Stevie bent solemnly over the bird, his bottom stuck in the air. And then he lifted it with his fat little hands, so gently ... so *tenderly* ... and he placed it in the cotton wool. It surprised me the way he didn't need to be told how to handle it. He could only have been four or five, but after he placed it in the box he took his pinkie, only his pinkie, and ran it ever so lightly on the bird's back.

'There, there,' he said, in a parody of a grown-up. Like a wee old man, he was. 'There, there.'

We soaked pellets of bread in milk and placed them beside the bird.

It was dead soon after, though Stevie didn't realise because its eyes were still half open, death coming somewhere between the poor thing opening and closing its lids. Stevie ran back and forward in play that afternoon, every so often remembering about the bird and running to the box to look. Eventually, he came to fetch me.

'It's not eating the bread, Mummy,' he said, subdued.

I came out to look in the box. Then I took his hand.

'I think the little bird is dead, Stevie,' I said softly.

For a second or two he said nothing, his eyes simply widening in amazement at the enormity of what had happened. Then his face crumpled.

'No!' he shouted. 'No, it's not!'

'I think so, Stevie,' I said and tried to put my arm round him. He pushed me away.

'You shouldn't have let it,' he said. 'You shouldn't have let it.'

'Sometimes these things just happen, Stevie. We did everything we could to make it better. You and me, we can bury it in the garden. Put a little cross made of sticks for it.'

'No,' he said, and he put out a plump fist and banged it hard on my shoulder in fury. 'It's *not* dead,' and he marched off to the garage and shut the door.

I left the dead bird where it was in the box, with the lid open, and let Stevie have his few minutes alone. When I went back out to get him, he was already out of the garage and playing on his bike. The lid of the box was closed.

I asked Alex to remove the box with the bird and he disposed of the body out the back somewhere, and put the box in the rubbish. Stevie and I never spoke about it again. He never asked where the box was. But he took the knowledge and buried it somewhere deep inside himself. Two days later we were driving in the car and I was stopped at traffic lights. The radio was on and I was singing along with a song when I heard his voice from the back seat of the car.

'But mummy ...' he said softly, as if we had been holding a conversation and this was just a continuation after a brief pause, 'Josie, *she'll* never die. Will she?' I turned round and squashed my top half through the gap in the seats to reach him, and he held tight to my neck while car horns tooted behind me.

* * *

My fingers tremble when I pick up the phone. I hold my hand straight and look at it, like it is an alien being, quite separate from the rest of me. The tremble fascinates me. It is part of me and yet I cannot control it, cannot, by sheer force of mind, will it to still.

I want to hear his voice. The wanting won't leave me alone. I know both that I mustn't, and that I will. It is only a question of when. The first time, I dial four numbers and then replace the receiver. The second, I dial six. I go to the kitchen. Flick the switch on the kettle. Look through the back window at the autumn leaves swirling through the wire fence into the back garden. I pour water on a tea bag, watch the water swirl brown in the cup like a peaty river. See the steam rise from it. Add milk. Leave it untouched. I look at my watch. 4.30. He will be home from school. The only person in the house.

I dial the code to bar my number being revealed. I hear the dialling tone buzzing. This time, I dial every one of the thirteen digits. Country code. Area code. Number. My heart thumps. It rings four times. He answers. I hear him as if he stands next to me, perhaps in the hall outside the open door. 'Hello.' It strikes me how like Alex he sounds. If he spoke for longer, I would hear the hint of the little boy breaking through the masculine tones, hiding in the uncertainty of the inflection, in the questioning tone. But in just one word, in 'hello', I hear only the deep register of the voice. I think it will be enough to hear his voice, but of course it isn't.

'Hello?' he repeats. The second hello is questioning, alert. I slam the phone down hurriedly, throwing it into the cradle as if it has burned my fingers.

Two days later, on his birthday, I dial again at the same time. He answers quickly, before the second ring is completed.

'Hello?'

I say nothing, move slowly to replace the receiver. I cannot speak.

'Mum?'

I hear the word, though the receiver is halfway to the base. It stops me short. Slowly, I lift it back, put it to my ear, wait.

'I know it's you, Mum.'

I cannot even say happy birthday. It is dangerous to have come this far. As soon as I speak, the old world and the new world will have merged. I know it is silly, like some pointless old superstition. Like not standing on the cracks in pavements. The rules of the new life are bound by magic, arcane rules. I am breaking the rules even phoning, but I cannot speak.

'Don't go, Mum.'

I move silently to the bottom step of the stairs and sit down, the receiver pressed still to my ear. 'I miss you. We all miss you. Grandma's doing okay, but she needs you. I hear her sometimes, crying. It's an awful sound, Mum. I hear her through the wall. Mum? Mum …? Dad's doing his best but …' he stops. 'Why won't you answer me? Mum? I know it's you. I *know* it's you.' I swallow hard.

'Why are you doing this?' he says suddenly. 'Why are you punishing me more?'

No. No. The words forms soundlessly on my lips and I shake my head. No, Stevie.

'You know, Mum, I can't do anything right. Not for Dad. Not for you.' His voice begins to fray at the edges. 'I can't help it that I'm not Josie.'

He has not spoken about Josie in years. She has always sat between all of us, a silent burden.

'I know you loved her and you miss her. But I loved her too. I lost her too. I lost everything then because she ... because she took you with her.'

Inside I am screaming. What have I done? Stevie, what have I done?

'I know Josie was special. She *was* special.'

He's crying now. Stevie is crying. I haven't heard him cry since he was a small child, since Josie died.

'But what about me? What about *me*, Mum? I'm your child, too. Josie wasn't the only one ... she wasn't the only one who needed you. You had *two* children. TWO CHILDREN ...'

He is sobbing. It's his birthday and he is sobbing, I think, as though that were the important fact. But his words are burrowing into me, like worms, invading me.

'JOSIE WASN'T THE ONLY ONE WHO NEEDED YOU!' he shouts, and then the phone clicks, the ringing tone buzzing, and I place the receiver down carefully.

I am beyond tears. Shock freezes everything inside me, the blood flowing in my veins is a chilly river of icebergs. That night, I go to Sean's firework display. The cold air nips my cheeks, the tip of my nose. I hear the sounds, the bangs and whirrs, the chatter. But in my head I see only a little boy's face, Stevie when he was four years old, wriggling in my arms on bonfire night, his mouth an open O of excitement and wonder. Seeing the world for the first time, the sparks of electric colour and the colossal noise, and the sheer vibrant joy of it all. His cheeks were pink with cold, his red woolly hat with the train motif pulled down over his ears and his scarf tucked into the neck of his jacket. He bounced in my arms, and hid in my neck, and I watched his face instead of the fireworks that night, watched the colours of the shooting stars reflected in the liquid mirrors of his eyes. I never felt such wonder, such awe in all my life.

'One for you, Cara!' shouts Sean and a whoosh of pink shoots into the sky, banging into cascading fragments of green and blue.

Happy birthday, Stevie.

CHAPTER THIRTY-NINE

Karen

I call round on Friday night. Steve lets me in. He says nothing, but opens the door to the sitting room and keeps walking by to go upstairs. Alex is sitting in the dark, with only the flickering television screen for light. The sound is turned down. He doesn't take his eyes from the screen.

He says nothing. I'm surprised he's this broken, this quickly. I expected more of him, to be honest. Mess with his head, that's the thing.

'Hard week?'

He turns and looks at me then, but says nothing.

'Mind if I sit down?'

Still no answer, so I sit on the sofa, flick the light on the table lamp.

Alex looks exhausted.

'About Josie ...'

'What?' His tone is suddenly belligerent.

'I have decided to say nothing ...' Something close to relief flickers in his eyes. I wait. 'For the moment, anyway,' I add.

'What do you mean "for the moment"?' He is out of his seat, standing over me and I admit it startles me. Maybe we're about to see Alex's limits. 'What's your game?' he demands.

'Things are tough right now for you. I can see that,' I say evenly. I stand up. I won't have anyone towering over me like that. 'So, like I told you, I have said nothing just now. But obviously I can't ...'

'What the hell are you playing at, Karen? Eh? What are you *playing* at? Saying one thing one minute, another the next …' His face is close to mine.

'I suggest you don't shout at me, Alex. I don't really think you are in the position for that, do you?'

My voice is quiet. I hold his gaze and I see curiosity flash across his eyes. He doesn't know where he is with me, which is the way I like it.

The door bangs.

'Is she making trouble, Alex?' Lily shuffles in wearing winter slippers, sheepskin bootees wrapped right up to her ankles. Her hip still buckles as she walks but her speech, though slightly slurred, shows an even bigger improvement than the last time I saw her.

'It's okay, Lily. Leave this to me.'

'I think you'd better go,' says Lily.

'Leave it, Lily,' warns Alex.

'What are you threatening him with?' asks Lily. 'Josie?'

Alex sits down suddenly, as though his legs have given way, and puts his head in his hands. 'Shit,' he says.

'Well?' says Lily. 'Is that it?'

'You know, Lily,' I say, 'you really shouldn't stand outside doors and listen to other people's conversations. You might hear something you don't want to.'

'You think you can tell me anything I don't know?' laughs Lily. 'Now what would that be, Karen? That you have your eye on our Alex, here? Well, knock me over with a cocktail stirrer. I'm an alcoholic – I'm not blind. Or senile, come to that.'

From the look on Alex's face, I'd say that's the first time Lily has described herself as an alcoholic.

'Lily, get out of here, will you?' he says, quietly, appealing desperately to her with his eyes. 'This isn't helping.'

'I'm thinking more clearly than you anyway, son,' says Lily. 'Now,' she continues, waving her stick at me, 'this thing about Josie.'

'You know about Josie?' I say.

'I know enough. I knew about the arguments between him and Carol Ann. She never said ... exactly ... what happened ... but I know enough. It doesn't take a genius ...' She looks at Alex with a kind of compassion.

'I ... Lily, I ...' says Alex.

'Look,' says Lily to me, 'Me and him don't always see eye to eye. But he loved his girl. That much was obvious.' She looks at him shrewdly. 'I just wish he'd made a better job of loving mine.'

I wish he'd made a better job of loving mine. Alex crumbles when she says it, his body imploding inwards. In the last six months, I have never seen him look more upset, not even when he was crying and talking about Josie.

Lily crosses over the room in front of me. 'I need to sit down.'

'Here,' says Alex, standing up. He reaches out for her hand, takes her weight while she lowers herself slowly into the seat with a sigh.

I sit back down, all of us silent, looking round at one another.

'Tell me, Karen,' Lily says, 'What would happen if your bosses knew you were throwing yourself at Alex here.'

'Lily, for God's sake!' says Alex. He throws his head back against the cushion and breathes out.

'Would you be suspended?'

I eye the old crow carefully. She has sunk backwards into the big cushions of the seat, looks shrivelled against their plumped-up fullness. She talks conversationally, like she's discussing the price of fish. 'You don't want some rambling old woman calling in at the station, spreading malicious tales. Think you'd better go now, Karen. I don't want Stevie getting wind of any of this.'

Alex jerks his head forward and looks at her open mouthed, then at me.

'I'll be in touch, Alex,' I say, standing up. 'I'll see myself out.'

'Yes, that would be best.' Lily points her stick at me from the depths of her chair. 'Go on,' she says. 'Bugger off.'

Well, well. In my bid to find out about Josie, I had almost forgotten about Carol Ann's mobile. It had lost charge and was lying at the bottom of my bag until I got round to checking the last of the numbers. And what did I find out? Our Carol Ann liked a flutter. Turns out she regularly called a bookie in town. Had a telephone account, apparently. How I would love to tell Alex. He wouldn't be able to believe it. God, I love it when men get a shock about the women they live with. Love it, love it, love it. Complacent bastards.

I can just imagine breaking the news. 'The thing is,' I would say, completely straight-faced, in hushed tones like I'm in a funeral parlour, 'she won £28,560 the day she left.'

'What?' he would say. 'WHAT?'

I would manage not to laugh. Then I would put my hand on his arm sympathetically and ask him if he'd like me to make him a cup of tea.

But of course that's just fantasy and the satisfaction would be short-lived. I can't tell him yet. Or McFarlane. It would change the case completely. Alex would know she was alive and McFarlane would assume she'd run off to open a Spanish bar with some ageing Julio Iglesias. In other words, Alex would be off the hook. And we can't have that quite yet. He needs to learn a little humility. Turn the screw till it won't turn any more. Turn it until it's so tight it's distorted, off the groove, caught between right and left with nowhere else to turn. Alex is screwed so tight he can't move. Relationships are just an exercise in control. Right now, I have it and he doesn't. He's going to end up doing exactly what I want him to.

CHAPTER FORTY

Carol Ann

One night Michael comes into McGettigan's and things change. There is no real explanation for it, but I know instantly that they have when he walks in the door. I am shocked by my own reaction to him; it has crept up unawares. There is a tension. Or maybe not tension exactly, perhaps that is the wrong word. Perhaps awareness is a better word. There is an awareness, an uncomfortable self-consciousness bordering on embarrassment. I see him come in the door and something rises in the pit of my stomach, like a pack of balloons being set free all at once, rising swiftly, lightly, into the atmosphere. I nod, almost diffidently, and then turn away, frightened I am betraying myself by the colour rising in my cheeks.

I go to the other end of the bar to clear glasses from a group of regulars, deliberately loitering to indulge in banter. Smiling, laughing, teasing. Michael walks to the bar. I feel him looking at me. My back prickles. I turn.

'What can I get you, Michael?' I say, walking towards him.

'Now that, I'm not sure,' he says.

I stand silently in front of him, looking at the black curl of hair that has flopped forward onto his forehead. Michael has hair like a gypsy. And greeny-grey eyes, like a stormy sea when the wind has whipped up, chopping the water with muddy colour.

It unsettles me the way I suddenly notice all his physical characteristics, things I already know but which somehow seem suddenly more intense, or more colourful, or simply more noticeable. Of course, I have always known his eyes are almond-shaped, but now there seems a perfection about the lazy arch of them. And about the angle his chest makes as it tapers to his waist. Am I really moving so far from my past life? Am I really moving so far from Alex? I have told myself for months that Alex is no longer part of my life. This is the first moment I have truly believed it and the reality scares me.

'Pint of Guinness, please.'

He watches as I pour. Guinness needs to be drawn slowly. I leave the glass to fill and busy myself. I feel as if every action is quite obviously, self-evidently, a sham. Wiping a counter that doesn't need wiping. Rinsing round an already clean sink. Michael watches me, saying nothing. I think he knows.

'Won't be a moment,' I say, nodding to the glass with its thick rim of creamy foam beginning to rise in the glass.

'Cara,' he says quietly.

'Yes?' I glance up.

'Come here.'

'What?'

I force myself to look at him.

'What's going on?'

'What?'

'What's going on?'

'Nothing.'

'Everything okay?'

'Yeah.'

'Sure?'

I smile a brittle smile.

'Sure.'

'Good.'

'Cara!' A voice calls from the bottom of the bar and I turn gratefully. 'Cara, what does a man have to do to get a drink round here, by God! Sure, I'm taking my custom elsewhere if you're going to spend all your time on favoured customers. What's that fella got, anyway?'

'Oh, be quiet, Davie Reilly, no other bar in a fifty-mile radius would have you. You're barred from the lot.'

There's a burst of laughter from the other end of the bar. Davie smiles with drunken surprise.

Sean comes through from the back where, for once, he's been doing paperwork

'Is that auld drunk giving you trouble, Cara?' he says with mock severity. 'Cause I'll bar him from here an' all, so I will. You hear that, Reilly?'

'Who are you calling an auld drunk, McGettigan?' Davie is leaning his elbow on the bar, grinning inanely, looking like he might slide right down it. 'Jesus, you're lucky you've got any customers left in this auld barn of a place.'

'I'll have no harassment of my bar staff,' says Sean, putting his arm round my shoulder. 'Or you'll be out the door.'

'And you've had enough, Mr Reilly,' I say. 'I'm not serving you any more tonight.'

'Ach, my God, you're a hard woman, Cara,' says Davie. 'Jist one more for the road.'

'Away home to Alice, Davie.'

'One more. One,' he says holding up a finger.

'I'll make you a cup of tea and that's my best offer.'

'Tay? My God ...'

The door opens. Sean's wife Molly comes in. Sean still has his arm round me and I feel him stiffen slightly but he doesn't move. Molly's eyes linger just a fraction on his arm, registering it, a sharpness about her eyes. Sean turns then, to head back out of the bar.

'I'll get the tea, Cara,' he says. Molly walks on past me, straight through to the back, leaving an awkward silence in her wake. There is a murmur from the top of the bar when she's gone, a whistle, a suppressed laugh.

'Fuckit,' murmurs one of the men with Davie, 'he can forget it tonight.'

'I think he can forget it most nights,' says Davie.

'Cara.'

Michael's voice is quiet. I turn to him and he nods towards the glass of Guinness, which is spilling over. I make a dive for the tap.

'God. Sorry Michael.'

Michael shakes his head, makes a calming motion with his hand. 'It's fine.'

I wipe the glass.

'Can you come to the beach hut tomorrow, Cara? There are things I want to show you.'

A sudden leap in my stomach. I have been alone in the beach hut with Michael many times, but suddenly the prospect seems different. Exciting, but laced with risk. I have never been one for danger, for understanding the thrill of the high wire. And yet here I am, walking it, the wind whistling round me, threatening to knock me off. Sometimes I don't know how I got here.

Thinking of Stevie becomes a kind of paralysis. I lost one child through tragedy and now, I'm beginning to see, I lost another one through my own blindness. It's as if the child I lost was more important than the one I still had, though of course I would never have put it that way at the time. But it was the way I acted. I see that now.

Harry thinks my torpor is because of opening up to him about Josie, reawakening memories of her. 'You've been through so much,' he says, 'to lose a daughter and a husband too.'

I am lying stretched out on the blue two-seater in my sitting room, a creamy cushion folded under my head, just staring at the ceiling. It still feels like a Wendy house in here, a plaything rather than home. Harry's words simply underline the fact that nothing is real, everything is a lie. I have told him about Josie. But how can I tell him about Alex … or Stevie … Harry does not really know who I am.

'I saw his shoes.'

Harry hesitates, unwilling to challenge me, wanting me just to talk.

'Whose shoes, darlin'?' he asks gently.

'Alex's. I came into Josie's room the day she died and I saw them sitting paired so neatly, and I was scared. I knew.'

'Knew what?'

I ignore the question, barely hear it.

'He didn't go to work that day. That was unusual. He said I was to go and lie down and he would look after Josie. She'd had a bad night. She was really, really ill. And then I woke up in a fright and I came in the room and I saw the shoes, sitting there. They hadn't been kicked off, you know on the spur of the moment. They had been taken off and put neatly together, and … and the laces were inside, all tucked into the shoes, instead of trailing outside, and I knew when he took off the shoes, Alex was doing something very deliberate. I knew.'

'Why had he taken off his shoes?' Harry seems bewildered.

'He was sitting cross-legged on Josie's bed. Cradling her.'

'I'm sorry Cara ... I don't understand ...'

'He was cradling her, waiting for her to die. You see? He knew she was going to die. Josie had a morphine pump, to control the pain. Alex turned up the morphine pump. He couldn't bear her pain any more. Then he climbed on the bed and held her and let her slip away in his arms. And when I came in and saw the shoes neatly paired, I don't know why I knew, but I did. I knew. So deliberate.'

I don't look at Harry. I keep looking at the ceiling, as if connecting with Harry right now would be like walking on the pavement cracks, or speaking directly to Stevie: a transgression of some unwritten rule. When I first went to Hammond, I used to make up a lot of 'rules'.

'She died and I wasn't there,' I continue into the silence. 'I'd been there all the way through. And at the end I wasn't.'

'Cara, she wouldn't have woken up. She wouldn't have been conscious, or known you weren't there. I'm sure of it.'

I nod.

'I tell myself that. But part of me ... I tried, but I can't forgive him. I feel like he stole her, even though I knew really she wasn't going to get better. It had to run its course, you know? Naturally. I always said if there was a God, if he wanted her back, he was going to have to take her from me kicking and screaming. I wasn't giving her willingly. But in the end Alex took her. He took her. He just gave her back. And he had no right. And now . . .' And now I've lost Stevie, I want to say, but of course, Harry doesn't know who Stevie is.

'Cara.' I hear Harry trying clumsily to get up from his seat but I don't take me eyes off the ceiling. 'I don't know what to say. I–I'm sure Alex didn't want to hurt you ... he just was doing what he thought best.'

'Things always had to be done his way, though. That's the thing. This was the one thing I needed done my way. I loved Alex, Harry. I loved him. But I said terrible things. And then there was the affair and ...'

'We love badly, Cara,' Harry murmurs, reaching me at last and putting his arm round me. 'I know that better than anyone. Those we love, we often love badly. Until it's too late. God, I know that. We reject them, but when they are taken away from us ...'

I cannot look at him. I roll my body over to lie on my side, facing the back of the sofa. 'What's wrong, Cara? Tell me. Please . . .'

My hands fly up to my face, covering up my expression, hiding like a child hiding behind spread-out fingers. Harry tries to pull my shoulder towards him.

'Cara …'

I shake my head.

'Cara,' he says.

I won't look.

'Cara,' he says urgently.

He puts his arm round me so that his head is against mine, facing the other way. And then suddenly he guesses. I feel his body stiffening with the shock of the thought.

'Cara, Alex isn't dead, is he?'

I can't answer.

'Cara?'

'No,' I say. 'No, he's not dead,' and then I turn quickly towards him and bury my head in his shoulder so he still can't see my face.

CHAPTER FORTY-ONE

Karen

Jack Thornton finally calls. At home rather than at the office, which is typical Jack. He understands things without having to be told. We go way back. He worked for the local rag when we first met, but now he thinks he's a big shot, working locally still, but for a national broadsheet newspaper. Jack is a slick dick in a suit, with an ego the size of Everest and a heart the size of a shrivelled pea. I like him. Apart from me, he's the most ruthless person I've ever met.

'Karrr...ren,' he drawls. 'Heyyy!'

'Not made it to head office yet, Jack?' I ask.

'I think we both know I am on my way, Karen.'

'Want a bit of help?' I take some ice out of my freezer and close the fridge with my foot.

'Got something for me?'

I hear the suddenly alert note in his voice and smile, trying awkwardly to force some ice out of a cube tray with one hand. It skites out at speed, shooting across the marbled work-top and slithering into the kettle. I chuck it into a glass.

'What's that noise?'

'Ice in a glass.' I open a bottle and pour. 'And that's gin.'

'Tut, tut. Drinking alone, Karen?'

'Yip.'

'Baby. Shall I come and hold your hand and keep you company?'

'My hand? You're a disappointment Jack. You used to be a little more imaginative.'

'I'm out of practice, Karen. You can teach me all over again.'

I take a swig of gin and consider. Jack's quite cute in a one-evening kind of way. But can I be bothered? Not really …

'Business,' I say abruptly. 'You know the Carol Ann Matthews case?'

'Yeah, I've been trying to get her husband to talk for the last two months.'

'No joy?'

'He won't answer calls or letters. I doorstepped him one time, but he didn't want to know. I even went back when I knew he wouldn't be there to try and get the old biddy ... forget her name ... the mother ...'

'Lily.'

'Yeah, Lily, but I couldn't make out a word she said.'

'Doesn't usually stop you, Jack. You just make it up, don't you?'

'Now, now, Karen,' he says smoothly.

'Didn't you go to the school gates to see if you could get the boy?'

'No, of course not. You know the position about talking to kids ...'

'Going soft in your old age, Jack. No head office for you.'

I root around in the fridge again, looking for lemon. No need to let your standards slip just because you're on your own.

'You're out of touch, Karen. Journos are touchy-feely these days.'

'I know. You've all given up the booze and gone bottled water. It's prawn avocado salad for lunch instead of a hot pie and a packet of pork scratchings. But you don't fool me. Underneath you're still the same squealing rat pack scurrying around in the dirt.'

'Kaa-ren!' he says, all wounded.

I gaze into the interior of the fridge. The end of a bag of lettuce, turning greeny-black and slimy. I chuck it in the bin. A soft tomato. Two cans of lager, a box of eggs, four fruit yoghurts.

'We have responsibility and conscience and heart,' he says.

'Yeah? Who do you employ to do that for you?'

'Margaret Forrester. Junior reporter.'

I laugh, spluttering on a mouthful of gin.

'Dead babies, road crash collects and battered wives?'

'That's about it.'

A half-lemon, wrapped in cling film, is stuck to the back of the fridge, welded on with iced condensation. I pull it out, tuck the phone into my neck while I cut a slice.

'Well, whoever she is, she won't do for this job. It's you or you don't get it.'

'I'm flattered. But you haven't told me what it is yet.'

'I think I can get you that interview you've been looking for with the husband of Carol Ann Matthews.'

'What? But he hasn't ever spoken – not to anyone.'

'See how good I am to you?'

'Seriously? Alex Matthews?'

'Yeah, but I need something in return. Obviously.'

'What?'

'I need a wee bit of pressure put on him. And I want you to exert it.'

I pad from the kitchen into my lounge and stretch out on the sofa with the phone, glass at my side. Jack is instantly jumping to conclusions about why I want Alex pressurised. As I knew he would.

'Jesus. Is she dead? Did Matthews do it?'

I can almost hear him sharpening his pencil.

'You might think that, Jack. I couldn't possibly say.'

'So he did, then?' says Jack. 'But why would he agree to an interview?'

'Because I tell him to.'

'So he wants to convince you he has nothing to hide? He wants to prove his innocence?'

'Aren't you a clever boy?'

'But you don't think he *is* innocent?'

'I told you, I can't say anything about that. But his marriage was quite clearly up the spout.'

I let a little awkward silence develop just to drive the message home. Lying on the sofa, I can see the ceiling paint needs doing. Shit. Should have got Gav to do that before I dumped him.

'Karen?'

'What? Oh yeah ... it's just useful sometimes to have a bit of pressure put on someone to see if they crack.'

'But it is true, though?'

'What?'

'I can't go implying he's guilty if he's not.'

'What if he is?'

'Well, that's what I'm asking. Is it true? We can't just go flying a kite.'

'Why not? You never let truth stand in the way of a good story before. For God's sake, Jack, I am the one who made up the quotes for that homeless bag-lady story you did all those years ago. What are you giving me this grief for?'

'Aye, well there's a bit of a difference between making up some bollocks about being homeless and accusing someone of murder.'

'Do you want the interview or not?'

'Of course I do, but ...'

'Well, I'm giving it to you.'

'Yeah, but you know my credibility comes into this,' he says.

I raise my eyes to the ceiling, listening to him.

'Your *what*?'

He's just trying to make me spill what I know.

'And I really need you to spell out what you know ...'

Knew it.

'... because, from a personal point of view, I can't do a story if I don't believe in it.'

Now I *really* know he's taking the piss.

'Jack.'

'What?'

'Cut the crap.'

There's a pause and then a snort of laughter from the other end.

'Okay. When and where?'

'I don't want to do this, Karen.'

I watch Alex pace the room, following him with my eyes. It fascinates me how much he's changed, how much less assured he is than when we first met. Six months ago he'd have told me to go to hell. Now he's wracked with indecision. He's walking up and down and up and down, trying to impose a rhythm, a pattern on his chaotic thoughts. He has no idea how much I want to hurt him.

'I know you don't want to do it, Alex, but I really think you should. Publicity often leads to a breakthrough. Besides, I know Jack Thornton. He's okay.'

'I'm not going to spill my guts to some reporter.'

'Calm down,' I say, getting up from the chair. 'Want some tea?'

He shakes his head.

I know why he's frightened. Alex can't handle being asked how he feels. He doesn't know what to say, mainly because he doesn't actually *know* what he feels half the time. His skin is muddy, granite grey, and there are dark shadows under his eyes. His expressions have become more fixed, stony and immobile, as the weeks have passed.

'When will he be here?'

I look at my watch.

'Ten minutes.'

'You didn't really give me enough time to think about it, Karen. I don't like this feeling of being pushed into something.'

I open up my mobile irritably.

'Look, Alex, I've told you what I think. I think it will help. I think we don't have much choice. Your wife is missing and we have no more clue where she is six months after her disappearance than we did the day she left. Now you can either give this a go, or I can call Jack Thornton and cancel. Which is it to be?'

I hold the phone out to him.

'Want to call him?' Alex says nothing, but turns his back on me and looks out the window, folding his arms. His shoulders are hunched into his neck.

'I'll take that as a no, then,' I say, and shut the phone with a snap.

Jack Thornton looks like Everyman's slightly dishevelled kid brother in a business suit, black hair curling over his collar, a faint, dark stubble peppering his jaw. Shirt puffing gently out of his waistband, trouser legs slightly baggy at the knees, gathering a little too much over the shoes. He must be thirty-odd now, but he has one those cherubic, youthful faces that hasn't aged much. Handsome in a conventional kind of way. Nice voice, Jack, smooth as fudge, and a smile sweet as warmed honey. I met him in the street once when I was with a colleague and despite the fact that he's attractive, she hated him on sight. 'I can't stand guys that smarmy,' she said. 'They make my scalp itch. I wouldn't trust him as far as I could throw him.' Well, who said anything about trust?

When he's being nice to you, you know you've got something he wants. The thing about Jack, I once heard one of his more pompous colleagues say, is that he has absolutely no moral compass. He has to guess at what normal people would think. So if you ever hear him expressing moral outrage, it's because he thinks he's meant to. That's what he thinks a normal person would think. You know, there's something about that kind of moral ambiguity that turns me on a bit. As long as I am the ringmaster, of course, and can control it. I guess I don't have a normal moral compass either.

'Lily wants to go and see that shrink that you told us about,' says Alex, watching out of the window for Thornton. 'The one Carol Ann went to.'

'What for?'

Alex shrugs.

'Thinks he might give some kind of clue about where Carol Ann is likely to have gone.'

'Tell her not to bother. I've got him covered and he's a waste of time.'

Alex is no longer listening. Thornton's car has just drawn up. Through the picture window I see him step out of his car, lift his suit jacket from the back of his seat and throw it over his arm. He comes round the passenger side and opens the door, lifting a notebook and tape recorder from the front seat. He sees me through the window and raises his eyebrows at me.

Alex shakes hands stiffly with him. Jack tries his reassuring smile and fails. They stand awkwardly. Alex looks down at his shoes. They make me think of two dogs, circling one another, sniffing. Alex doesn't like intruders on his territory. Jack thinks he can take him any day.

It's clear Jack wants me to leave them to it.

'I'm sure Alex can manage without you holding his hand,' he says lightly. 'Can't you Alex?'

Alex shrugs, like the matter is of complete irrelevance. But he holds my eyes with steely intensity when I say I'll make tea. I make it fast. The minute I walk back in the room, I know there's an atmosphere. Jack is sitting forward in his seat. Alex is staring belligerently.

'So there hadn't been an argument between you and Carol Ann?'

'No. There hadn't been an argument,' Alex says flatly. He takes a mug from me and glares at me accusingly.

'Thanks, Karen,' says Jack, as I place one on the table in front of him.

'Forgive me for being a bit personal, Alex,' Jack says, 'but to write the story, I need to understand everything that was going on, you know? So how would you describe your marriage to Carol Ann?'

Good for Jack. He *was* listening the other night.

'What do you mean, how would I describe it?'

'Well, were you close? Were you happy? Is it possible Carol Ann left to be with someone else?'

'No.'

'Why so sure?'

'Look, what is this? I thought you wanted the facts about Carol Ann's disappearance? You want a marriage guidance report?'

'You seem very jumpy, Alex.'

'Jumpy? I'm not jumpy. I'm fucking irritated by your questions.'

Christ, I think, watching Alex, he's his own worst enemy. As I knew he would be. Perfect, really. They're getting right up each others' noses. Just as well I wouldn't let Jack send Margaret Forrester. She'd have oozed gooey sympathy over him, which wouldn't have been good for any of us. Of course, if this had been a woman, Jack would be handling it completely differently. And if it were a good-looking woman, he'd end by getting her number.

'Do you miss Carol Ann?'

'What do you think?'

'Can you think of any reason why she might have gone?'

'No.'

'Do you worry that people suspect you might have something to do with her disappearance?'

'You're the first to suggest it.'

Jack raises his eyebrows, pen poised. He waits until Alex looks up at him.

'Do you believe she's still alive?'

For a moment, Alex stands on a cliff edge, teetering. I can almost see him consider throwing himself off, abandoning himself to freefall, to the mercy of wind and tide. His head sinks into his hands. He's not sure of anything any more. Any minute now he's going to give voice to his secret fears and say she's dead, and then he really will fall, down, down, down into the void. I watch him with held breath, waiting for the launch. And then at the last minute he musters every bit of strength, the effort rippling through him like a physical current, and he steps back from the brink.

'I really don't know any more,' he says quietly.

CHAPTER FORTY-TWO

Carol Ann

The beach hut has become the focus of every dream I have ever had. Everything I ever wanted and never got will be soothed when I finally live inside those walls. It represents peace and security and happiness. Perhaps a little loneliness too, but when it gets down to it, you *are* on your own in life. I'm used to living on my own. I lived on my own when I lived with Alex.

Michael is coaxing it into life, like he shares the dream, almost as if he knows what this is about. I cannot get used to opening a door when I go to see him, instead of having an empty space that is open to the wind and the rain and the sheep and the smell of wet grass. I walk through the doorway like Alice in Wonderland going down the rabbit hole, knowing that transformation lies on the other side. When I close the door, it is another world.

A radio is playing in the corner. Michael smiles at me and puts down his tools. He is master here.

'See?' he says beckoning me into the kitchen area. The world behind the door is a miniature world, like a doll's house. Everything in miniature. And yet I like that, the feeling that life in here is cut to necessity. I left my old life with nothing but myself. Already in my new life I have accumulated too many things for living in the beach hut. Some of them will need to go. Maybe I have surrounded myself with things to give a feeling of permanency, of roots, but I prefer it here, in the beach hut, where my living will be an impermanent kind of living. An acknowledgement that life really is temporary.

'Look,' Michael says. The kitchen is yellow as I asked it to be, with deep green tiles, the colours of a Spanish lemon grove. He points out the short kitchen work-top and cupboard next to the tiny sink. The sink is stainless steel and though it has been fitted, it still has the labels from the suppliers stuck to it. The smell of dung and dampness has been replaced by the smell of paint and newly sawed wood. 'It's nice wood,' he says, his hands running lovingly over the grain. His fingers are long, thin, sensitive. For all his height, Alex's hands are unusually short and square.

When he looks up at me, Michael laughs.

'Your eyes are shining.'

'It's beautiful, Michael. Thank you for everything you have done,' I say, walking to the window.

'You have beautiful eyes.'

I flush, ignore it, pretending I haven't heard. Then I feel embarrassed in case he thinks I am snubbing him. I do not know what to say. I feel like I did when I was a teenager. Gauche. Inadequate.

'Won't be long till it's finished,' I say.

'A bit to go yet.'

'But still ... I can see it. How long before I can move in?'

'A month, maybe.'

'January?' I walk to the window, look down on the silent sea, the sound now tamed behind the glass. But if I open the window, I will let it in, that glorious sound rushing towards me at the bottom of the rocks.

'Won't you be lonely?' he asks.

'Not really. Maybe. Sometimes.' I turn from the glass. 'Friends will visit.'

'Harry.'

'Yes.'

'Is he ...'

'No.' I smile. How could he think ...? 'He's a very close friend.'

'I see.'

'I'm like the daughter he never had.'

'And Sean,' says Michael, moving over to the window beside me. 'He'll visit.' He perches on the window ledge.

'Yes.' I think of Molly. 'Maybe.'

'And perhaps ... perhaps I can visit sometimes, too,' he says. 'If you need anything you can ... you can just phone.'

'Thank you, Michael.'

The room is shrinking further, getting smaller. He is so close. Michael lifts my hand from the sill and holds it in both of his. I cannot imagine why I ever thought him shy. He is so much in control now. So calm. He leans over and kisses me gently on the lips. I have the curious sensation of falling, tumbling and tumbling, right down to the bottom of the rabbit hole.

CHAPTER FORTY-THREE

Karen

'Alex Matthews is a man on the edge. His body is hunched with tension as he sits in the comfortable home outside Inverness that he shared with his wife Carol Ann, who has now been missing for six months. "No," he says testily, when asked where Carol Ann might be, he has no idea. Neither do Carol Ann's teenage son, Steven, her mother, Lily, or the police.

Increasingly, there are concerns for the safety of the forty-two-year-old woman who worked as a waitress in her local café, and as a volunteer in a charity shop. Murder cannot be ruled out, says a police source close to the inquiry. But police have drawn a blank at finding a suspect, a motive or a body.

Alex Matthews stares with cold blue eyes when asked if he worries that he might now be considered a suspect. And there is a long silence when asked if he believes his wife is still alive. "I really don't know," he says eventually.

But what he must know is that rumours are circulating locally about the state of his marriage to Carol Ann. Locals talk of a quiet couple who kept themselves to themselves, particularly after the loss of a seven-year-old daughter, Josie, to cancer, about five years ago. Matthews is defensive when asked if he and Carol Ann were happy together. It's nobody's business but theirs. But increasingly, questions are being asked about whether the state of the Matthews marriage could be relevant in the search for Carol Ann. Matthews– '

'Yeah, okay Alex, okay, I get the picture.'

I sit up in bed, squinting at the bedside clock. 1.30 a.m. He's been to the late-night garage for the first edition, has ended up calling me on my mobile. He's shouting down the phone, stabbing the words at me like knives.

'Thornton has made me sound shifty and suspicious, like I am some bloody nutter who bumped his wife off and buried her in the compost heap.'

'Don't exaggerate Alex, it's not that bad.'

'Not that bad? Fucking hell, Karen ... you wouldn't be saying that if it was you. And was it you told him about Josie?'

'Do you think your neighbours didn't know about Josie? Do you think journalists don't talk to neighbours?'

Alex ignores me, ranting on. 'What are other kids going to say to Steve at school when they read this shite? This is your fault, Karen. You advised me to do this. You said Thornton was okay and ...'

'Alex, just cool it, will you? Give me a minute to get myself together ... to think ...'

'Bit late for thinking now.'

'Look, you might not like what Thornton has said, but it does no harm having it out there. We wanted publicity for the story and now we've got it. It might lead to some kind of breakthrough.'

'Will it, hell. We wanted people to concentrate on the idea that Carol Ann was alive so that they would think about where they could possibly have seen her. We wanted them to look out for her. We didn't want them to write her off as being dead already, dumped somewhere by her old man. It's completely the wrong message.'

'I think I need to come and see you tomorrow, Alex. There's nothing we can do right this minute.' There's a noise at the other end, a bang.

'What was that?' I say.

'It's me kicking the bloody table, Karen, that's what it is.'

'Well, you'll wake Steve and Lily. Alex, it's one-thirty in the morning,' I say pointedly.

'If I knew where that bastard lived I'd go round there right now ...'

'Don't be stupid, Alex, what good is that going to do? Stay away from Thornton. Don't even phone him. I'll deal with this. I'm telling you, it's the last time I'll trust him with anything.'

'Too late for me.'

'I'm not happy with him either, but I think you are making too much of this, Alex. We'll sort it out tomorrow. Try and get some sleep.'

'I'm not going to get any sleep after this.'

'Try.'

Silence.

'I said try. Okay?'

The phone clicks.

I reach out and snap the bedside light off and wriggle down tightly into the duvet.

Good boy, Jack, I think, smiling into the darkness.

CHAPTER FORTY-FOUR

Carol Ann

We have our routine, Harry and I. He still visits each night after the graveyard, but I notice he spends less time with Patsy these days and more with me. Unloading his guilt has helped. It's not that he has forgotten her any, not a betrayal. It's just that gradual, natural change of focus from the dead back to the living. The readjustment of the lens from microscope to telescope.

When I watch through the curtains now, he walks to the grave and bows his head for a minute. Sometimes, he pats the stone as he leaves. I have the tea ready in mugs for his arrival. I take pleasure in having a biscuit that will be to his taste, a bourbon cream or a Viennese sandwich. Something special on Fridays and Saturdays from O'Dow's, the small, cramped delicatessen in Balgannan that smells of blue cheese and herbs. I love that shop, with its wooden floor and its smell of the past, and the shelves going all the way to the ceiling, shelves that need stepladders to reach. The display of biscuits is in the dark, back corner away from the natural light of the window. Most times, I choose plain chocolate with stem ginger. That's Harry's favourite. I like to see his face when he sees them on the plate. Like a boy's face.

The night I confessed about Alex, then about Stevie, I thought I had spoiled everything. The two lives had merged and I did not see how I could go on pretending that Alex was dead when one person knew the truth. When he left that night, I panicked. Perhaps I would have to leave *this* life too. Perhaps I should go right now. I ran upstairs to my bedroom and began to stuff things into a bag and then halfway through changed my mind and took some out. I must keep calm. I must think. Think.

Over the next few days, Harry watched me a lot. Whenever I glanced up, he was looking at me. He smiled when I caught him, and looked away, but I was conscious of his scrutiny. He never once asked about Alex. But one night, I asked him.

'Harry, what I told you ... you won't say? You know, to anyone in the village?'

He merely shook his head.

For the first week, it is all I think about. But nothing changes. Harry comes in each night. I go to work at McGettigan's. After a week, I begin to relax a little. After two, it is not exactly as though we never had the conversation, but it is pushed to the back of my head. I have become adept at compartmentalising difficult things, putting them in a box and locking them away.

Michael shows me the finished bedroom. Soft pink, the colour of a pale summer dawn. The bed is higher off the ground than beds usually are, to accommodate storage units beneath. Above, there are several shelves. He has used the space so cleverly. Underneath the window is a short, slim cupboard, at seat height, and on top he has made a padded seat with a pink cushion. I can sit there, with my feet tucked up in front of me and look through the window onto the beach below.

He has done the same in the sitting area, put bench seats under the full length of the window. Sometimes, I sit there in the evening with my legs stretched out in front of me, watching him work. The beach hut is a beacon on the hill, like a lighthouse in the surrounding darkness. It feels comforting to sit enveloped in light, looking out into the pitch blackness outside the window, the nearest light across the hill in Harry's place. I can hear the sheep bleating plaintively, forlorn and distant behind the new, double-glazed glass.

Michael is a meticulous worker. Precise. He measures and cuts and builds with a neatness that is somehow at odds with his bohemian looks. His dark curls fall onto his cheeks as he sands wood, his muscular shoulders taut with effort, his eyes focused on his materials. I like to watch him work; I like the creativity of what he does, the physicality of it. Watching something grow from nothing, from the power of his hands as well as his brain. I like the curl of the wood shavings and the smell of the varnish and even the whine of the drill. It is the sound of a dream being built.

I made my excuses and left after he kissed me. Took flight like a maiden aunt, all blushes and breathless panic. But he came into McGettigan's as usual that night and we spoke in the way we always do. Neither of us have mentioned it since. There is time, all the time in the world, to work out what there is between us.

We talk little as he works, but the silence is companionable, not awkward. Occasionally, he catches me watching him and smiles. Sometimes, he says something functional like, 'We need more paint,' or, 'I'll go to Balgannan for some varnish tomorrow.' At 8.30 I make him tea and he stops working, sits on the floor with his back to the kitchen unit that divides the kitchen from the sitting area. His long legs stretch out in front of him, black round-toed boots layered with a thin film of dust and wood shavings. The round toes of the boots strike a familiar cord, ring bells I try to silence.

'I like your company,' he says.

I smile.

'You don't talk much,' I chide.

'No.'

He sips tea from the mug.

'People talk too much,' he says. 'Too many words for too little substance.'

'That's probably true.'

'I only talk when I have something to say. And I don't have any difficulty saying what I need to say to you.'

I have a sense of panic them, a mixture of longing and dread. Please don't, please don't, oh please ... I wouldn't know what to say if he said out loud what I secretly hope he is thinking.

'I love the colour of the pink wall. You were right to persuade me to go lighter. That pink ...'

'I really like you, Cara.'

Fear wraps round me, clinging to me like a heavy, wet towel. The room seems so small.

'I like you too, Michael,' I say lightly, pretending this is a conversation about friendship.

'More than like.'

'I ...'

'You don't need to say anything right now. I just want you to know.'

'Michael, I'm a lot older than you. If I was ... if you were ...'

'Not *that* much older.' He tilts his head back against the cupboard and rubs his nose with the heel of his hand, leaving a black streak of dust. 'How old are you?'

'Probably old enough to be your mother. How old are you?'

'Thirty.'

'If I had been a precocious twelve-year-old I could be your mother.'

'Were you a precocious twelve-year-old?'

'No.'

'There you are, then.'

It is true the age difference would be considered nothing the other way round. And there is something so compelling about Michael. He is deep enough to drown in. It would be so easy. So easy to lie down on the floor where he sits and put my head on his lap and look up at the sky and see the stars for the first time in years. He would stroke my hair and everything would follow naturally, very, very naturally. Like the movement from one season to another.

The wanting inside me is confused. I want the intimacy so much that I am not sure if I want Michael. Perhaps it is just what he seems to offer that I want. I think if I were with Michael he would be mine, always. But didn't I think that once about Alex? I can scarcely remember.

I am not free to accept the possibility of those bonds with Michael. Even now, I am not free. You can remove yourself physically, take yourself away, but the greatest prisoner is the mind. You will be joined to your past across time and space until you set your mind free. Mine is ensnared by fine threads, like fragile, silver cobwebs that wrap round and round and round. I have not been able to cut them. For the first time since I left, I cannot deny that.

I cannot understand it, either. Here, in this room, is exactly what I craved: the possibility of a new life. A new order. The chocolate box has been passed to me and the one I imagined, the best in the box, is safely nestling there amongst the dark tissue. All I have to do is reach out and take it. It's mine. But I can't.

I have been staring out into the dark night through the glass, unaware that Michael has stood up, that he is at my side.

'Cara?' His hands on my shoulders. The gentle pressure turning me round.

'I have to go. Harry will be at my place soon. We watch *Newsnight*.'

My voice sounds shaky, unnatural.

'Stay,' he whispers. He leans his head forward, till his mouth is next to my ear. 'Stay,' he whispers again. His fingers gently brush my hair aside, and he kisses my neck.

I close my eyes, my head momentarily tilting back involuntarily.

'I can't,' I say.

He draws back, hands on my shoulders and looks at me. I cannot return his gaze.

'Are you frightened of me, Cara?' he says suddenly, sounding a little bewildered.

I shake my head.

'No, Michael. I'm not frightened of you.'

I hug him lightly, my cheek brushing against his, and then walk quickly to the door.

'I am frightened of myself.'

A cold blast hits me as I open the door and I step through it, out into the darkness, back into the other world.

CHAPTER FORTY-FIVE

Karen

The morning Thornton's story appears, McFarlane wants to know if we should be cautioning Alex Matthews. He strides purposefully up to me and spreads Jack's article over my desk. Typical. Sits on his backside all week, then squeals when a journo concocts a double-page spread of manure. Manure that I helped him dig, which makes me feel even more contemptuous of McFarlane. Pointedly, I shift the paper slightly out of my way, move the corners of it to release my coffee cup underneath.

'We don't have a body, remember?' I say.

'I wouldn't say that, Karen,' says Mackie lasciviously from the other side of the room. Both McFarlane and I turn and glare at him and McFarlane ushers me into his office.

'What's going on, Karen?' he demands.

'Nothing. What do you mean?'

'As far as I can see, that journalist has got more than you ever did.'

I wave my hand dismissively. 'Oh, don't take any notice of that. It's Jack Thornton. You know what he's like, makes it up as he goes along.'

McFarlane stares at me.

'You look awful.'

'Yeah, thanks.'

'What's the matter with you?'

'Nothing's the matter,' I snap. 'I've just … not been sleeping that well.'

'Well, there certainly must be some reason why you've made such a mess of this.'

'I'm not part of the inquiry any more,' I say. 'You took me off it remember?'

McFarlane ignores me, picking up the paper and beginning to read.

'"Murder cannot be ruled out," says a police source close to the inquiry… Who's that then, Karen? Who's this police source close to the inquiry? And what's all this about the Matthews marriage being in trouble? You never said anything about that to me or to Sergeant Kennedy. Never mentioned a dead daughter. Never said that there were rumours locally about Matthews bumping her off. If I think for one minute that you've been helping a journalist rather than Kennedy …'

He's beginning to rant, working himself up as he goes along. I say nothing. I can't very well tell him that Thornton is repeating a load of shite that I fed him and that Carol Ann won twenty-eight grand on the gee-gees. McFarlane's thin, hawk face is pushing across the desk at me. It's making me feel crowded and I want to reach out my hand and push it back across his side.

'I could have a murder case on my hands here, but we know so little about it that even some local hacks are asking questions that we don't have the answers to. They've left us standing!'

'She's not dead.'

McFarlane throws the paper back on my desk.

'You're a police officer, Karen! Have you lost your mind to that psychic? We deal in facts. Evidence. We don't base our cases on the hunches of the junior officer investigating them. You have landed us in a very embarrassing position here.'

'She's not dead,' I repeat. 'Over two-hundred thousand people go missing in this country every year.'

'I know the figures better than you do, ' snaps McFarlane. 'But the media don't think this is just another bored housewife going off with her boyfriend. They're crawling all over this. I've had the BBC on, local papers, national papers…' He looks at me expectantly. When I offer no explanation, he shakes his head.

'It's becoming clear, Karen, that you're not ready to be thinking about CID work.'

Shit, shit, *SHIT*! Thornton was a stupid fucking mistake.

'That's not true. You *know* I'm one of the best in here.'

'I'm more impressed by Mackie's performance recently than anything you've done.'

Mackie! My face must show my disgust. For the first time, I suddenly realise who Mackie reminds me of. So unbelievably obvious that my subconscious must have worked hard to suppress the comparison. Lee Mackie is big and fat and sweats like a pig. He revolts me. He reminds me of my father. McFarlane looks curiously at me, then sighs. 'Karen,' he says more evenly, 'Go home and get your head together. You are your own worst enemy sometimes.'

On the way home, I switch on the car radio. McFarlane has wasted no time in responding to the press reports. He's a politician, always covers his back. Carol Ann liked to go walking at a pond close to her home and he has decided to bring in a specialist diving team to search it. The fact that he didn't even tell me when we spoke shows how much he wants me sidelined. It makes me feel belittled and angry. My foot surges on the accelerator pedal.

'A tremendous amount of effort has been put into this inquiry,' McFarlane is saying. 'The inquiry to date was reviewed yesterday and the decision was made to bring in an underwater team from Strathclyde police. Carol Ann was a well-respected member of the community and we intend to keep searching until we find out what has happened to her. The search and inquiry will continue to be monitored at the highest level.'

Well respected. He means middle class. The lights ahead turn to red and I slam on the brakes. I hit the off button and his voice fades. If only it was that easy to *really* get rid of people.

My heart lurches when I hear Alex's voice coming from the interview room in the station the next morning. I glance quickly down the corridor, then stand outside for a moment, listening. I can hear Kennedy from CID being quietly threatening.

'Tell me again when you first heard Carol Ann was missing.'

'But I've told you three times already,' Alex is saying.

'Tell me a fourth.'

'I was working late. Steve, my son, called me.' Alex is sounding robotic now.

'He told me his mum wasn't home and wanted to know if I knew where she was. I said no, but she was probably still at the hospital. I didn't think much about it. I left the office about seven and when I got home she still wasn't there.'

'And what was the last time you saw her?'

'About four o'clock. In the hospital.'

'You didn't row?'

'No.'

'Mr Matthews, did you harm Carol Ann?'

'No.'

Alex's temper is shortening. I can hear it.

'Have you ever hit your wife?'

Silence.

'No.'

No, through clenched teeth.

'So she just packed her bags and went?'

'She didn't pack her bags. I told you that. She didn't take anything with her.'

'No clothes?'

'Not as far as I know.'

'No jewellery, no make-up, no handbag?'

'Nothing.'

'She wouldn't have got very far would she, Mr Matthews?'

I can hear someone coming, so I move swiftly down to the toilets and bang the door open. I wait behind the door, listening, until the footsteps have gone then peer out into the corridor again. Nobody. Quietly, I move back to the interview room.

'...phone you?' I hear Kennedy say.

'No.'

'Did she ev–' Kennedy begins to say, but Alex is still talking.

'Anyway, she left her mobile.'

Kennedy stops. 'She left her mobile at home?'

Shit. I hold my breath.

'So why didn't you tell us this before, Mr Matthews?'

'What? I *did* tell you. Of course I told you. You've got the phone.'

'Who has?'

'Karen.' Alex sounds bewildered.

'Karen McAlpine?'

'Yeah.'

I move from the door and back into the toilets, running cold water into the sink and splashing it on my face. My face looks grey in the mirror, eyes pink. I look down into the running water, pouring so fast from the tap that it sprays upwards, splashing my jacket. The phone ... Hammond ... Doug ... the money – it's all going to come out.

CHAPTER FORTY-SIX

Carol Ann

In early December, the first snows come. When I look through the window, the tree in the graveyard is bowed with the weight of it, the long arm arching wearily down to the stones. Sean brings dusty boxes of decorations down from the loft to the bar and we hang twists of tired red tinsel round the mirror, and garlands of silver bells above the gantry. Sean hums as he works.

'There now,' he says cheerfully, 'is that not grand looking, Cara?'

The tinsel gives me a strange feeling inside, a twist of sad happiness. Like when you open boxes of old decorations and think of childhood Christmases, and you have to feel sadness for the ones gone before you can feel happiness for the one approaching.

Sean uses December as an excuse to drink. Molly appears in the bar most nights, her lips tight, eyes watching him, warning him. One night I watch Sean put his glass to the optic and then salute her with it. There is an ugliness about the gesture. I think of me and Alex, the way we are. The way we were. Maybe when love first comes it brings the best of you with it, and when it takes its leave, the disappointment leaves the worst of you behind. My eyes flick surreptitiously between the two of them. Molly, giving no indication that she has seen anyone other than Sean, turns on her heels and leaves.

Sean holds a Christmas party the second weekend in December. It's an annual event and the bar is heaving with locals from miles around, some from Balgannan even. We can barely keep up, running out of glasses, frantically washing and serving. Michael is standing at the side of the bar, where the sink is. He catches my eye and smiles.

Sean is flying. 'A drink for yourself, Sean,' the customers are saying, and he's drinking with them, buying the regulars booze in return. He ordered some mistletoe for the party and he pins it above the bar, and circulates round the room, holding it above customers. There's an old guy with a dog in the corner of the bar and Sean holds the mistletoe up and shouts, 'Give the dog a kiss!'

'Here,' shouts Sammy Barnes, who is sitting at the next table. 'That's no way to talk about my missus!'

And Sean laughs like it's the funniest joke in the world.

Michael leans across the bar.

'Cara, it's finished.'

My system slams to a halt, my stomach tumbling in ever-slowing circles like a washing machine coming to a halt.

'What?'

'The hut,' he says, and the life rushes back into my body. 'I had my day off today. I finished it.'

I can hardly hear the last bit above the noise.

'What did you say?' I shout.

'The beach hut is finished. I did the last of the painting and the carpet is being laid tonight. Come round tomorrow morning.'

I drop the glass into the sink. 'Michael, that's fantastic!' And I lean across the bar and pull him to me.

'Whoa!' someone shouts. 'Sean! Sean, your bar staff are kissing the customers!'

'Cara May, me darlin',' roars Sean, 'Where are you? If you're givin' out kisses I'm coming for one mesel'.'

I let Michael go and turn to wash some glasses, laughing at Sean. But the customers are stamping and cheering and shouting, 'Come on, Cara, come on now, Sean is lookin' for you.'

'I'm too busy,' I yell at him.

But Sean is advancing on me with the mistletoe, convulsed with bonhomie and booze. I back down the bar as he comes towards me, but eventually he's got me stuck in the corner and he throws me over with mock passion, till my back's bent and everyone cheers as he smacks me on the lips. I stand up, hardly able to breathe with laughing, and push him off with a slap. I look up. Molly is standing behind Sean. Sean turns.

'Molly, me own sweet darlin',' shouts Sean and advances on her. He's too drunk to interpret the cold anger in her eyes. 'In Dublin's fair city where the girls are so pretty, I first set my eyes on sweet Molly Malone,' he bellows, but Molly's having none of it. And in the end, I can't blame her. My friends used to think Lily was funny when she was in party mood. A hoot. But they weren't trying to carry her upstairs at the end of the evening to put her to bed. They went home to their mums who weren't such a hoot, but who were sober.

Everyone goes a bit quieter when Molly walks off the bar. I see customers at the back trying to see what's going on, what the reason for the lull is, then in seconds, the noise and the chatter resume. Sean goes after her. I leave a pint to pour and pop into the back hallway off the bar.

'Molly, it was nothing at all. I'm sorry if I embarrassed you. Honest, it was nothing like it looked. It was just a laugh, a bit of fun ...'

Molly looks at me, her eyes hard, two turquoise icebergs of hurt.

'Fun? Sure, I'd like a bit of that. Eh, Sean? Bit of fun. Wouldn't that be nice? I guess that's why all the local men go for you, Cara May. No ties, no responsibilities, and lots of fun.'

'What?' I feel the colour suffusing my cheeks.

'Aw, Jesus, Molly,' says Sean.

'You're a man's woman, aren't you, Cara May?'

'Molly ...' repeats Sean, sharply.

'The merry bloody widow,' says Molly bitterly and walks to the stairs.

I hear her words in my head all night. I'm glad when the shift ends, when the doors are finally locked. I look round the bar, strewn with scraps of tinsel from the garlands, mistletoe berries squashed underfoot, their juices staining the wooden floor in dark, damp patches. Sean is lying flat along the bench seat, snoring. I clear up the glasses mechanically, brush the floor with an old broom kept behind the door. I feel empty inside.

I shake Sean gently to wake him when I'm finished.

'Sean.'

He snores, and I shake his arm more firmly.

'Sean, I'm going home now. Away up to your bed.'

He wakes with a start, sits bolt upright, looks round him to get his bearings.

'Jesus, Cara.'

'I'm away home, Sean.'

'I'll take you in the car,' he says, though he's sunk enough to run his car on pure alcohol instead of petrol.

'No you won't,' I say quickly. 'I fancy the walk anyway. Go on up to your bed. I'll lock up and let myself out. I've got the spare keys.'

Sean rubs his face. 'Are you sure now?'

'Sure.'

Sean lies back down on the bench.

'Go away up to your bed, Sean.'

'Aye. I will,' he says, 'I will.' I hear him snore again as I close the door behind me.

The snow has hardened in the night air, topped with a crisp sugar film. It makes me think of the crystalline coating of the sugar mice we ate as kids. Pink mice, green mice, sweet crispness. I shiver, walking too slowly for the cold, taking small teetering Bambi steps on the treacherous surface.

My steps are slow but my mind is moving fast, whirring through the evening events like a video on fast forward. I feel hurt by Molly, misunderstood. Even this new person I have created has been rejected. Stop the frame. There's Michael. Leaning over the bar to me, telling me the dream is realised. What do I feel about Michael? I feel pulled towards him, as if on elastic, but I also fear that any minute now that elastic is going to be released and I am going to shoot back, away from him, unable to reach him. Right this minute I'd like to be with Michael, just sit in his stillness and be. Be whatever it is that I am. I shiver, as much with the thought as the cold.

Most of the houses are in darkness, but a few have left their Christmas trees lit in the front windows, twinkling a light outwards into the street, sending a message of welcome. There is a back light on in my house. Strange. I thought I had switched everything off when I left. There is something about the house that makes me uneasy. It does not sit quietly somehow, in repose, the way an empty house normally does. There is no tangible reason to feel any alarm and yet I have a sense of anxiety as I walk gingerly up the icy path. My heart beats faster as I put the key in the lock. I push open the door and it swings silently. There's someone in here. I know it. I stand on the doorstep, peering in, listening, waiting, too frightened to enter.

There is a thump. The familiar sound of dragging footsteps.

'Harry!'

I come through the door and snap the hall light on, closing the door behind me with a bang.

'Bloody hell, Harry, you gave me the fright of my life. What are you doing here at this time?'

Harry's face is taut with unease, rigid with something close to shame.

'I'm sorry, Cara. Forgive me. I've done what I thought best. If it's not the right thing ... please ...'

'Harry, what are you on about?'

I hear a sound from the sitting room, someone walking across the floor. The door into the hall opens.

'Hello, Carol Ann.'

My heart stops.

Harry looks from one of us to the other and then heads for the front door, closing it quietly behind him.

'Alex ...' I whisper.

CHAPTER FORTY-SEVEN

Karen

I watch the dawn break on the hill above town, a pink, painful eye forcing the sky open. The car is freezing cold and my neck is stiff from leaning against the door, dozing. Crumbs litter my lap and the floor, fallen from a half-eaten garage sandwich that lies stiffening in the open packet. A grease spot stains my black trousers. The light filters through the darkness in rays, warming the grey buildings below.

I didn't mean to stay out all night. It simply went past the stage I could go home, somehow, even though I live alone. Perhaps I should simply drive and not look back, never look back. Isn't that what Carol Ann did? Kept on going. Became someone else. She is alive, of course. On some level I have always known she is alive. They won't find her in the pond, those specialist divers. I peer out into the diminishing darkness through the side window and I wonder where she is. Right now. Where is she watching the dawn rise? What new life has she created?

Perhaps I could do the same. At one point it looked like her old life could be my new one..Maybe there's still a way. I take a cigarette out of a box, then change my mind, throw the carton onto the seat beside me. The first pack I've bought in four years. I used to smoke twenty a day before I gave up.

I close my eyes, drift, turn the engine on for the heat, switch it off, drift again. Here in the semi-darkness, shadows of memories whirl in my head like Catherine wheels, moving faster and faster until they career so fast they seem motionless, their speed invisible to the naked eye. They whirl across my brain, shadows from the past jostling with new shapes that collide and explode. They take me over. Once, it terrified me, the thought of the shadows sucking me in, swallowing me up. I fought hard for my identity, for my existence. But I am tired. They suck me in and spit me out and I no longer care enough to resist them.

Just after nine, I head to Alex's office. In the glass swing doors I catch sight of my own dishevelment, the bed-head hair and crumpled clothes, but I don't care.

'Alex Matthews,' I say at reception. The receptionist looks at me. 'Police,' I add brusquely.

'I'm sorry. Mr Matthews is away for a couple of days.'

'At home?'

'My understanding is he's away on personal business.'

I walk from reception without saying anything, feeling a kind of desperation. A week ago, I felt in control. Alex wouldn't have dared move without consulting me. Everything has changed.

I can't go into work. There is only one place left I can go and I drive there instinctively without really making any decision about it, parking outside and looking up at the office. He walks in front of the window, a neat, dapper figure. My feelings for him are entirely confused, a mixture of contempt and neediness. If anyone can help me, maybe he can. And the cunning part of me, the part that never rests, says perhaps having a psychiatrist's report will help get me out of the shit at work.

I dial his number and ask Sally to put me through. He walks to the window while we're talking, looks down at me from above. 'Tomorrow?' he suggests, and I catch my breath because tomorrow is a lifetime away and, hearing me, he says, 'Very well, then. Lunchtime. It will have to be lunchtime.'

CHAPTER FORTY-EIGHT

Carol Ann

In my head, seeing Alex is like glass shattering into tiny fragments. The cracks shoot in every direction across the surface of the glass and then slowly, slowly they fall inwards, gradually building momentum until the whole thing simply implodes. The glass is so real I can hear it, the gentle tinkle of the first fragments, then the crescendo of the rest.

I battle at first to keep my face smooth as the glass, but the emotions shoot across it, sending cracks and fissures across the surface. Love. Hatred. Pain. But mostly guilt. Guilt that I am forced to face when faced by Alex. Lily is real. Stevie is real. Alex is not dead. Self-evident? Well, of course. But it's amazing what simplicity you can use to tame the complexity of the brain. You just close one of the doors in there, put a barrier across the entranceway, like rope across a forbidden room in a museum, create chambers in your brain that you simply don't allow yourself to enter.

Alex and I sit in silence. The conversation is too big to begin, too complex to know how. He looks pale, strained.

'How did Harry find you?'

'He went to the library and got help to look online. Did some detective work from old newspaper cuttings, apparently. Didn't take him long to figure out. He short-circuited the police, came straight to me.'

'The police?'

'Christ, Carol Ann, what did you expect? That you would walk out and we would do nothing?' He shakes his head. 'We didn't even know if you were alive or not. And then the police started pulling me in for questioning, thinking I'd … thinking I'd murdered you.' His voice drops to a murmur and the full horror of what he's saying makes my hand fly to my face.

'Oh my God, Alex. What happened …'

'Never mind that just now. It's not the important bit.' But neither of us seem able to tackle the important bit.

He looks round.

'Why here?' he asks. 'Why Ireland?'

I shrug. 'Why not?'

'You look amazing.' His face crumples and he covers it with his hands. 'You get away from me and you look bloody amazing.'

I can't go to him to comfort him. I simply can't. I don't know how.

'How's Stevie?'

'Missing you.'

I hesitate, terrified to ask.

'Lily?' My voice comes out small, shrivelled somehow.

'Holding her own.'

I breathe out.

'She's staying with me and Steve.'

I can't take that in. I blink at him. My mother staying with Alex. 'Me and Steve', like a unit.

'She's off the sauce.'

'I should go away more often.'

'She's been desperate about you, Carol Ann.'

The name makes my heart sink. Carol Ann. It is like a call to responsibility.

'They've missed you.'

'And you?' I know I sound bitter. I can't help it.

'I've missed you, too,' he says, his voice low. 'I didn't know how ...'

'How what?'

'How ... cold ... things are when you're not about.'

'They seemed pretty cold to me when I *was* about.'

'I know.'

'Alex, how did we get in this mess?'

He shakes his head silently.

I shiver.

'Are you cold?'

'Yes.'

He gets up. 'What kind of heating is it?'

It makes me smile, despite everything. Christ. In the middle of this, he wants to know what kind of heating it is. He can't mend my heart, so he'll mend my radiators.

'The kind with a dial,' I say dryly. I go to the hall, turn it up. 'The radiators don't work very well.'

'Is there a key with them?' he asks.

'What?'

'A key. To bleed them. You need to bleed them to let the heat through.'

'Oh, to hell with the radiators, Alex.'

Alex blinks at me and sits down. We sit apart.

'Why can't we ever speak about anything important?'

'I don't know,' he says. He is sitting hunched forward in his chair. 'There never seemed much point. We saw things differently.'

'That's the point about talking, Alex,' I say sarcastically. 'You try and come to an understanding of the other person's point of view.'

'That wasn't going to happen though, was it?'

'Not if you don't listen, no.'

'Oh, and I never listened?'

'Yes, frankly.'

'Whereas you were perfect, Carol Ann.'

'No, I wasn't perfect.'

'Too right you weren't.'

'Oh, go home, Alex.'

For a moment, I try and imagine what I would feel if he did simply walk back out the door again. Is that what I want?

Alex tuts, and sits forward in his chair, resting his forearms on his legs. It is so Alex, that stance.

And then maybe the realisation that we are about to start arguing in the way we always do focuses his attention on what really needs to be said.

'This is about Josie, isn't it?' he says quietly. 'This,' he says indicating the room, the house, with his hand.

Even the mention of her name on his lips moves me close to tears. Josie was a long time ago. A lifetime ago. And yet she was only yesterday. Still she drives us.

Alex looks at the floor. 'I did ... I did what I did because ... I loved Josie.'

'You never even gave me the chance to say goodbye in my own way,' I say. 'I left her alive and when I came back she was dead. But you sat and held her while the life ebbed out of her. You gave yourself a privilege you wouldn't give me.'

Even just saying it lances some of the anger, the huge backlog of resentment that only grew bigger because it wasn't allowed expression. Alex runs his hands through his hair.

'I'm sorry,' he says in a low voice. 'But I couldn't ... Carol Ann, I can't explain, I can't say anything that will make you understand ... except I loved Josie and I've found it so hard to live since … with ... with what happened ... it's eating me inside. Eating me. I can't get rid of it. But I loved Josie. I loved her so much.'

He looks so tortured that this time I cannot help but move to him where he sits. For a moment the seesaw of love and hate tilts back in love's favour. I put my hand on his back awkwardly.

'I know you loved Josie, Alex,' I say quietly. 'Inside me, I know that.'

The acknowledgement makes him break. He sobs into his cupped hands, shaking, and I hold him until he stills.

'You realise this is the first time we have ever spoken properly about what happened to Josie? After all these years.'

He nods, taking the hankie I offer him.

'That's not healthy.'

'Maybe not.'

'I'm sorry,' I say quietly.

'For what?'

'For what I said ... for the words I used ... after Josie. I was angry with you. I am still angry but ... but I didn't mean that, what I said. I was ... distraught.'

He takes my hand, but doesn't look up at me.

'Come home, Carol Ann.'

'I don't know.' I feel confused. I'm not sure where home is any more. Home is no longer simple.

'Why did you go? Why did you just disappear like that?'

'I felt such a failure.' I drop his hand, sit back, folding my arms round myself. 'And I couldn't bear to feel it any more. I felt useless as a wife. As a mother. My daughter was dead. My son was angry and, God knows, he had every reason to be, we were so wrapped up in Josie. My mother was an alcoholic ... and ... and then ... and then she got the stroke and I saw the rest of my life disappear and I just couldn't cope.' I look at him. 'I guess that makes me a not very nice person, running out on my own mother.'

Saying it out loud makes a wave of shame overwhelm me. I left my mother when she'd had a stroke. She needed me and I turned round and walked. What does that make me?

'It was like ... like part of me just shut down.'

'I didn't know you were going to a psychiatrist. Why didn't you tell me?'

I raise my eyebrows quizzically at him.

'Okay. Okay,' he says, holding up a hand. At least he has the insight to acknowledge he wouldn't have understood.

'Come home,' he says again, and it's then the thought hits me with full force.

'There's no choice, is there?'

'What do you mean?'

'It's over,' I say, going over to the window. The air is cold over here, a draught sneaking through gaps in the panes. Outside, the snow has begun to fall again, white flakes looming towards me in the blackness. I feel cold inside and out. The old and the new lives had to be separate. It was the rule, like not standing on the cracks in the pavement. But I stepped on a line and now I am being swallowed up.

'My pretend life is over. I can't pretend that my old life doesn't exist any more.'

'How could you ever?' he asks in bewilderment. 'What did you tell people?'

'That you were dead. That I was a widow.'

'Bloody hell,' he mutters, shocked.

Alex comes over to the window. Stands side by side with me, looking out at the snow.

'We are tied together, Carol Ann,' he says quietly. 'I can't cut that, can you? It's just the way things are.'

'I know.' My voice is barely a whisper through tears. I must face reality and I am grieving already for the things I will leave behind, the buds that will never fully flower. Harry. Sean. Michael. Independence. Dreams. The beach hut. A whole other life. And perhaps even grieving for myself, the person I have become. I don't know if this person exists back in my old life. Perhaps Cara will simply dissolve back into Carol Ann. I can't yet be sure.

But I don't want to be Carol Ann again. I don't want to exist in the crumbs of her life. I don't want to go back just because there are some kind of bonds of familiarity that I am too frightened to cut. Rebellion flips inside me. There *is* a choice, always a choice. I turn from the window to face him in a way I seldom ever did.

'The affair,' I say.

'What?'

'Oh, come on, Alex. If we can't be honest now, there's no hope.'

'It meant nothing.'

'That's a comfort,' I say dryly.

In my mind I think of the beach hut. The snow will be piling up on the windowsill right now, but it won't last. The salt from the sea below will see to that. I picture it on the hill, dark and silent, and I think of Michael waiting there tomorrow, waiting expectantly, eager to show me the realisation of a dream that he doesn't yet know has shattered already.

Desire is like snow. One minute it's there, concrete, tangible, beautiful with possibilities. The next, you touch a single, falling flake and it is gone, simply dissolved as though it never existed. A small drop of residual water as detritus of what might have been. Desire is fragile, changing like a landscape in different seasons, dependent on time and mood and constantly evolving.

Michael. Alex. Who do I desire? I am no longer sure. I want to reach out to Michael. Still I want that. But I think perhaps he is like falling snow. Beautiful, but not really there in any substantial sense. Or am I confused? Is it Alex who is not there really? I consider telling him about Michael. But what's to tell? Nothing happened. Or did it? I don't know if infidelity is only physical. Maybe real infidelity is not about sex. Maybe real infidelity is about sharing dreams.

'She was just … it was ….' Alex stumbles.

'It was *what*, Alex?'

'*I don't know.*' He runs his hand through his hair, a mixture of despair and exasperation.

'Did you love her?'

'No, of course not.'

'Why of course not?'

'Because I loved you, but …'

'But …?'

'Nothing.' He sits down next to me, leans his elbow on the arm of the sofa, his body sloping away from me.

'But what, Alex? The reason we're in this mess is because we don't ever discuss things. Come on, you loved me, but what?'

'I was angry.'

'Oh, now we're getting somewhere. Why? Why were you angry?'

'Because of Josie,' he says, so quietly the fight goes out of me. 'Because I wanted to protect her and I couldn't. And I was frightened. Frightened of her suffering and of her dying. And after she went, I couldn't cope with any of it. With losing her. With what I'd done. With what I'd done to you and to me. And the least of it … the *least* of it was the affair.'

'Not to me.'

'I know,' he says. 'I know.'

There is silence.

'It blotted everything out,' says Alex, turning to me. 'For a little while.' His voice drops even further. 'It made me feel kind of alive again in an unreal world, a world where you and me and Stevie didn't exist. And Josie. Especially Josie. None of us existed. What I had done didn't exist.' I can feel him looking at me, tugging at me with those eyes. I have avoided the emotional commitment of looking directly at him, but I am drawn now by his pleading.

'Can't you see, Carol Ann? Can't you *see*? We both ran away … we just did it in different ways.' His voice trails away. 'That was just my way. My way of wiping out who I was and creating someone different. For a while I could pretend I wasn't me. I was someone free, with choices and possibilities. But in the end the deceit just made things worse. Because I wasn't this other person. Underneath it all, I was still just me. And I still loved you. And Josie was still dead.'

Choices and possibilities. I understand that. I understand it so perfectly that I am amazed those words have come from Alex's lips. And I am amazed that suddenly in a life that was so dismal, so trapped, so powerless for both of us, I am the one who has created choice for myself.

'That night … that night at the Christmas party,' Alex is saying, and I close my eyes against the memory. 'I knew then. I knew it was over. I'm sorry it took that … that you had to … that I made you …' But I don't open my eyes and his voice stumbles and trails away. I lean my head back against the chair, keeping my eyes closed, listening to the silence that ripples towards me in waves, and in a moment I hear his voice resume.

'When we came home that night, I lay in the dark and it felt like … like death. Everything had died. And I wanted her back, I wanted Josie back, through the wall from us …'

'Don't.' I keep my eyes closed, as if by not opening them I will shut him out. But his voice continues, gently, persistently.

'She was beautiful, Carol Ann. She was ours and she was beautiful, wasn't she?'

In my darkness, I can still hear the tremor in his voice. A tear runs slowly from my closed eyes and a moment later I feel his finger running up my cheek, wiping it away. And I know that I have to open my eyes some time. Open them and face him.

'Yes, she was. She was incredibly beautiful.'

'And I can't … what I came to say was …' He stops, fighting for control, grasps both my hands, and in that contact I feel a relief and a longing, a longing for the familiar, reassuring, physical presence of him. 'What I came to say was … that I can't bear thinking that what was so beautiful to both of us ultimately destroyed us. It's not right. Not right. You know, Josie … she loved us … both of us … we owe it … we owe it to her …'

My voice has been ripped from me by the sound of Alex, tears running silently down my face in a torrent now. Cleansing tears that wash the grief and anger and resentment that have sat in a muddy, toxic, silt inside me for years. Yes, Josie was beautiful and she was ours. And he is right. How ironic if Josie destroyed us.

'Carol Ann, remember Josie's funeral? Remember? When we grabbed each other's hand?' I didn't think Alex was even conscious of doing it that day.

'You remember that?'

He looks at me in bewilderment. 'Remember? How could I forget that moment? Carol Ann, that instinct – that's what is real. The rest of it is just … baggage. And, okay, sometimes the baggage seems too heavy to carry around, but it connects us, too. It contains everything that we are. We are the only two people in the world who can fully understand what Josie meant. We're bound by her.' I look down at his hand, wrapping round mine.

When Harry first found out about Alex I said I did not know where to begin to explain to him about my old life. With Josie? With me and Alex? With the first time he walked in out of the rain, and sat at a corner table in a steamy café, watching me? And right now I understand why I didn't know where to begin. In a way there *was* no beginning. In my life, Alex simply is. Timeless, ageless, and mine.

Alex is a vindication of my past. He gives it meaning. Everything that has been is tied up in him. Stevie. Even Lily. And of course, Josie. Josie who loved us and broke us. Josie who came close to destroying us but is somehow here in this room rebuilding us, claiming us as her own. The very thought of her makes me reach out to Alex and lay my head on his shoulder. She broke us and now she heals us.

Outside, it has begun to snow again, flakes driving against the window and dissolving instantly, trickling down the pane in another form, a tiny river that gathers in tiny puddles at the bottom. Later tonight, when the temperature drops, the pool of water on the outer windowsill will freeze again into ice. It can be what it once was, solid rather than liquid, only different. Not quite the same. Like Josie, like her spirit. And I see now as I lie against the man I have spent my whole adult life with, and watch the snow whirl against the windowpane, how primitive and how resilient love is. Even when it undergoes transformation it can endure, reshape, and survive in another form.

It is afternoon, just before the light fades. The hill path is lined with snow still, but the beach and rocks near the water are clear, swept clean by the salt from the sea. Further back at the sand dunes, the long, straggling grasses are choked with ice at the roots. The beach hut looks neat and trim now, the walls washed blue, the black-tiled roof dotted with white.

I feel so nervous leading Alex here, but he has no idea how important this is, the test of it. He has to understand. He has to see the beauty of it, the possibilities. If he looks round disparagingly, if he asks me what I was thinking of, how I could have sunk so much money into it, somehow it will be a sign.

The gulls cry and the waves whisper below as I open the door and I think perhaps Josie is still with us, calling. And then silence as the door slams shut. 'Wow,' says Alex, looking round. 'It's like a doll's house. Could you really have lived in it?' He walks to the window. 'Fantastic view.'

'I love it so much.'

Something in my voice makes him turn and he looks at me for a minute before smiling and turning back to the window. He watches the waves below, then takes off his jacket and throws it onto a chair. I smile when I see he's wearing jeans and a white casual shirt.

'You were wearing a white shirt the first time we met.'

'Was I?' He seems pleased that I remember.

'Not like that. Not casual. With your suit. It was soaked through.'

'You were wearing pink, a floral chiffony shirt thing with tight jeans.' I stretch out on the floor. The place smells of newly laid carpet.

'I was wearing blue, actually.'

Alex shakes his head. 'I remember,' he says, and something in his voice makes me raise my head from the floor. 'Top few buttons undone.'

He winks.

I laugh. It seems like a long time since I laughed with Alex.

'Open the wine.'

'Ma'am.'

He walks through to the tiny kitchen. 'My head's almost hitting the ceiling,' he calls as he opens the bottle.

It's strange having Alex in the beach hut. Two lives merging. The only man who has been here with me is Michael, and I feel a little sad at the memory.

'Is there actually a bed in this place?' Alex calls.

'Is that some kind of chat-up line?'

'Just asking.'

'There's a single one.'

'Cosy.'

'Don't get ideas. Yours is the floor.'

'What?'

He reappears with two glasses and I take one and smile, raising it silently to him before taking a sip.

He is standing above me.

'There are window seats,' I say.

'I'm fine here.' He sits on the floor next to me, his back against the window seat. I swing round to sit beside him.

'Harry says it's when you lose something that you realise its value.'

Alex leans back and considers.

'Harry could be right.' The light is falling fast, disappearing into the horizon.

'It's going to be all right,' he says, as if he can see into me.

'I'm frightened.'

'What of?'

'Of going back and things not changing. Of becoming Carol Ann again. The old Carol Ann.'

Alex takes a sip of wine.

'I can never be her again. Not in the same way.'

'I know,' he says. 'Neither of us can be the same.' He looks around. 'Keep this place. A reminder for both of us.'

'You'll come here with me?'

In answer, he takes my glass and puts it with his own on the windowsill. He leans across then and kisses me, a kiss both strange and familiar. His lips are warm and soft and taste of red wine, like long ago.

CHAPTER FORTY-NINE

Karen

Hammond's grey blue eyes watch me intently when I enter the room. He wears a deep turquoise shirt, matching handkerchief tucked into a dark grey jacket. He must have a closet full of those stupid handkerchiefs. No plain white shirts for him. Everything about him is so restrained, apart from his peacock colour schemes. I guess he needs some outlet from the dreariness of spending his days with nutters. It must be a bit of a relief when he gets someone like me coming in.

Of course, I don't tell him everything. But enough. The formal letter about my suspension. He wants to know why I didn't follow the rules and I say because they're not my rules. That's what people like him don't understand. Middle-class folk with easy lives. What kind of life would I ever have had by sticking to the rules? Who was going to save me if I didn't save myself?

'In my job, Karen,' says Hammond. 'I see that childhood is very, very important. It is not simply a cliché. It really, really is. So let's talk about that.'

He senses my discomfort, swivels his chair round sideways to look out the window, so that he sits side-on and is no longer looking directly at me. There is something deliberate, almost calculating about the movement.

'Beautiful tree, that,' he says, looking out at a magnificent fir tree across the road, its tips tinged with frost. 'Yes,' he continues. 'Family. Mothers. Fathers. Siblings. Do you have a big family, Karen?'

'No. One brother.'

'Mother at home?'

'Yes.'

'Father?'

'Yes.' My heart begins to hammer.

'Which of them were you closest to?'

'Mother.'

Hammond continue to look out the window, as though only half listening. 'Still alive?'

'Yes.'

'And your father … tell me about him.'

'He … he had an accident. He's in a wheelchair.'

'What kind of accident?'

'He fell downstairs.'

Hammond merely nods. 'Did you love your father as a child?'

'No.'

'I see.'

'Why did you ask that?'

'Because you defined him in terms of his handicap. You offered nothing else.'

'So I didn't like my father. So?'

Hammond shrugs.

'Why didn't you like him?'

'Lots of reasons. He drank too much.'

'Was he an obnoxious drunk?'

'He was an obnoxious everything.'

'How did he make you feel, Karen?'

He uses my name softly, gravely. Intimately even. His voice caresses me, but the question explodes somewhere behind my eyes, emotions shooting into my brain like coloured firework rockets, propelled by anger. I close my eyes, squeezing the colours out, trying to bring back a grey uniformity in my vision.

'How did he make you feel?' he repeats.

My eyes are closed still. I am so tired. So many sleepless nights, the shadows dancing, a moving screen of dark menace against the grey wall. I told myself they were only the shadows of passing cars, moving headlights rising and dipping in the darkness, but something inside did not believe it. Something inside told me that *he* had sent them, that one day he will come back. When I was a child, he said he would own me always. I could never escape him.

'Powerless,' I say. I am almost surprised at the sound of my own voice. I tilt my head back, resting it against the chair.

'But he is in a wheelchair, you said?'

'Yes.'

There is someone else who makes me feel powerless now. Alex. I cannot forget the way he made me feel. It changed everything. I crave it, the way I felt that night, the strange, unfamiliar shiver of tenderness, the delicate, exquisite fear of surrender … Hammond's voice cuts in.

'A person in a wheelchair is usually the one who feels powerless. Your father is a very strong character, perhaps?'

'Yes,' I say shortly.

'You mentioned an accident. How did it happen?'

My eyes open.

'You are tired?' asks Hammond. 'Still sleeping badly?'

'Yes.'

'Close your eyes again, then,' he says soothingly. 'It's okay to close your eyes.'

I feel a flash of irritation. I don't need his permission.

'The accident?' says Hammond.

'He fell downstairs.'

'Was he drunk at the time?'

'Yeah, he was drunk. Drunk and violent.' I feel myself drifting. Yes, Alex makes me feel powerless. Is that what love is? Is love surrender?

I don't know if I have ever loved anyone in my life, really loved them. Apart from my mother. And even then, if I am honest, the love is tinged with a little contempt for her weakness. I was the one who had to sort things out, though I was the child.

With my eyes closed, I can see him again. My father, I mean. He and Alex drift in and out of my consciousness, first one then the other. Six months after I threatened him with the cricket bat, he had my mother by the throat on the upstairs landing. There was a scorch mark on his shirt and he said she had done it deliberately. She was taking the mick. Thought she was being clever. Well, he'd show her. He'd show her once and for all.

My brother was out, but I heard the row from my bedroom. She couldn't even scream out. I heard the little choking coughs coming from her throat and I knew that he would go too far, that she was on the way out. I grabbed the bat and rushed out into the hall, whacking him across the back with it so that he dropped his hands. My mother fell to the floor, coughing and spluttering. It was the livid fingermarks round her throat that made me lose it. His dirty great fingerprints were pawed all over our lives, marking them, tainting them with his filth.

He turned on me then, but I had the bat as a shield.

'Come on then, you old bastard,' I whispered, high on adrenaline. 'Come on, then.'

I backed towards the stairs, leading him on. I could smell the sourness of sweat and alcohol as he came nearer, hear the sound of his laboured breathing. The least exertion and he always heaved and spluttered.

'If he made you feel powerless, was he violent towards you?' Hammond's voice makes my eyes spring open. So many questions. So many tiring questions.

'To her first. To my mother.'

'He hit her.' I notice his voice does not rise at the end in a question.

'Yes.'

'And then he hit you.'

'I could hear the gurgle in her throat, bubbling, choking ...'

'You stopped him?'

'Yes.'

'Well done, Karen,' he says softly. 'You were brave.'

Yes. Well done, Karen. That's what I thought. But nobody ever said it. Not my mother, though it was for her I did it. Not my brother, who never knew but always suspected.

'How did you stop him?'

'With a cricket bat. Then he fell downstairs.'

He had lunged at me and I hit out with the bat. He ducked but tripped and I kicked out to help him on his way. He toppled then, right down the stairs, bouncing almost on his head and somersaulting right over. There was silence when he reached the bottom. My mother crawled to the top of the stairs. Her eyes were wide and frightened and she began to whimper. He was lying sprawled at the bottom, unmoving.

'You must have loved your mother,' Hammond is saying. I only grunt in reply.

'Why did you love your mother?'

'She was always frightened.'

'That's a strange reason to love someone.'

'Is it?'

'You knew how she felt?'

'I wanted to protect her. To make it okay. For her not to be frightened.'

'And that's why you hit your father with the bat?'

'She'd have died if I hadn't.'

'You saved her life.'

'That's what I said.'

'You hit him and then your father fell downstairs. Is that the way it happened?'

'I suppose so.'

'Suppose?'

'Yes.'

'He stumbled?'

'Yes.'

'Because he was drunk?' Alex. Alex. If only the tenderness had been real, been for me. I had to lash out against the pain, just as I did with my father. I lash out at anything that has the capacity to hurt me. If only you could understand. If you could only see … Things could be different. I can feel myself floating into sleep, have not the energy to resist. Hammond's voice is becoming more insistent.

'Because he was drunk?' he repeats.

'Yes.' I handled everything. I made my mother change into a polo neck before the police called to hide the marks of the struggle. She was shaking from head to foot and the policeman said she was in shock and called the doctor, who sedated her. It was left to me to tell the police about the fall. They took a blood sample from him and found him four times the driving limit. Hardly surprising he stumbled.

He came round but he never recovered. He was left paralysed and without much speech. I told my mother we were finally free of him and tried to get her to put him in long-term care. But you know what the silly bitch said? She said it was her fault and she loved him and it was up to her to take care of him. Well, don't expect me to do the same, I told her furiously. Don't expect me to stay and help.

If that's love, then you can keep it. The biggest thing you can have in life is freedom, emotional freedom. That's why I hate the effect Alex has had on me. There is no freedom; only dependency. That's the way it is for my mother. I go round to see her sometimes, but I don't bother with my father. He just sits there drooling most of the time, grunting incoherently. My mother always looks tired and strained, but in a way she's happy as Larry because he's completely dependent on her and she gets to look after him without him lashing out at her. He makes his displeasure known as he always did, but he's her child. He needs her.

The doctors say his brain is damaged, that he doesn't take much in, but I'm not so sure. Sometimes, I think his black eyes are as vicious as they ever were. Especially when he looks at me. I went round to see my mother after I got the suspension letter. I didn't think he would listen. I try not to see him when I talk, pretend he is part of the furniture, simply an inanimate part of the room like the old settee or the print of New York City that I gave my mother that hides a damp stain on the wall. But I think he understood what I told her.

My father still has strength in his arms and I watched him bang his cup against the frame of his chair as I spoke to my mother. A crash of breaking china. There was a cold violence about his action that I knew was deliberate. He held the handle in his hand like a trophy, the broken slice of cup tumbling to the floor, the tepid tea running in a torrent onto his grey, old-man jogging trousers, dripping onto the carpet below. My mother rushed for a cloth then and I turned from him in despair, trying to block out the cold glittering blackness of the triumph in his eyes.

Hammond says he has another appointment, that he has only fitted me in during his lunch break. We must stick strictly to times if I am to become his patient. It annoys me a bit. He must see this is an emergency. He tells me to make another appointment with Sally and I say I'll think about it. Afterwards, I sit outside in the car, looking up at the office. Part of me says I don't need him. The other part says he's my only chance.

CHAPTER FIFTY

Carol Ann

The house is packed up. A sprawl of cases and plastic bags in the hall. It has the look of a holiday home again, a bare, scrubbed space that waits for new fingerprints on the door handles, new noise to drift up the stairwell from one floor to another like slow, creeping mist. I lived simply enough. There's not much I want to take, except my new clothes. Cara's clothes. When I go home, everything in Carol Ann's wardrobe is going. My phone beeps as Alex drives. A text message. I reach down to my bag at my feet, lift it out, and my heart leaps. Michael.

'Who is it?' asks Alex.

'No one you know.'

Normally it is Alex who says that to me.

A shadow crosses his face. What I say is the truth, but it is evidence of a life he knows nothing of. A new friend, on a new phone, whose number my own husband does not know. Perhaps he thinks I am trying to hurt him, punish him.

'A friend,' I say, touching his arm. 'Just a friend.'

Read. Click.

One word.

Stay.

* * *

Alex sits in the car while I see Harry. I am crying before he even opens the door.

'Cara,' he says, and holds me close. 'Cara.'

His eyes go up to the road.

'Why is Alex not coming in?'

'I'll get him in a minute. I asked him to give us time.'

'Come in, then.'

We go into his sitting room and I wonder if it's the last time. I think Harry does, too. Neither of us sit.

'You're not angry?' Harry asks.

'I'll tell you in a year.'

'I didn't want to meddle, Cara. It took me a while to decide, but just ... I just thought you needed a helping hand.'

'How did you find Alex first?

'I went to the library in Belfast. Looked up the cuttings of Scottish papers online. It wasn't hard. Though the picture of you ... my God, girl, it looked nothing like you.'

'That was Carol Ann,' I smile.

'You'll always be Cara May to me.' A tremor shoots through his face. 'I'll miss you,' he says.

I nod. '*Newsnight* won't be the same,' I say.

We stand in silence a minute. Tears are pouring down my cheeks.

'You saved me, Cara,' he says.

'We saved each other.'

'I have something,' he says, and he limps across the room. I stand in the sitting room as he slowly thumps his way upstairs. I tilt back my head and close my eyes, unable to bear it. I don't want to leave him and yet I need to get out of here, get it over with.

He has Patsy's ring box when he comes back.

'The emerald is the nicest,' he says. 'Take it.'

'I can't, Harry. Please ... I can't ...'

He isn't listening. He open the box and takes out the ring. 'Fits you perfectly,' he says. 'Patsy would want it. I want it. Patsy, she ... she'd have loved you, Cara. Sometimes, I imagine the two of you together.'

I put my arms round his neck.

'Thank you, Harry.

He kisses the top of my head and puts his hands on my arms.

'I'll not bring Alex in, Harry.' I can hardly stand. ' It will only prolong things, make it worse.'

'Get on the road, girl,' he whispers, trying to smile through tears. His voice is broken. 'You've a long journey.'

'I'm keeping the beach hut.'

He smiles.

Alex puts his hand on my knee as we drive off. My last view of Harry is of him standing with his stick on the doorstep, waving, the snowy hills at his back, the blue-washed walls of the beach hut in the distance, glowing in the winter sun.

CHAPTER FIFTY-ONE

Carol Ann

I return home when the first snowdrops are pushing through iron-crusted earth, pure and white, a symphony of gentleness and resilience. I gather a handful for Josie from the base of the cherry-blossom tree. I do not want formal flowers wrapped in cellophane. No hot-house posies or cultured blooms.

Stevie does not own a suit, but he wears school shoes instead of trainers without being asked, and borrows a tie from Alex. I look at him, and I love him.

Lily wears a smart woollen coat but smells of booze. It's the first time, Alex says defensively, since she became ill. Lily looks at me tentatively, a cold light of shame in her eyes and in our silence. I notice she avoids me, sitting beside Alex as though seeking refuge. She sits in the front of the car beside him; it is easier for her to manoeuvre her leg. None of us talk, but in the back Stevie holds my hand and periodically squeezes my fingers. The last time he held my hand he was a little boy. Now he holds it for my sake, not his. He holds it like an adult, but his face is pinched and white like a child's.

It is the first time we have been to see Josie as a family. It is the first time since she died that we have *felt* like a family. It is a rite of passage, a moving on, a new kind of unity. In my bag, my mobile vibrates. I have set it so that it will not ring out because I know who it will be. Michael.

And I know what he will say. Come back. Lives do not separate that easily.

I left Alex sleeping the morning after he arrived; his exhaustion was such that he never even stirred. Outside, I phoned Michael and left a garbled message on his voicemail, which was a mistake. I should have waited until I saw him, but it was urgent. I needed to get him to come immediately to the beach hut. I walked, he drove, and he was there before me, standing at the window as I climbed the hill. There was only a thin line of snow left, like a tide mark, well up the beach at the long grasses. He did not turn when I closed the door behind me and I stood, waiting.

'You lied,' he said finally.

'I'm sorry.' I touched his arm but he refused to turn to me. 'Michael, I got caught in a web of stuff that I couldn't ... I couldn't tell you.'

'Chose not to tell me, you mean.'

He bit his lip, watching the sea tumbling, iron-grey and white. I could actually hear him breathing heavily with anger.

'Part of me actually wants to ask you to stay,' he said bitterly.

'I can't stay.'

'No more than I can ask you to.' He turned towards me. 'I wouldn't know who I was asking. Everything about you has been made up.'

'Not everything.'

'I was in love with a made-up person.'

In love? Oh God.

'Michael, I really liked you. That was true. Everything I said about how I felt was true ... it wasn't a lie ... it was ...'

'This,' he'd said, waving a hand round the beach hut. 'I thought ...'

Michael shared the dream, but it was dissolving before his eyes, melting down from a magical ice sculpture into a pool of muddy water.

'I never meant to ...'

What did I never mean to do? To lie? To hurt him? To become someone else? But I *did* mean to become someone else. I *did* mean to create another life. And that has had consequences I never foresaw. When you create a new life, you think you'll leave problems behind. But you just create new ones. New ties and responsibilities. New dilemmas. A whole new complexity to replace the old one. And then, when the old life catches up …

'I felt …' I take a deep breath, forced to try and make tangled thoughts concise. 'I felt I was dying. Inside I was dying. Slowly. For years and years and years. The loneliness was just … overwhelming, really. I was so lonely I wanted to live on my own, because that was less lonely than living with someone else. But everything was so complicated I didn't know how to do it. I couldn't untangle the mess, I could only cut it and walk away. I daydreamed about that all the time, about walking away. The fantasy kept me going. And then one day, it all … everything just fell into place, like the numbers on a slot machine … ping, ping, ping … and I knew it was the day I had to go. Really go. I just walked and kept on walking. It was like the person I was didn't exist any more. I was trying to create a new one. But the old one never quite died.'

'Shite,' Michael said. 'Shite.' His voice sounded alien. Just the sound of it made me wince. He turned to the door.

'I can't love you any more because the person I loved doesn't exist. She never did. How could I ever trust you? I just don't know who you are. But I guess that's no surprise. You don't know either.'

I realised I had never seen him angry before.

There was only the brief, strangled call of the gulls as the door opened, a blast of frosted air, and then silence. Four hours later, he sent the first text message. Stay.

But I didn't stay. Because running away from emotional ties just created a space for new ones to spring up unbidden. They would be tested too, those new ones, and what would I do then – keep running? Keep pursuing freedom until it turned into loneliness?

So now I'm here, laying snowdrops loosely on Josie's grave, scattering them like white stars on the frosted mound where she lies. We stand together, saying nothing, but Lily cries softly, sad, old-lady tears that mourn wasted years and lost chances. I move to go to her but Alex gets there first. Stevie looks round desperately, as though for escape, his face thin and wolfish. He is too young still, this impostor in a man's body. I run my hand gently up and down his arm.

'Time to go,' I say, sensing his need to be out of here.

Alex is already leading Lily to the car.

I run my hand unthinkingly over Josie's stone before I leave, then suddenly become conscious of the action. It makes me think of Harry. Harry in the whitewashed cottage, far away in another life. My finger traces the indentations in the stone, spelling out her name. J. O. S. I. E.

'Come on,' I say to Stevie, and smile. He looks relieved, puts his arm round me and holds me briefly before letting go.

Lily moves so slowly that we catch them up before the gate. Another car is parked behind us now. The driver sits, back to the cemetery gate. I see eyes watching us in the driving mirror. At first I cannot be sure if it is a man or a woman, but as we get closer it becomes clear it is a woman. The electronic window of the car moves down.

'Hello, Alex.'

'Steve,' says Alex, 'take the keys and help your grandmother to the car.' He looks at me. 'Go with them,' he says quietly. He nods reassuringly. 'I'll deal with this.'

I walk forward and turn my head back curiously. A young, dark-haired woman is at the wheel, attractive in a hard, provocative way. She blows smoke from a cigarette out the window.

My phone vibrates again. Text message from Michael. Two words: come back.

I become aware of Alex's voice, hard, urgent, aggressive, and I glance up from the phone.

'What are you doing here?' he is saying. The tone stops me getting in the car. I switch off the phone, lean my arm on the roof of our car and wait for him. Lily mutters something to Stevie as she gets in. Alex keeps glancing over at me. I know he wants me to get in too. He repositions his body slightly, turning sideways on as if he doesn't want me to hear.

It is the woman I watch. I cannot hear what she says, but I can see her face through the windscreen. Her mouth twists slightly, mockingly, when she talks. I can see the tension in Alex's shoulders, the way he stands, a hunched anger. He keeps moving his head back in irritation when the woman blows out her smoke, then repositioning himself at the window.

I do not know her name but I know one thing for sure. There is something between them. There is intimacy in their anger, and knowledge. Alex's eyes flick up at me again and away. The woman appraises me coolly. And suddenly I realise I won't be passive, won't be appraised any more. My new life taught me that at least. I walk towards the woman's car.

'Alex,' I say quietly, 'we're waiting. Time to go.'

He looks at me, then holds out a hand. I take it, feel the solid power of it enclosing my fingers. 'Yes,' he says. 'Time to go.' The woman starts the car engine.

'Alex ...'she calls when we are halfway to the car. Alex turns his head but keeps walking.

'What?' he says.

'See you around.' She grins then, sticks her cigarette in her mouth and puts the car into gear.

I get into the driver's seat when we reach the car, a small gesture. Alex gets in the back but exchanges a look with Lily which I catch in the mirror. We drive in silence for a few minutes and then I say, 'Do you remember that on Josie's last birthday before she died, she had a white iced cake with pink roses and pink and white striped candles?'

'The magic candles!' says Stevie from the back, as if remembering a half-forgotten delight.

'She loved them,' murmurs Lily.

We saw them in a joke shop, and every time you blew them out, the flame suddenly re-ignited, magically, from nowhere. Josie lost her puff trying to blow them out that day, the flame continually dying then bursting into life again, and eventually she could try no more because, what with the effort and the laughter, she had no more breath left to give. We all watched her, hearts sore and full, but simultaneously caught up in the infectious trill of her laughter. Eventually, we stuck the burning candle flames in a cup of water to extinguish them.

'A little bit of magic,' says Alex softly, quoting Josie.

I look sideways at Lily, sitting beside me in the front seat. Here we are, the four of us, two in the front and two in the back, an invisible cord running between us. And each time one of us tries to cut that cord, it joins again, miraculously, like the re-igniting candles on Josie's cake, tying us all back together whether we want it or not. A little bit of magic.

'We all sang "Happy Birthday",' says Lily vaguely.

'You always sang to her, Mum, remember? When she was little.'

'She only sings "My Way" now, with Frank,' says Alex, not unkindly, and Stevie smiles, glancing at him as if there's a private joke running between them.

'*Bheir me o, horo van o*,' sings Lily softly, ignoring them, doing her own thing as always. The men look out the back windows, Stevie clearing his throat self-consciously and Alex fixing his eyes on some notional spot in the middle distance, but I join in with her in the final verse, which was always the most beautiful of all.

'When I'm lonely, dear white heart,
Black the night or wild the sea,
By love's light my foot finds
The old pathway to thee.'

And then I look up and catch Alex's eye in the mirror.